MW01625832

SALT FORK STATIONS

To Kenny,

So good to see you!

—[illegible]

SALT FORK STATIONS

ROCK NEELLY

Hydra Publications

ISBN: 978-1-948374-70-5

Hydra Publications

Goshen, Kentucky 40026

www.hydrapublications.com

To my Marie, Vicki Marie, my wife

The Salt Fork Stations

You have left me to linger in hopeless longing,
Your presence had ever made me feel no want,
You have left me to travel in sorrow.
Left me to travel in sorrow

You have left me to linger in hopeless longing,
In your presence there was no sorrow.
You have gone, and sorrow I shall feel as I travel!
Ah, the pain, the pain, the pain!

--Francis La Flesche

"The Weaver's Lamentation"
The Osage Tribe
Rite of the Wa-Xo-Be, 1930

Author's Note: The Stations of the Cross were said to have been set by Mother Mary outside of her home near Jerusalem. There, she followed a path to each as she traced the journey of her Son's Passion. Christians have followed this tradition since, visiting and praying at each of the fourteen stations in remembrance. Most Christians see the stations in the stained-glass windows of their churches each Sunday. In this novel, I have used each station as a marker and chapter along our way. I have added Resurrection.

1. **The Arrest**: Jesus is arrested condemned to death.
2. **The Weight**: Jesus carries His cross.
3. **Dust**: Jesus falls for the first time.
4. **Mother**: Jesus meets Mary on His way.
5. **Kinship**: Simon of Cyrene helps Jesus carry the cross.
6. **Kindness**: Veronica wipes the face of Jesus.
7. **Sorrows**: Jesus falls for the second time.
8. **Benevolence**: Jesus meets the women of Jerusalem.
9. **Darkness**: Jesus falls for the third time.
10. **Unveiled**: Jesus is stripped of His clothes.
11. **Stigmata**: Jesus is nailed to the cross.
12. **The Passion**: Jesus dies on the cross.
13. **Release**: Jesus is taken down from the cross.
14. **Burial**: Jesus is placed in the tomb.
15. **Resurrection**: Jesus rises from the tomb.

A Prayer Before the Journey

The old man said, "Don't let life's inherent sadness steal away your faith in good things."

The young man met the old one's eyes, saying, "Has your life been good?"

The old man's eyes turned inward on memories he had hoped not to dredge to the surface again. He moved past them. "At times, it was, yes," he answered. "There were, indeed, moments of happiness and joy. Enlightenment, even. When I saw the way things could be. Should be. Certainly, there were days when things were as good as I could have imagined."

The young man wanted to know more but could see the conflicted emotions on his friend's face and asked no more. He knew of the darkness that had followed.

Though the two had known each other but a short time, the same blood coursed through their veins. Thoughts others might find difficult to express needed no words between them. The blood spoke louder than the tongue. Today, it told them that this meeting would be their last. The blood told them there would be a parting, yet there was no trepidation.

The two would not waste their final moments together discussing things that did not matter. They spoke of love and joy. They spoke of loss and sorrow. They spoke of how glad they were that they had met and were friends. They spoke of how they'd known from the very first second their bond was resolute and timeless.

The old man and the young one did not speak of enemies and misdirected anger. Time was too short to waste on people who did not understand, those who did not matter.

The two did not mince words, and there were none they would have liked to have taken back. Every word seemed perfect for its time, and the young man would reflect on them for the remainder of his life. The old man would not need to.

They spoke of rivers and of oceans, of birds on the wing, of clear mountain mornings, and the laughter of children carried on the wind. They spoke of the women each had loved; of their parents and their friends now gone; of those whose paths had intersected with theirs for perhaps a single moment but had left a lifetime impression; of those who time and detour had taken away too soon, of wine, song; and good companions; of nights when life seemed it would go on forever.

When the sun had fallen that last time and they realized their time was at an end, the two shed tears as men may do when they do not care what others think. Then, they held each other in an embrace, no longer worrying about artifice. They knew they were family in the truest sense and their paths would cross again in the hereafter. As the great tribes of the plains believe all family will once again gather around the council fire in the sky, they, too, believed they would be reunited when their sorrows were gone and their sins forgiven.

Then, the young man bade his friend farewell. He left with no regrets, and the old man, now at peace, remained. Each knew destiny would now complete the circle. Both were ready.

It was a good day to die.

Amen.

Arrest
Wichita Kansas
November, 1963

"Wake up, booger face," the raven-haired girl said, using her index finger and thumb on each hand to pinch at the sleeping boy's cheeks.

Chris Fairchild opened his green eyes, groggy and confused.

His fourteen-year-old sister leaned over his bed. Her fingers began to poke his cheeks.

The boy pulled back away from her. He could see a poster of Fess Parker as Daniel Boone looming above them from the wall above his desk. The hallway light was on, but not the light in his room. The boy was confused. Piper never woke him for school. His mother always came in and softly called to him as she sat on the edge of his bed. The change jarred him. He was immediately uncomfortable with the change. The boy sat and up and turned to the window.

"Hey, Piper, what gives? Why did you wake me? Is it still night?" he asked. He rubbed his eyes, pushing his sister's hands away, trying to regain some control over his bossy sibling.

Piper nodded, moving gangly, all elbows and legs, to the closet, dragging their father's Army duffle bag onto the floor. She also set Chris's tiny suitcase down. "Yep," she said, "it's still night. Daddy did something awful. Mom just got off the phone with Grandpa. She's crying and she told me to wake you up. We're headed to the farm."

Two contrary bits of information entered his mind. The boy initially dealt with the one that made his stomach jiggle inside. "What did Dad do?" Then, Chris added, "And why are we going to the farm? It's Wednesday. We have school tomorrow."

"Don't know. Mom just said he done something real bad. And anyhows, it's past midnight, so it's technically Thursday. Mom said no school for us for the rest of the week. She said for you to pack yourself for the whole weekend. You're almost eleven, she said, and can do it your big self." Piper's teeth grinned out from her freckled cheeks. "I told her you'd forget underwear and socks."

"I can pack myself. I'll even remember my toothbrush," the boy replied back, irritated, but starting to be excited at the prospect of going to the farm and missing school.

"I'll be back to check on your progress," Piper said as she marched out, her nightgown flowing after her bare feet.

Chris slipped out of his bed and moved first to the bathroom.

After taking care of business, he grabbed his toothbrush and comb. He wrapped both in a Kleenex and put them in the bottom of his suitcase. What should he pack? He figured clothes for four days, but that was just three nights. They'd come home on Sunday. Chris decided to be prepared. He packed four pairs of underwear, four pairs of socks, two pairs of jeans, one pair of brown trousers in case they went to church, a shirt, a sweater, two undershirts, one white tee and his favorite article of apparel, a corduroy pullover with a rawhide, lace-up neck like the cowboys wore on *Bonanza*. His shirt was green, just like Little Joe's. Chris rolled each article of clothing like his father had shown him and stuffed them all in the bag.

After that, the boy packed a big stack of comic books in his suitcase.

A few minutes later, Piper reentered. "Why aren't you dressed?"

"I figured I'd sleep in the car."

Lillian Fairchild entered at that moment, nodding in agreement. "That's fine, but Chris, put on socks and your tennis shoes. We need to go. Piper, did you see if Chris got everything?"

"Just fixing to, Mom."

Chris examined his mother's face as she watched Piper inspect his bag. Her makeup was smeary, and her eyes were red. Both were telltale signs that she had been crying, all right. Kids always recognize stress in their parents, and Chris saw telltale signs with his mother.

Lillian was a dark-haired woman with pale skin. Tonight, blue shadows encased her deep-set eyes. She was tall and willowy. People said she carried herself gracefully. Tonight, she looked anxiety-ridden and exhausted.

Chris examined his mother. He always knew to watch her hands. Right now, she was picking at her thumbnail. The boy recognized that motion. It made him worry. Things weren't good. He stood there, watching her with his own anxiety.

"Well, how'd he do?" Mom turned impatiently as Piper dug through his bag.

"No belt, no coat. It's snowing a little outside and it's cold."

Mom gave him that look.

"I was going to wear my coat," Chris said.

"Pack him both his black and brown belts. I don't know how long we'll be there. Make sure his dress shoes are in there, too."

Chris' ears perked up at that. More than four days maybe? He stood there. His mother looked at him and raised her shoulders in impatience. "Chris, go get your tennies on. Piper, get Chris's coat."

With the bags in the trunk, they piled in.

Piper pleaded to sit up front, but Chris did, too. The children awaited Mom's ruling.

Chris managed a negotiated settlement and was allowed to sit in the middle.

"But it'll be dangerous," Piper said. "Plus, it will be too crowded if he wears that big ole coat. Chris needs to sit in the back."

"Piper, there's plenty of room if you want the whole back seat" was the parental reply.

"Yeah, Piper, pipe down," Chris added, knowing she hated that expression.

His sister glared at him, but she let Chris get in first.

The boy offered up a consolation and removed his coat to give Piper more room. He couldn't help but shiver as he slid across the seat. He rolled the jacket into a pillow.

Once in, he leaned against his mother's side and snuggled in.

Lillian rubbed his head. "You tired, baby?"

Chris nodded, and she smiled, but the boy saw the sadness in his mother's eyes as she did. What had Dad done to make all this happen? It had to be big to get his children out of school and have Mom miss work. The boy waited as Piper slid in beside him and closed the passenger door.

The ride to Oklahoma was just over two hours long. They would travel out of Wichita, down past Medicine Lodge, into mesa country and across the state line at Kiowa, continuing on blacktop for four miles into Woods County before taking a turn south onto a dirt road. Five miles more approached the old "troll" bridge and the farm's long, curving drive.

Mom started the car and they backed away from the garage. She inched into the street and away from their home. Chris would remember the moment later, surprised he would never see that house again. If the boy had known the finality of it, he would have given the structure a last look back. But the truth is he did not give it a thought.

"I get to run the radio," Piper said. She leaned in, intentionally bumping her brother with her elbow, but he ignored it, having just won the battle to be next to Mom. He allowed Piper a tiny bit of payback. Chris knew she got over things quicker that way.

As Mom guided the car over the surface streets of their neighborhood onto Wichita's west side and the highway south, Piper played DJ. She punched one button and then another. Finally, she found a song she liked.

"I love this song."

Trini Lopez's "If I Had a Hammer" chimed through the dashboard speaker. Piper sang along. "If I had a hammer, I'd hammer in the morning," she wailed. Her pitch was wobbly and even a bit screechy, but her singing was always so joyful people did not seem to mind.

Chris did not join in. He was sleepy and he didn't sing well, anyway. He noticed people frowned when he sang. Chris could tell people did not like his singing. The boy noticed things; Chis was smart. When people frowned at what he was doing, the best thing, he figured, was to stop doing it.

When the song ended and Piper's warbling ceased, his sister once again began twisting the dial. Muffled voices from distant lands drifted to their ears. Chris heard cities mentioned by the DJs: Dallas, Denver, Chicago, and even Cincinnati. AM radio late at night was a wonderland, his dad said, but not one Chris knew much about. His father talked about it sometimes, about pulling in radio signals from far away while he was on his epic drives across the country. His father loved driving. His father loved cars.

His mother's car was a 1959 Rambler. It was a green and crème four-door. The tires were white-walls and the interior a billiard green plastic with floor mats to match. The dashboard was lit in red and white. It was a good car. His father, Henry Fairchild, was a mechanic, and an excellent one at that. Before his dad bought this Rambler, it had been junked after the engine blew. His dad saw the clean new body of the car. He had it towed to behind the repair shop where he worked, and little-by-little, Henry rebuilt the engine like new. Chris knew his dad was kind of a genius at figuring out how things worked. Henry could fix things like nobody else. Chris's mom said Henry could also break things better than anyone, too. Chris remembered when she said that. The boy guessed tonight was one of those breaking things sort of nights.

Chris knew his family didn't have a lot of money, but they always seemed to have good cars. In fact, they were alone in the neighborhood in having two cars. Most families had but one.

Mothers did not need them if they stayed at home, and most stayed at home. But Lillian had her own car. Of course, that was because she was the only woman on her street who went to work every day. She went to both work and to night school. His mom was working on her college degree at Wichita State on Tuesday and Thursday nights. Those nights, he had to eat Piper's dinners; they were usually pimento loaf sandwiches and chips. Chris did not like Tuesday and Thursday nights, especially because Piper decided what shows they watched those evenings. Piper liked romantic shows. He read comic books when her shows were on. During the week, Dad was gone down to Oklahoma City. Henry arrived home around their bedtimes on Fridays.

Piper turned up the radio, raising Chris from his reveries. "Dominique" by the Singing Nun filled the car, and once again his sister sang along. "Dominique, a-nique, a-nique, a-nica…"

After the song was over, Chris reached up and turned the radio down.

Piper frowned, but before she could act, he spoke. "Mom, what did Dad do? Was it bad? Why do we have to go to the farm? I don't understand."

His mother was slow to respond. As Lillian turned to him, Chris saw tears rim her eyes before she returned to staring at the ribbon of highway. Another car, its high beams adjusting as it approached, sped by. Chris could feel the turbulence. He watched his mom's face. She didn't speak for a long moment.

Finally, with a tremor in her words, Lil spoke. "Honey, I don't think I'm ready to talk about it just yet. It will get me too upset and I don't want to be that way because I'm driving." She took a tissue from her left pocket and dabbed her eyes.

Piper jabbed him again. "Yeah, just go to sleep, poop face."

"Piper!" Mom said, "you apologize."

His sister laughed, "Sorry, Brother. Your face isn't as ugly as poop." She turned the volume back up. She punched a button. "Oh, this is Dad's station, country and western."

Skeeter Davis's "It's the End of the World" played. Next up, Jim Reeves sang "Make the World Go Away."

Afterwards, Chris leaned forward. "Mom and I don't need any more sad songs; do we, Mom?"

His mother scuffed his head again. "No, and we don't need any more 'world' songs', either. Find us a happy tune. Chris, your turn."

The boy was delighted. He took his sweet time, pushing buttons and twirling the dial. Finally, he found the perfect song, "The Ballad of Jed Clampett."

All three of the passengers sang along.

Piper got some of the words wrong, but Chris knew them all. He remembered things very well. He brayed the whole song.

When he finished, Piper gave him a clap on the arm, high praise from her.

Mom even managed a tight-lipped laugh.

Afterwards, Chris felt elated to have brightened his mother's mood at least for a moment. As Piper resumed the DJ duties, the nearly eleven-year-old leaned back and watched out the windshield as big snowflakes swirled into the car's wipers, the bright lights making it seem like the three were seeing stars coming at them. The highway was a streak of black as the land's contours changed; the November hillsides of bluestem grass, sagebrush, and fallow milo fields slid away in the darkness. He remembered seeing a road sign that they were coming into Medicine Lodge. The farm was but an hour away, he thought, and then he went to sleep.

Chris awoke to the smell of bacon. He lay in the bed in the south bedroom of the farmhouse. The bed was a double, and the boy was covered by "Grandma's Hugs." That's what the family called the orange sherbet-colored satin comforter that lay over him. Chris took the time to rub his cheeks against it, to smell the fragrance of

Grandma's rosewater perfume on it; he took satisfaction in knowing he had it and Piper did not.

But the aroma of the frying bacon soon got the better of him. Chris bounced from the bed around the corner to the kitchen, not a distant walk in the tiny house.

Grandpa Jeff was at the gas stove with a skillet of bacon on the burner. A cigarette hung from his lip, so Chris knew his mother and grandmother were gone someplace. Smoking at the stove was something Jeff would not have done had Grandma been home. Truth was, he would not have been cooking, either. Jeff did smoke in the house, but only in the far seat of the kitchen table with his ashtray set on the edge of the windowsill, the smoke rising up out of doors.

"Look who's up," said Jeff. "I figured it would be Piper who'd get around first, beings the north room gets a little chillier."

"Further away from the bacon smell," Chris replied.

Jeff smiled. "True enough. Go get you some Tang out of the fridge. Grandma made some up before she and your mom left for Oklahoma City."

"Why'd they go there?"

"To see about your pa, I reckon." Jeff turned from the stove and went to the window and tipped his ash. He seemed to think about it twice and then extinguished the cigarette in the green depression-era glass tray.

"Grandpa, what did Dad do? Piper said he did something bad." Chris poured his Tang and looked to see if his grandfather wanted some too. The glasses were the old containers for chipped beef with the labels soaked off. The rims of the glasses had five-sided stars.

Jeff shook his head and motioned to his coffee cup.

Chris took the pot off the stove and carefully filled Jeff's cup.

"Well, boy, I think your momma wants to talk to you about all that when she gets back, but I'll tell you what little I know. You know Henry, your daddy, works for Addy's Motors, right? Master Mechanic, they call him. Henry Fairchild, Master Mechanic. Anyway, some fella brought his brand spanking new Cadillac

Deville in for servicing. That feller wasn't supposed to come back and get his car for a couple of days. Owner told Addy he'd be out of town.

"Your daddy loves cars, Chris. He told your mom he'd never seen such a car. He told her that with his one phone call. They's give that to prisoners. He said it was the most beautiful car he'd ever seen. Anyways, your pa just couldn't resist taking that Caddy out for a drive. And things led to things. Your dad took that fine ride over to a bar to show some friends. Just for a lark, I'm sure. Then, they's gets to drinkin'. And your daddy ends up keepin' the car overnight."

Jeff removed the skillet from the burner and turned it off. He moved the bacon to a plate with a paper napkin on it. He blotted the grease off the crinkled slices with a second napkin then moved down the entryway, where the refrigerator faced the door. Jeff grabbed an egg carton and carried it to the stove.

After the pause, he took a sip of coffee and surveyed Chris's eyes.

"Anyhow, the fella who owned the Caddy came back early the next morning. His car was gone when he showed up at Addy's for it. Addy, your pa's boss, he's an all-right guy, I think, but he knew the score and he knew Henry probably had the Cadillac. But Addy didn't let on that he knew your dad had it and called the cops and reported it stolen."

"Did the police arrest Dad?"

"Yessum. They charged Henry with grand theft auto. Now, Chris, it's just a big misunderstanding. Your pa was planning on bringing back that car when he went to work that morning and have it back in place before Addy got there; only he overslept.

Chris wrinkled his brow. "You mean Dad got drunk."

Jeff nodded. "You gonna eat one egg, or two?"

"Two."

"That-a-boy. Now, go wake up your sister and tell her to get in here to put the toast on. We'll be having breakfast as soon as these eggs are done."

After breakfast, Jeff washed up the dishes with Chris drying and Piper putting them away. This process had been their system for a while now whenever the children came to the farm. Chris was too short to put away glasses and dishes in the cupboard, so he always dried.

"Get a move on. This is a workday," Jeff said, "There's chores to do."

"Causin' every day is a workday on a farm," the two children said in unison, reciting one of Grandpa's favorite litanies.

"You two, you go gather the eggs after you're done drying and putting the plates away. Piper, you know where the baskets are."

Piper nodded. Gathering eggs was their favorite activities, like Easter morning every day.

The farm was expanded now to about nine hundred acres and the farmyard itself was at the northern most point above the pasture and was shaped as a small, self-contained triangle. It extended about two hundred yards to the east to the back of the barn and corral, about seventy-five yards south to the dog pens and the gas and diesel tanks, then back to the house on the west side. Behind the house, along a sloping hill, a deep wood blocked the north wind with stands of elm, locust, and along the meandering quarter-mile drive in, a line of towering cottonwoods.

As far as the buildings went, there were four. The house squatted against the hill, a tiny, five-room structure with a tin roof and slatted sides. It had been originally a single room structure of roughly twenty by thirty, but Grandpa's uncle, who'd been its first inhabitant, added the south room when he married and started a family. A generation later, Grandpa himself added the north room, along with a mudroom and bathroom once they got inside plumbing.

The largest structure on the property was the barn. It was a traditional red two-story, steeply gabled building with room for tack and tools inside. There was also a hay loft, four stables, and a place to park the tractor, although most times this space was instead filled with bales of hay just like the loft. Hay was baled in the spring and summer to feed cattle come cold weather. South of the barn, a large, rectangular corral with thick six-by-six posts was used for cows nearing delivery or horses needing to be shod. Most times, the horses were left in the north pasture closest to the barnyard. Chris loved to hear them whinny in joy as he lay in bed. It was one of his favorite sounds to wake up to.

The garage was the building farthest south. It was big enough for two vehicles, although Chris could never remember seeing his grandfather's Chevy truck parked inside. Inside the garage, one side held Grandpa's Oldsmobile 88. It was black with white trim, fins on its rear end, white-walled tires and black seats. It was three years old and only had twenty-three thousand miles on it. And that was after a trip up to South Dakota to see the Badlands, the Shepherd of the Hills, and Mount Rushmore last year.

Grandma Gwen did not have a car. In fact, she had never driven a vehicle, a fact Chris found astounding. He couldn't wait to drive. It seemed to him that anyone would want to get their driver's license as soon as they could. And in Kansas and Oklahoma, kids could drive at age fourteen once they got their learner's permit. Young drivers needed an adult beside them unless the reason for the outing was a farm errand. Chris figured anything could be a farm errand.

His eleventh birthday was next month, so he wouldn't be fourteen for three more years, but he couldn't wait. Driving seemed to him the ultimate freedom. Chris sometimes wondered what it would be like to drive his grandfather's Olds. The 88 was a huge car, long, black and sleek. It reminded him of the Green Hornet's car in the comic books. The boy decided he would prefer to get a Slug Bug, one of those Volkswagens he saw in Wichita with teenagers driving them. Maybe a bright yellow one.

Since his grandfather left his truck out at night , the far side of the garage was empty and instead was rigged with a rack for hanging and butchering either deer or cattle. Jeff rented freezer space in Alva to keep a side of beef when he did butcher, which was about twice a year. Chris's Uncle Landon almost always shot at least one deer each fall, and most time Jeff did, as well. The boy viewed one butchering session and that was enough for him. He liked hamburgers, but the boy did not like where they came from, at least not to watch.

The chicken coup was the last building in the barnyard. The chicken coop sat in between the garage and the barn. It was a rectangular building identical in construction to the original house, white slats, and a tin roof, but much smaller. It was only about fifteen by ten with its single door facing the house. Chickens were only cooped up at night and had the run of the farm during the day, except Grandma Gwen kept them at bay from the lawn around the house with a wire fence. A gate with a curly-que grill closed the yard but opened with the slightest of tugs.

Chris and Piper entered the chicken coop with baskets in hand. Most of Grandma Gwen's chickens were out pecking in the barnyard, but there were four that scampered this way and that upon the children's entrance. Grandma kept about thirty chickens on hand at any one time. Grandma would catch, kill, and pluck them clean herself when fried chicken was on the menu. The rest, except for the big brown rooster, were hens for laying. Most of the hens produced an egg every other day, so the children hoped to get enough eggs to fill at least the empty dozen carton from this morning's breakfast.

Piper, being older and a bit braver, shooed the chickens away from their nests, which were perched on three shelves along the north wall, but today all the hens were in a dither. They frantically flew and jostled past Chris and Piper as the two children opened the door.

"What the heck?" called Piper as she ducked under the clucking cluster going out over her head. "What's got them all excited?"

Chris saw what it was. A black snake, perhaps four foot or longer, wound its way along the back wall of the coop. It had an egg in its mouth, its jaws distended impossibly far.

"Go get Grandpa," yelled Piper, but Chris was frozen in place, his eyes locked on the snake's glassy yellow gaze.

Piper repeated her call, but Chris did not respond, so she shoved him out of the way, throwing her basket to the ground as she stepped over the concrete foundation. She found Grandpa at the barn running water into the trough.

"Come quick. There's a huge snake eating eggs in the chicken coop."

Grandpa left the water to run and ran into the barn.

He reappeared a moment later with a long-handled hoe.

Piper was already retracing her steps to where Chris now stood outside of the coop.

Grandpa arrived just after her. "Where is it, Chris? Did you keep your eyes on it?"

"It swallowed the egg and then went down that hole." The wide-eyed boy pointed to a gap at the far edge of the wooden shelf and the concrete foundation. "It went down there."

Piper corrected him. "It slithered down there."

Chris shrugged.

Grandpa looked at him. "Did you get a good look at him? Did it have rattles? Was it a copperhead?"

"Nah, Gramps. I've seen pictures of those. This was a big ole black snake. Shiny black with a brownish white underbelly. It was maybe three or four feet long. Rat snake, pretty sure."

Grandpa spit. "I figured as much, but there's been rattlers around before. A fella has to be careful. There's been snakes here long as there's been people. I try to give them space, but we can't be havin' one start eating eggs. I'll see if I can't get a rat trap down in that hole there and maybe catch us a rat snake. What do you think?"

Chris picked up his basket. He stepped over the foundation onto the red clay.

His sister looked at him. "You're not going in there and gather eggs now?"

"Sure, snake's already eaten. Snakes only eat once or twice a month. Now would be the safest time ever, right Grandpa?"

"That's right. I've got to go and turn off the water at the barn. Then, I'll come stand watch for you, Piper. Or maybe Chris will gather all the eggs today. He seems to take a lot of scarin'."

Chris smiled, stepping onto the second shelf. He found an egg in the first nest and placed it carefully in his linen-lined basket.

Cherokee Strip
September, 1893

Tanner Station sat his sorrel horse in a gully cut between two dunes due north of the Salt Fork branch of the Arkansas River. It was September 16 of 1893, and it was Oklahoma territory hot, which meant ten degrees hotter than hell. The sun beat down and the meager wind could not find him, hidden as he was in the thicket of sand plums. His pocket watch told him that it was just past noon and the land run had begun. In less than an hour, his sister, Avery, and her husband, Everett, would be coming. Riding horses alongside the two in the buckboard were Tanner's father, Billy, and Everett's father, Max.

The two elder men and Everett were registered for the run and lined up along with thousands of others along the northern border of "M" county of the Oklahoma territory. They were boomers, those who rushed away at the rifles' roar from the union troops stationed along the northern border. Each man was licensed to stake out 160 acres of land in this the largest of territories to be settled by a land run. It was the clan's hope to claim three contiguous parcels of land and create a nearly five-hundred-acre ranch along the river.

However, the competition was fierce. The town of Kiowa was only fourteen miles away, and the five thousand men on horses and wagons at that starting line would be bearing down on this dirt, too. Hardtner, closer to where Tanner now sat, had fewer boomers, perhaps fifteen hundred. And while the territory was enormous, forty-eight miles wide by fifty-eight miles from north to south, there was not enough land for everyone.

So many people and not enough land led to cheating. Many people hid in the territory ready to jump a claim as soon as the noon race began. They started the race "sooner" than they should have, thus the name. There were boomers and there were sooners.

Tanner, hiding in the brush, was technically a sooner, a derogatory term and one that would start fights for years after the run. His brother, Carson, was also a sooner, also hiding on as-of-yet unclaimed land. The younger brother hid in a copse of trees directly a mile north and east of his older brother. Tanner, only sixteen and not the head of his household, was not legally able to register and Carson, two years younger yet, certainly not. Both now kept watch on the prized property to stop any claim jumpers from staking out the parcels the Stations and Harts had targeted. The boys' father, Billy, told them to ward off any sooners.

The elder men and Everett would be there within the hour. It was only nine miles south and two east to the property from the starting line in Hardtner. Both older men rode cow ponies, not fast, but sure of foot and good for the long haul. The team leading the buggy was also built for durability and strength. That very team of horses had pulled the family from Virginia two years ago to Missouri and later to southcentral Kansas in the last year. The Stations and the Harts believed they would be the first to their land, if the two Station boys, Tanner and Carson, could fend off any sooners who might seek to steal it. The boys' father had been clear; the young men were not to be aggressive with anyone who had a registration claim in hand, at least at 1:00 p.m. or later. No one could expect horses to ride 11 miles in 110-degree heat in less than an hour.

Indeed, the temperature was unbearable. Tanner stepped from the horse to the south side of the berm. The river was but a trickle at this time of the year, but it ran, even in this drought. That was gold for raising cattle. Getting land along the river was vital to survival for a small ranch in this stretch of mesa country. The lanky teen sat on his haunches, rolled, and smoked a cigarette, staring with narrowed eyes across the sandbars far downstream.

From the river's south bank, Tanner saw trouble coming, but he expected it. In his life, if trouble was traveling his way, it inevitably arrived on schedule. Sometimes early.

Several men rode out of a cut in the red-dirt south bank and onto the sand bar. The men's horses splashed through the pool hiding in the shadow of the bluff.

They stopped to let their mounts drink.

The water was deep enough at the center of the pool that one horse began to swim.

Its rider took the moment to leave his holster on the bank and lower himself, hat and all, under the river's flow. The hole was good and deep, perhaps a hundred feet long and forty feet wide. That there was water here, even in September in a drought year was a good sign. Cattle would likely always have a place to drink here, even during the worst of times.

It would be a great place to start a ranch. That was if the Stations and the Harts could claim it, and if the three riders now crossing didn't take the land Tanner had vowed to keep. He watched them from his hiding place, but in five minutes, they landed in their saddles and aimed north once again. The riders surprised him by crossing the sandbar and continued to trot north. Tanner knew that the riders' current path would take them directly to Carson. He made a calculation with a shake of his head, not liking things. The older men would still not be here for some time. Then, wiping his brow, Tanner mounted up.

The older boy made sure to stay well behind the three riders as he hoped and prayed other sooners wouldn't jump the river claim he'd left unprotected. Tanner didn't like leaving it, but Carson was just a boy and not up to facing down three grown men.

Tanner had surveyed the claim in the last two days and knew the land. He swung his sorrel to the east, following a sandy dry stream bed. His horse crossed again to the west, and he gave it his spurs to hurry along.

He rode fast for three-quarters of a mile, figuring he was now ahead of the other three.

The teen dismounted and brought his rifle with him as he edged to the rim of the hill. Below, he could see Carson. The boy knelt against a treefall that left him a bit of cover from the approaching men. Tanner could see his brother knew the three were approaching. The riders also saw Carson, and one who appeared to be the boss, a barrel-chested man in a dusty black shirt, led the way. The three men spread out as they approached.

Tanner took a chance leaving cover. He was directly behind the men.

They did not turn, intent on the boy who knelt behind a tree trunk ahead of them.

Tanner ran across the bare quarter mile. As he closed the distance, he could hear them.

The big man called to Carson, "Boy, I see you there. We intend to lay claim to this land. You're gonna have to move on. Now, go on. You don't want no trouble with us."

Tanner heard Carson's words across the fifty yards between them. "Mister, you ain't got a valid registration. And you ain't no more right to this land than I do. I got me a good pocket watch. It's ain't been even twenty-five minutes since noon. Ain't nobody got a horse fast enough to get here from Hardtner in that time. Kiowa, neither. And for sure not from the south where you come in from. It's near on thirty miles from the starting line down there."

"Don't matter," said the big man who turned to reveal a half-moon scar etched from his left ear to his mouth. He leaned forward, his rifle tilting across his saddle. "You ain't got legal standing here either, son. By my count, we have more guns than you have. And we've been using ours since before your mammy was wiping your ass. We don't want to hurt you. Now, scat."

Tanner stood behind them and jacked a shell into his Henry

repeating rifle. He didn't speak. The shell clicking into the chamber did all the talking.

The other three men turned as if their ears were linked with barbed wire.

"Looky here," the scarred man said. "Another snot-nosed kid. You lookin' for trouble?" His voice gave no indication of fear, just anger at being defied, if only for a second.

Tanner ignored the three riders. "Carson, you got that scattergun cocked back?"

"Yessum."

"Both barrels?"

"Yessum."

"Buckshot like I told ya?"

"Yessum."

"If these fellas commence to raising their guns," Tanner said, his voice flat, "you just let fly with both barrels at that big scar man's belly. Let me worry about the others."

The scarred man seemed to wither a bit with the thought of Carson's shotgun aimed at his guts. The boy couldn't be more than twenty yards away. It would be hard to miss with both rounds from that distance. But he made a show of bravery by turning his back to Carson and faced Tanner. "Who are you? What gives you claim to this land over us?"

"Don't matter. What matters is who gets here first from Hardtner," Tanner grinned. "Let's see who of the boomers gets here first, legitimate-like, shall we?"

"Maybe we don't have that kind of time. You willing to pay the piper?"

"Costs a nickel to find out," Tanner replied. "Oh, you asked my name. I go by Tanner Station. What's your handle?"

The big man did not answer.

With the mention of Tanner's name, the second rider, a scruffy bearded poke on a churro pony, leaned to the man beside him. "Buck, it's that, kid. The kid who killed the two Comanches trying to rob that stage up on the trail out of Abilene."

Tanner had heard the talk before: whispers that ended as he walked into a room, stares whenever he walked into a store, or kids pointing at him as he mounted his horse in Wichita or Dodge City. Tanner was used to hearing his whispered name. He was used to the narrowed eyes. He was used to heads shaking in disapproval. The rumor mill thought him to be a gun hand. A well-known gun. His reputation with a six-shooter had grown to outlandish proportions.

There'd been articles in the Kansas press about him. How he'd killed Indians trying to rob a stage. How he'd gone down to New Mexico territory as a killer for hire. How many a man gone missing in the Cherokee Outlet ended up in a shallow grave after the boy killer robbed and killed him. All the stories had grown larger than life. None he'd heard were accurate. But right now, Tanner was glad for the effect they had.

The three men, believing they were being braced by a stone-cold killer, backed away.

The big man ducked his head, reducing the moment's pressure. "It's a big country. We'll move on."

And they did back away.

Their horses trained to back on roped calves all finished the maneuver without the three men having to turn their backs to the Station brothers.

Once the riders were more than an easy rifle shot away, they turned south and moved away at a trot.

Soon, they veered west, away from any land that the Stations and Harts had plans on.

Tanner relaxed a smidgen, though he could still feel his heart through his shirt.

Within a half hour, Everett and Avery Hart arrived in the buckboard.

The two older men, Billy and Max, stepped from their horses.

Carson and Everett mounted theirs, and together with Tanner, the three rode to the first of the claims, the one near the river bend. Then, leaving Tanner alone at the pool of water, Everett and Carson went back west to the second river site, a property bounded on the south by the Salt Fork and to the north by Hackberry Creek. The claim was near where the riders had headed, but Tanner saw no one. They'd moved on.

An hour later, Everett Hart, his father, Max Hart, and the father of Avery, Tanner, and Carson, Billy Station rode south to the registration office in Alva and registered their claims. The families became landowners before nightfall.

Now, all they had to do to keep it was hold onto it for five years.

Staking the claims was a huge accomplishment, and the family felt ebullient. It was full-on night before the three men returned from registering their claims. By this time of year, mid-September, the days were shorter. Summer was at an end. Those long sultry evenings the Stations had known in Virginia growing up and even last year in Missouri melted away in memory. The heat here was oppressive, even with the sun gone and a full moon looking down. Moonlight tinted the foliage yellow and dimmed the red of the dirt under their feet. Everyone was exhausted from the day's exertions, and yet it had been the best day for all of them since before losing their land to the Reconstruction. All of it that had come before had been one long road ending in a furious race to this piece of land. They felt gratified in their fatigue.

By the time the menfolk returned to the farm, they and the horses were done in. Everett and Tanner sat on the sandy bank with the five horses tethered in shallow water.

Carson used his shirt to soak the horses' backs, and they whinnied in fatigue.

Avery had a fire going on the sandbar. A Dutch oven of beans and ham hocks was heating on stones near the coals.

The two fathers, Billy and Max, were both asleep their heads cradled on their saddles. Neither man was yet fifty, but they had ridden almost forty miles that day in terrible heat. It was a day that would do in the toughest of cowpokes, and neither of these two men were horsemen. They had, however, held their own that day when many younger and stronger had failed. Their nap before a midnight dinner was well-deserved.

Everett, a stockier version of his father, dark-haired and serious, slid a bottle from his boot. He took a swallow and handed it to Tanner.

The teen also gave it a pull. Tanner was lanky, six-three, gaunt and sandy-haired. His eyes were green and right now those eyes had deep circles under them. Everyone, including him, was in serious need of rest.

Everett, five years older at twenty-one and the two families' leader, took the bottle back and looked at his brother-in-law. "If that fella Carson told us about, the one with the scar, had decided different, what would you have done?"

Tanner looked out at Carson and the horses. The moon danced not on land but on the water. It radiated gold like a future foretold by a gypsy woman giving good news. "Sometimes, you don't get to decide what the fiddler plays," Tanner said, softly.

"You'd have let fly with that Henry?"

Tanner shrugged.

Everett raised an eyebrow. "I was there that day at the stagecoach. I saw you in action," he said. "I know the truth."

"I am my brother's keeper, am I not?" Tanner said without emotion.

Everett chuckled but did not respond.

When dinner was ready, Avery woke the two older men from their slumbers. Everett and Tanner helped Carson bring the horses in and line-picket them for the night. Then, the five ate a simple meal and split two cans of peaches in syrup for their dessert. After, Everett handed the whiskey to his father and onto Billy. The patriarch of the clan took a drink.

"My boys here," Billy said, "they didn't get to see what we seen today, to hear what we heard when we went into Alva to register the claims. Boys, did you know two men were killed today by the Union troops? I guess the first man jumped the gun and crossed the line before the bugle started the race. A union officer shot him. A deaf fella saw the first man jump the line and he started early, as well. Another soldier shot him, too."

Billy shook his head and took another swallow. He passed the bottle to Max. The whiskey was two-thirds gone. "Those blue bellies are blood-thirsty bastards."

"Father, watch your tongue." Avery stood and let her skirt flare, as did the flush in her cheek with her father's words. She did not abide violence or profanity.

Billy laughed. "Sorry, Daughter, but we know it's true. We know what them Union troops did in Virginny. We buried those they slaughtered, your mom and me, fore ya'all kids were born. Max did, too. Sherman and Grant, drunks, just like those soldiers today. Drunk killers."

Max, a slender, more elegant man than his son, Everett, had been born to a well-to-do Virginia tobacco farmer and had been educated in private school. The war had taken all his kin, except for his wife. Then, Reconstruction took his wife and his land. Finally, all he had left was Everett. Everett and a future in the American west.

For a short time after the war, Max and his wife, Marleen,

forged a life together. They moved from the big house on the plantation to the town of Orange to find work. Their only child, a son, had been born the first year in town, 1872. Everett had the same bloodlines but not the same financial security in his childhood as his father. His parents ended up as storekeepers waiting on people who'd had them over for dinner five years prior.

Max nodded silently at Billy's berating of the Yankees. Max was quiet for the meal but now spoke to the sights they had seen in their race south in the land run. "We also witnessed horses killed by the heat, all up and down the range. All those well-heeled fellas who brought in their quick Kentucky thoroughbreds, well, those horses were not bred for hundred-degree heat and a ten-mile run. No sir-ee. They dropped, leaving those rich fellas sitting on the seat of their fitted trousers. Most of them within sight of Hardtner and Kiowa. They didn't even get to file a claim."

"They'll buy their way in," said Everett. "Same as they do everywhere."

"The way of the world," Billy added.

Max said, "I heard hundreds of folks took the train, hanging from the rooftops, but it was not allowed to go over fifteen miles an hour and could only stop every five miles."

Billy added, "Claim office feller said some jumped to stake a claim three or four miles out, once the train got a bit ahead of the horses. A few folks got busted up."

Avery spoke for the first time as she gathered spoons and plates. "I wouldn't want to jump from the Atchison-Topeka and the Santa Fe at any speed."

Everett laughed, imagining it. "It wouldn't be very ladylike."

"We heard from someone whose brother jumped. He was back in Kiowa getting a splint on his broken leg," Max said.

Avery finished the conversation. "Then, I'd have to say, compared to a lot of others, we did very well for ourselves. But there'll be lots to do for many weeks to come, so we better get some rest. Carson has got the jump on the rest of you." She smiled down on her little brother, three years the younger. His eyes were closed, and his hands still held a can of peaches balanced on his belt buckle.

"Tanner," she said, "you see to the fire. Everett, you can help me with the dishes down at the river. Dad, you and Max want to get the bedrolls from the wagon?"

She put her hands on her hips, her gingham dress clinging to her hips in the night air. Avery brushed her black hair away from her freckled face and smiled at her husband. "Put that bottle away. We've work to do tomorrow."

Everett stood and swooped to put his arm around her. He pulled his seventeen-year-old wife close and kissed the top of her head. "Anything you say, dear. Anything you say."

The next day and every day for the next few weeks were the same. Residency was required on the staked claims, so the families quickly set up a lean-to in the northernmost claim. They cut saplings, sticking the sharpened ends into the dirt, taking the thatched top of leaves and limbs, weaving it into a tent-frame of sorts up top.

Tanner and Everett removed the buckboard roof and using twine, created a haphazard ceiling for the lean-to, wrapping the fabric frame around the tied limbs. The structure would not be fit for cold weather and the winter that was coming, but it would at least show habitation if the family was challenged for the claim.

Tanner kept the scar-faced man in his head, wondering if he would come back. Knowing the northern claim was the location where he and Carson braced the three riders, Tanner volunteered to sleep here. The lean-to was only big enough for one. Its crude discomfort was his to endure and Tanner moved his bedroll from the back of his saddle to the roughhewn shelter.

On the eastern most flank of the two claims that bordered the river, the families decided on a dug-out for Billy and Carson. Here in the sandy soil, the digging was easy. They found a place at the middle of the one hundred sixty-acre claim. There, the sand dunes, covered with bluestem, some six-foot-tall, created a berm away from view, and wind. Here, they dug into the largest sand dune they found.

They cut saplings again, but this time longer ones and laid them across the span at the top of the dune. With the roof braces in place, they cut sod squares covered with bluestem grass and moved these to form a sod roof over the dugout. The one problem was that the opening to the shelter was a full ten-foot wide and faced north. The days were quickly shorter. The first frost, they guessed, was less than a month away and maybe only a week or two from arrival.

Tanner split what logs he could find and fashioned a wall of sorts to block the winter's chill. It would stop wind, but not cold.

Eventually, the men created a second dugout for the animals. The roof of what the family cheerfully called "the barn" was assembled in less time and one could see up through the thatch to the stars, but it seemed to be enough to shelter the stock in the coldest of weather.

Most of the time in October's early chill was spent in building a sod house on the western side of the farm. It was nearly the same distance from Tanner's lean-to and to Billy's and Carson's dugout. The site was determined as closest to the river bend, but where they found the soil to be red clay and not the river's sandy composition.

Carson carted buckets of water by buckboard to and from the river all day. Tanner spread the water over new sections of soil hour after hour. Everett followed and cut the bricks from the land. Avery spread them on bluestem grass patches to dry in the sun.

While the four youngest worked against the clock on the sod house, the two elders spent their days hunting and fishing. It was their job to provide food for the table. They still had some canned goods, but there was a time coming where food would be hard to find. It was up to the two old men to keep bellies filled before the snow flew.

Billy was the better fisherman, having been a seaman and starting his life in a sea-faring city in Ireland. He soon found that there were both catfish and bass in the hole at the bend in the Salt Fork. His day was first spent by filling a can with worms and then baiting several cane poles with hook and line down by the river.

Max, the better shot, found the surrounding woods and prairie had plentiful game. Deer and rabbit were plentiful. He shot turkey, quail, and on one occasion, he bagged a prairie chicken. Between the fish, fowl, and on the first of October, a small deer which Max and Everett butchered, the family did not feel the pangs of hunger.

Finally, by end of the second week of October after four weeks of continual labor, the walls of the sod house were tall enough that even Tanner would be able to stand inside.

Then, the men set to felling trees. They used three of the sturdiest they found as stanchions to support the peak of the gable to the house. The men split logs, notching them and fitting them to support the corners of the dried mud walls.

Carson and Avery, being the weakest, worked behind the others filling red mud as mortar into every crevice.

Eventually, it was decided to go to town and buy two stove pipes.

Billy went into Kiowa and while none were available on his first visit, he prepaid the general store owner out of their meager reserve and was able to ride into town and retrieve the stove pipes in the third week of October.

By then, Everett and Tanner had created stone and mortar fireplaces for both the dug-out and the sod house.

Once the stovepipes were fitted into place, certainly the sod house, and to some degree, the sandy dug-out could facilitate a small cooking or heating fire. Tanner's lean-to was only fit for warmer weather and would be abandoned come the cold.

The hearth in the main house was none too sturdy, and they resolved to get a Franklin stove when they could afford one.

Finally, they felt the structure, now called the cabin or main house, as home.

With nothing more than a buffalo coat tacked above the entryway as a door, Everett carried his bride across the threshold into their home for the first time on the last night of October 1893. Of course, the married couple would be sharing the tiny home with Max, and in cold weather with at least Tanner, if not Carson and Billy, as well. But through the first week of November, the Indian Summer weather held, and Max stayed at night at the dug-out with Carson and Billy. Tanner was alone at the northern claim in his lean-to. The weather was now too cold at night to sleep on the prairie under the stars.

Snow fell on the eighth of that month, but by that time, the family was well-installed upon the land. They burrowed deep and bided their time for spring to plant crops and try to raise enough money to buy a start-up cow and bull to begin a herd. Times were tough, and the Oklahoma territory's winter was much more difficult than those in Virginia. There was a ten-day stretch when all five slept every night huddled around the stove in the sod cabin when temperatures tumbled into the teens and stayed below zero at night. On balmier nights, the four men crammed into the dug-out to give the married couple some nights alone.

By late February, Avery began to show a tiny bump. She was sure she was pregnant. The two had conceived the child during that last week of Indian Summer in the fall of '93. They named the baby Autumn, but she would born on August 1st, the hottest day of 1894. The six would by next summer be seven.

The Weight
Woods County, Oklahoma
November, 1963

Mom didn't return to the farm Thursday evening, but she called to say she and Grandma Gwen would be back on Friday night. That was fine with Chris and Piper. In the women's absence, the two children fed the dogs (fun), rode in the pick-up to the west pasture to count the livestock (fun), mucked out the manure from the horse stable (not so fun), got to ride Big Red up to get the mail (incredibly fun).

Big Red was a full sixteen hands high, Grandpa Jeff said. What that meant Chris did not know, but he planned to look it up in the *World Book Encyclopedia* when they got back home. Big Red was a gentle giant of a gelding, and the two children felt relatively secure in the saddle.

They walked around the barnyard, and then on their own, they rode Big Red up the quarter-mile long driveway out of their grandfather's view.

Piper rode full in the saddle, leaving room for her little brother jimmied in behind the saddle horn. He didn't mind being tightly wedged in, but the boy was more than a bit afraid.

Once to the mailbox, Piper leaned down and opened the box, grabbed the mail, which included this month's green stamps book, and closed it gently. When she turned Red, he bounced them a little more on the way back, moving into a trot, eager to return to the barn.

Grandpa waved at them and let Piper lead Big Red around the farmyard one more time. The two children clip-clopped around the dog pens, the coonhounds braying at them from their cage, then past the chicken coop, the rooster giving deference to the horse. They looped around the coop in a Figure 8 to the barn, up along the north edge past the garden, and to the edge of the orchard, the peach and apple trees now leafless for winter.

Once Red was back in the corral, Grandpa showed the two how to curry him down and how not to get kicked by the horse while doing it. Not all horses were as nice as Red, he said.

That evening, Piper took possession of the satin comforter.

Chris had hoped in vain she would forget about it, but no such luck. Going to sleep was not quite as sweet as it had been waking up wrapped in "Grandma's Hugs." He longed for the gliding feel of the fabric as he lay down with his comic books, but the boy fell asleep before his grandfather even came in to tell him to turn out the light.

Friday was typically the day Grandpa ran into town for supplies and to the hardware store. Usually, he dropped Grandma off at the hairdressers and then shuttled her to the grocery store, but today the two children and the skinny old man rolled a cart through IGA and picked out the food for the following week.

"Might as well go ahead and to get a turkey," Jeff said. "Looks like you two are staying through next week."

"What about school?" Piper asked. "Don't we have to go back?"

"Aw," Jeff laughed, "missing two more days ain't going to hurt you two smart kiddos. Next week, your school is out Wednesday for teacher's meetings and then it's Thanksgiving. You want for me to give you homework? I have books you should read. I'll give them to you when we get home."

Chris moaned. "Thanks a lot, Piper. I have plenty of reading to do already; I have three *Detective Comics* with the Batman back on the bed."

Even Piper laughed at that.

With groceries purchased, they hurried home to put the turkey in the freezer.

At dark, the women folk were still not home. Jeff fed the children fried baloney sandwiches with chips and apple sauce.

The children helped with dishes again.

Afterwards, Chris lay on his bed, looking at his comics.

His grandfather walked into the room and dropped two books onto the coverlet. "Here you go. These are a couple you should read. Better than that stuff."

Chris picked them up. *Son of the Phantom*. Chris read the first title. "What's it about?"

Grandpa sat on the edge of the bed, "It's kind of like Tarzan. Guy lives in the jungle and really gives it to the bad guys."

"How about this other one?" Chris said, "*Riders of the Purple Sage* by Zane Grey. I guess it's a cowboy story, huh?"

Jeff patted his grandson's head. "Yeah, it is. The best one ever. Get your pajamas on. You can read the first chapter in whichever one you want to get into first before you go to bed."

"Can I read to you?"

Jeff smiled. "No, I 'spect your mom and Gwen will be walking in any moment. I want to get a couple of things done 'fore the women get here, pickin' at how I left the place." He smiled and left the room.

Chris read the first chapter in the phantom book, trying to stay awake for his mother's return, but the womenfolk had not arrived before he yawned and turned out the light.

When Chris awoke in the morning, he could hear his mother's voice in the kitchen around the corner from his room. He lay still and listened. The boy knew the grown-ups would stop talking about important stuff if they knew he was awake. The house was small and his bed was close to the door.

"The judge wouldn't extend bail until Henry's priors report

arrived from Delaware. And even then, the lawyer said to expect it to be five thousand dollars. Ten percent down is five hundred bucks. I don't have that kind of money."

Gwen said, "Your father does, honey. We'll get Henry out. You're going to have to go down to Oklahoma City and take care of this on Monday, Jeff."

"Dad, I can't ask you to put out five hundred dollars for Henry's stupidity," Lillian said.

Jeff replied, "Yeah, it only costs me if he jumps bail. No reason for him to do that. Henry should be able to get the charges reduced. Took a car home and returned it in the morning. Hardly a felony rap,"

Chris could hear Grandma Gwen stand and move to the stove. She must have been refilling coffee cups. "That rich fella who owned the Cadillac is connected. Owns the biggest nightclub in OKC, I hear. They run slots and tables in the back. Cops know and let it ride. Everybody in town knows and since everybody gets their share, nobody does nothing." She paused. "That rich guy wants the judge to throw the book at Henry."

Then, Piper bounded around the corner. She saw Chris lying in his bed, eyes wide open, listening, but before he could shush her, she rounded the corner, and the adults abruptly shifted the conversation.

"There's my baby girl," said the children's mother. "Did you miss me?"

"Terribly, Mom. Those boys treated me just like, just like," she paused, trying to think of just the right phrase.

Chris stuck his head into the room. "Like the brat she is."

Everyone laughed.

Mom sent the kids to wash their hands to get ready for breakfast. Chris's mind was tumbling with all the information he had garnered before Piper blew it. But he still ate. Grandma's cooking was a lot better than Grandpa's.

As they finished their pancakes and Tang, Jeff said, "Get a move on, kids. We have to finish the chores before we run into Hardtner.

Your grandma wants to get her hair done, and Saturday is a busy day at Merna Dawn's. She only had one appointment left. Merna'll have to hurry on Grandma's hairdo if we're going to get back in time for the Sooner football game."

On Monday, Jeff and his daughter, Lillian, left the kids in the care of their grandmother. It felt extra special to Chris. He couldn't remember ever missing school like this without having been sick. Somehow, missing a Monday felt like a much bigger deal to him. He felt like a criminal, and he had to admit it was a bit thrilling. Chris knew enough not to mention his emotion. He knew Piper would report his words back to Mom.

The kids did the chores as they been taught, including mucking out the stalls after Uncle Landon moved the horses to the corral. He saddled his gelding, Blackie, and rode out to check on the livestock. Landon lived in Hardtner with his wife, Etta Jane, and his daughter, Libby. Libby was only three, and Chris didn't think little kids were much fun. Piper thought them adorable.

Uncle Landon, Lillian's older brother, was a quiet man. A true cowboy, he felt most at home in the saddle. He was a long and lean man, big on doing and shy on speechifying. Landon had served his country in Korea. The war made him quiet, although he had not been a talker even before. Chris didn't know him well. Not many did. The thin cowpoke was a man of few words. Often, it seemed like he might speak, but he would just squint and light a cigarette. Mom told Chris that Landon lived on mashed potatoes out of C-Rations cans for a whole winter in the war and had vowed upon his return never to eat mash potatoes again. But with that vow, Landon helped Grandma Gwen maintain a huge summer garden of fresh veggies. Everyone benefitted from his hours of hoeing. They grew few potatoes.

Lanky and always in black boots, Landon was good with a rope. Plus, he was a crack shot. During quail season, which was right now, he could always be counted on to bring dinner back. He didn't hunt much, though. A cowboy's work was never done, and Landon was a busy man. Chris figured Landon felt the same about him as Chris felt about babies. That was okay, too, Chris calculated. He was getting bigger, if slowly. Someday, when he could help with round-up, Landon would talk to him. Grandpa called it "earning your spurs." Chris could not wait for that day.

To Chris, his Uncle Landon was a dead ringer of those cowboys in the Ace Reid-drawn "Cow Pokes" cartoon strip. The boy did not share the observation with Uncle Landon. Chris was a little intimidated by his uncle, but he also watched him carefully. Most impressive to the boy was that Landon never had a wasted movement. His ability to be still, whether it be a fishin' or just sitting on the top rung of the corral fence with cigarette smoke drifting past his face, fascinated the boy.

After the kids finished the outside chores, they both headed in and took a quick bath. Afterwards, Gwen went to making apple pies. Piper helped.

Chris moved to his bed and read more about the phantom. His grandfather was right. The book was much better than a comic book.

But an hour before lunch, the smell of the baking pies drew Chris from his bedroom.

"Well, look who shows up now that there's food to eat," Gwen smiled. "Got some snacks just coming out of the oven." She took hot pads and removed a dozen tiny, baked rolls of pie dough and then sprinkled them with sugar and cinnamon.

"You need to wait a few minutes so you don't burn your tongue. They're hot."

Piper piped in. "Won't it ruin his lunch?"

Chris groaned. Why did his sister always butt in?

Gwen laughed at her grandson's reaction. "He can have one,

maybe two, and we'll wait to have lunch until an extra half hour goes by."

By late morning, Uncle Landon returned, and the children went out with him and helped curry the horse. Landon left them to it and went to the house to talk to "Ma," as he called her.

Just at dusk, their grandfather's Olds rolled up the drive, but without Lil.

With ham steaks on the table, Jeff explained to Gwen, Landon, and the kids about what had taken place. "That judge, Judge Hiram Spence, he don't like that rich guy who owns the Caddy as much as you two let on. I think the judge is a bit of a prude. He knows that rich fella runs a club with illegal gamblin'. I don't think the judge abides gambling, Gwen."

"And he shouldn't. He is sworn to uphold the law."

Landon laughed. "Rich take cares of rich."

Jeff smiled. "Anyhows, me and the judge got to talkin', and I mentioned how I hated to come down here and handle this right in the middle of quail season, and his eyes plum lit up. Turns out the man's a hunter. I thought he might be. Saw a photo of a dog in the judge's chambers when we got back in to see him. Good lookin' pointer, it was."

"So how did that help, Grandpa?" Piper asked.

"Well, darlin', it's the way the world works. You scratch somebody's back and they ease up on ya if they got you in the squeeze. I told the judge about the sand plums down on the Salt Fork and how they just overflowed with coveys. I could see His Honor start thinking."

"What about, Pa?" Piper asked.

"The judge agreed that grand theft auto was a pretty big stretch for leaving a car parked in your driveway overnight. Turns out Henry's story is that he drove it home to eat but had a couple of beers with dinner and decided that he shouldn't drive the other man's car after having alcohol. He decided to not drive it back until the morning. Just a misunderstanding, he said."

Gwen tutted. "And Judge Spence is buying that malarkey?"

"He is, long as he gets a quail hunt out of it."

Chris smiled. "When is he coming to hunt? Tomorrow?"

Jeff smiled and forked a cut of ham into his mouth. "Judges are busy, Chris. He won't be down until next Saturday."

"And tell the kids where their momma is," Gwen said to her husband.

Jeff spoke with his mouth full. "With Henry. I got him out for $500, but he can't leave the city limits. Lil stayed with him, although I'm not sure I would want her with me if I was Henry. Looked like he was about to get an earful once I drove off." He smiled and took a drink of tea.

"Why she ever let him take that job in Oklahoma City is beyond me. It's just been trouble since day one," Gwen said.

"'Cause Addy's Car Shop paid twice what anybody would pay in Wichita for a skilled mechanic like Henry, especially with a rap sheet from back in Delaware," Jeff replied.

Gwen frowned, and Chris made a mental note to ask his sister what a rap sheet was.

"It's only until Mom finishes her schooling," Piper added.

Jeff nodded, "The girl's right. Addy's is the biggest and best mechanic shop in Oklahoma, probably. He's mad at Henry, sure, but Addy won't fire Henry if we can get this quail hunt to go down just right."

"And how does that work, Jeff?" Gwen said.

"Well, I think it's time Chris learned to shoot. The judge is going to want to have someone along and nothing says we're good, wholesome folk like having the clear-eyed, innocent son of the accused walking alongside the judge when he's bagging a few quail."

Chris smiled big. "I'm ready."

Jeff mussed his hair. "Good, boy. We'll start you shooting in the morning."

Chris was surprised that in the morning his grandfather emerged from his bedroom, where he kept his weapons high up on the wall, with a .22 rifle in hand. Chris had never seen that gun before. The boy had seen the men with shotguns, usually twenty gauges for quail. Chris had also seen Uncle Landon with a deer rifle, but he'd never seen this smaller weapon.

"This is a .22 Hornet," Jeff said. "We're going to shoot shorts in it today. Let you get used to shooting, but first let's go outside and familiarize you to the gun. No bullets for now. There's etiquette involved. And safety is the main thing."

Chris was disappointed. He thought he'd be shooting the shotgun right away. His face must have given away his emotions because Jeff took his shoulder and directed him outside.

"Gotta learn how not to kill the judge before you can learn to hunt alongside him, boy. Now get a move on."

Later that morning, Chris did get his first chance to shoot. But only with the .22 at Hamm's beer cans on the fence posts south of the dog pens. He learned to take a breath and breathe out slowly as he squeezed the trigger. The gun was bolt action and held six shots in its clip. Before long, Chris was hitting cans with regularity from fifty feet away.

When Jeff moved him back to the sloping ground before the garage, he missed every time. Chris was discouraged, but Jeff let him move closer once again before they quit and he put a beating on the beer cans, hitting them five times.

"Chris, boy, you're a natural, I'd say. It is nice that the gun has almost no kick for a little guy like yourself. The shotgun you'll be using, a .410, is still a light gun. It'll be different. You don't get to aim and squeeze like you do here. A bird gets up, or a dozen get up and they're gone if you take as long to aim as you do."

"Do I get to shoot the shotgun tomorrow?"

"Nah, I don't think so. We'll work on this 'un again tomorrow. See if you remember your safety lessons. Then, we'll see if you can snap shoot with the .22 and hit maybe one of those tree trunks out there. You can do that, you'll be ready for the .410."

"Gotta be ready by Saturday, don't I?"

Jeff smiled and nodded. "Now, show me how to make sure the weapon is unloaded before we head to the house. I'm starvin'."

Oklahoma Territory
March, 1894

The drought broke with the spring rains in '94. The lowlands near Hackberry Creek flooded and the menfolk used the time to cut hundreds of clay bricks from the sod beneath the new grass. It was a tedious process, but one speeded by not having to haul water from either the creek or from the river.

Carson and Billy spent days moving finished bricks from the flooded plain onto higher land, laying them upon the bent stalk of bluestem grass in the pastures.

It was decided with Avery due to give birth in the summer that a second house would be built, this one on the northernmost claim, nearer the woods and close to Tanner's lean-to. That required moving the bricks the better part of a mile. The backboard was repurposed without its seats, carrying loads of bricks after they cured in the Oklahoma sun.

Billy and Max began to learn the art of becoming masons. This new structure was to be much larger and to have two rooms, a central living quarters, and a back bedroom, with a fireplace in between to keep both rooms warm. More importantly, they framed the corners of the structure with thick beams so that as time and finances allowed, they might replace the sod, which softened and became muddy in rainy times, to a wood paneled frame house. Another major improvement to the first house is that they sold one horse, Max's, at his insistence to buy a tin roof. It was decided the four men would live here away from the married couple.

Carson spent his days gardening and as soon as the last frost was safely gone, he planted corn, beans, potatoes, and other vegetables. He also chopped the wood for cooking each day. The boy had changed from the insecure and scared fourteen-year-old into a thick-bodied, heavily muscled, young man. His hair was sandy blonde, his eyes blue. Carson looked more like his father with his broad-shouldered frame. Tanner, much thinner, favored their departed mother.

Carson spent his evenings exploring the river, now flowing with water. He often brought catfish, bug-eyed and bulbous, back for nightly meals prepared out of doors by Avery. With the weather warm, the family spent little time inside the one room cabin by the river. Most nights, they camped a mile north at the site of the new homestead. Carson often was away from the family, camping under the stars by himself.

Once the frame of the house was in place, the two older men kept busy each day mudding and placing bricks. Everett suggested he and Tanner ride to Texas. Everett was the thinking man of the family. He had an idea that might help them get some cattle on the cheap, and after explaining, the family agreed the two young men should ride south.

Everett and Tanner took the two best horses the next morning and rode across the Oklahoma Territory into central Texas. There they met cattle herds moving north. They were easy to find, as they stirred huge clouds of dust on the horizon. Those clouds could be seen from more than thirty miles away. There was no hiding large herds moving north.

The two young men waved and greeted the cowboys as they approached the herds. Friendly calls returned with tired smiles. Most of the dusty, beat-up men greeted them warmly, glad to have someone new to talk to after weeks on the trail.

Everett did the talking. He made his pitch and handed the ramrods his hand-drawn maps, showing the men how to get to their land, where the grass was high, the water plentiful, and most importantly, there was no grazing fee. Everett would trade passage through for cows still young enough to procreate. He offered time enough to rest the herd, as well. No cash was Everett's selling point. It was music to the ears of the ramrods in charge of getting the herds north. Most dreaded the grazing fees of the Cherokee Nation or the exorbitant rate of the big ranches. Several handshakes left the two young men hopeful a few herds would head their way.

Everett and Tanner arrived back after three weeks of living out of their bedrolls with smiles on their faces. It looked certain at least five herds headed north would rest up and fatten on their lands in trade for cattle. Without money to buy a herd, it looked as if they might be in the cattle business before the fall.

The Oklahoma Outlet had been used by the cattlemen of Texas as a stop-off for nearly thirty years. After the Treaty of 1866 with the Cherokee, cattlemen used the strip as a place to rehydrate and fatten their herd after the long trail to the Kansas railheads from south Texas.

In 1866, 600,000 cattle moved through the strip. During the next twenty years, more than five million cattle had watered there, many along the Salt Fork. But in 1882, the Cherokee Tribe began to ask for a dollar a head for cattle crossing their land. While the two sides finally agreed at forty cents a head, cattlemen moaned. This fee was a huge expense.

A herd of two thousand head, which was average sized, would now cost $800. With the labor cost of a cowboy at thirty dollars a month, the toll by the Cherokee suddenly was a huge and despised expense, especially as the money was going to Indians. Many Texans balked at doing business with Indians at all. Eventually, a lease was worked out on the part of the many Texas cattlemen who couldn't, or wouldn't, bear such a toll, and the Tribe was paid $100,000 for the cattle herds to have permission to cross the territory.

However, even though the path was now clear with the Cherokee, the homesteading of the territory meant even more trouble for the migrating herds. In fact, some new Oklahoman ranchers were beginning to fence their land to block the herds. Everett had heard the talk. He reckoned the ramrods knowing there was a home away from home at the river was a comfort worth aiming for. Especially if it only cost a few cows. Cash was always in short supply before the herd got to the railhead. Everett was the first small rancher to barter with the cowboys driving the herds north, but he wouldn't be the last. Many a Boomer owning a farm followed Everett's and Tanner's lead to trade grass and water for livestock.

When the first herd arrived in the latter part of June, Avery was heavy with child and uncomfortable in the heat, but Everett was beaming when the herd moved on north after a week's grazing leaving four calves and four mature cows behind. The Stations and Harts were suddenly ranchers. And on August 15th of that year, Autumn Eve was born. Everett smoked a cigar by the river with his father, Max. Life had never looked better to the new dad.

By the time the last herd had passed through to the railroad hubs in Dodge City and Wichita, seven different ramrods had paid in cattle and the farm now had forty-five head. The cows were old, maybe with only a year or two of fertility left in them, but they carried the ranch's brand, an F within a flowing river of two capital S's. The Salt Fork Stations, as they began to call themselves, butchered one cow for winter meat, salting the beef into jerky which could be made into a salty stew. They would not go hungry.

Autumn Eve proved to be a difficult child in her first winter, which was blessedly mild, but nonetheless she was an infant who slept but two hours at a time for most of her first six months. That winter the four men were very glad that the north place was built. Of the men, only Everett suffered from lack of sleep due to the child's wailing.

Avery was spent most of the winter, sleeping whenever the child slept.

With the herd now easily their most valuable asset, the men took turns riding and watching over the cattle. The herd was unusual in that almost half of them were less than a year old. The other half were quite old. They also had no bull to protect the herd from predators, like wolves or coyotes. Indians and rustlers were also a concern that kept Everett awake at night.

Everett prayed that they would not get a sub-zero stretch of weather and that the calves would not freeze to death. He didn't worry nearly as much about the cows which carried more fat and thereby held more body heat. But the grassland had been cropped short by the passing herds, some of which were massive in number. There was little cover for the young ones. The land farthest east, near the dugout, still held pockets of grass, and the sand dunes offered shelter from winter winds.

Tanner and Carson moved the herd in among the sand dunes out of the worst of the weather during snow and cold. The two, who wintered in the dug-out in fair weather, took turns checking the herd at night. There were still rumors of buffalo wolves on the plains, though the Station boys had never known of anyone who'd lost cattle to one. Cougars, however, were a different story. One occasionally still saw a track for one of those big beasts.

It was a difficult time. The older men needed Everett's help in hunting to keep the family in meat by hunting. Carson and Tanner had to break the ice at the river each morning to allow the cattle to drink. Everett worked to excess, his face now as lean as Tanner's so that people thought they were brothers, not brother-in-laws. But Everett, as father to the newborn and now clearly their leader, let the Station boys guard the herd at night, so he could spend evenings in the main house with his new family. Carson and Tanner did not complain.

When the weather finally broke and green shoots started appearing on the prairie, all of the Salt Fork Stations breathed a sigh of relief. The herd had survived its first winter. Now, the trick was to furnish the herd with a bull so that the cows might provide yet more calves by the fall. One young calf looked to be a future sire, but he was still too young. So once again, Everett and Tanner rode south to the herds, finding partners satisfied with last year's deal and traded in advance to bring a young bull north in exchange for use of the river ranch.

Upon Everett's and Tanner's return in April, both Billy and Max moved to Alva some twenty-five miles south, taking jobs in town to earn some actual cash which the family had not possessed to any degree in the last two years.

Billy went back to his Dublin days and worked in a saloon. He learned to deal Faro and Blackjack at The Hole, an afterhours gambling joint on the southside of the burgeoning city.

Alcohol sales were forbidden in Indian Territory, but now that the land runs had essentially homesteaded the entire Cherokee Nation, the laws were flaunted, if not outright ignored. Saloons were common but were kept on the "wrong" side of the tracks. Out of sight and out of mind seemed to be good enough for the women-folk of Alva. And if the women did not object, then the men were pleased. By the end of 1894, there were at least as many saloons in Alva as there were churches. And more men attended them than the churches. Women held their tongues as long as drinkin' and whorin' stayed on the southside of the train depot.

Max found work at a general store, using his experience behind the counter in Virginia five years before as a reference toward employment. He and Billy worked opposite shifts and rented a one-room apartment with a single rollaway bed. Most times, they slept opposite shifts. They lived cheaply. The goal was to save enough to buy furniture for the two cabins on the ranch before winter. The first item would be a rocking chair for the crabby Autumn Eve. It became more important in June of '95 when Avery announced that she was again with child.

One day, not two weeks after Avery had made her announcement, Carson and Tanner, fresh from weeding the garden, rode to inspect the herd. Finding the cattle grazing peacefully, the two young men stopped along the Hackberry Creek. The bluestem at sunset was near purple as long shadows stretched from the cottonwoods. A wind, with maybe still a hint of northern chill, rustled the prairie grass as the late afternoon sun lit it lavender and blue. The cottonwoods whispered in their high limbs. The air was crisp, the breeze soft. It was perhaps the best day since they had arrived here twenty months ago.

"Tanner, you ever get tired of all this?" Carson asked.

"What do you mean, little brother? Tired of days like this?" He smiled and nodded his chin up to the heavens above.

"Well heck, you know what I mean. I guess it's fine, but..." He made the last word seem a penance. "Seems like we work all the time. When's the last time we ever did anything for fun?"

Tanner pulled the tallest stalk of bluestem free from a plant and stuck it in his teeth. He was tan and his green eyes glittered a bit in the late afternoon sun. He pushed his flat, crowned hat back on his head, squinting at the sun on the western horizon. "We fish and we hunt. We sleep on our own land. Our father, and his father, spent the years of their youths, the years we're living, either in debtors' prison in Ireland or shanghaied and out to sea against his wishes. You and me have it pretty good."

"Yeah, but Pa saw the world. He saw England, India, and the Horn of Africa. He's worked on a ranch in Australia. He's been to New York City and Boston. He's seen the world. I seen the world from a sharecropper's cabin in Virginia and a tenement in St. Louis I've lived in a mud hut for the last two winters. Don't you git what I'm seein'?"

Tanner shook his head. "We're making our own way. You forget why our father saw the world the way he did. I'll have him tell you again next time we're together about how we came to be Stations instead of Donahues. It's a wonder, the story is." Tanner's voice grabbed his father's brogue from memory unintentionally.

Carson said, "I know I'm not quite full grown. But I'm bored. I wouldn't mind seeing a girl. Or going to town with some change jingling in my pocket. Maybe getting to go see a rodeo or a horse race. Maybe get in a fight."

Tanner raised an eyebrow. "A fight, eh? Now there's ambition if ever I heard it."

Carson turned to face his brother. Tanner had him by four inches, but not by many pounds. Tanner's lean arms and legs had a suppleness, and Carson knew he would lose a wrestling match with him now, but the day was coming when he would be stronger of the two.

Knowing the load would eventually shift his way, Carson spoke his mind. "You and Everett went out west when you were my age. On your own, you two. Fought some Injuns, you did. And *you* even kilt two of 'em. I don't see why I'm destined to be stuck here for the rest of my life."

"Firstly," Tanner said, his face now dark with disappointment, "we don't talk about that day. Our sister doesn't cotton to violence. Our mother was Quaker, and our sister holds those beliefs dear to her heart. We don't abide violence and we certainly don't aspire to fighting."

"Says the Injun killer," said Carson, suddenly with iron in his neck, his chin jutting. He turned his face toward his older brother. "You talk about peace. But when that fella with the scar came callin', you talked pretty big."

Suddenly, Tanner swung his boot through the grass.

Carson thought Tanner planned to trip him and whirled out of the away, but the boot was not intended for him. It rushed through the clump of grass beside the boy and swept a prairie rattlesnake, coiled and ready to strike, into the air.

The snake untethered like a lariat as its mouth, fangs extended, stabbed only air just past the younger boy's leg, missing the meat of his calf by less than six inches. The rattler landed just feet away. It coiled its blotched body again, looking all the world like a tightened muscle. The snake gave its distinctive warning.

Carson leapt away. "Holy Christ, what do I do?"

Tanner said, "Shoot it. You wanted some excitement. There's some."

Afterwards, they walked back with the snake dangling from Carson's hand.

Tanner led the two horses, both flighty with the snake's scent heavy in their nostrils.

Tanner looked at his brother, "Remember, little brother, when you go looking for excitement, sometimes you find it."

Later, at dinner with the family eating the snake meat pulled into strips and cooked on willow sticks, Carson retold the story without recalling the conversation which had taken place during the moments before the snake's appearance.

When he got to the place in the story where he drew his gun, Carson said, "I kilt it dead to rights, I did." He snorted with emphasis at Everett, Tanner, and little Autumn Eve, but then broke into a grin. "But it took me four shots."

The whole family laughed.

After a spell, Everett said, "There's a lesson there, Carson. Today was a glorious day. As beautiful a day as God ever gave us. And yet there was a snake in the grass. Had Tanner been my height, he wouldn't have reached that serpent with his big ole boot. A shorter man might not have been able to kick that snake out of harm's way. 'Twas lucky for you, it was him, not me. We all need to remember there's always trouble out there in the grass."

Avery punched her husband on the shoulder, and the baby squealed in delight. "Ev, you leave the boy alone with your preachi-fying. It was a snake in the grass, simple as that. He kilt it and now you got a full belly. So you just go on."

Everett raised an eyebrow. "There's always a snake in the grass, ain't there, Tanner?"

Tanner didn't reply.

Tanner did ponder Carson's complaint over the next two days and finally when the work seemed to slack off a little and rain settled in, he suggested the two of them ride to Alva and take in the sights for a couple days, not that it took even two hours to see the sights in the small city.

Tanner told Everett his plans. He could tell his brother-in-law did not approve. Everett's drive to make the ranch a success was nearly puritanical in its dedication. And this occasion would be the first time anybody had taken a leisure day other than Christmas and Easter over the last two years.

Everett frowned, but he kept his tongue inside his mouth and agreed to watch the herd by himself for the next two days.

Tanner and Carson rose early the next morning, did their chores fast as they could, and after a quick lunch of biscuits and dried beef, the two waved to Everett as he left the cabin toward the herd. Then, they rode to Alva.

Five hours later, they arrived.

Billy, their father, did not usually start dealing cards until nine in the evening, so he was available to have supper with the two young men when they shuffled in unannounced at the small house that he and Max now rented.

"Yes, heaven's yes, we'll go to out to a fine meal," the stout Irishman said to his sons. "Max, change out of your mercantile clothes and put that apron away. We've to take these hungry boys for some beefsteak."

While Carson and Tanner scrubbed their faces and brushed the dust from their clothes, Max changed from his mercantile clothes and apron.

Billy put on his best white shirt and a fresh collar. He deftly anchored the collar to his shirt with a stud in the back.

As Tanner looked out the bedroom window, Max called to him from the mirror. "Tanner, I believe I met the man you and Carson stood to ground the day of the land run. A man with a scar like you described came in the store a week or so ago. Asked for a line of credit. A thoroughly unpleasant fellow, I must say. Melvin Harris was his name. Rides as a ramrod for the Miller 101."

Everyone knew of the 101. Founded by Colonel George Washington Miller, a veteran of the Confederate Army, in the same land run as the Stations ran in 1893, the patriarch and his three sons lay claim to land near Ponca City. The colonel had soldiers who served under him likewise stake claims on adjoining land only to sell the claims back to Miller.

It was a huge operation, one that in many ways precipitated breaking the grazing fee contract with the Cherokee Nation. It was said that the colonel and those who worked for him were ruthless and relentless in getting what they wanted. However, Ponca City was a two day's ride due east of Alva. The Salt Fork Station and its concerns were too distant even to rise to the consciousness of a land baron, even one beginning his own country in the territory outside the United States, at least for now.

Tanner waited to see if Max had more to say about this Harris fella, but Max was not a talking man. He was, however, a dapper one. Tanner stood in silence, watching Max straighten his tie, adjust his vest and comb his hair. The elder man turned from the mirror, having finished. "There, that should do," he said.

Billy stepped in the small dressing room, pulling his black coat onto his shoulders. "You're speaking of Mel Harris, the bastard with the scar. Aye, I met him, as well. Well, you know the Millers have the biggest ranch this side of Texas. Over Ponca City way, it is. Harris works for the Colonel but comes all the way to Alva to wreak havoc. Harris runs with some trash. Buck Wells and Charlie Crups, both of them drunks and thieves. Harris is a troublemaker, and the other two follow his lead. Harris is smart enough to know that he can't raise hell close to home. The colonel wouldn't stand for it. Or that's the talk at the card table. Tanner, Carson, my boys, you crossed a bad one. Stay well clear of him. If you see him coming, I recommend crossing the street and heading the other direction. The man's a heartache, he is."

Carson raised his eyebrows at Tanner, but he said nothing. Of course, Tanner did not comment. He never did. And as they left the house for the evening, Carson noted his brother did not take his .45 Army Colt. Carson, however, stuck his 1849 Pocket revolver in the small of his back. His father's warning would not be lost on him.

The four were soon at a table in The Bull's Corral, a restaurant owned by Kat Dodson, the same man who ran the afterhours saloon where Billy worked.

Together, the four men feasted on slabs of prime rib, potatoes with gelatinous gravy, and thick hunks of bread slathered with butter. Beer was brought by the pitcher.

Carson, not having drank alcohol before, soon had a rosy glow on his cheeks. His sandy hair was mussed, and he bore a wide grin Tanner had not seen on his brother in quite some time.

"Carson, your brother here tells me you've been somewhat on the glum side, my boy," Billy began, several drinks freeing his Irish tongue. The gift of gab was upon him.

Carson frowned at Tanner across the table. "It's not that. The farm is just dull. We work all the time and nothing changes. You and Max are here in town. You live in a nice place. You eat good. Me and Tan, we just see cows and mud." He paused. "And get bossed around by Everett."

Max guffawed. "We don't eat like this every day, boy."

Billy laughed. "Cows and mud, eh? Do ye remember all the men running from that starting line coming on two years ago? How some died trying to get a piece of that mud? To raise cows?" He finished his glass and nodded for his youngest son to fill it. "Listen, boy, this meal cost me tonight's pay and then some, but Tanner thought you needed a bit of sunshine in your life. Eat up. Drink up.

"But before that full belly puts you to sleep, let me tell you how we came to be here. I know you've heard it before. You all have, even Max here, but it bears retelling. For it's how you got your name. The name Station. Because your blood is that of the Donahues."

Billy took a drink, settling in. "I was raised in Malahide, a coastal village outside Dublin. We were poor, but saying we were poor Irishmen is redundant. Do you know that word? It means saying the same thing twice. My father was a fisherman; Ned Donahue was his name, and he was a good man. Your grandfather was, but he was but a fisherman in a country filled with 'em, but ever the worse for our lot, he was a fisherman on another man's boat. Ned, he could barely keep us fed in good times. In bad weather, when the boats couldn't get out of port, we didn't eat unless we had fish from yesterday's catch. And in the winter, it was a common thing to hear your stomach complain.

"I was the oldest of four children, urchins if ever the word had meanin'. And as soon as I could, my mother found work for me, but bein' barely twelve and smallish, the pay was hardly enough to help at all." Billy's eyes looked inward as he remembered his younger days.

"I took to stealing. First from markets. Just enough for me to eat myself, but going home with a full belly to my sisters and me mum gone hungry didn't sit well in my heart. Soon, I took to tryin' to steal enough to feed the family, but it was difficult to get enough for five under my coat. And the storekeepers began to know my face well enough to run me off long before I got me pockets filled. Off to greener pastures and down to the city, I took to stealing better things, things that could be sold. And for that, you need somebody to sell to. Of course, there is always somebody in the business of buying stolen merchandise if the price is low enough. The fine art of fencing, and I'm not talking swords here.

"My fence was a man called Bernie Riordan. Bernie lived over in Portmarnock. It was still a backwater town, but there was a castle there for tourists to explore during good weather, so Bernie made his living selling stolen goods, watches, and jewelry. Stolen from tourists, sold back to other tourists. Black market on a small scale under the table of the meat counter, if you believe it.

"I got in some scrapes. It was a rough crowd I ran with. More than one mate I knew ended up in the canal as fish food. You get caught stealing from the wrong ones, well, they had no patience with it. They never caught me, they didn't. Though I was smallish, I was fast, and a pretty good pickpocket after a time.

"Now by this time, I'm sixteen and I can hold my liquor, or think I can, and me and my best mate, Martin, get soused. We end up late at night in the taverns near the docks of Malahide, which were the only ones who would serve us, most of the village knowing we were thieves and as liable to steal their pocket watch as give them the time of day." Billy smiled at his line, used before in the telling of this tale.

"Coming out of that bar that night, I got blackjacked on the head, both me and my mate. Except they hit Martin a little too hard. Cracked his skull and died, Martin did. I heard about it from the one who killed me friend the next day. He laughed telling me. Me in shackles held below deck on a freighter. British bastards shanghaied me.

"I spent five months swabbing the decks and working in the kitchen on our first go. It was bloody hot in the kitchen below deck on a freighter in the East Indies, I'll tell ye. The captain, an arse of a man named Javitts, kept me chained below deck when we came into port in Italy, and later in Siam. Finally, I learned to not fight the bit. I began to act as if I had warmed to the job. I told the occasional joke. Told people about how my life now was infinitely better than the hell of being beaten nightly by my father, which was partially true. Eventually, I was no longer the newest kidnapped crewman. The pecking order had moved on, and I moved up.

"Javitts finally gave me some freedom. I was promoted to above deck and some poor shanghaied Indian out of Bombay who progressively lost his bronze color out of the sun became the new galley boy.

"When we finally made it to the end of the world, the west coast of Australia, bloody Captain Javitts went so far as to give me some coin and tell me to go ashore, get drunk and get lucky. Javitts told me to be back in thirty-six hours. The captain warned me if I was late, he'd send his Shanghai boys to find me with their knives, not their saps. He told me those things before he met with the dock laborers to unload our cache. And that beast meant it, so I went down below decks, dressed in the best set of rags I had to wear, slipped into the captain's cabin, and stole his watch, his monocle and his knife, a nifty folding blade that tucked into a tusk handle. I carry it to this day." Billy removed the knife from his pocket, unfolded the blade and stuck it in the bread in front of them. He showed them the *J* initialed on the knife's handle.

"Then, I left the ship in Denham. The port's a shithole, a port on Shark Bay, and they mean it. Great whites there waiting for a man thrown overboard, I tell ya. The town was just as bad. Full of thieves. Just like I had been, like I obviously still was. And I knew Javitt's men, they'd be coming for me as soon as the captain found the knife and the watch missing. They'd kill me if they found me. I didn't wait around. Didn't even stay for one beer. Nope, I departed the city, heading inland on the first wagon headed east. Paid my coin for a ride inland.

"Eventually, I found my way to Home Valley Station. That's a cattle ranch. It's damn near as big as Ireland, boys, but not as green. Hardly a bit of color there. Red as the clay on our farm, it is. But a bit bigger. Fifty-five hundred square miles, that station is. That's the same as three and a half million acres. How's that compared to our puny five hundred?" Billy looked to the bar. "Raymond, this pitcher is empty! How can you let me and my sons go dry, my friend?"

Ray, the bartender, raised an eyebrow, having been eavesdropping on the story Billy told. He called across the room to the little Irishman. "Seems to me, Billy, the only person wagging his tongue enough to be dry would be you. Make sure you're in shape to deal cards tonight or it'll be my carcass for not cutting you off."

Billy wagged a finger at the barkeep. "Beer will never do me in, dear Raymond. Whiskey, yes. She has been known to knock me off my feet in the latter rounds, she has, but beer, I'm able to drink it all night and still shuffle a deck with the best of them."

Max stood, smiling, patient with his roommate holding court. Billy seldom drank at home, only allowing himself a beer or two each shift between his turns at the tables. Neither men spent their hard-earned pay on booze.

Max brought the refilled pitcher to the table. "Billy," he said, "before the beer ran dry, I think you were at the biggest ranch in all of Australia."

Billy laughed. "Oh, big, but not the biggest. Anna Creek Station puts Home Valley to shame. It's almost ten thousand square miles, twice as big as Home Valley. Anna Creek is as big as New Jersey or Lake Michigan."

Carson laughed, thinking his father was joking.

"Boy, I do not joke. The cattle ranch I worked on was half that size, most of it desert, but still big enough that a man on a horse couldn't ride 'cross it in two weeks. And you couldn't have, anyway, because it was always so bloody hot and dry, a horse would have died."

"Speaking of dry," Billy poured beer into his glass and wet his whistle. "I worked two years there. Cook's assistant again to start and eventually working in the barn and corral with the horses and later with calving. But Australia is no place for an Irishman. Too hot, too brown. Everything dead for eleven months a year. Yet I knew I couldn't go home. Javitts would always be looking to put a blade to my neck and start sawing.

"So going to America became my plan. Eventually, I made my way to Perth. Then, I signed on with an American freighter. And although the captain of that ship was nearly as bad as Javitts, I kept my nose clean, jumped ship in New York and found my way to Ellis Island.

"Now, Ellis Island would take another whole night to tell of, but, by the time I finally got to the front of that teeming line of humanity, I decided to fib a bit. I decided to tell the man filling out my papers I was from Australia, having come from Home Valley Station. I left off my last name, going with Bill Jackson, not William Jackson Donohue. I felt sure the man would ask for identification, which I didn't have. It had been more than five years since I'd left Ireland, and three years since I landed in Denham off Shark's Bay. But I was afraid of Javitts and was sure he would have word on the street for a Billy Donahue in the Irish neighborhoods of New York.

"I wasn't taking any chances of giving the immigration man my real name, no, not me. I had a plan. But the joke was on me. The clerk fella was so bored with filling in papers that all my fast talking only confused him. Afterwards, when I looked at my citizenship document, it read *Billy Jackson Station*. Ain't that one on me?" Billy laughed, his eyes glazed with drink.

"I was always a cautious one," he continued, "I left New York just like I did Denham. The first day, I headed south. Ended up in Virginia and eventually went to work in Lunenburg. I met Max there. But more importantly, I met your boys' mother there, God rest her soul." Billy's eyes glistened with the memory.

"We started our life together, Maddie and me, finally saving enough to buy a bit of land, but then the war came along. We lost everything in the bad times. The Yankees burned the crops, the house, and the barn. Madilyn died not long after you came along, Carson, and we've been scraping by since. The road ain't been easy. The Cherokee Strip ain't easy. But this here situation is the best I've had, and I been on this Earth going on fifty-five years now." Billy paused for a drink. He took Carson's hand first and then grasped across the table to Tanner's extended hand. "Boys, you're young and I know you think red clay ain't much for a man to claim to be his'n, but just think if we didn't have it. I know you've heard Everett say things could always be worse. And he's right there. Things could be much worse."

Billy put four twenty-dollar gold pieces on the table. "Carson,

son. This is all I saved this year in town, sparing what I spent for us to eat tonight. You take it, Son. Figure out what you want to do with it. You're a man now. I trust you to make the right choice with it. It was for our family, but that's you. You're my family. You decide how it should be spent."

Carson, weary of his father's long-winded story and slowed by his first night of drinking, tried to push the coins away, embarrassed to be so singled out, but his father pressed the heavy coins into his hand. Billy folded the boy's fingers over the money. "Take them. Go back to the house and get some sleep. I have to go to work."

Dust
Woods County, Oklahoma
November, 1963

Judge Hiram Spence arrived around 9:00 a.m. on Saturday morning under much scrutiny from the farmhouse. Chris watched from the kitchen window, his head above the green ashtray, as the judge's woody station wagon pulled up just outside the tiny, fenced yard.

Jeff, who had been smoking at the window since dawn, stepped out to meet him. Later, the boy's grandfather would tell people about Judge Spence's rig, a 1947 Mercury Woody Wagon with a wire kennel for his two dogs set up in the back. Behind the two-bench seats in front, the back seat had been replaced with storage for shells and an ice chest for storing birds for the ride home and a rack above which held three shotguns, all over-and-unders, so fancy that no one in Woods County had ever seen the like, Italian guns, all filigree on silver, buffed, finished barrels and engraved scrolls in their wood stocks.

To Chris, the whole scene unfolded like something out of a movie. The boy sat at his grandfather's window seat with Piper standing behind, bent and looking over his shoulder.

The two children stared with fascination as the judge opened the rear of the station wagon and let two liver and white German short-haired pointers from the vehicle.

The dogs raced in excitement around the barnyard with their bobbed tails shaking with ardor. The chickens went into panic mode, except for the rooster, who was never afraid of anyone, but the dogs paid the birds no mind. Instead, they raced up toward the trees where they urinated multiple times, marking their new territory.

Chris gawked out the window, taking it all in.

After perhaps two minutes, he returned to his bedroom and put on his lace-up boots. He laced them tight and then double knotted the bows so they wouldn't come untied while he was in the field carrying a gun. Then, the boy put a heavy flannel shirt over his white undershirt. He carried his orange hunting jacket under his arm back to the kitchen.

Judge Spence was, by then, in the kitchen, standing near the sink, sipping coffee. It was only his grandparents and Piper with him. His mom had gone to stay in OKC with Henry for the weekend. Jeff had thought things would go smoother without his mother around as a reminder of the *quid pro quo*. During the discussion on Friday night, Chris had asked his mom what the strange expression meant, and she said, "Cheap bribe."

Jeff had then laughed at Lil's definition. "Nothing cheap about quail hunting the way the judge does it," he replied.

Now, as Chris entered, the judge was laughing with Piper and Gwen. Jeff introduced him. "Judge Spence, this here's your hunting partner today, my grandson, Christian Fairchild."

The judge set his cup down on the drain board of the sink and stepped forward. "Pleasure to meet you, Master Chris," he said with a smile, extending his hand.

Chris who had been drilled on how to properly shake hands the night before by his grandfather, took the man's hand and used his best firm grip as he said hello.

"You hunt a lot, son?" the judge asked.

"No, sir," Chris replied. "This will be my first day in the field."

Judge Spence raised an eyebrow. "You're not going to shoot me, are you, Chris?"

"No, sir, Grandpa says shells are expensive and I have to save them for quail only," Chris said, solemnly, waiting a beat before smiling.

Judge Spence's eyebrows raised with amusement before smiling in return. He turned to Jeff and winked. "Well, he'll do. Yes, he will. He'll do just fine."

Jeff smiled at his grandson and turned to Gwen. "We'll be in for lunch 'fore 12:30."

Gwen nodded. "I'll have some hot food for ya'all ready. Judge, are you fine with some fried quail for lunch?"

"I cannot wait. Thank you for your hospitality," the judge said. "Now, let's go huntin'."

Judge Spence was a different type of man than Chris had met before. His hands were smooth and his nails shiny and white-tipped, almost like his mother's. His hair was cut just so, and his temples were gray, but the rest of his hair was jet black, like the detectives on TV shows. His boots were lace-up like Chris's but fabric halfway up, like they were military style, maybe, but they were all khaki, not camo or green, like the boots the soldiers over in Vietnam wore. The judge wore his hunting vest over a sleek, brown suede long-sleeved tunic. The vest was orange, and the judge also sported a matching orange felt cap. A single long pheasant feather extended far behind his head. Uncle Landon would have laughed at it, Chris was sure.

Jeff had his dog pen loaded on the pick-up, so they left the judge's Mercury parked.

After the judge loaded the dogs, he and Chris rode together on the tailgate as Grandpa took them to the south pasture over east. Chris knew this part of the ranch was where the coveys were the best. The sand plum thickets and bluestem grass here was prime cover. One of the best places was where the remnants of an old dugout rose out of the sand and bluestem. An old tin roof toppled into a deep cut hole glinting sunlight, giving away its location when the sun was right. Chris watched for it as they approached.

Once there, the judge released the two dogs, Pecan Pie and Plum Puddin', from the cage.

Jeff waved to the two hunters that he'd pick them up at the end of the mile section.

The boy and the judge each trailed the dogs by about thirty yards as the animals moved in slashing forays in front of them. One would move forward at a forty-five-degree slant, move up twenty to thirty yards, and then cut back toward the two hunters. Then, as the other was cutting back, the second would slash forward the other direction, cutting the field into pie slices, little by little. It wasn't long before Pecan Pie locked up, his left paw tucked, and his eyes locked on the clump of bluestem three yards ahead of it.

"Here we go, Chris," said the judge. "You're about to get in your first quail shootin'. Be ready. It'll happen fast."

Plum Puddin' began to back the larger Pecan Pie, sliding behind the pointing dog.

Suddenly, faster than Chris could imagine, the world was filled with quail. The flapping of the wings was loud.

The judge shot a single barrel, missing, but then a bird tumbled with his second shot.

Chris did eventually shoot, but he was way behind and so late that the birds were fifty yards away before the pellets of his .410 rattled the tree branches of the cottonwoods.

Judge Spence laughed as Pecan brought the quail to him. "Good boy, good boy." He turned to Chris. "Quail are fast, aren't they?" He pointed to the dog. "Chris, see how Pecan here has what they call a soft mouth. Pecan can pick up the bird with his mouth but doesn't damage it as he brings it to me. Some dogs have to be taught, but not ole Mr. Pie here. He could bring you a raw egg and not break it."

Chris felt red-faced at his initial poor showing. Quail hunting was going to be hard. The judge seemed to read his mind.

"Don't worry. We all miss shots," said the judge, kindly. "I missed my first one, too. We both missed our first shot. It gets easier. The birds split up. We'll let the dogs work them and we'll pick up some singles. When Plum Puddin' goes on point, get ready. Get your gun up to your chest, not aiming, but ready to place against your shoulder. And then there's this. When a whole covey of birds gets up, you mustn't get flustered. You can't shoot them all. Just pick one. That's the trick. It's just you shooting at one bird."

———

They walked the half mile section and each shot twice more. The judge got both of his, but Chris missed his.

As they neared the pick-up, he could see Jeff smoking a cigarette, leaning with one boot against the passenger door. He held his twenty-gauge loosely down his left side as the two hunters approached. Chris was conscious he could not shoot to his left where the vehicle lay.

But then Plum Puddin' locked on a bird right at the crest of the river's last dune before open space.

The boy raised his gun.

And the bird flew, but unlike the others he had missed, this bird flew straight down the berm, like an arrow heading away.

Chris aimed and fired. His shot wasn't perfect by any means.

The quail altered its flight with the shot, heading high into the air, before giving it up, glancing off the trunk of a cottonwood as it plunked into the grass. He could hear both the judge and his grandfather laugh in approval.

Pecan Pie lumbered in and brought the bird to the boy.

After each hunter had bagged one more quail, the judge suggested they take a break.

The two men moved to sit on a large fallen cottonwood trunk and sipped coffee from a Thermos; each smoked a cigarette.

Chris took a sip of water and sat on the tailgate. He nibbled on a Milky Way bar his grandmother had given him to stick in his pocket on the way out the door. The judge now had five quail, and Chris two.

The judge motioned for Chris to bring his canteen and come sit beside the two men.

"Chris," the judge said, "you're getting the hang of it. Got two in the bag. I think you'll be limiting out, if not today, then within a month of huntin'. Don't you agree, Jeff?"

Grandpa Jeff nodded, smiling, but not speaking.

"What grade are you in, Chris?"

"Sixth."

"Where's your school?"

"Wichita."

The judge frowned.

Jeff interceded. "Things work out; we intend for the kids to go to school in Hardtner after the holidays. Kind of depends."

The judge nodded. Chris had trouble keeping his face impassive. Going to school in Hardtner meant living on the farm. It was the first he had heard of this possibility.

The judge patted Chris's knee. "That sound good to you, boy? Living down here. Too bad you can't get him into an Oklahoma school."

Jeff shook his head. "Not one close. Talked with the superintendent. They allowed that Chris can go to Hardtner; his sister over to Kiowa. Got the feeling they were glad to get the kids. Not a lot of families out here no more."

Judge Spence acknowledged Jeff's words. "What do you think about that, Chris?" the judge asked again.

"I guess it all depends if you put my dad in jail."

There was a moment of silence. Chris watched his grandfather give him one of those disapproving looks with his gray eyes. The boy didn't like getting those looks, he knew that.

The judge considered Chris with one eyed narrowed for a second. "I guess the boy ain't a bullshitter, is he, Jeff?"

Jeff took a sip of coffee. "Reckon not."

"Yes, I guess it is about that. Chris, your daddy did something real stupid. Was it 'steal a car stupid'? No, I don't think so. It's a misunderstandin' stupid, though. And the man whose car went missing, well, he's got a say in this, too. Being a judge, I have to balance both sides, considering the law. Like that."

"Does my dad have a lawyer?"

"Yes, he does. A good one. Your grandfather saw to that."

Chris pondered that for a moment. "What good are lawyers if judges do the decidin'?" Chris asked. "No disrespect, sir, but I don't understand that part."

"None taken, son. Lawyers make sure the judges remember all the parts of the story and remind us of any other times this happened so we are aware of past judges' decisions that might be relevant…" the judge paused, looking for a word, "in helping me make up my mind."

Chris nodded. "Judge Spence?"

"Yes, boy?"

"I think I want to be a lawyer when I grow up. Reminding judges of things to help keep people out of jail seems like a good thing to do."

The judge laughed. "It is a noble calling. I was a lawyer before I became a judge."

"You were?"

Judge Spence laughed. "Yes, why, what'd you think? You think I was born a judge?"

Chris took a swig off his canteen. "Nah, I figured you were born a quail hunter."

The judge laughed long and full. He tossed the remaining dregs of his coffee into the grass and turned to the boy's grandfather, smiling broadly. "Jeff Hart, that son-in-law of yours, Henry Fairchild, is trouble, pure and simple, but he can't be all bad if this young'un is his offspring. This boy is a keeper. Yessiree."

That following Friday night was the first time that the children's father was allowed to leave Oklahoma City and come to the farm for the weekend. The judge allowed Henry to come under his father-in-law's recognizance. This legal stuff, Chris decided, had a lot of big words.

Henry arrived at 7:00 p.m., swooping into the kitchen, grabbing Lillian for a big smooch, then turning and wrapping his right arm around Gwen's waist. "Dang, it is good to be here, but I'm starvin'. I'm hopin' Grandma saved me something. I figure I missed supper about an hour ago." He looked to the living room where Piper stood. "Come here, little girl," he said.

Piper flew into his arms. "Oh, Daddy," she said, bursting into tears.

Chris followed, but with more reserve. The truth was he wasn't sure if he should be glad to see his father or be mad at him. The boy did take the hug and while lingering in his father's embrace, he felt the strength in the man's arms and his strong mechanic fingers brushing through his hair. It was reassuring, and yet he felt somehow repelled. Chris was afraid to like something he felt could be taken away. He was uncomfortable with the competing feelings and tried to push the negative thoughts out of his mind.

After Henry wolfed down a meal, the six of them gathered around the table to play dominoes until the children's bedtime.

Henry eventually put the kids to bed, this time both in the same room.

Chris was forced to move to his sister's room so his parents could have the South room. It would have normally been worse, but Chris once again lay claim to Grandma's satin comforter, so Piper's cover-pulling seemed inconsequential.

On Saturday, Chris trailed after Henry and Jeff as they walked and smoked.

The two men wandered down to water and feed the dogs.

Jeff let the hounds out of the pen for a while each day, and the two coon dogs scampered across the barnyard, yelping with joy.

Chris ran water from the hose, spraying out the pen, rinsing out the two bowls, refilling the bigger one with water while Henry scooped four cups of food into the second.

Henry turned to Jeff as he knelt. "I know you stood up for me. I made a big mistake. I heard from Lil you footed the attorney and put up my bail. I won't forget it."

Jeff nodded. "Family takes care of family."

Henry likewise nodded. "I know I ain't blood. It ain't the same, yet you took care of it after I shamed you. I appreciate it."

"Taking care of you is taking care of them," Jeff said, flatly, pointing his chin at Chris.

"I'll do what I can on the weekends to show my appreciation and thankfulness, Jeff. Over time, I'll make square with whatever money you're out," the boy's father said. "How can I help?"

"The money ain't important," Jeff said. "Living right is. You do that and we're square. Though I thought you might volunteer up some help. I could use the oil changed on both vehicles, the Olds and my pick-up. I got filters and fresh oil cans in the garage. And later, Landon's coming out. The old Allison Chalmers is burning some oil. Thought maybe a master mechanic from the big city might take a look at it."

Henry reached out and shook Jeff's hand. "Of course, I'll get right to it. I got me a first-rate assistant, too." He put his hand on Chris's shoulder.

Jeff didn't speak. He winked at the boy and headed off the barn. Then, he turned and yelled behind him. "Chris, leave the dogs run for another half hour, then pen 'em back up, okay?"

"Yes, sir," the boy called after him.

With the older man gone, Henry opened the garage door and backed the Olds out. Keys were always left in the ignition on the farm. Chris's father expertly placed two lifts on the garage floor, a dirt floor thickened by two generations of repairs and spilt oil.

After, Henry drove the Olds up onto the two lifts, placed the car into park, and turned off the engine. "Come on, get your butt on the ground under here with me, Chris."

Henry proceeded to show his son how to remove a drain plug and let the thick, viscous fluid drain into a bucket. While the oil bled away, the boy's father slid out and stood, lighting a cigarette. "How about that grandfather of yours? Jeff having the oil and oil filters ready to go, eh? Putting your dad to work? Gonna get that bail money back in free labor, it looks like."

Chris nodded. He was out from under the car but still seated on the ground. "Dad," he said, "why'd you take that car home? Did you not know it would get you in trouble?"

Henry raised an eyebrow as if in thought. "Well, I can tell you for sure I wouldn't do it again after all the trouble it has caused. No, buddy, I didn't think it was such a big deal. It's just, well, how do I put it? You'll find this out someday. Every man has that *one thing* he has a weakness for. I guess fat guys have a weakness for ice cream. Some guys like ladies, can't keep away from them. Lots of fellas have trouble with drink. It's like that thing is in first place with them. With me, it's always been cars. I've loved them since I can't remember. I loved moving fast in one, seeing how they work, making them run better, go faster."

Henry stopped and stubbed the cigarette out under his boot. "And that Caddy was the fanciest car I ever had the chance to be in. I just wanted to drive it around for a tiny bit, and then I thought my buddies needed to see it. I wanted to show off a little bit. I made the mistake of going by to see them."

"And you drank some beer and then couldn't drive it back?"

Henry agreed. "Yeah, it's bad to drink and drive. I had to leave it because I couldn't drive drunk. At least I did that right."

Chris nodded, but he wondered why his dad's one thing was cars and not his family.

On Sunday night after his father returned to Oklahoma City, Chris lay in bed, having dozed off reading a comic and having finished both books Jeff had given him, but then awaking to voices in the living room. It was his mom and his grandfather talking.

"Dad, I really want to finish my degree at Wichita State. I got my professor's permission to complete the work I missed during Henry's mess. I can finish over the holiday break. In January, I can go back and finish my last semester. Then, I'll have my master's. I can get a job at double the pay. Maybe we'll all move to Oklahoma City at that point."

"Lil," Jeff said, "you know Gwen and I got no problem with the kids living here and going to school up in Hardtner, but I guess the real question is what Henry's going to do."

"What do you mean?"

"Lil, he's a good man when he ain't drinkin'. Problem is when you ain't around, he drinks. And you ain't gonna be down there to keep him in line. You think he's gonna behave himself with the kids here and you in Wichita? It's still November. You're talking to May. Half year on his own? On probation? Henry?" Jeff shook his head. "He's supposed to work and go home. Just those two things. You think Henry'll do that every night if you're not around?"

"You think I should quit my schooling to babysit him? I've been going to night school for two and a half years. I'm so close. The extra money will make a big difference. Dad, you know Henry loves me. He loves Chris and Piper. He won't do anything to jeopardize our family."

Jeff's voice was low. "He wouldn't, not sober, he wouldn't."

Lil seemed to take that answer as an affirmative. "Then, it's decided. I'll go to school up to Wichita on Tuesdays and Thursdays again. I can stay with my friend, Connie, after school and get my work done the next mornings. I can help out around here, Fridays through Mondays. Maybe find some work in Kiowa a couple of days a week."

"That'll work," said her father, knowing enough about women to know when the die had been cast. "But what's this Piper told me about you moving both of the kids up a grade? You think Chris is ready for seventh grade? He's a small fella already."

Chris heard a glass set down on the coffee table and realized his mom was having a glass of Jeff's homemade wine. "Piper will do just fine. She's a social girl. Always finds friends, no matter what."

"And what about the boy?"

"Chris is bookish. So smart for his age."

"So smart for any age," Jeff agreed. "But he's tiny. Like me, I figure. Smallest in his sixth-grade class. And you want to move him up a grade? A city kid going into a country school. He's gonna have a tough time of it. I can see it coming."

"We both know Christian can do the schoolwork, Dad. And although it's sad to say, Chris didn't really have any friends back in Wichita, not close ones. My thinking is moving him up to seventh grade is just one less year of his social awkwardness. He's going to be a great adult, but he doesn't really have anything in common with kids his age. They want to play Cowboys and Indians, and he wants to discuss Jules Verne. Next year, they'll still want to discuss *Wagon Train* and he'll be reading Voltaire."

Jeff laughed. "Whoever the hell that is. That reminds me. He tore through that Zane Grey book. I need to get him some more of those. They got a stack of used ones at the barbershop over to Kiowa. He reads a few of them might make him want to play Cowboys and Indians."

"I doubt it," Lil said, laughing.

The following Monday, the first week of December, the kids joined their new classes. Chris was in seventh grade at Hardtner, and Piper moved up to ninth grade in Kiowa. Ninth grade was in the four-year high school building. Jeff took both kids to school each morning, more than an hour driving morning and night.

Chris's homeroom classroom had fourteen students, ten of them boys. Piper's school was much bigger and had over one hundred students. She switched classrooms and subjects every hour. Piper came home that first day full of stories at supper. She had six classes every day; English, math, biology, social studies, history and then gym on Monday, Wednesday, and Fridays. Choir was on Tuesday and Thursdays.

Chris watched and listened to his sister tell about her day and her new teachers. He knew the conversation would come to him next. He had none of the enthusiasm his sister did. Piper's face, her nose covered with freckles, lifted with excitement as she mentioned two new friends, Meg and Linney, and how she wanted to go into town over the weekend to see them.

Chris tried to think what he would say.

As Piper finally took a big drink of milk, his mother turned to him with a question. "Christian, how about you? How was your first day?"

"It was okay. One kid made fun of Dad. He said he'd heard my dad was Clyde Barrow. He asked if your name was Bonnie."

Gwen tutted. "That's a mean thing to say. I'm sorry, Chris. That's bad manners to be so awful. Whose child said that to you? I'm sure we know their elders. Everybody knows everybody in Hardtner."

Chris shook his head and didn't answer the question. "It was okay. I told him he was wrong. I said Daddy was no old Clyde Barrow. I told him Daddy was Pretty Boy Floyd."

Jeff laughed. "Good one, Chris. Might as well laugh as cry."

The boy could see the stress in his mother's eyes as she picked at her thumbnail. He regretted the story and changed the subject to his history class which was covering World War II and the Battle of the Bulge.

Later after dinner, Chris lay on his belly on the living room floor by the gas stove, writing in his Big Chief tablet. His mom came in and stood over him. "What are you doing? Homework?"

Chris looked at his mom. "No, making out a Christmas list."

Lillian looked surprised. "Really? And what's on this list?"

The boy smiled at his mom. "I decided I wanted one of those cap gun toy rifles with the lever handles. Like John Wayne carries. Maybe even a holster and a six-shooter, too. I'm living on a ranch now. Figure I ought to be a cowboy. What do you think, Mom?"

Lillian smiled, but the boy thought he could see doubt creep into her eyes, if just for a moment. "Yes, honey. I think Santa can arrange some cap guns for you. I'll get some stamps and we'll mail him your list to the North Pole this weekend. Is that okay?"

"That's great."

"Now, go get your jammies on. It's a school night."

Oklahoma Territory
February 5, 1899

Six years had passed since the Salt Fork Stations clan had made their home along the river. Led by Everett Hart, the family's fortune, like its herd, had continued to increase in size. While some neighbors without Everett's complete dedication to the land failed during lean times, the Salt Fork Stations prospered. Everett rued that they had no money to buy nearby farms up for sale during these lean years. But they survived.

So far, they had been lucky. The winters had been kind, the grass accessible, even during rare snowstorms; the cold survivable, the droughts short, and the few Cherokee uprising not in their neck of the woods. The family had avoided sickness, accident, and rustlers. Each spring found them with more cattle than the year before. Times, though still hard, were good.

Max and Billy continued to live in town but had rented a house. It was far from grand, but seemed luxurious to the two mature men, among the oldest in Alva now, which was essentially still a booming cow town. The three-bedroom, two-story house set directly across from the Presbyterian church.

Often on weekends, Everett and Avery would board their buckboard and head south into town. They would leave the ranch Saturday at noon, arriving in time to dine out on Saturday evening and take in church on Sunday.

Billy always worked Saturday nights and that left his bed for the girls, for now there were three of them; Autumn Eve, Viva May, and Madge Millicent, ages four, three, and two. Everett and Avery became popular as after-church lunch guests around town. The meager social circle of Alva seemed to see potential in the two. The best families vied for their graces. Their star was on the rise.

Everett had offers to join the cattlemen's club, Avery, the ladies' auxiliary, and there was talk Everett would become the youngest deacon of the relatively new Presbyterian congregation.

The ability for the couple to have a "city life" was due, of course, to Everett's complete confidence in Tanner to run the ranch. He and Carson were grown men now. The two were strong and handsome, albeit in completely different ways. Tanner was lean, dark, and quiet, a contemplative man if ever there was one. And of course, there was his reputation for violence, untested now for more than half a decade, but still resonant in the community. Tanner's reputation of violence was like someone who carried a disease but did himself not suffer from it. And people shunned him in much the same manner. Tanner did not mind. He was more comfortable on the ranch, out among cattle than with people at a social function in town.

Carson was the opposite of his brother. Now grown, he was quick with a laugh and a joke. He was blonde and stocky to his brother's trim build. Carson was known to have a short fuse, the opposite of his brother's unending patience.

When the ranch could spare him, Carson often slipped away for a day or two and came back with fatigue deep in his eyes and the smell of saloon whiskey on his stale clothes. There were rumors he frequented the whores south of Alva's railroad station. Carson lived for those nights in Alva south of the tracks. However, back on the ranch, he did not speak of his exploits. Avery, on occasion, scolded her youngest brother for his sinful life, but he seemed unrepentant and would not discuss what he did, with whom, or where. Unlike his younger brother, Tanner never went to town unless Everett had specially asked him to attend to an errand.

The three girls were Avery's delight in life. Autumn was the oldest and the nurturer from the start. Viva, like her name, was the exuberant one, always laughing, and Madge, the baby, was clingy. However, it was not her mother, Avery, to whom she clung. It was Autumn. The prattle and chatter of little girls filled their lives. None, not even Tanner, seemed immune to the laughter. Carson was their favorite and he played on the grass with them often, wrestling them, letting the three of them pin his massive shoulders to the ground. Indeed, times were good.

And the rising family fortunes were distinguished by the community for one more reason; they now had a hired hand. Morrie Renfro, a cowpoke slightly younger than Max and Billy, now worked the ranch. Renfro was the best cattleman of them all. He was a veteran of the Indian Wars of the Kansas Plains and had battled for the southern states in the war between the states. Renfro took a bullet in the hip at Vicksburg in 1863. The Confederate doctor needing to stop his bleeding, cauterized the wound and saved his life, but in doing so, damaged the joint so severely that the soldier would never walk without a limp again. Now thirty-six years after the war, he used a cane and struggled to walk.

However, on a horse, Renfro's locomotion was a different matter. He rode magnificently. He excelled in managing a herd. The man was also a wizard in the training of both dogs and horses. Renfro's inability to walk, brand calves, or even carry provisions now prohibited him finding employment with the trail herds coming from Texas, but after one ramrod stopped to rest his cattle on the Salt Fork spread, Renfro found a job with Everett. The Harts and Stations treated the old soldier as family. He lived in the dugout, now improved with a tin roof and a cookstove. Bunk beds raised above the dirt floor sufficed to house him and whichever of the clan was working the herd with the wounded Johnny Reb.

With Renfro, now the cattle ranch had a man whose job it was to watch the herd and tend to it each day. His addition gave both Carson and Everett the free time they desired, although both rode alongside Renfro most days from dawn to dusk.

Tanner spent the most time with the old soldier. He did not strive for a day off each week, so many weekends, it was Tanner and Renfro riding herd and tending to the livestock.

The rest of the family began to regularly spend its weekends in Alva.

Carson often rode into town with Everett and Avery but would leave them and the three little girls on the buckboard at the outskirts of town.

Everett would spend the afternoon on errands, but he did not frequent the same locales as his younger brother-in-law. Everett would never set foot south of the train station, and Carson saw no reason to go north.

Carson did not even bother to see his father, except late in the evening when the son would stop to watch his father deal cards. When Billy took a break, the two would have a beer, but their relationship had cooled. Carson was on a path that neither wanted to discuss.

The weekend of February 5th, 1899 was the first time Everett brought the family to town since the Christmas Sunday service. There had been snow most of January, and Baby Madge had been croupy. It seemed every Saturday the clouds darkened, the winds blew, and the tree limbs rattled on the north side of the house. Staying in, safe and warm, seemed prudent with three tender girls to tend to. Everett was not a man who took chances, not with the ranch, not with his cattle, and not with his four ladies. He played his cards close to his chest, and he kept his ladies warm in his home, and in his heart.

The homestead now included a wood-framed house, a barn and corral. There was also a crowded chicken coop, and Everett now raised pigs kept in a sty out beyond the barn on the east side. Everett placed the sty at the farthest point away from the house to protect from the smell on the prevalent west wind. The farmhouse itself now consisted of a central room with a hearth, two bedrooms, one for the parents and the baby, the second for the two older girls, who slept together in a double bed. These two rooms were added to the main cabin, which was split side-by-side with a sitting room of sorts divided from the kitchen table and stove by a half wall. The entire house had a tin roof, leak-proof and secure. By current standards in the region, the house was perhaps one of the finest in the surrounding forty miles.

The territory, by now, had grown up a bit. Neighbors were plentiful, many now the second owners of the homesteads. More than half the original boomer homesteaders were now gone, replaced by steadier, more durable farming types. During good weather, frequent gatherings sprang up, complete with roasted pigs, pie contests, the occasional horserace, and of course, music played with guitar, fiddle, harmonica, and banjo for the younger folk to dance to. The older women would keep plates filled, and the men would nip from bottles in their hip pockets or from flasks stuck into their boots.

A sense of community was beginning to form. There were plans for a one-room schoolhouse to open in the fall at Rose Hill six miles south of the Salt Fork Ranch. Children were plentiful in the territory. The McCrackens, the Sternbergers, the Strawns, the Campbells, the Finneys, and others, all had children now, most a bit older than the Hart girls. Everett and Avery frequented the parties and were popular, especially Avery for her cooking. Everett was too stiff for most of the men to become close friends. Tanner's reputation as a gunman and his stoic manner kept him outside any forming social circles. Carson was the most popular of the clan and often danced with the ladies and drank with the men. His quick wit and smile made many a young woman's heart skip a beat if he should look her way.

Tanner could usually be found just beyond the firelight at these gatherings, tapping his toe lightly to the banjo.

Carson, on the other hand, would be in the middle of the dancing, twirling all the women who were up to shaking a leg, married or not. The times were not so hard as they had been, and the inhabitants of the Cherokee Outlet now took some time for joy in their lives. Even Everett allowed himself the happiness to see the smile on Avery's face.

Avery herself, without trying, had become the most popular and influential woman in the northern part of the Cherokee Strip. Motherhood in those hard lands stripped the beauty from many a woman. But not for Avery. The half-decade of hard years and the birthing of three girls seemed only to soften Avery's features. There was not enough to eat for her to have gained weight, and even after three children, she still had her figure. Her face, now perhaps a tiny bit fuller, was etched with the beginnings of lines, which only emphasized the symmetry of her high cheekbones and full lips. Her face, always freckled in youth, became less so as she reached her mid-twenties. Her demeanor was friendly and kind, but she was intolerant to talk of violence. She forbade men to swear in her presence. She was devout in her religion and true to her man. Her world, however, revolved around her girls.

Avery was quick to laugh, and many a traveler stopped by the Hart household for water and to chat with her, usually when Everett was in the field with the cattle. She represented a wholesomeness and a joy to the Cherokee Strip that was hard to find. Her husband modelled the work ethic of the ranchers. Indeed, Everett was the symbol of a hard-working puritan dedicated to the land. Difficult, silent and strong, Everett displayed the ethos of the territory perfectly.

It was not that Everett was disliked. Most in the community thought him very much the good neighbor and honest fellow. However, while Avery seemed to glow with the land's bounty, Everett seemed fraught with the need to wring every possible benefit from it. He worried incessantly. Creases formed on his forehead. Like Tanner, his face was now a permanent burnished brown, mostly lined with worry. His upper body was thick and the weight he carried would have turned to fat on a lesser man, but on Everett, it formed a barrel of muscle. When he could be goaded into a wrestling match, there was no one in the territory who could best him. However, he never sought matches and never bet on himself when he did. Some thought the only match to Everett's skill at wrestling might be found in Carson, his brother-in-law, but to anyone's knowledge, the two never faced off against each other.

To find Everett at rest was rare. Avery's husband was the hardest-working man in the entire Cherokee Strip. He never borrowed, never slacked, never got drunk, and never spoke ill of a neighbor. He attended every barn-raising, fishing derby, or pie bake, but he was always just a bit separate of the festivities. While Max, Everett's father, with his breeding was popular and always good for a story of old Virginia days, his son was never the life of a party.

In many ways, he was quite like Tanner in his minimal interactions with neighbors. However, while Tanner stood outside the circle, Everett was alone within it.

Avery would often look to her husband and find him standing straight-faced while the other men heehawed at some joke. Avery loved her husband, but she knew he was always alone in a crowd. Distant in his intensity. There was something of a loner in him which hadn't been there in his youth, she knew. She had the girls; he had the farm, and both were a worry. However, Avery found joy in her daughters. Everett, with no son, stood apart, alone in his disquietude regarding the ranch. He spent his every second in worry about possible calamities. Most of all he worried about an heir, someone to whom he could hand over the herd and the land. Who would take the reins when he could no longer do so?

Avery worried that she would not be able to give Everett the son she knew would complete his life. And without a son to whom to give the ranch, Avery knew her husband had a void none of the girls, as much as he loved them, could fill. Though he loved them, in truth, all he had was the herd and the land. That red dirt was everything. It provided for his family, and thus he worried about its care night and day.

And yet with all his concern, when calamity finally did strike, Everett could do nothing.

Avery pressed her husband a bit to take the family to Alva that first weekend in February. Yes, it was cold, but the weather was clear. The skies were blue, calm, and nonthreatening, although the west wind was cold.

Finally, Everett relented and agreed to leave the ranch and the herd to Renfro and Carson's care. Tanner was away but due back from Enid anytime with a new stallion shipped in from faraway Iowa. It was Everett's first major purchase, a stallion to be used as breeding stock. While Everett on his own would have preferred to stay home to see the arrival of the yearling colt, he understood the social advantages of getting to Alva and rubbing elbows with more prominent citizens. Plus, a trip to town would make Avery happy.

The ride into town that fateful Saturday was different, as Carson did not accompany them, and it was always easier for Everett if his more talkative brother-in-law joked and told stories to the little girls on an all-afternoon ride into town.

On this day, behind two sturdy steads, Avery chatted and questioned the girls, leaving Everett in thought, a silence familiar to the girls. The trip to town was uneventful, if cold, and dinner in town that night at a restaurant was a rare moment spent away from the children. Max was to babysit while Billy dealt cards. The evening went as planned. The girls, in bed early, slept through the night, tired after cold ride in.

Sunday morning crept in with a storm front arriving from the west with the dawn.

Walking across the street to the Presbyterian church the next morning on February 6, the wind was decidedly bitter cold. Avery decided to leave the little girls home with Max and Billy rather than bundle them up. The cold bite of the wind was shocking to the senses, and the mother felt better with the girls playing beside the stove than getting them out in the gale.

Everett was antsy about getting back to the homestead by nightfall, but it was a twenty-five-mile ride on the buckboard. More than three hours in that bitter wind with the girls made Everett nervous, but staying away for another day made him even more nervous.

Crossing the street to the church for the service, Avery advocated staying another day to let the weather pass. Cold was one thing, but thirty-mile-an-hour winds were another. Everett thought the children could be warm enough bundled under his buffalo rug in the buckboard.

Avery disagreed.

The married couple squabbled about it momentarily as they walked the short distance across the street in the minutes before the church service began.

Two couples with whom they were friendly held seats for them in the second pew of the chapel. Kendrick Bailey and Mort Jeffers and their wives waved them to their seats after smiles and handshakes.

Then, the service began. Everett was not a religious man, but he was a patient one. He was dutiful in church, closing his eyes, standing on cue and mouthing words from the hymnal as beckoned by the preacher in the pulpit up front. Whether he heeded the call was anyone's guess. His religious views were yet another thing he kept to himself.

Afterward, Kendrick Bailey and his wife, Allison, persuaded Everett and Avery to brave the cold and join them for lunch. At least their carriage had an enclosed car for the women.

Kendrick bade Everett to join the women below, but the rancher would have none of it, insisting on joining his friend up top. In his heart, he knew going to lunch was a mistake. Everett needed to convince Avery to make the difficult and cold journey home. But he was dissuaded by his new friend and the thought of a delicious luncheon.

The Baileys lived west of town by about a mile, owning forty acres; a gentlemen's farm, Kendrick called it. He also owned a piece of the railroad depot in Alva and was known to invest in cattle futures, which was new, possible because of the telegraph line that now ran to town.

At lunch, Allison Bailey was shocked that Everett would even consider putting his children in the back of a buckboard for what would surely be a bone-chilling ride north to the Salt Fork ranch. The thermometer on the rain gauge out the back window showed the temperature to now be at nineteen degrees. By the time Allison served coffee, the gauge showed sixteen degrees. Avery forced Everett in front of his friends to admit that a four- or five-hour ride in that kind of cold, what with thirty mile an hour gusts and the beginnings of dark blue clouds on the western horizon, was out of the question.

Kendrick took the couple back to Billy and Max's abode. Flurries danced in the air, and Everett was concerned a blizzard would soon be upon them. He would be stuck in town.

Max attempted to calm his son. "Tanner is there, Carson is there, and thank God, Renfro is there. They are all good cattlemen. You know what they're doing. They felt this weather coming on before dawn. They've already bunched the herd. They'll have moved them into the hollows in the sand dunes east of the dugout. They'll have moved the young ones to the corral up at the main house, and come dark, they'll move them inside the barn. We've talked about what to do. They'll do what you've told them all those winter nights over the last four years."

"I'm not there. When there's finally a blizzard a-comin' and the herd needs me, I'm here in town. Helpless."

Billy passed Everett a cup of coffee. "My boys will do ya proud. It'll be fine. We don't have even an inch of snow on the ground yet. Don't worry about a blizzard when there's been nary a flake. Let's not worry about something that hasn't happened. Remember that God, not us, is managing. You just came from church. Things will be okay, Everett, you'll see."

As the men talked, Avery rounded up the girls for an afternoon nap. She picked up the toys from their morning in front of the stove, then moved them off to Billy's bedroom to sleep.

By the time she had returned, Everett had the beginnings of a terrible anger coming on him. Anger at what, she was not sure, but soon he spoke, and she realized his developing rage was directed at her younger brother.

"What if Carson isn't at the ranch?" Everett said, his cheeks crimson, his eyes dancing with nerves and too much coffee. "What if he waited until we left and then slipped away? What if he's just ten blocks away sleeping off last night's whiskey? What if he's hungover and has decided that it's too cold for a ride back to the ranch with a bad stomach and a throbbing head?"

Billy's voice likewise rose a pitch. "You've no call to speak of my boy like that. Carson told you he would watch the herd and he will. You said he and Renfro were at the ranch when you left yesterday afternoon, and Tanner was due back by early afternoon. You've no reason to besmirch Carson. No cause at all."

Everett shook his head. "Carson asked me not a half-hour before we left if I thought it would be okay to leave things to Renfro, seein' as Tanner was due back yesterday afternoon. I told him no, under no circumstances was he to leave without Tanner there."

Billy nodded. "Well, then, it was settled."

"What if he waited until we left and then followed us into town?" Everett's mind was full of worry and apprehension.

Avery took her father's side. "Father's right. You don't have any reason to think Carson is not pushing cattle into the barn as we speak. Apologize, Everett. Your words were hurtful and offensive." Her hands were fists on her hips. Her dark gray velvet dress hung to her heels and one black boot tapped the floor with emphasis.

Her husband nodded an apology at Billy, but then escaped to Max's room to change out of his Sunday-go-to- meetin' clothes. When he came out, he was dressed in his heavy coat, gloves, and with a kerchief tied around his neck pulled up to cover his ears.

Avery looked up from peeling potatoes in a bucket in the kitchen. "Everett, you're not considering heading back to the ranch now. You won't make it before dark at this stage. It's a fool's errand. It is probably no more than five degrees out there now and will be below zero by nightfall. And if you look out the window, it's snowing pretty bad right now. It's all we need is for you to get lost out there in the middle of a snowstorm."

"Not headed to the ranch. Too late for that," he said.

Max looked up from lighting his pipe. "Then, where are you headed, Son? It isn't fit for man or beast out there."

"I'm headed south of the tracks. I've heard Carson spends time at McKinney's. It's a favorite of his. If he's holed up in town, I figure he'll be there."

Avery threw a potato at him, striking him in the back. "That's a place for sinnin', and you'll not be discussing such a vile location in my presence, Everett."

He picked the potato up and walked across to the bucket and dropped it back in. It hit with a bang.

Avery shushed him and looked to the closed bedroom door. "You'll wake the babies!"

"I'll leave quietly," he said.

"You do that," she replied, curtly. Avery stood from her labors, and unable to shout, she hissed a whisper at his back as he reached the door. "No husband of mine goes to visit a whorehouse. Not and then sleeps in the same room with me. If you're leaving to go there, be prepared to sleep in the front room this night."

"Avery, I'm not going to date any of them. I am going to see if your brother is there. And if he is, I'm going to beat the living tar out of him. That I swear," Everett said, flatly, as if he was pronouncing a fact. He opened the door. Icy wind burst through as Everett exited, and in his place, a dozen plump snowflakes spun in a helix into the room. They descended in despair, leaving wet dark ovals on the wood floor like so many tears.

And of course, Carson was exactly where Everett thought he would be—well, not exactly. In his mind on the way there, Everett imagined dragging the younger man from a bed upstairs, a woman screaming obscenities as he pulled Carson down the stairs. Instead, Carson was downstairs at the bar, playing solitaire with a beat-up pack of cards. A bottle of whiskey, yet half full, sat next to him. An incorrigible-looking youth wearing a sooty bowler leaned next to him on a bar stool. The young buck was maybe a year younger than Carson's twenty years.

Everett was surprised. He quickly rearranged how things would go in his mind.

As he stepped to the bar, the door swung wide, allowing a gust of cold to fill the room.

Every eye in the place turned to see who had brought the chilled ill wind. A dozen lost souls stared at Everett with dead eyes, including one prostitute in the corner with only one eye, a patch covering the left side of her face and temple.

Carson glanced up from his deck, nodded, realizing who and what was coming at him. In reaction, or rather non-reaction, he lifted a black ten and placed it on a Jack of Diamonds.

Everett grabbed his brother-in-law by the arm. "Carson, what the hell? You're supposed to be at the farm."

In response, the young man reached into his vest. He brought out a pocket watch different and much nicer than one Everett knew he owned. "According to the time, so should you. I thought you were returning by Sunday evening."

"Avery insisted it was too cold for the girls to make the trip."

"Guess one of Billy's offspring has some sense," Carson opined, wryly.

The youth beside him, with a dull look on his face, laughed at his partner's jest.

Carson turned his head to acknowledge there was a third-party present. "I'm sorry. Everett, this is Pokey Arthur." He turned to Pokey. "And this overly righteous fellow, Pokey, is my brother-in-law, Everett Hart."

"Charmed," Pokey said, tipping his hat, revealing a headful of greasy hair.

Everett nodded. "Ahem, Mr. Arthur, could you give me a moment with my kin here?"

Pokey nodded at the bartender, "Maybe I should step away and order a round of drinks. I could do that if you're buying…" He left the words there like a bribe.

"Sure, just go away," Everett said, reaching in his pocket for a dollar coin.

Pokey Arthur laughed, snatched the coin from Everett's palm, and stepped away.

"When did you leave? Tell me you waited until Tanner was back," Everett said under his breath. His exasperation was rising, and his face, red from the cold, now was flushed with anger.

"Tanner was due back by late afternoon Saturday. Hey, you were the one who sent him to Enid for that stud."

"You left before he got back?"

Carson sighed. "Just like you did. Getting all high-falutin, are you? Got your long johns in a wad? Come to town to make nice with the society folk figuring you could leave the herd and ranch to the hired help." Carson paused as he spit out the last words, "No, not quite. I ain't no more hired help than you, Ev. You got that?"

"Get your things. You're coming back to your father's house. You'll sleep there with the rest of the family. Then, you and I can head back to the ranch come first light."

"I ain't headed anywhere. I got a room booked upstairs and when one of the better-lookin' ladies, at least one with two eyes, gets free, I plan to book her for the night, iffin' to just keep warm. Drafty accommodations here down south of the tracks as you might imagine."

Everett paused and looked around. No one was paying them any mind, except McKinney the owner, who had stood two drinks in front of them. He was waiting to get paid. Pokey and the first dollar were nowhere to be found. Everett frowned, but he took a second coin out of his front pants pocket and left it on the bar.

"Carson, you better get your stuff because if I go back to the house without you, you know what will happen next. You think your Quaker sister will let that stand for the night? You? Here?" Everett laughed briefly, imagining the scene. "You know Avery'll be back here herself and create a stink like this place has never known, and from what I've smelled thus far, they're familiar with stink."

Carson laughed, dryly. "What? You don't like my friends?"

Everett smirked, "That's what they are? Pokey Arthur? I heard tell of him. He gets his spending money running north to the state line to Dodge or Wichita and stealing money off of old ladies by knifepoint. Pokey's got him a reputation."

Carson nodded at his companion, who had now returned. He was now chatting with the one-eyed whore in the corner. "Aw, he's not so bad."

"He's your running buddy these days? He finance that new pocket watch? Or did you take it off somebody you done bush-whacked? You helpin' him rob folks to get enough money to come to town drinkin' and whorin'?"

Carson laughed. "You pay me twenty dollars a month, less than a 'poke gets on the trail. Plus, I don't get much chance a-spendin' it out on the Salt Fork. I ain't been in town since before Christmas. I got a little saved up. Intend on having some fun tonight, even it bein' Sunday."

Everett wouldn't let it go, nodding at Pokey chatting up the whore. "You run with that creature? A guy who threatens women for money and is proud enough of it that he has *KNIV* on his left knuckles and *BLAD* on his right? Is he that dumb or does he just not like the letter E?"

Carson chuckled again. "It's funny you should say that because I asked him once if the U.S. Marshal ever put out a warrant for him if he wanted it to say Woodrow Arthur, his given name, or Pokey Arthur, you know, like everyone knows him."

"And what did he say?"

Carson took a big swallow of his whiskey shot and said, "He tipped that ratty ole bowler at me and said 'Pokey, P-O-K....E."

Everett and Carson both laughed. The moment lightened for a second, but Everett moved back to the attack. "You gonna get your stuff?"

"It's all at the livery. Horse is boarded up and warm. Guess you got a point. Can't have Avery coming down here like Carrie Nation over to Kiowa. She'd piss people off enough I wouldn't be able to come back. And I intend on coming back every chance I get."

Everett nodded and finished his drink with a single gulp. It was terrible, rotgut stuff.

Carson stood and measured himself next to his brother-in-law, nigh on seven years older and perhaps ten pounds heavier. The younger man sized up the other. "You know it would be a hell of a fight."

Everett grinned slightly on just one side of his mouth. "Short one, too."

Carson gave a jovial shake of his head and then moved to where Pokey was standing with the prostitute. Everett thought Carson was going to tell his friend he was leaving, but Carson only told the whore to get off his coat.

Outside, the weather had turned into hell on Earth, albeit one of cold and ice, not heat and flame. The wind roared with such ferocity that neither man spoke for the rest of the journey home. They both knew the other would not be able to hear the utterance such was the cacophony of the storm. The snow had now arrived with a vengeance. It whipped sideways and back. Drifts were already piling up in the corners of storefronts and in the tiny yards of the homes. A foot-high drift extended from the entrance of the Presbyterian Church across the street.

The two men trudged through the white wave that swamped the tops of their boots.

Cursing, Carson slid his boots off his bare feet once they were on the porch.

Everett couldn't help but smile for an instant at Carson's blue toes. His mood soured again as the door opened.

Avery bade them to enter. Her stern eyes chastised both men.

Inside, Carson sloughed off his sister's inquiries about the last twenty-four hours.

Everett also declined comment.

Avery entreated her husband to respond, but Everett did not want to start a second argument, this one in front of the girls. Feeling he had to say something, Everett remarked he couldn't ever remember this much snow coming this fast with this kind of cold.

Avery frowned and herded the girls to the bedroom, away from the men.

His observation was markedly true. For this storm marked the beginning of what would be called Great Arctic Outbreak of 1899. The storm that began while Carson and Everett were in McKinney's Saloon was a blizzard that would drop over forty inches of snow in just as many hours. And on Tuesday, when the storm passed, the bottom would fall out. The temperature by Tuesday evening would be seventeen below zero. Everett wished he was home, but he did not believe in fairy tales and knew things did not go right just because you wished them so.

Mother
Woods County, Oklahoma
February, 1964

On Saturday, Grandpa Jeff agreed to take Piper into Kiowa to a new friend's house. It was a warm day for the weekend before Valentine's Day, and two teenage girls were doing cartwheels in the yard as the pick-up truck pulled into the drive.

"Who's *that*?" Chris exclaimed, pointing at a redhead, her face flushed after completing two cartwheels into a round-off.

Piper gave him a disgusted look. "Shannon Gill. She's a sophomore. Wh-y?" she finished, making the question into two syllables.

Jeff laughed. "Cause, evidently, he likes redheads."

Chris blushed, and Piper said, "Yuck."

She closed the door with a slam and was gone.

Jeff rolled down his window. "Be back for you at 2:00. You be ready, ya hear?"

The older man smiled at his grandson, lit a cigarette, and then rolled the crank until the window was just about two inches from the top. He blew smoke out the gap. "I understand the sentiment, Chris. I surely do. Something about a redhead, ain't there?"

Chris brushed it off. "Where we going first? Hardware store or to get those .22 shorts you promised me?"

Jeff laughed. "I don't know. Guess you're callin' the tunes, lover boy. Where we goin'? 'ceptin' to hell in a handbasket?"

"Just drive. Stop teasing me."

Jeff nodded and they headed to the gun shop for two boxes of rounds.

At supper the following Monday night, Piper was animated with news from school. "I'm going to be in the high school musical. *The Sound of Music*. Mom, didn't you see the play?"

"I did," said Lillian. "At Starlight Theater in Kansas City. I heard they are going to make a movie about it. What part are you going to play?"

"Oh, really a part of the chorus. I'm Gretl Von Trapp. I do sing a couple of lines by myself, though. My friend, Shannon, is the lead. She sings a bunch of songs."

Jeff said, "That's the redhead, ain't it, Chris?"

Chris blushed, and his mother glanced over at him, confused at the private joke between the two males at the table. Lillian said to her daughter, "I'll have to get out my record player. I have the soundtrack album to the play." She smiled at Chris. "Honey, you used to listen to that quite a bit. You were always asking me to put it on when you were just bitty."

Piper's eyes got big. "Chris, my music teacher is going to come to your school on Thursday. She's looking for a little boy in the third or fourth grade to play Kurt. No kid in Kiowa wanted to be in it. You're little enough you could still do it."

Chris winced at the comment about his size.

Lillian raised an eyebrow. "I'll bet you know all the words, Chris. 'Doe, a deer, a female deer…'."

Chris, though pained, replied in his reedy tone, "Ray, a drop of golden sun."

Piper beamed. "Grandma, can I call Shannon after dinner? You'll have to help me find the number."

Grandma Gwen smiled benevolently. "Yes, if you eat up and help me with these dishes. Now, enough talk. Get back to eating, both you children. Jeff, you, too. What are you smiling like the Cheshire Cat for?"

On Thursday, Chris got the part of Kurt in the Kiowa High School musical. Jeff agreed to pick Chris up from elementary school in Hardtner each day at 3:00 and make sure he was at play practice by 3:30 in Kiowa when the high school ended each day. The arrangement with his teacher let Chris leave math twenty minutes early. He got sneers from the ten other boys in his class. Chris had a ninety-nine percent in math, so his teacher didn't mind.

Barton Meeks, the boy who had ribbed Chris about his father on his first day, continued to tease him. The attacks intensified after Chris's teacher announced he had received a part in the play. Bart was the largest boy in the seventh grade. He wore cowboy boots to school every day, which increased the height gap over Chris, who wore soft-soled Buster Browns. Barton was stout with the beginnings of a belly and would be a natural lineman for the football team in two years. He wore his father's old duster jacket, faded with sun and rolled up at the sleeves. His Wrangler jeans dragged the ground at the heels of his boots.

At lunch recess at school a week into rehearsals, Bart moved close to Chris during the regular kickball game taking place on the muddy interior of the school track. "I figured out something. You think you're better than us, don't you, city kid?"

Chris frowned, trying to figure out a way to respond that would not cause Bart to become physical. The smaller boy avoided eye contact, noting the frayed muddy hem on Bart's jeans gathered around his boot heels.

"Maybe you should sing it," the bigger boy laughed and bumped Chris with his shoulder.

All the boys stopped to watch the confrontation. They bunched around the two.

Chris narrowed his lips. "They were just wanted someone who could learn the words."

"You sayin' I'm stupid? That I cain't learn the words if I wanted?" Bart moved close to shove Chris. He slammed the butts of both palms into Chris's shoulders.

Chris was staggered by the assault. "No, someone small enough to play the part."

"Oh, I didn't know it was a baby's part." Bart's voice was now loud, a taunt.

Chris could see there was no way out of this confrontation. He knew that running would probably involve other boys to slow his escape. He stood his ground, fearing the worst.

Bart lunged at him, but Chris was the more agile of the two. He slipped out the way of Bart's bear hug and through his quick sidestep accidently tripped the bully, who fell headlong into the grass. Wet circles formed at Bart's elbows and knees. The bigger boy stood, enraged.

"Now you're gonna get it, you little shit," Bart said. His voice was a shout, and two teachers standing on the sidewalk by the building, noticed the circle of boys yelling, "Fight! Fight!" They began to run toward the ring, but they would not be in time to stop the first punch.

When they arrived, Chris was sitting on the ground, his lip bleeding.

Bart towered over him, glaring. "Get up, you little baby. Tell me you're scared. Sing it, or maybe you should just cry."

Chris did not stand until a teacher interceded. The first grabbed Barton Meeks. "Stop fighting! Principal Farley will have something to say to you two! Come with me! Now!"

The second adult to arrive was Chris and Barton's teacher. Mrs. George picked Chris off the ground by taking the boy by both hands and pulling him to his feet. "Are you okay? Let me look at you. Split your lip, didn't he? Well, come on."

At rehearsal that afternoon, Chris could not sing his parts without his swollen red lip beginning to bleed again. Piper, often his nemesis, was now his staunchest defender. "Tell me who did it, little brother. I'll pound him. First, I'll pound him, and then I'll get some of the Kiowa High School boys I know to pound him, too. Right into the ground."

Chris shook his head. He didn't want to rat out Barton, not for any sense of comradeship or boy's code of honor. No, he was afraid it might get out he'd told high school kids about Barton hitting him and it would extract some method of revenge. Chris could see a rumor like that backfiring. It might end up with him getting another punch. Or maybe something even worse.

Chris was miserable, but having Piper dab a wet paper towel to his lip between her scenes made him feel a little better for the sympathy. It had been a rough day.

Soon, a gaggle of high school girls, including the play's leading actress, Shannon Gill, were in a semi-circle around him. Each noted the continued blood on his lip, a watery red dribbling down to his chin.

The attention from the five high school girls was something new to Chris. Their demand for the name of his attacker was enticing, like sirens to a sailor. He finally broke down. "This bully in my class, Barton Meeks, he's been after me since I got to school last month."

Shannon Gill suddenly looked as if it were she who had been punched in the mouth. "That's my step-brother."

Piper looked in surprise at Shannon and then at her brother.

Shannon shrugged and then said in explanation. "My mom got married again after my dad died. Barton's her new husband's son. We live in the same house."

Piper, always able to discern changing moods, grabbed Shannon. "It's okay, Shannon. It's just boys being boys, They're always fighting. Chris, you'll be okay, right?"

Chris nodded, knowing there was a new gravity to the situation, but he didn't quite grasp it. He guessed Piper did not want to lose Shannon's friendship. He didn't want that to happen, either. It wasn't Shannon Gill's fault.

The high school music teacher called the cast of high schoolers back to the stage, leaving Chris to sit in the bleachers nursing his bloody lip. He didn't sing at all that evening.

During the time, the boy sat there reflecting on his getting hit, the attention it had received, and his grandfather's words in the pick-up on the way to rehearsal: *"You made a mistake today, boy. When you're a little guy like you and me are and you know a big ole feller is going to start a-wailing on you, you get in the first lick. Sometimes, you're still going to get whipped, but at least you'll have got in one good poke that way." Jeff lit a cigarette and leaned over to look at the boy's bloody lip. "If he comes close enough again, you kick him in the nuts. See if he still has any fight in him after that. Okay, Chris?"*

The next morning, Chris was reluctant to go to school. Granny Gwen had thought her daughter needed to know and called Lillian in Wichita.

Chris was called to the phone and asked if he was all right. At this stage, he was tired of the whole thing. The night before, he had gone to bed only to wake up to a monstrous fat lip. It got in the way when he ate, and the orange juice he drank caused his cut to sting.

Grandma Gwen sat him down to look over his wound before he went to get in Jeff's truck. Chris tried to avoid his grandmother's scrutiny, but she was playing the nurse, poking his lip and stretching his cheek out, peering inside.

"I don't think there is any damage to your teeth. Does it hurt?" she asked.

"Yeah, it hurts. It hurts more when you do that," he said as she pulled his mouth even wider to look at his bottom teeth.

Chris's bottom lip showed a straight black line with purple swelling around it. The place above his top lip was sanded red from the abrasion of Barton's blow. Chris didn't want to go to school. He didn't want the teasing he knew would come with his temporary disfigurements. And most of all, Chris didn't want further victimhood at the hands of Barton Meeks. He knew well enough that Jeff would have none of shirking off a fight, so the boy didn't even ask to stay home.

But things went quite differently than Chris imagined.

When Chris arrived to school, he slipped inside. He slid into his desk and pulled out his reading book. There, he kept his head down, pretending to be absorbed in the printed pages. Several students stared at his lip, but no one spoke to him. However, the attention toward him was less than he thought it might be. Chris was not sure what was going on, but as more students entered, Chris realized he was not the center of attention in his class of fifteen.

Just before the bell, Barton Meeks arrived, the last student inside before Mrs. George closed the door. However, it could not be said he walked in; Barton limped in. There was no other word for it. The large boy was gimping on his right leg, and he held one arm tight to his side. One of Bart's eyes was blackened and there was a scrape along his jawline.

Chris was a smart kid. He quickly put two and two together. Shannon Gill had gone home and told her stepfather Barton beat up a little kid at school. And Bart's dad, in turn, had whipped the boy beyond all permissible levels of punishment. Chris wanted to smile, but one look at Bart made him reassess any joy in the situation. Bart was in pain, a lot of pain. Chris could see the bigger boy had pain in his ribs, too. Chris frowned. Getting punched in the mouth was bad, sure, but he wouldn't wish a beathing like Bart had received on anyone.

At recess, Chris noticed Bart stood at the side of the grass field, away from the other boys. Neither he nor Chris participated in the kickball game. Chris watched Barton and could see the bigger boy was in obvious distress. Chris cautiously moved beside him, staying out of range of a swing, but there was no fight in Barton Meeks today.

"Your dad beat you, huh?"

Bart stared over with hate. "No thanks to you for ratting me out to my bitch step-sister."

"I'm sorry. I didn't know Shannon and you were family. My sister caused a stir at rehearsal last night, and Shannon heard about it. Are you hurt bad?"

"I'll live. You just mind your own."

Chris squinted toward Barton. "Look, this is stupid. You're the biggest kid in the class, bigger than most of the eighth graders. Everybody's pretty much afraid of you. I'm the smallest and the newest kid in our class. I'm not worth beating up on a regular basis, particularly if you're gonna take a whipping every time. We should do like they do in the cowboy and Indian movies. Smoke a peace pipe, you know."

Bart looked at him and closed one eye. "You're just scared of me."

Chris smiled. "I sure am. But we'd both be better off if this situation got ended right now. I don't want the reputation of a squealer. I really didn't know about you and Shannon being related. I'm real sorry you took a whuppin'."

Barton looked at him and considered the proposal. He narrowed his eyes while he pondered the idea. Then he nodded. "Okay, I guess you're right. We're both better off iffin' we don't fight. I guess I'm sorry I took a poke at you." He smiled and then grimaced, as it caused him a twinge of pain. The bigger boy paused. "Now what?"

Chris pondered. "My grandpa bought me two boxes of .22 shells to shoot this Saturday. You want to come over and shoot at some beer cans?"

On Saturday, Chris rode with his grandfather and his mom to pick up Barton Meeks from Hardtner. His mother looked at him, sternly. "You know, you don't have to be friends with this boy after he punched you in the face."

Chris touched his lip, which had healed some, but was still sore to the touch. "It's okay. We decided on a truce. I don't think we're ever going to be best buddies or anything. Today just gets his father to leave him alone and gets me out of hot water at school with the rest of the boys."

Jeff agreed. "It's a good move. Mutually beneficial, they call it. That means good for both of you. Boys are boys. They fight and then they get over it. Shooting some guns together is a good way to put things to bed. It's a smart move by the boy."

Lillian nodded. "Just don't let him shoot you. And don't you shoot him."

"Mo-om," Chris complained, and then they were there. Chris slid out of the backseat of the Oldsmobile, ran up the sidewalk, and rang the bell.

Lillian and Jeff could see it was Barton who opened the door.

The two boys spoke for a second and then Chris retreated to the car. He motioned for his mother to roll down her window.

She did. "What's wrong? Can't he come over?"

Chris shrugged. "His dad wants to know if we're Jews."

Lillian's mouth dropped open. "For the love of…he really asked that?"

"Yes, ma'am."

"And you know we're not. What did you say?"

"I was afraid I'd laugh and cause a problem, so I came back here. I told him I'd go ask you." Chris smiled and then raised an eyebrow. "Pretty strange, huh? What should I say?"

"Pretty rude is what it is. Maybe I should march right up there…"

Jeff cut her off. "That won't help matters none, Lil."

Lillian nodded. "I know, Dad." She looked to Chris. "I should just make you get back in and let's head home." Lillian was incensed.

Jeff said, "That's baloney. Chris, you go back there and tell him we're not Jews and ask him if he's ready to go shoot." He looked to his daughter. "Today ain't about anything other than making things easier for Chris at school. Also, we want to make sure Barton don't take any more lickings from his father. Nine out of ten people in this town would think that Jew question is bullshit, but we're navigating a situation to make things better for both these boys. Okay, Lil?"

She nodded.

So did her son.

Then, Chris went back, and Lillian could see her son say something after which Barton yelled back into the house.

The larger boy lifted something to his shoulder and carried it to the car.

Jeff exited and took what appeared to be a rifle case from Bart and put it in the trunk.

After Chris introduced his mom and grandfather, Barton sat in the backseat beside Chris.

As they pulled from the curb, Bart spoke. "My dad said it's okay to come shoot, especially if you're providing the bullets. But he said if you're Catholic, I can't stay for lunch."

Oklahoma Territory
February 5, 1899

By late afternoon at the Hart and Station's spread, Renfro was worried. Tanner had not arrived home. Carson had left Renfro assuring him his older brother would return. The sunlight was muted, both from the incoming front on the western horizon and the dimming of the day.

Renfro spent the afternoon on horseback, bunching the herd into the hills around the dugout as best he could. The cottonwoods were bare, and the wind rattled their branches like bones in a box. The hobbled cowpoke could only bear an hour at a time in the wind, which was probably forty miles an hour in gusts. Sparse snowflakes flashed past his face in the dying light. When he felt the cold too acutely, he retreated inside the lean-to for a cigarette, bringing his horse into the shelter of the stable, bunching in a corner with his dog, Stu.

Then deciding he was on his own, the cowman, his horse and dog working in expert partnership, cut the yearlings one at a time from the herd.

Once separated, he roped each and brought the bawling youngsters into the larger dugout, which was little more ten feet square with a tin roof. There were four horse stalls in the shelter, and he forced four of the animals into each stall. It was noticeably warmer in the stable, not because of the quality of the shelter, but because the sixteen heads' body temperature began to warm the space once Renfro reached capacity. The absence of wind was a palatable thing.

After each stall was filled, he decided to fill the entryway with three cows, which calmed the panicked calves. Renfro felt good, knowing the most vulnerable of the cattle were now safe.

With nineteen of the herd of roughly 160 animals sheltered, it was now full dark. Unhappy, but unable to work the herd in night, Renfro rode into the fury of the northwest wind to the main farmhouse.

In the barn, he cared for his horse, planning his next move. If Renfro was correct, behind this wind was an incoming blizzard. Renfro felt the snap in the wind and heard the deathly moan through the barn walls. The cowpoke had lived long enough on the plains to know what followed such a powerful front: snow, and lots of it.

Inside the main house, Renfro built a fire in Avery and Everett's stove, allowing his dog inside. He opened a can of stew and split it with Stu.

Both rested while Renfro smoked a cigarette and drank freshly brewed coffee from the now fully heated stove. The kitchen was warm, and Renfro's nose and hands began to ache as the blood again flowed through his gnarled knuckles. He watched out the window and could see the snow begin to accumulate. The wind had not abated, and the snowflakes danced at the window before abandoning him with his thoughts. He poured a second cup of coffee and had a second cigarette. During that time, Renfro contemplated his next move.

The cowpoke carried a lantern, not bothering to light it. The gale outside would certainly extinguish it before he could walk to the barn, which was his destination. Inside, the wind still made lighting a match and catching flame to the lantern wick difficult.

After two tries, he was successful.

As he fed the horses, Renfro considered the corral. Perhaps he could fit fifty head into it, but there would be little protection from the wind. If that was his only play, the herd would be better bedded down in the sandhills, amid the dunes. However, inside the barn, Renfro made similar calculations. If he moved the tack and saddles to the loft and tossed all the bundles of hay out into the snow, he might get about fifty head inside the structure. Inside right now, Everett's horse, as well as Avery's, and two ponies for the girls occupied three of the stalls in the stable area. He could move a pony into each of the bigger horses' stalls and situate a couple of head into each of those vacated areas.

The large bundles of hay, perhaps three hundred of them on the floor of the barn had to be moved outside. Hobbling on his injured hip, Renfro stacked the hay against the exterior walls of the barn, insulating as best he could. Next, the crippled cowboy spent several hours moving all the farming equipment from the ground floor to the loft after the hay was outside.

Sometime around midnight, the barn was clear. Renfro was tired. He curried his horse a second time and gave it grain and water along with sugar cubes. The dawn was going to bring a difficult day and he needed both he and his steed to be nourished and rested.

Together, Renfro and Stu, who followed in his footsteps to avoid the deepening drifts, crossed the farmyard. The wind howled and drifts against the eastern sides of the chicken coop, the barn and the house were now more than a foot deep. The snow falling from the sky was prodigious. Renfro feared for the cattle, hoping the wind and its deadly ability to cause hypothermia would cease. However, he did not believe the storm would abate anytime soon.

Inside, he drank several glasses of water from a pail and smoked two more cigarettes as he loaded a full complement of coal into the stove. Then, he rolled out his bedroll and laid on the floor next to the stove. Stu curled against him. Together, they slept.

A false dawn created an eerie light upon the world of white when Renfro awoke. He could see the snow was nearly a foot deep across the farmyard and perhaps twice that or even three times that in tailing drifts along the barn and chicken coop.

In the dim light that seemed to emanate from the snow itself, he stirred the coal in the stove and revived the flames with a small stock of coal. He reheated the coffee from the previous evening. He let Stu out to urinate, which Renfro also did. The cold was shocking in the wind. This storm was different, it seemed to him. Usually, snowfall brought a milder temperature than the initial front's passing. However, this morning was noticeably colder than last night. There was no time to waste. He quickly fed the dog another half can of stew. Renfro himself ate some hard tack and a can of peaches before dressing. He did not take time for the cigarette he craved.

Uncomfortably, the cowpoke raided Everett's closet as his own meager stock of clothes were in a trunk at the dugout, approximately three miles away. He appropriated an extra pair of socks, two extra shirts which fit over his easily as Everett was much stockier than Renfro. As he tugged on his boots and coat, covering the rest with his duster, the cowboy stared into the mirror in Avery and Everett's bedroom. All the bulky clothes did not help his looks.

He grinned at his ridiculous figure. Renfro was not much to look at: a no-account cattle tramp, a greying veteran of the Confederate Army, and a damaged man, unable to walk any distance without limping in pain. His face was thin, his body lean, his mustache long and unfurled like a ratty yellow rag. Renfro knew he was second rate to most folk, but today he would earn his keep. His job was to save the ranch's herd. He hoped he was good enough.

Renfro took a towel from Avery's closet and tied it around his head over his ears. Then, he took a section of twine and tied it over the crown of his hat and under his chin, securing his cowboy hat to his head. Next, he tied another towel over his nose and mouth, leaving only his eyes exposed to the elements. Renfro found little solace in the fact that he would be riding with his back to the gale on his way to the herd. Renfro knew he would be in the elements for many hours on this day, and he knew the price of being in this kind of cold for so long. The cost of this bitter cold was frostbite. Humans did poorly in this kind of weather. He put the thought from his mind. Fear and trepidation could not be a part of this day.

After feeding grain to the horse once more, he saddled it

quickly, placing a second blanket over its neck, much to the horse's irritation.

The horse fought the covering until Renfro lifted a reluctant Stu onto the blanket.

Then, the cowboy rose to the saddle, holding the dog against him. Their warmth was a comfort to each other. Then, he left the shelter of the barn.

The horse naturally headed away from the wind, walking in rhythm with the rider directing him with only his knees.

Renfro gave the horse time to get to the herd. He knew how much effort would be expended in the cold. He needed the horse fresh.

It was tough going in the snowfields. The drifts once they reached the dunes were regularly over three feet deep. The cold was bitter and vicious. The wind was a wicked thing, malicious and without relent. The endless white, even without sun, hurt the cowboy's eyes.

The herd was now down in the dunes and was beginning to be covered in layers of snow. Renfro fired his sidearm several times, and most of the cattle rose to their feet, but with reluctance. The western flank of the herd did not rise. The hypothermia of being in the wind for the night had taken its toll on them. He feared the downed animals would be dead very soon. He counted more than ten head lying in the drifts, heads down.

The cowman moved into action. He stepped inside his quarters. The lean-to's furnishings were meager enough; a bunk bed, a table and two chairs, a stove, and the trunk holding Renfro's worldly possessions. In less than five minutes, he had them all out in the snow.

Next, he moved into the downed cattle. With his lariat tied to his saddle horn, he placed a loop around the closest steer's neck. Then, with his horse backing his play, Renfro pushed the animal's hindquarters up as his horse pulled hard at its head.

Slowly, they raised the animal.

Renfro moved the steer into the dugout where he himself

normally slept. He pressed the animal to the far wall and went for the next one. This one could not be roused. It was too far gone. He left it. The next one was also already dead.

Altogether, in the next two hours, he and the horse, with Stu nipping at the cattle's feet, moved eight frost-bitten cattle into the lean-to. He dragged his trunk across the closed door.

Now, he checked on the yearlings stuffed into the stable and saw they were scared and wild-eyed but stable. Using his slop pail, he watered them, and they drank. He nodded that this was the first positive sign of the day. The cowpoke closed the door and tied it shut.

By now, it was full light, and the snow still came at them sideways. The knife's edge of the wind was deadly, he knew. Four head were down, dying or dead. The remaining one hundred and forty-odd cattle in the herd had again gone to ground. This time as he emptied his gun, several more head did not rise. Renfro did not bother trying to get them up. The situation now was desperate. He had to get the standing herd across three miles of foot-deep snow laced with three-foot drifts before dark. Renfro began to work the cattle out of the shelter of the sand dunes. They did not want to go. It was only with Stu biting at the cattle's heels and the skill of the horseman that he was able to move the herd out of the cottonwoods into the flat.

As they left the dunes, Renfro counted four dead and another six down that he was leaving to certain death. He lost another ten as he marched them into a forty mile an hour headwind for half a day.

By the time he reached the eastern edge of the main place, the snow was now better than eighteen inches deep on the flat. At the stream bed narrows, the snow was perhaps four feet deep and the herd wallowed. The drifts were deeper than their legs, and many started to give up. Renfro used his bullwhip to force them into the breech. He broke the drifts with his horse, moving back and forth through a gap under a scraggily crab apple tree.

Soon, a narrow pathway formed through which the entire herd passed. The cowboy looked back and saw he lost two more head in the monster drift. He abandoned them.

Rising out of the gully brought them into such a wind as he had never faced in his life. Renfro lost his hat and pulled the towel over his head as best he could. It, too, blew away, and so he faced the wretched cold and wind with his bare face, now numb to the onslaught.

But the farm lay below him less than a half of a mile away. Renfro forced the cattle downhill. It was the first time they obeyed without reluctance in the nearly six hours it had taken to drive the herd those three miles. He drove them across the flats, alternating drifts and windswept, the snow at its most thin there. The cowboy noticed his horse faltering after busting through the towering drifts of the streambed. Its nose looked frostbitten. He patted the animal's neck. The steed was simply done in. The horse began to wobble in fatigue.

Pulling away from the cattle, Renfro dismounted and led the animal to the barn. There, he exchanged his saddle from his horse to Everett's, leaving his exhausted animal in the stall, checking to see there was water.

Autumn's pony sidled up to the shivering animal.

Renfro's horse nuzzled back, and Renfro knew it would be all right.

Renfro's face ached once he was inside the barn. Outside in the wind, he had felt nothing on his face for a long time, but inside out of the storm, he felt his eyebrows and the bridge of his nose. Skin came away in patches, leaving blood on his cowhide gloves. He pulled the towel from around his ears down his forehead down to wipe away the blood and then saddled and mounted the second horse. Pulling the towel over his forehead over his nose and mouth, he grimaced but once and then got on with it.

Renfro rose to the saddle of Everett's big gelding and headed back into the gale. He feared the herd had surrendered to the snow and wind and he would not be able to get them to their feet again. They were not a quarter of a mile away, but he could not see them as he left the barnyard. The snow had not abated, and the day's light was waning. Everett's horse was not nearly the cattle horse as his, but it was a powerful and moved through the snow with authority.

In the less than ten minutes he'd been gone, most of the cattle were, indeed, down, their faces turned against the cyclone. This time, it took him firing the shotgun he kept in his saddle scabbard to move the herd to its feet. He stopped counting the number left behind in the drifts.

The dog nipped again at heels of those cattle still moving.

Stu and Renfro pressed the herd forward into the barnyard. He figured he still had over 100 head with him, but now he was too tired to count. Without his horse and its superior cattle skill, it was more difficult to get the herd to go in the direction of the corral. He realized he was sloppy and making mistakes.

Stu barked at one stubborn steer, and Renfro heard an uncharacteristic crack of the air with the sound. It must be very cold. He had never felt this kind of cold before, but he had been told by cowboys from Montana way about cold that could crack and snap sound itself like ice. That effect would begin, they had told him, when the thermometer fell to twenty below. It must be that now, Renfro reckoned. Yes, the temperature, remarkably, had continued to fall during the day. And the snow continued to pelt them, seemingly falling in clumps at times and at other times like tiny ice pellets hitting them like the load of a quail gun.

In time, Renfro finally had all the remaining cattle in the confines of the barnyard. It had taken him an hour to move the herd the last two hundred yards. After returning Everett's gelding to its stall, crowding the two horses and the pony together for warmth, Renfro loaded the cattle into the barn, needing nothing more than his lariat, his command, and his bullwhip. He no longer needed the horse, but he ached for his cane, which was still in Avery and Everett's house by the stove. Soon, his hip hurt so bad he felt tears well up from his eyes, freezing in the folds of the towel.

Standing in the now full barn of braying beasts, Renfro realized with the temperature still falling that any of the animals left in the barnyard or corral would be lost overnight. He made some decisions.

Stu looked played out but continued to help.

Renfro dragged additional steers, one at a time, into the chicken coop, much to the displeasure of the hens. Only five head would fit.

As he forced the last big cow's ass inside the shed, the hens squawked at him, angrily, but despite their protestations, each bird remained inside out of the howling tempest, some so bold as to alight upon a cow's back.

Renfro laughed grimly at the birds. "Bitches," he called to them and shut the door tight with its latch.

There were still roughly fifty head in the corral. They had little life in their step, and all of them showed signs of frost bite on ears and noses. Renfro needed shelter. Any kind of shelter.

Out of time, out of light, and out of energy, the cowboy pressed on. He forced the remaining herd to the eastside of the barn, finding a place windswept and clear. He marched them grudgingly to the spot. He himself fell, as his bad leg gave way, but he rose and pushed the cattle tight to the barn wall, huddling them tightly. Out of the tempest, it felt much warmer, but when he yelled at the catatonic animals, Renfro could hear the crack of the air in the deadly chill. It was so very cold. The light of the day had completely surrendered.

Renfro now made another decision. In a move to insulate the

herd, which was quickly bedding down, the cowboy began to move the stacks of hay from the northside of the barn. He broke the bundles apart and piled it on the herd. Normally, cows would never abide something on their backs, but these poor critters were so far gone, they never budged.

Renfro had another idea. He took a tarp Everett used for shade in the corral during hot summer days. He spread it over the animals. Then, he covered the canvas with more hay. It worked. The animals stayed beneath it.

Seeing success, he tromped as fast as he could in the deepening snow with his bad hip and exhaustion to the house where he stripped all the beds and even took his bedroll in hand. Before he left the house, he called Stu to him. With the dog inside the house, Renfro closed the exhausted pooch inside. He had seen the frostbite on Stu's ears and nose. The hound had done his job for the day. It was time to get Stu inside and let him rest. He heard the dog scratch the inside of the door, wanting to accompany him, but Renfro thought the scratch perfunctory, and that Stu was truly glad to be staying behind.

Carrying those five blankets, one tablecloth, and his bedroll back, Renfro felt the ache in his bones. It had been so hard to come back out into the storm this time. But he did. Renfro moved into shadows on the east side of the barn.

With the last of his energy, he spread the blankets, tablecloth, and bedroll over the dazed herd, now huddled against the barn's rear wall. Renfro covered as many as he could reach. With at least half of the fifty covered, he tossed hay over the blankets, creating a layer of insulation. There was no more he could do. He stood for a moment just trying to catch his breath. There was little sound, except for the constant wind and his breath, which came in ragged gasps.

The fringes of the herd were now all covered in blankets and hay. The internal portion were not since he could not reach them all, but he hoped they would create enough body heat to survive. Renfro had done all he could.

The cowboy was so tired he could hardly make it across the barnyard to the house in the dark maelstrom. Renfro pondered as he walked the fifty yards back to the house if he should have cleared the house of furniture and driven the remaining herd inside the ranch owner's home. He thought it might have saved a few more, but he was not sure how Everett and Avery would have reacted to the destruction of their home. Nonetheless, he felt the cattle had a pretty good chance of survival as he had left them.

Inside, Stu raised his head from the floor where he'd been sleeping. The house was cold, in fact, very cold, but the absence of wind was a Godsend. The dog whined a little and licked at his front paws, which Renfro could see were red and raw from the cold.

Inside, the cowboy opened Avery's medicine drawer. Finding a salve, Renfro tugged at his gloves with his teeth, fumbling to remove them. His fingers no longer responded to his mind's commands.

Using the butt of his hand, he treated the dog's toes, ears, and nose. Then, he rubbed the salve over the raw strip of his own face. In the bedroom mirror, he could see the skin across his nose and along his brow was bleached and bleeding. His fingers were red and ached terribly. His fingertips were numb and had no feeling, and that worried him greatly.

It took him quite some time with his fumbling hands to light a match and rekindle the stove. Soon, though, he had created a steady flame. Heat eventually filled the room.

The cowboy took a pot and filled it with water and placed jerky to boil to softness. He set it on the washboard as he went to the pantry to search for some beans. He meant to feed the dog and himself but woke hours later on the floor beside the dog. It was nearing the dawn, and it was still snowing. He restoked the fire. Heated the broth and beans. Stu and Renfro ate. And then they slept, still as death.

———

It snowed for another day, and the cold lasted for another day after that. The cattle on the backside of the barn were covered in a deepening drift. Renfro heard lowing, however, and knew that some of them were still alive in there. There was little Renfro could do except climb the ladder to the loft and drop feed down to the horses and the cattle inside the barn.

Outside the drifts were such that on the second day; he was able to walk with makeshift snowshoes into the loft without a ladder. The drifts would have to be over twelve feet high for that, he reckoned. Renfro had never spent four days inside in his life that he could remember, but he was stuck there all that time.

By the morning of the third day, he was so bored that he retrieved the two head of cattle down down in the gully, dragging them to the closest cottonwood. Then using block and tackle, and Everett's sturdy horse, he hoisted the frozen beasts into the tree. Renfro started a fire. With a roaring blaze to hold the arctic air at bay, he butchered each steer and hung the meat, high in the loft.

It would be four days before the cold snap ended. Carson and Everett reached the ranch that afternoon. Both men were amazed to find Renfro butchering beef and managing the herd, which was now back out of the barn, the chicken coop, and feeding on hay in the corral and north pasture. One look at the old soldier's scarred and scabbed face told the story of the day, the blizzard, and its difficulties.

For his part, Renfro told the story matter-of-factly as he awkwardly rolled a cigarette. His hands were clumsy, and their tips were still blue and numb. Everett had no words to express his appreciation for what Renfro had done. He patted the old man's shoulder and slid his holdout one-hundred-dollar gold piece into the man's palm.

None of them had any idea where Tanner was. They could only hope he had found shelter in time on his way back to the ranch. But awaiting his return, they ate well, indeed, on fried steaks. Even Stu got steak. Everett knew, looking at Renfro's already scarring face, that the old cowpoke had saved the ranch. His family was safe in town and the herd was safe here. They were secure. Everett thanked the Lord for bringing that old Confederate to the ranch to stay.

That February storm is still the coldest in Kansas history. Oklahoma was not yet a state, so there are no official records, but it likely the worst storm in the territory's history, at least since white men arrived. There were over 100 deaths over the region to hypothermia, and over half a million cattle died of exposure. Temperatures were later reported at forty-seven below zero in Montana, ten below in Galveston, and twenty-two below in Kansas City. Georgia got a foot of snow as far south as Atlanta. Heavy snow fell in New Orleans and the Gulf Coast of Florida. Fruit trees throughout the southern states were generally lost to frost and died.

By Tuesday, Valentine's Day, the storm had reached the East Coast, where thirty to forty inches of snow fell all the way north to New Jersey. It paralyzed New York and Philly. After the snow came the horrible cold. Within ten days the snow was gone, and sixty-degree days were soon upon the territory, but the damage to the Outlet's herds was done. It took years for many a rancher to recover. Some who were highly leveraged to banks did not. The Salt Fork Stations had survived. Except there was no news of Tanner and the territory still largely impassable. Everett's mind was in a panic. Where was his brother-in-law, and what had happened to the yearling colt he had sent him to fetch home?

Kinship
Woods County, Oklahoma
March, 1964

Those who attended the Kiowa High School musical during the spring of 1964 became aware that Christian Fairchild could not sing a lick. But he was excellent at memorization and delivered his lines flawlessly and with great spirit. All in all, the play and the singing was a rousing success. Shannon Gill received many accolades for her lead role. Barton, her step-brother, even delivered a dozen roses to her onstage afterwards. Her mother had driven all the way to Medicine Lodge to get them.

March in Panhandle, Oklahoma is a fickle month. It can reach the sixties one day, then snow the next. That March, new shoots of grass grew on the prairie, and the cattle were grazing contentedly. However, that weekend, the forecast was for heavy rains. Storms in Oklahoma can bring deluges of rain, hail big enough to kill a horse, and of course, tornadoes.

Jeff and Landon spoke as they sat in squat positions, looking over the field. Each smoked a Camel cigarette and tipped the ash into the cuff of their pants. The habit kept ash off of Grandma Gwen's linoleum floor inside the kitchen and prevented grass fires in the parched summer months outside.

"Figure we go to the trouble of moving them in close to the house?" Landon suggested.

"Reckon so. We get six inches of rain, and you'll have standing water in the pasture. We won't be able to get to them for days after that. Don't want to lose calves over it."

"Probably be nothing."

"Probably."

"Can't risk it, though."

"No, can't risk it."

"Better go saddle up. I need to gas up the truck."

"Reckon so."

It took most of the afternoon for Landon on horseback with Jeff in his Ford to push the herd into the north pasture just south of the barn.

Of course, being it was a Saturday, Chris rode along with Jeff, bumping along in the truck. He grinned most of the day, watching Landon slap cows on the rear with his hat, and Jeff cut off those rascals that tried to sneak out the side.

The biggest challenge of the day was to get the cattle past the cattle guard, which they were conditioned to avoid. Jeff put down two sheets of plywood over the gaps in the metal grate, and eventually, the herd, led by an old mossy-back cow, trod across the gate into the pasture.

All the while, the herd complained vociferously.

Landon took time to count each head as it passed through the gate, letting Jeff and the boy push the cattle across with the truck.

"What's your count?"

"One eighty-six."

"Me, too. One short."

"Think we counted wrong?"

"Probably."

"I'll count again."

A pause.

"Still got one eighty-six. You?"

"Same."

"Damn. I ain't gonna get any tractor work done today. Figure we left one out there?"

"Probably."

"Okay, I'll mount up. You and the boy take the west side. You can get there sooner. Honk if you find her. I'll fire a shot if I do."

"That'll work."

Chris and Jeff drove back through the gate and with more speed this time, which meant more bumps. They hurried to the far west side of the pasture toward the Hackberry.

Chris bounced around on his side of the bench seat. Eventually, he began to laugh. Jeff after a moment began to, as well.

"Think I'm going to bounce your butt out of the truck?"

"Probably," Chris said in a kids' baritone, imitating the two men.

"Think you're funny, don't you?" Jeff asked, grinning wide.

"Reckon so." Chris paused for effect.

And they laughed.

Later, they concentrated on looking for the steer. Jeff criss-crossed the pasture several times, cutting roughly fifty yards off the field with each scissor cut. As they made their third turn, they heard a pistol shot from afar. Landon must have had found the missing animal.

Jeff steered that direction.

Soon, they saw Landon sitting astride his horse. He nodded at the steer, which was up to its belly in a pond near the east fence line. The steer's rear was underwater, and it munched on swamp grass, newly sprouted on the underside of the bank. The animal looked content.

"Ain't gonna want to come out of there."

"Nope, not gonna wanna."

"Gonna fight us, you figure?"

"Probably."

"You drop a rope around him and tie it to the hitch. I'll pull him out," Jeff suggested.

Landon just nodded and began to maneuver his horse in position to rope the steer.

Jeff backed the truck to the water's edge. Chris, with his head craned out the side window, watched as Landon tossed once, missed, twice, missed, and three times, loop floating through the air over the steer's extended neck as he munched away.

Landon dismounted and brought the line to the truck, where he tied a knot to the trailer hitch.

Jeff waited in the cab until Landon nodded at him. He dropped the stick into granny gear and began to move forward.

The steer fought it, but it had met a torque ratio it could not best. Soon, he followed along behind the truck, even with some slack in the line.

It took them ten minutes to get to the cattle guard with the truck inching forward in low, but Jeff smoked and told Chris to keep an eye on the animal in tow.

Landon rode on ahead.

"Is Uncle Landon the best cowboy you ever met, Grandpa?" Chris asked.

"Well, he's a helluva cowboy, your uncle is, but he ain't the best I ever saw," Jeff said.

"Who, then?"

"There was this cowpoke who worked on the ranch back when I was just a young-un. Taught me to throw a rope, as a matter of fact. Man named Mr. Renfro. He lived in that little shack we now call the woodshed. Back in the day, we called it the bunkhouse. My father built it for him after one real cold winter. Renfro could do things with his horse and his dog that I've never seen any cowboy do."

"Like what?"

"I expect he could have made cattle dance if he wanted to."

"Was he good with a rope?"

"That's a funny thing. He couldn't hardly throw a rope by the time I knowed him. Didn't have any feeling in his fingertips. Got 'em frostbit in that bad winter, 1899, before I was born."

"He had a cow dog?"

"Yessir! In fact, he had two. Old Stu was getting up in age by the time I was walking around, so Mr. Renfro had him a second pup named Brew by the time I was up and around. Old Stu and Brew. Stu taught that pup to work cattle. I saw it. Damnedest thing I ever saw. One dog training the other. Yessir, Mr. Renfro was the best I ever saw. Had the best horse and dogs, too."

"Mr. Renfro?" Chris asked.

"Oh, yes, it was *Mister* Renfro. Once, I busted my spur as a kid. I yelled for Renfro to get out of the barn and help me. My father heard me call him. I was rude. A kid bossing a grown man around. Pa came out of the house a-hummin'. Paddled my ass." Jeff paused to light a second cigarette off the butt of his first. "How's that cow doin'?"

"Fine," Chris replied, looking back, "just trailin' along."

"Dad laid the belt to me good, and when he finished, my father stood me in front of that cowhand and said, 'That man is *Mister* Renfro to you, boy. There'd be no ranch if it weren't for Mr. Renfro. He's the best cowman in Oklahoma. Maybe in the whole west. You ever take a look at his horse and see those raggedy ears? See how that old dog, Stu, limps? See the scars on Mr. Renfro's face? All of those happened on the day he saved this ranch. You show him some respect, son, or next time I'll whip you for real.' And then Pa made me apologize to Mr. Renfro for being a stupid little bastard. I'll never forget it."

"Did he accept your apology?"

"Hell, yeah, boy. Mr. Renfro was quite the gentleman."

Oklahoma Territory
February 3, 1899

Tanner Station knew he was in trouble long before the snow began coming at him sideways. It all started with a horse, a horse Everett had seen up in Wichita at a horserace when he'd shipped some cattle there by train and sold them. Thoroughbred horses had fallen out of favor for ranch work in the west after the debacle of the Land Run of 1893, when imported Kentucky purebreds died in the heat.

Smaller, but more durable, stock survived the triple digit run. Plus, ranchers out in panhandle country had no money for fancy horses with fancy names. But horseracing was very popular, and when Everett saw a horse called National Anthem win three days in a row at the cattlemen's monthly meetings at the stockyard races in Wichita, he decided he wanted in on the game. Of course, Avery thought investing in a racehorse a risky proposition. But Everett's plans were not to race the horse, at least not primarily. He needed the horse to win a race or two to gin up its stud value and then he would take fees for siring.

For once, Everett took a risk, something he was not prone to do. As Avery argued against it, Everett reasoned they had money in the bank for the first time, something they had not had in the five years prior. This three hundred could bring them ten-fold that over the next decade. Everett finally convinced his wife the risk was worth the bet.

When he next took the cattle to market in Wichita by train, he used the money from the sale of the cattle to buy rights to a colt off of National Anthem the next season.

The following spring, Anthem Song was born. Like his daddy, Anthem Song was no small critter. His pappy, National Anthem, stood at more than seventeen hands high, towering over the average working horse on the plains, which often stood at just over fourteen or fifteen. That meant he was eight inches to a foot taller, and on National Anthem, it was all legs. Everett had watched that stallion's pappy out-stride every horse he came against at those Wichita races, and Everett was gambling a horse off that bloodstock would be a good investment. A mare would give him foals, a stallion would bring him cash from stud fees.

The owner was willing to take a low price for a foal not even yet a glimmer in National Anthem's eyes. The man who bought Everett's cattle had a good mare and negotiated her offspring in the next season for some free steers.

Near on two years later, that colt was ready to come to his new home. Everett's bet on the future was now a stallion the color of burning coal ash with a mane black as sin.

A yearling, the horse was a big enough to leave the confines of the horse farm and come to the Salt Fork ranch. Everett hoped to make good money on Anthem Song until 1910 or longer. There were few things the ranch owners in the Oklahoma territory would splurge on, he knew, and good horse flesh was their biggest weakness.

Tanner left to get the yearling, which Everett simply called Anthem, on the Wednesday morning before the storm. The animal was to arrive by stock car in Enid on Thursday night on the Atchison line. It was an easy two-day ride there by horse.

The lanky cowboy planned his path to head east from the ranch, skirt round the Indian encampments at Cherokee, trace the bottom of the great salt flats to Cherokee's east, and spend the night, camping near the general store at Jet, where the military still housed a unit of forty horse soldiers in case of any uprising or runaways from the reservation. Tanner would picket his roan at his campsite. There was no need to utilize Joe Wolf Walker's livery there. Tanner would save the two bits. In the morning after coffee over a small fire up in the willows, Tanner would head over to the general store, deliver a handwritten order from Avery, and then ride on to Enid to meet the train. He'd pick up the supplies coming through on his return.

———

The first two days went as planned, but upon his arrival in Enid, a telegram awaited him. Anthem Song had been delayed. The south-bound train had been stalled by strong winds which had derailed two cars south of Wichita. The horse would not arrive until the next day. The high winds had also downed the telegraph lines after Tanner's note had been received, so no additional information was available. Tanner, who stayed at an Enid hotel for the night due to the increasing cold, was sitting on his hands impatiently awaiting the colt to arrive.

———

When the Atchison, Topeka, and the Santa Fe finally arrived in Enid late Saturday, Tanner's throat was raw from sitting and smoking all day.

A young fella, with papers for Tanner to sign, met him after disembarking from the train's cattle car.

Tanner inspected the colt and signed for him. Anthem Song was now theirs.

Tanner and the colt's handler hurriedly moved the yearling down the gangplank onto solid ground. Tanner could tell Anthem was jittery with energy after two days in a cattle car. They moved the yearling to the livery corral as the sun faded in the west. Tanner marveled at the colt's size. At a year old, he was nearly as big as Tanner's own horse already. Anthem would be a monstrous stallion when full grown.

In the corral, Tanner removed the colt's halter and allowed the horse a measure of freedom. The colt stomped around as if on parade. Anthem shook his black mane and bellowed to announce his arrival.

Tanner sat on the rail and watched the animal with an appreciative eye.

After a quarter hour, he had the stable boy bring fresh water and a bucket of grain to both the colt and his horse. Next, Tanner sent the boy to buy the both of them dinner. The boy deserved it for the good care he'd given a stranger. They ate fried chicken as friends.

Tanner nodded in approval at the horse. Everybody needed to be well fed before they left on the trail home in the morning. He certainly was. He paid the boy to feed grain to the livestock once more before stabling them for the night.

Tanner was now running a day late and hadn't even started for home. He considered whether to send a telegram to Everett, but he knew the message would not make it to the ranch. The only alternative was to send it to his father in Alva. It seemed a waste of money, and Tanner's funds were low after an unplanned stay at the hotel. He chose not to bother with the telegram. He slept at the hotel for a second night.

Before dawn, the boy, good to his word, was up and had saddled his horse. With Tanner's help, the two arranged a halter with a long running line on the colt.

Tanner and Anthem left Enid with the first light at their back. It was colder than Tanner liked, but Anthem was full of piss and vinegar and ready for exercise. The colt seemed to enjoy blowing steaming air into the morning light. Anthem was strong, and they made good time.

Just past dawn, on that raw-bone morning, they were underway. The wind was an assault, but the sky was clear. It was cold, maybe thirty-five degrees, but the windchill made Tanner pull his bandana up over his ears. He'd told Everett he would be back to the ranch by noon Saturday, but here it was already Sunday morning, and he was two-day's-ride away. Tanner did not want to push the young colt. Anthem was a big investment. Tanner thought the colt looked tough and strong, but the gale was bitter, and the cowboy had no idea about the horse's durability in that headwind. It would be a two-day trip once again and he would have to spend the money to put both horses in the livery at Jet.

Day one was uneventful, although increasingly cold. The colt needed no prodding to move west. His gait equaled Tanner's horse's.

By nightfall, they were coming into Jet and back to the fort. Tanner didn't worry about missing the fort in the night. The salt flat on his right was easy to discern and its soil much different than the prairie. If Tanner kept its barren ghostly white to his right and the wind in his face, he would see the lights of the fort as he and the two horses approached. It was much colder now, and a few flakes hung in the air briefly in front of his numbed face before they flashed past in the moonlight still visible through the racing clouds.

The wind worsened all the while, and Tanner's face ached with cold. The road seemed longer now than the passage to Enid had been. Still, they would reach Jet before midnight.

The cowboy and the colt arrived in full darkness. A roadhouse was the first structure they passed, but few were inside as the fort's captain has recently banned all soldiers from entering the building. Fixed card games, fights, bad liquor, and venereal disease were all it had to offer. Tanner steered clear.

A quarter mile past, he saw the swinging lights of two lanterns, one in front of Joe Wolf Walker's dilapidated house and next to it, a listing barn he used as a livery. Tanner was happy to see the structure still on its feet leaning into the wind. He dismounted roughly fifty yards from the stable entrance, wanting to give his aching legs feeling again before ducking into the stable door and arranging quarters for the night.

As Tanner approached, he heard raised voices above the gale's howl. Downwind in full darkness, he knew they could not hear or see him approach. Tanner dropped the reins and halter, knowing the horses would stay close, wanting to get in out of the wind just as badly as he did. The voices came to him across the wind. They were full of crisis and chaos.

"Help me get her bloomers down, Charlie."

Tanner heard ribald laughter in return. Then a deeper, more assured voice after, "Get the whore on the ground. You two hold her. I go first."

Tanner could hear a woman's muffled objections to the assault. The lean cowboy could see only little in the gloom, but he scrambled back to the horses.

In two strides, Tanner was back to his roan and grabbed his Henry long rifle in his left hand. With his right, he removed the thong from the hammer of his pistol. As he returned to the rape just beginning, Tanner raised the rifle.

Nearing the four, he crept toward the closest lantern's illumination. The wind's volume hid his approach. Arriving to the fray, he saw a man forcing a young woman to the ground. His hand covered her mouth, muffling her shouts. Her tan sprawling legs caught the lamp's glow.

Tanner stepped forward, but none of the three men noticed him, their attention on the woman. Tanner wound up his leg, and using his heel, he stomped the prone man's ribs at the kidney. The man bellowed and fell off the girl.

The young Indian woman pulled free and scrambled to a standing position.

The two standing men whirled to brace Tanner, reaching for their weapons, but they did not clear leather, seeing the Henry aimed at their chests.

The third man, whose britches were around his ankles, rolled to his back. His paw reached down for the pistol in his holster just beyond his reach. The man's face was hateful.

Tanner recognized the face. It was the scarred face of Mel Harris, the cowboy he'd braced the day of the land run so long ago. He moved the rifle barrel until it touched Harris' scar. He rested the barrel on the man's cheek.

Harris slowed his hands to a stop. He then raised his hands and nodded his head, understanding. Harris bobbed his chin, in essence asking for permission to pull up his britches.

Tanner shook his head.

A sickening smile hung on Harris' lips.

With the rifle barrel off him, Charlie Crups took a step to the left, moving well out of the lantern's glare.

Buck Wells stepped laterally to the right.

Tanner placed the business end of the Henry on Harris' heart. He asked the girl without looking at her, "You okay?"

First, the Indian woman only nodded, but then she realized her savior did not dare look her way. "Yes," she said, hesitantly. Now standing, she tugged her leather dress down over her leggings and knee-high moccasins. She picked up a heavy walking stick from the ground.

As she gathered herself, Buck Wells stepped farther from the lantern glow and reached for his weapon, but it was the young woman with the speed.

She swung the staff up from the ground with all her might. It cracked under Wells' jaw.

Wells dropped, hitting the ground nearly as quickly as the pistol which fell from his limp hand. Blood already trickled from his mouth where he'd bitten his tongue.

Tanner, however, had never taken his eyes off Harris.

Harris, in turn, had not stirred. His eyes glowed in the lantern light.

Tanner watched them glint over his rifle sight. Charlie Crups, he could see, in his peripheral vision. Crups' hand began to creep slowly until Tanner said, "Tich, tich, you're going to get your ramrod killed you move that hand another inch."

"Don't be stupid, Charlie!" Harris barked. His man relaxed his arm and came back to a standing position.

The girl held the walking stick like an ax, ready to swing.

Harris' eyes seemed to be almost crossed as he stared at Tanner over the Henry's sight. "Why you want to get involved in something like this, mister? Just an Indian girl. You just like messin' with my fun?"

"Why you want to die over an Indian girl?" Tanner replied.

"We'll kill you," was Harris' reply.

Tanner nodded with his chin at Crups. "He might have a chance at it. You, not so much. I figure I got one for sure shot in this melee, and it's going in your heart, iffin' you got one."

Harris shrugged, his body still frozen on the ground, his pants down. "Okay, then. She's not worth the fuss. Just an Indian whore."

Tanner asked of the girl, "You got a horse?"

"Yes."

"Go get it." Tanner moved his eyes to the men's guns on their hips. "Harris, tell your man to drop his gun belt."

The Indian girl spoke. "The scar man has my gun. He just took it from me."

Tanner smiled. "Where is it?"

Harris nodded down at his dropped pants.

The girl gathered the unconscious man's gun. Then, she stuck both her gun and Harris's in her belt.

Tanner nodded. "Charlie, you drop your belt, too." He then said to the girl. "Get Charlie's, too. Take care to stay out of reach."

She did.

"Now, go get your horse 'fore these two get too impatient and do something stupid."

The girl disappeared into the barn's door.

"We'll follow you. It ain't like this is over," Harris growled. "Don't matter that you're wearing a mask. I'll figure out who you are. You'll get yours."

It wasn't till then when Tanner realized the bandana around his face had kept his identity hidden. The men did not know who he was. Tanner decided to let that stand. It was just as well they wouldn't come to the ranch for retribution.

Charlie was starting to feel his oats again. "We'll be comin' for you. You'll die tonight."

"Follow if you want. Gonna be cold out there a-huntin'," Tanner said. He was already worrying about being out in the open in the coming blizzard. First things first, he decided.

Harris laughed.

Crups joined him, nervously.

Neither paid their fallen companion any mind. Buck Wells lay on the cold ground; blood issued from his mouth and nose.

The girl appeared a moment later at the barn door, returning with a large mule. She struggled to put a large double pack across the mule's broad back, a double-folded tent roll extended across the mule's rump. The girl took the reins and led the animal clear of the men.

Tanner backed away from the two men, and the girl followed. They hurried back to his horses in the pitch black and wind.

Once there, they both mounted quickly.

"Come on," he called.

The colt pulled at his tether, fighting Tanner's insistence they head back into the wind's fury. Tanner said to the girl, "They still have rifles. They'll be right behind us."

Tanner and the Indian girl raced away from the light to the west, directly into the wind.

Anthem seemed to like the chance to run, and instead of trailing Tanner on his steed, the colt plowed alongside them.

Into the cyclone they ran.

Tanner watched the girl hunched over her mule, struggling to keep up with the two horses. She kept her head down out of the wind. He slowed to allow her to keep pace.

She glanced up, realizing it.

Tanner realized he had not taken time to look at her face until he saw her there, glancing up at him, what little light there was reflecting off the snow which now covered the ground. Her cheekbones were high and wide. Her eyes, deep set and dark, looked up at him in concern. Tanner saw tears leak from the corners of her eyes, etched in the fierce wind.

Tanner knew they were in for it. It was much too cold to go all night. The ranch was still forty miles away, and he'd be damned if he'd take trouble into another man's farm or ranch, not with those two mangy dogs on his trail. But with the girl and the colt with him, staying out on the prairie in a storm, twenty-degrees, falling temperatures, and a forty mile an hour wind, was not an option.

He quickly devised a plan in his head. "Turn north," he yelled over the gale.

The girl nodded.

After a quarter mile with the wind now buffeting their left sides, he slowed his horse.

The mule seemed relieved and fell into line behind him.

Tanner slowed more, letting the girl pull alongside.

"You think they follow us?" she asked.

"Yes. Harris, Scar, he is a very bad man."

She nodded. "I know of him. He gambles at my father's sometimes."

Tanner nodded. "You're Wolf Walker's daughter?"

"Yes. Do you know my father?"

"Yes, I've boarded there at the stable a time or two."

The girl's mouth pursed. "My father is a good man now. He has given up the whiskey."

Tanner didn't respond to her words.

Later, he said, "I've heard people call you Injun Mary. Is your name Mary?"

"Marie."

He nodded. "I'm Tanner Station."

"Where are we heading?" was the reply.

"Into the night, away from Harris and Crups."

"Is your ranch close?"

"No, nowhere we can get to tonight."

"Then, where? We are headed to the salt flats. There is nothing out there."

"Yeah, so that's the one place those two varmints won't think to look for us."

The girl pondered for a second but then countered. "It is too cold to stay out on the flats."

"Yes," he agreed. "We'll go a mile or two out then head west."

"Into the switchbacks?"

"Yes."

"There is nothing there but quicksand and mudslides down the canyon walls."

"Normally, yes, but it is too cold for those right now. We should be able to find shelter out of this wind someplace where no one will look for us. The canyon walls are steep there."

The girl considered this statement, her eyes peering up at him from the folds of the blanket she now placed around her shoulders. "I have a tent," she said.

Tanner smiled. "That's very good news," he replied.

And then they rode.

It was easy to find the switchbacks, even in the pitch black of this stormy night. By the time they turned back west, it was snowing full out. They couldn't see more than fifty feet ahead of them, but there was really no need to. The wind was now an evil demon plowing its way east. All they had to do was face into it.

As they reached the end of the salt flats, snow now drifted away from the leading canyon of the switchbacks. The wind whined like a widowed woman down the choked canyon offering entry into this godforsaken land.

The switchbacks were the only unclaimed land in the territory. It was ten square miles of plateaus, canyons, and cliffs. Few trees could be found anywhere in the whole region. Those cedars that did grow here were twisted and gnarled by constant wind along the canyon walls. The slopes were steep with erosion, and no one had ever bothered to map the territory, as rainstorms and flooding would change the landscape at least once a decade.

Mostly, it was bare land, devoid of life, except for scrub, dwarf cedars, and snakes. It was one of the few areas in the whole territory that no one had ventured to homestead during the land run. No one was that crazy. The land was that bad, that dangerous. The homeless with nothing to lose had still avoided this place. It was easily the least traveled place in the territory, and that was considering the sand dunes at Winona and the salt flats they had just passed.

When Tanner and Marie arrived at the towering cliffs at the edge of the salt flats, they dismounted to get their bearings. They led their animals deeper into the first of the canyons.

By now, the fury of the storm in the twisting crevice confused Tanner. In the swirling snow, he could no longer tell in what direction they were headed. The wind seemed to come from every direction at once.

When soon, that canyon petered out, they were forced to veer left or right. He chose left, thinking the wind might be blunted by the steep rise of that side's wall. His wish was not granted. The snow was now piling up. They busted through calf-high drifts as Tanner searched for a port in the storm. It was dark and the snow whipped their eyes, dulling the world's features. He had to find them someplace soon.

Finally, Tanner found something that would suffice. A large cedar had been uprooted by erosion from the plateau above some time ago. The tree had sagged, then plummeted from the canyon rim, creating an arch of limbs and deadwood, still attached to but also extending almost ten feet away from the red clay wall. The cliff, against which the tree clung, was over a hundred feet tall, he figured. Tanner had no way of knowing in this pitch darkness. All he knew is the dead cedar offered sanctuary.

"Here," he yelled, indicating the cedar.

She nodded.

As he moved Anthem and his horse into the natural stall of deadwood against the canyon wall, the girl pulled the large double pack from the mule. She tugged the large, rolled canvas from its hold, and Tanner led her animal away from her into the enclosed roof of broken limbs. The mule nuzzled in between the two horses.

"We will need three large poles for the tent. It is what you call a tepee. Big enough for us and a fire," Marie called to him over the wind's constant din.

Tanner nodded and waded into the darkness at her request. There was plenty of wood here, but finding three long enough limbs for the teepee might be tricky, especially in this darkness. However, as he scrambled around, Tanner realized the snow on the ground seemed to reflect some light. Tanner soon discovered a stand of scraggly locust trees nearby. He felled them by busting their slender trunks over with his foot and then cutting the remaining trunk bark away with the heavy blade off his belt. Soon, Tanner had three poles nearly ten feet long. They were none too straight and none too sturdy, but they would have to do.

When he dragged them into view, Tanner saw Marie nod in

approval. She was gathering wood from around the base of the tree's blasted landing area for their fire. He saw that she had already gathered a dozen large flat stones from the dead creek bed, as well. At least they would have a fire, he thought. It might not be enough to warm them. He couldn't remember ever being warm. It was so cold. It didn't get this cold when it snowed. This blizzard, this snow, seemed different, malevolent almost. He and Marie might freeze to death, but at least Harris and his henchman wouldn't be able to find them. No one would come up the mouth of the switchbacks in a blizzard after him and a no-account Indian girl.

Tanner himself had a large tarp he used as a pup tent when camping on the prairie. He pulled its roll loose from his horse and draped it over the cedar, using his tall frame and long arms to drag the tarp with its straps over the horses. Then tying the ropes, he pulled the two facing ends taut, tying them to extended limbs, and with the butt end of his Henry, he drove two wooden stakes into the frozen clay for the remaining two straps on the tarp. The horses were, for now, out of the worst of it. At least snow couldn't pile up on them. The animals had a roof over their heads.

Marie had swept a place free for them to place the tent. Now, he helped her unfurl the teepee, tie a thick line around the poles' three ends, and then plant the opposite ends of each into the ground. He stretched the posts as far as they would go against their ties.

Marie rolled the teepee around the inside of the poles. While he lifted it, she fastened the tent to the poles, using rawhide ties to secure it to the posts. Tanner could tell her hands were clumsy with cold. Their faces were close together, and she nodded in apology for her slowness.

He merely blinked and nodded. He understood. Speech was not needed.

After completing the bottom ties, Marie pointed to the top ties.

Tanner stretched tall and tied them high and tight. Now, he stretched the tent tight as he forced their bases outward and upward. The tent poles shuddered as they stabilized, and the thick buffalo skin rattled in the wind.

Marie nodded her approval. "It is good."

Tanner grinned through his cracked lips. He noticed the tent had a hole on the backside high up and pointed at it.

"For smoke," she said. "I will build a fire now."

"I'll take care of the horses."

She nodded and began to carry the stones into the tent.

By the time, Tanner stripped the saddle off his roan and placed blankets on all three animals; he could smell smoke emanate from the teepee. Tanner fed each animal from his meager grain bag. He rubbed his hand across the back of each equine. His roan, the colt, and the mule had all performed admirably this day.

With the tarp trailing over the cedar arch and angled toward the ground, the horses were up against the cliff and out of the wind. The base of the tent was almost against the tarp, creating a cave of sorts beyond for the horses. They seemed content for now. He examined each, especially the colt. All three were tired and glad to be in shelter, however, meager. They were placid and tame. He didn't bother to hobble their legs. None could get out of the cedar tree stall without banging into the tent, and Tanner did not believe they would try.

Tanner retreated to the cedar's broken base and gathered what firewood he could find. To his surprise, there was quite a lot. The tree's trunk and primary structure was leaning into the cliff wall, but its limbs were broken and scattered on the ground and were still visible above the snow, for now. He gathered numerous armloads. Tanner feared all available fuel would be covered with snow by morning. The wind and the temperature chilled him to the bone.

By the time he finished, Tanner realized he was shuddering with cold. Finally, he allowed himself to descend to his knees and crawl into the tent but not before retrieving his Henry and a box of shells from his saddlebag. Inside, he was surprised by how warm it was.

There was no wind. He had forgotten a world with no wind. His teeth chattered and his shoulders shook as he sat on his haunches.

Marie looked at him with alarm. "You are close to freezing to death, Mr. Tanner." She tugged the blanket off her shoulders and placed it around him, even over his head. She tugged his hat free and set it aside. "Move to the fire."

He did, but the shuddering did not stop. His teeth chattered and his body quaked.

Marie assessed the situation. She took his bedroll and spread it beside the blaze, against the cliff wall, against which she had laid the river stones. Warmth radiated into the tent; the smoke swirled up through the hole in the tent's top. Still, his body refused to warm. Marie motioned for him to lie down. As he did, she lifted the blanket from him. He lay, but it seemed his knees would no longer stretch. His body was frozen in a ball.

The Indian girl gently pressed his back to the ground. She pulled his legs out, extending them flat, pulling his thoroughly soaked boots free of his feet. She lowered his knees until his body was prone on the bedroll. Then, she lay across him, stretching the blanket over them, covering even their heads. She clutched his shaking body, her head against his heart. Her hands held his shoulders; her fingers massaged away the spasms in his neck.

Tanner started to speak through his chattering teeth, started to object to this kindness, this intimacy with which he was so unfamiliar.

"Shush," she said, her ear hearing his rapid heartbeat. "Be still. Let my body warm yours."

And he did.

Kindness
Woods County, Oklahoma
May, 1964

Six months had passed since Piper and Chris had moved with their mother to the ranch. In all that time, the children had not once been back to Wichita to pack their things or say goodbye to the house they once knew. Mom told them she and their father packed up things into a trailer one weekend in January and everything was now in a storage garage. Neither child seemed to miss their old life. They just moved on as children can; they lived in the moment.

Mom went back to WSU two days a week and was now only weeks away from completing her master's. Henry, their father, only visited the farm twice. Most times, their mother went to Oklahoma City to see him, but it was not every weekend. Piper said there was trouble brewing between Jeff and Henry and they'd had words. Chris didn't know about it, and surprisingly, he didn't care.

Life for Chris was good. School was no longer a source of anxiety. The truce with Barton was holding, and because of it, the other boys left him alone. Chris did not miss his father. His grandfather was enough; however, Piper missed her mother when she was back in Wichita two days a week, but that would end soon. Lillian's graduate thesis was submitted, and there was little school left for her to do. Now the talk was of moving to Oklahoma City. It made Chris's stomach hurt.

One May morning, the two children entered the henhouse with Grandma Gwen leading the way. No one had seen the rat snake in months. Every day upon entry, Chris would pull the rope his grandfather had tied to the big rat trap up out of the hole to see if the snake had finally been lured to its death. Every day, he lifted the rope and saw the trap smeared with SPAM and grease, but the jaws of the trap were always empty. Today, however, was different. Chris knew it as soon as he lifted the rope. He called to Gwen.

"Hey, Grandma," he called, moving like he was reeling in a big fish in with his Zebco 404.

Gwen and Piper jumped upon seeing the snake, long and dead, coming out of the hole. The black snake, lustrous even in death, was long enough that Chris had to raise his arms high to keep the tail off the ground.

The hens panicked at the sight of the serpent and hurried out the hole in the far wall. They squawked their disapproval as they departed.

Grandma stood her ground and waved her empty egg basket at the dead creature. "Cursed are you above all livestock and all wild animals! You will crawl on your belly, and you will eat dust all the days of your life."

Chris nodded. "And now you're dead."

Piper looked at Grandma Gwen. "What was that you just said?"

"A Bible verse, honey. Now, go fetch your grandpa. He's down filling up the car. He needs to cart this snake off. I can't stand the sight of it."

Henry didn't come up for the weekend after they found the dead snake. For once, Chris wished to see his father. He wanted to brag about catching the snake.

Curiously, Lillian did not go to Oklahoma City that weekend, either. Lillian said she had to take care of graduation stuff, but Piper told Chris their mother was mad at their dad.

Chris asked if he had stolen another car, and Piper raised an eyebrow at him.

"Boys really don't understand relationships, do they?"

Chris laughed. "Like you do. You haven't even had your first kiss."

"Yes, I have," replied Piper.

Speechless, he watched her leave the room. Chris pondered just who his sister might have kissed, but he mainly watched his mother for signs of stress. There were plenty. He spent a quiet weekend, reading Zane Grey books his grandfather had borrowed from the barbershop.

A week later when the children's mother's car came down the driveway on Saturday morning just before lunch, Chris saw Grandpa Jeff crane his neck out the window then grind his cigarette out as he did so. The boy could not remember his grandfather ever extinguishing a freshly lit Camel before. Mom had just left for OKC last night. For her to be home again this morning was a surprise. Chris could see it on both Jeff and Gwen's faces. Jeff moved to the door to await his daughter.

"Move out of the way, Jeff," his wife said to him. "Our daughter's got troubles or she wouldn't be back. I'm going out to get her." Gwen wiped her hands on her apron on her way out the front door. She met Lillian at the gate.

Lil folded into her mother's arms.

Jeff joined them and held both in his arms.

After a time, Jeff put his arm around Lillian's waist and guided Lil into the house.

All five family members assembled in the kitchen for a group hug without words being spoken. The embrace of the five was deepfelt, and Chris felt the old pain in the pit of his stomach. Things were wrong; what they were he did not understand, but he knew they were wrong. Whatever had happened was momentous and tragic. Chris felt bewildered.

Jeff finally took his daughter's hand and led her to the kitchen table. He poured her a cup of coffee. Their eyes met.

"What's happened?" he asked. "Should I send the children down to the dog pens to water the animals?"

Lillian shook her head. "No, they need to hear this, too. Let's all sit down."

Chris watched her mother and was not sure he'd ever seen her in quite this way. The word "resolute" came into his mind. He'd read the word before but had never used it in a sentence. He understood it now. Lillian looked resolute. Her face was drained of color, and deep blue rings circled the bottom of her eyes. Chris noted the lines in her brow and at the corners of her eyes. They seemed new and severe. He moved his gaze to Piper and saw a mirror image of his mother, the same features: the wary, guarded tilt of the head, the emotional red spot on each cheek, and the same deeply serious eyes. He realized his sister was becoming like his mother. Chris worried for an instant he would be like his father. He'd rather be like Grandpa Jeff.

Finally, Lil took a sip of coffee before speaking. "You know I'm graduating in a few days."

Everyone nodded.

"And while I haven't told anyone," she said, moving her eyes lovingly to each of them for a long second, "I want you all to know that I have been offered a job with Haskell Indian Nations University in Lawrence." She paused for the children. "That's outside Kansas City a'ways."

Piper raised her eyebrows at the prospect of moving, and Chris thought of her revelation regarding her first kiss. Was Piper going to lose her first boyfriend?

"I haven't decided to take it yet, but it is a really good opportunity. I'm one of the first women in the country with a master's in social work with an emphasis in Native American Studies. It's a great school and a great town. I'd be the assistant to the provost at the university, and they'd pay for me to get my Ph.D. I asked Henry to speak to his probation officer, but he doesn't want to move from Oklahoma City."

Chris now understood the tension between his parents. Mom wanted to move, but his father didn't. He didn't want to leave OKC.

Lillian hesitated. "And given your Uncle Tanner's history, Dad, they know our name. It may have caused them to make the offer to me."

Gwen gave her a shush, and Lillian shrugged. "It's the truth, Mom. Tanner Station is still known by the Cherokee."

"We won't talk of him in my house, Daughter," Gwen replied.

Lillian nodded, noting her willingness to obey.

Chris leaned back. What uncle? He had never heard the mention of an Uncle Tanner, especially one who'd done something bad. What was the expression? A black sheep. That was it. He had a black sheep for an uncle. Chris tried that on for size. The boy decided he liked the romance of it.

"Does Dad want us all to move to OKC?" Piper asked.

"Yes, but my job will pay twice what his master mechanic job does, and he can get a very similar job in Lawrence. His skills are needed everywhere."

Jeff lit a cigarette then blew out the match. He rubbed its tip of the ash into the ashtray, letting smoke trail out the partially opened window. "Seems simple enough. I could make a call to the judge if it's the probation officer. Judge Spence would allow Henry to leave the state more'n likely to keep the family together, I'm thinking."

Lil shook her head. "Henry just doesn't want to go. And last night he told me he would divorce me if I took the job in Lawrence." Her eyes rimmed with tears.

The word stung the group like Lillian had struck a hornet's nest with a hammer.

Piper began to cry, and Lillian joined her. Piper leapt to her feet and ran to the north bedroom, her wails reverberating throughout the house.

Gwen followed.

"You know he probably just lost his temper, Lil," said Jeff. "Men say things they shouldn't when life takes sudden turns. Most of 'em don't handle change, not well they don't."

Lillian took a cigarette from her father's pack, something Chris had never seen her do. "It's worse than that." She turned to Chris.

"Maybe you shouldn't be hearing this, honey. Why don't you go check on your sister?"

Chris nodded and stood from his chair. He walked around the corner and paused at his grandfather's cushioned rocker. He listened intently.

"Like I say," Lil said, blowing smoke toward the window gap, "it's worse than that. He told me there's someone one else. Another woman. He'd rather be with her. Told us to go to Lawrence without him. He needs a fresh start."

"Was he drunk? Either way, he's a damn fool." Jeff's voice was bitter and angry. His tone carried a rasp that Chris was not familiar with. He would not want to hear that tone in his grandfather's voice coming at him, Chris knew that.

"When is he not drunk, Dad? He works on his cars and then starts drinking as soon as he's off. He's running with a real bad crowd. Pool hall losers. Gamblers. Crooks."

"Then perhaps you're better off moving with the kids to Lawrence. Or maybe you want to get your feet under you up there and leave the kids here."

"No, I thought about it all night. There's no reason for us to be split up anymore. Me spending time in two places. My job will be enough for us to live. I'm going to accept the job. Dad, I'm going to file on Henry. Ask for a divorce. My marriage is coming to an end." Then, she burst into tears.

Chris realized, eavesdropping as he was, that he was picking at his thumb like his mother. And in more surprise, he also noted his grandmother was standing beside him.

Gwen put her arm around him. "I don't think you were meant to hear that."

Chris nodded. "But I did."

Gwen smiled kindly and took his hand. "You'd have figured it out soon enough. It's okay." Then, she returned into the kitchen with him in tow. "I think we are going to need a girl day around the house. Jeff, you take this boy and don't come back until supper. You hear?"

Jeff raised his eyebrows. "Where you wanting us to go?"

"Now, that's up to you. Finish what chores you need done and git, you hear?"

———

A half hour later, Jeff and Chris headed east on the county road away from the ranch's long driveway and their mailbox. They crossed The Troll Bridge and soon were in Capron.

From there, they drove south, zig-zagging mile sections. Dust plumes trailed them, and the pick-up rattled its shocks on the washboard bumps created by the past winter's snows.

Jeff did not speak, and the boy sensed he should not, either, not until his grandfather first changed the rules.

Finally, his grandpa spoke. "You got any questions about this morning?"

"Where we heading?"

"Cherokee, right now."

"Why?"

Jeff smiled at him patiently and said, "I'll tell you later, but right now I need to ponder matters a might. I don't want to say something about your father I shouldn't."

"You can say anything to me, Grandpa."

"Well, rightly, I can't. There are things one man cannot say to another about his father. Those would be called fighting words. I don't want you to reflect badly upon my words later."

Chris did not understand Jeff fully, but he was quiet until they came to the four-way stop in Cherokee. They rolled past an impressive red brick building with limestone blocks and stone crosses over four white garage doors.

"That's a great building. What is that?"

"That's the Cherokee Armory. I helped build that back in the day, 1935 or 6, I think. Must have been '36. It was a WPA project. That was when the country was in a big depression. It holds the National Guard now. But when we built it, I think it was for something else. Those were hard times." Jeff's voice trailed off, and Chris could see his question brought memories to his grandfather. He waited.

"I kinda thought how I wanted to address things with you about your father. So let me get them said as we get where we're going."

"Which is where?"

"A surprise. Now, let me ramble a bit and see if I can make some sense for you." Jeff paused for a bit. "See, the way you decide to look at the things I say will affect how you interact with folks the rest of your life. Listen up and then you will get your turn to talk."

Chris nodded.

"I am not saying I know the answers to anything I'm fixin' to say here. But it's food for thought. Here goes." He rolled down the window a peep and lit a cigarette. "There's a number of ways to look at folks and to see how they's behaving. Some see all babies as born without fault. People are naturally born good, and it's their lives, the stuff that happens to them that makes them make mistakes. To treat other folks bad.

"'Course some folks have things go good, so they live good. Treat other people good. Some people get bad breaks. Take it out on other folk."

Chris nodded.

"Some folk believe the Bible says that we're all born with bad in us. That babies are born bad, at least part bad. And we all spend our lives trying to get better. Some of us are more successful with that than others. I've never been a church-going man, but I've read from the Bible some and know that religious folk take great stock in asking forgiveness for their sins and trying to do better. There's that.

"Then, there's folks out there who believe that people are just smarter animals. That we're driven by animal urges, like a bobcat or an elephant. We just are better at getting stuff done because we have better brains, the ability to talk and, for some reason, thumbs."

They both laughed as Chris held up his hands and examined his thumbs, suspiciously.

"Then, there's those folks in India and such who believe we keep coming back time and again, paying for our past lives' mistakes, getting born again and again. They call it reincarnation. For example, you act real bad in this life, you come back as a shit beetle or such."

They both laughed again.

"What do you believe, Grandpa?"

"Ain't about me today. Today's about you. And your mom and sister."

"I don't know what I think."

"You don't have to have it all figured out today. It's just something for you to ponder."

Chris scratched his chin. "Are we talking about what kind of guy my dad is? What made him not want to be with Mom anymore?"

Jeff pondered the boy's question for a minute. "Maybe you'll get to where you can think on that someday. I was just talking about folks in general. Why don't we leave it there? Especially since we're getting close to where I wanted to take you."

Chris examined the landscape. It was different than anyplace he'd ever been. It was flat and white. The dust that rose around them now was flat and flaky, like snowflakes.

Jeff eased the truck over to the side of the flats close to where the land went from normal to otherworldly. It smelled different, too. Like dry stuff. Like death. No, that was wrong. It smelled like no life was there. Chris decided that was different than death.

"What is this place, Grandpa?"

"This here's the great salt flat. Let's get out and walk out there a'ways. I brought a shovel. Fetch it from the bed of the truck."

Chris did, and the two walked perhaps a couple hundred yards out onto the flat.

The boy could smell the alkaline in the air. He stopped and

turned completely in a circle. The flats seemed to go on forever. Far into the distance, he could see another truck out on the flat, barely visible in the distance.

"Can we drive way out there?"

Jeff shook his head. "Got stuck out there once. It gets soft. We'll stay close for your first visit. Maybe you can come back someday with Piper. Right now, why don't you put the shovel to use? Make a circle about a foot across. Draw it with the blade tip. Then, dig down, straight down around the edges. I'll take a turn if you get tired. When we dig down a'ways, we'll pull up the ball. I'll show you a surprise."

The boy followed his grandfather's instructions. And as he dug into the crusty soil with the spade, he felt a rocky connection or something below the surface.

In a minute or two, Jeff took the shovel and dug deeply around the ball of dirt.

Eventually, the old man freed the clump from what held it in place.

Then, the two of them, using all four of their hands, pressed down into the earth, brought the ball to the surface, and tipped it over on the ground.

Chris looked at his grandfather. "Good thing we have thumbs," he said with mirth.

Jeff laughed and squatted down and began crumbling dirt away from the globe of dirt.

Chris wasn't sure what they were looking for, but he joined in.

Soon, they found treasure, large crystals of salt, perhaps four inches long and intersecting like a helix. Some were broken, probably from the spade, but others were perfect in design.

"Can I keep them?"

"Sure," Jeff said, standing and picking up the shovel. He waited while the boy gathered the salt crystals in the hem of his T-shirt. The older man lowered the tailgate so the boy could set the salt crystals down. Before he did, Jeff handed the boy his handkerchief, and Chris carefully wrapped the salt in the cloth. With the treasure secure, Jeff gently closed the tailgate.

"There's someplace else you need to see. Come on." He motioned the boy to get back in the truck. Jeff started the vehicle and drove along the western fringe of the salt flats for perhaps two miles. It was surprisingly flat and smooth, like new freeway.

"Now, where are we going?"

"Just shush."

And in a minute, they had arrived. Ahead, Chris saw a second place unlike any he had seen before. It was a bramble of scrub brush, sickly and malnourished by the salty soil. But beyond, he saw a maze of canyon mouths, twisted cedars along the towering walls, and tumbled red clay boulders the size of Jeff's truck. His grandfather stopped, and the two, without words, exited the truck and walked off the salt flat to the entrance of the canyons. It was like the delta of a river, cut and broken with erosion and time.

"What is this place?" Chris asked. "It's scary. Weird."

"It is, isn't? They call it the switchbacks. Ungodly place. Back in the day, Cherokee who ran away from the reservation used to hide out here. You know about Butch Cassidy and the Hole-in-the-Wall Gang?"

Chris shook his head.

"They were outlaws back in the day. Hid out in the mountains up Wyoming way back in a place where the law couldn't get 'em. They called it Jackson Hole. This here's like a small one of that, I guess, except more dirt-red and sickly."

"Who owns it?"

Jeff shook his head. "Don't rightly know. The Devil, I guess. Nobody else would have anything to do with it. Can't even hike back in there. There's quicksand, and see that clay boulder? They fall all the time without warning. It's just a mess."

"It's kind of beautiful."

"Maybe. Some might say so. Them 'twas lost up those canyons might beg to differ."

"Did you ever go into the switchbacks?"

Jeff smiled. "One time, just for a little bit. Heard a story about a fella who hid out up there. Turns out he met a woman of all things. Made me want to check out the place for myself."

"What happened to the man and the woman?"

"Didn't end well."

"Was it your Uncle Tanner? How come nobody ever talks about him?"

"It was him that hid out here, but my mom, Avery, Tanner's sister, made me promise to never talk about him. Reckon I'll abide that, at least for today."

Chris frowned.

"I don't know about you, boy, but I'm hungry," Jeff said, trying to change the melancholy mood that was beginning to set in. "Let's head over to Jet. There's a good café there, and I know the owner a bit. He makes a decent bacon sandwich."

The fella did make a good bacon sandwich. They ate lunch, and Jeff even let Chris have coffee with milk and sugar in it.

As they arrived back at the ranch, Piper ran out

"Mom's on the phone with Judge Spence. Grandpa, you need to come, quick."

Jeff slammed the truck door and strode toward the house. He flipped the gate latch back, and Chris had to dodge the rebound of it as he followed behind.

"Can't Henry leave us be for the evening? Damn troublemaker," Jeff grumbled.

Inside, Gwen looked shell-shocked, and Lillian's eyes were rimmed with tears. Chris's first reaction was that his father must be dead.

Lillian reached out and pulled her son close as she handed the phone to her father.

"This is Jeff Hart. How are you this evening, Judge Spence?"

Chris could hear the judge's voice through the receiver.

"I'm fine, Jeff," the judge said, "but I'm calling with some bad news. Henry's been involved in a robbery. That's what the sheriff is telling me."

Jeff was quiet.

"Tonight, Conway Twitty was to play the Civic Center, sold out show. Two men entered the box office brandishing guns just as the show started."

"Henry one of them?"

"No," the judge replied. "But he was seen in a vehicle out front. Later, that car was reported as stolen."

"They get away with much cash?"

"Quite a sum."

"Anybody hurt?"

"There was an altercation. Patrolman on the scene tried to stop it. Shots were fired. One of the robbers and the officer both went down. That deputy's going to live, thank God."

"Henry's been arrested?"

"No, just one man was arrested. The second of the two who carried the guns did get away in the car with Henry and a bag of cash. Don't know much more at this point. But the arrested man has identified Henry as the wheel man. The second man is named Reynolds. Oscar Reynolds. You know of him?"

"No. Any idea of where Henry and this Oscar are headed?" Chris could hear the fierce anger in Jeff's question. His words were even, but the rage behind them was evident to the boy. This situation was real bad. The worst ever.

"Mexico, we figure," said the judge. "But you should be on the lookout. There'll be a marshal's vehicle out to your place on the prowl for the next few days. I wanted you to know. Maybe even FBI to talk with Lillian."

Jeff paused for moment, reflecting on G-men coming to the house. "Thanks, Judge Spence. We'll call authorities if Henry contacts us. You'll keep us informed if y'all find him?"

"Yessir, we will. And I'm sorry for your family, Jeff."

Jeff hung up.

Lillian and Piper slid into old man's arms. Both sobbed, and Chris felt tears coming.

He went to his room so no one would see him cry.

Oklahoma Territory
February 3, 1899

After a time, the spasms of cold left Tanner Station's body, yet Marie still held him, her head to his chest, her legs astraddle his long torso. Soon, she could feel his excitement below her.

"I'm sorry," he said, embarrassed. "Been a long time since I been this close to a woman."

"You may have me," she said, almost shamefully. Her eyes were cast down.

Tanner shook his head. "You do not have to pay me back with your body. You don't have to pay me back at all. I ain't like them. I don't need a woman that way, not by force, no way."

The truth was he had only been with a woman one time. It had been on his first trip west with Everett. Tanner lost his virginity in Kansas City before the fateful stagecoach trip west. The young lady had charged him a dollar. Tanner never told anyone, and if Everett knew where Tanner had gone that evening before the trip across the Kansas plains, he never let on so.

Marie lifted her eyes to his. "It is all right. I have been with men before. When I was younger, my father sold me to pay off gambling debts. Those days are past, but the soldiers still say things. Horrible things."

Tanner frowned. "I'm sorry those things happened to you. But you say your father is off the booze now?"

"Yes, he is better to me now." Marie sat up and shrugged. "Back when my father sold me, he was too drunk, and he gambled too much. Now that he is old and has the stable, he is better. He stays sober. It is better."

Tanner nodded, looking up at the girl's face as she leaned against him. He did not speak.

"You won't have me because of those nights when my father gave my body in trade?"

Tanner didn't reply.

"You won't even say no?" the girl asked.

Tanner shook his head. "No, I just don't say much. Most folks never speak their minds, anyway, so it don't matter what they say. It ain't what they're thinkin'."

"With you that is true?"

Tanner laughed. "Mostly, I don't never say anything, so, yeah."

Marie joined him in his laugh. She rose and put a log on the fire. "Some summer nights," she said, "my father still holds a game out under the cottonwood trees. Or when it rains, he will put a table in the barn. Usually, it is for men who have caused trouble in town or those who are banned at the other places for attempting to cheat or because they drink too much. Some are soldiers who play for a few hours but cannot get leave to Jet or Cherokee."

Marie came back to the bedroll and lay beside him. She put her head on his shoulder, and Tanner felt his heart reach out to her. "My father does not often play," she said. "He just takes a cut and sells whiskey and cigars."

"That was what happened tonight?"

She nodded.

"Did you know those men who attacked you tonight?"

"They were playing cards at my father's earlier. With two other men. Mel Harris was losing and began saying things about me. Ugly things. Father sent me to the PX at the fort to get some coffee and sugar. We did not need it, but he wanted me away from Harris. Buck Wells and Crazy Charlie, too."

"Charlie Crups?"

"Yes."

"And they caught you coming back?"

"Yes, the PX was closing because of the snow. Harris said even though they'd lost their money they could still have some fun with me, and that is when Buck Wells grabbed me."

"Lucky I came along when I did."

"Yes, I was yelling for the men inside the stable to help me, but I guess the blizzard kept anyone from hearing."

Tanner nodded. "Maybe not. Maybe they were scared. A lot of men wouldn't want to go out and brace Harris, Wells and Crups, especially after they had a bellyful of liquid courage."

"You did."

Tanner smiled. "Didn't take the time to think about it first of all and didn't know who was doing the dirty deed when I barged into trouble."

"Would it have made a difference if you'd known it would be Harris and the other two?"

"Expect not," he said, embarrassed. "But I'm not saying I'm a brave man." He laughed. "I should check on the horses. Get them some water."

Marie nodded. "I will get some food around."

When he came back, her clothes were lying across his saddle. She was wrapped in her blanket. Tanner knew she was naked underneath the blanket. She smiled at him. "We should dry your clothes by the fire."

Tanner laughed. "Expect we should."

After they finally ate hours later, Marie and Tanner lay together naked on the bedroll, wrapped in the Indian blanket. They made love a second time. Then, spent and with full bellies, they slept, their bodies intertwined and warm despite the raging storm outside.

Tanner woke once in the night and placed more wood on the fire. The tent felt even colder. He dressed and checked on the horses. They were fine, but it was dangerously cold outside. The snow had choked the canyon and was nearly three feet deep around the tepee.

Tanner ducked in through the flap and moved to the flames, warming his hands. "Still snowin' to beat all. Three feet deep. We're not going anywhere tomorrow. Maybe for two days."

Marie gazed up at him from her bed. "We have plenty of coffee and sugar."

The lanky cowboy smiled. "Have to find something to do inside for a day or two."

With the dawn, the cold was so intense the two feared for the horses' welfare. They rearranged the tarp and slit the rear of the teepee so the two structures became one. Marie saved some coals but utilized snow to cool the flat stones which composed their makeshift hearth.

The two of them moved their firepit to halfway between them and the animals, then rekindled the flame.

Anthem, of the three, seemed the most uncomfortable with the fire, but after Tanner marched the yearling out for a quick walk, the bone-chilling deep freeze and the howling wind created within the animal a sense of acceptance for the smoke and flames ten feet from his stall. Merging the tarp stable and the teepee into one larger structure definitely reduced the temperature within the canvas dwelling to uncomfortable climes.

It was so much colder that when the two weren't feeding the fire, cooking or brewing coffee, they were under the blanket huddled together. But certainly, they would have also been there had the weather been warm and pleasant. They made love all day.

Their bodies seem to have found a home with one another. They lost count how many times they had coupled.

On the third morning when they awoke, Marie lay in his arms.

Tanner said to her, "You are my woman now. You must come back to my house when the cold spell breaks."

Marie looked over at him. They were the same age of twenty-two. That age, for a woman, was late to be married or to have a child on the plains. Marie had expected she would end up pregnant from one of her father's card players some night. She could not believe her good fortune to have found a good man and to learn of him with the world held at bay by snow and now cold.

"You know it will not be easy," she said. "I am a Cherokee, a full-blooded Cherokee. People look at us as beneath even the negroes. You will become an outcast. You will be alone."

Tanner laughed. "Lady, you got it dead wrong. I have always been a loner up till now. With you by my side, I finally won't be alone. It'll be the two of us against the world."

Marie smiled at the sentiment. "These last three days have been easy. No one knows about us. But when you are living with an Indian woman, things will be different. I cannot go to the places you will go."

Tanner again laughed. "I don't go anyplace. I live far from anyone and anything. My brother, Carson, sleeps in the other room of our little cabin. It will be fine."

"What about Harris, Wells, and Crups?"

"I figure they sobered up. They don't even know it was me who pulled you out of there. Remember, I was wearing a kerchief over my face. Anyways, neither of us are worth the trouble. Got no money. Don't want no trouble. They ain't gonna bother us once we're hitched."

"Hitched?"

"I figure the Baptist preacher in Cherokee can marry us today. That is, if you're willin'?"

Marie nodded. "Yes, I will marry you." Her face was thoughtful, but she then smiled.

Tanner nodded. "Good. Now that that's settled, I'll get the horses around. The bitter cold is breaking. It's still cold, but we don't want to be in these canyons when the thaw hits. I figure in a couple of hours the sun will be high enough to get us out of the shadows of the canyon walls. We can work our way of the switchbacks, head north and over to Cherokee before dark. Depending on when we get in, we can find the preacher after supper or in the morning." He paused and smiled. "Want to get hitched today?"

On Thursday, they made the ranch, but it was near dark. The two rode into the north homestead, but the cabin was dark. Carson was not there. It did not surprise Tanner that his brother was absent. He figured Carson was at the main house, as it was much better built than this shack and thus much warmer. But Marie seemed pleased enough to see her new home. He left her to get acquainted with the place as he took the three animals to the small stable.

Tanner figured Everett was chompin' at the bit wondering what had happened to Tanner and his prized stallion, Anthem. Amazingly, both he and Marie were fine. The three animals were fine, as well. Not a touch of frostbite on any of them. They had been very lucky.

So, as it got light in the morning, he'd ride to the Hart household with Anthem in tow. Tanner wondered how the family would take the news of his nuptials. Avery would be happy for him, and she'd probably go to trying to convert her new sister-in-law to the Quaker faith right away. Carson would see it as an imposition to him staying in the next room from Tanner and his bride. Everett would take it hard. Everett was always conscious of what the people in Alva would think. Tanner marrying an Indian squaw would be the talk of the town. It would hurt Everett's social standing, probably. Not that Tanner gave a damn about that, but he knew Everett enough that he would resent Tanner for it, even if he never said so.

As far as Billy and Max, they'd be happy for more grandchildren, although they might have to come to the ranch to see them. Tanner could not imagine bringing Marie and children into Alva. He would not subject them to the scrutiny and sidewise looks they would get.

When Tanner emerged from the stable, he saw Carson dismounting near its door.

The younger sibling smiled in the dim moonlight at his older brother. Carson laughed, seeing him. "Thought you were froze over in a snow drift and we wouldn't find you till spring."

Tanner nodded. "Coulda happened. Bedded down in the switchbacks till the cold broke."

"In the switchbacks? Why in the world did you end up there instead of the fort?"

"Had some trouble with Mel Harris and his crew again."

"Any shooting?"

"Naw, put a lump on Buck Wells' noggin and lit out."

Carson nodded. He looked inside. "The colt okay?" He looked inside and then turned to his brother. "That a mule?"

"Yeah, I got a woman inside."

Carson grinned, knowingly. "Here we are all worrying about you and you've been keeping extra warm with some legs wrapped around you." He laughed. "She must be pretty good for you to bring her back to the ranch. What's that costing ya?"

Tanner shook his head. "Be careful what you say. I married her this morning."

Carson stepped back out of the stable, surprise on his face. "Married her?" He laughed. "Who is she?"

"Marie Wolf Walker. Preacher Ben over to Cherokee got us hitched this morning."

Carson raised one side of his lip in disgust. "Injun Mary. The whore? You're kidding me, Brother? Hell, man, tell me you didn't marry her? You can win her for a night in a poker game."

Tanner stepped forward in the darkness and his chest bounced off his brother's.

Carson stumbled back into his mount. If he hadn't, he would have fallen. Carson's hand moved to his weapon. His fingers trembled there.

Tanner shook his head. "Sorry. That was wrong of me." He

extended his hand. "Shake and then we go in and eat some supper? I'll introduce you to Marie."

Carson tossed his head back in disbelief. "What? You expect me to come inside, eat with you two, and then sleep in the next room while you hump your squaw? I don't think so."

"Those are unacceptable words."

"They're mine. I'm keeping them."

"And you're one to talk," Tanner said, "Like you don't frequent prostitutes."

"I don't marry them and bring them back to Avery and the little girls." Carson paused. "But them kids and Avery are still in town, anyway. Too cold still for the girls to ride back. Snow's too deep, too."

Carson drew up his reins and threw a boot in a stirrup. He rose to his saddle once again. He sat astride his mount and stared down at his older brother. His eyes held no respect at all.

Tanner said, "You headed back down to the main house or out east to Renfro?"

Carson sneered. "Not that you give a good goddamn, but Renfro's laid up at the main house with frostbite. Everett's tending to him. Old man saved the herd, but he's losing parts of his ears and can't feel his fingertips. Scarred his face up something fierce, too. We lost over forty head to the freeze. The rest of us are okay. Thanks for asking."

"I'll ride over in the morning and bring Anthem." Tanner did not know what else to say.

Carson nodded. "I came for that rubbing alcohol. Everett thinks it'll keep Renfro's wounds from getting infected. Mind getting it 'fore I head back?"

"Surely, but I wish you would reconsider and come in and break bread with us."

"Brother," said Carson, with a resolve Tanner hated, "that will never happen."

Sorrows
Lawrence, Kansas
September, 1964

School started after Labor Day in Lawrence, Kansas. This year, Chris was at the same school as Piper. Piper entered Lawrence High School as a junior, but Chris skipped a grade again to become a ninth grader. He was twelve years of age and would have been among the smallest seventh graders at the junior high down the street. Those children were the same age as he.

Lillian felt Chris's brilliant scores on the eighth-grade tests, which she insisted he take although he was just then completing seventh grade at Hardtner, should allow him to take challenging classes at the high school level. His lack of social skills, she reasoned, would not be improved as the smallest child in the eighth-grade class. Better to be seen as a super-smart odd duck at the high school than a runt at the junior high.

Chris enrolled in five classes, plus drama club: introduction to literature, chemistry, algebra, American history, and biology. The school nurse exempted him from gym class, and he joined the debate club instead. Here he developed his first real friendship. His debate partner, Patrick Lakke, was from the East Coast, the son of a New York attorney who'd come back to Lawrence to oversee his ailing father's manufacturing company. Patrick was short, though not nearly as short as Chris, and he spoke with an NYC quickness that made him seem untrustworthy to most Lawrence teens, and their parents. He also had long hair. He was perhaps the first Lawrence teen to wear his hair in a Beatle cut. Patrick was therefore shunned by Kansan girls. He wasn't particularly cute, anyway, and his intelligence intimidated most classmates. But for now, they rejected him based on his hair's length. Many young lassies in less than two years would refuse to date a boy with a flattop, which was now all the rage for boys.

Patrick, a pudgy boy with a sallow complexion and acne, never fit in at the high school. He prided himself on his East Coast upbringing. He was brash, brusque, and rude at times. None of those traits endeared him to either teachers or students at Lawrence High. There were rumors he dealt marijuana, but he never used drugs. It was the hair.

Patrick, whatever his faults, was brilliant, a quick speaker with a precise mind, and most importantly, without a debate partner. Chris was brilliant, tiny, mostly silent, and also without a partner. It was a debate team made in heaven. Patrick was a year older, and as a sophomore, he knew the ropes of debating.

Debate topics for the upcoming season dealt mostly with the new Civil Rights Act of 1964, which had been signed into law in July. Most Kansans, said Patrick, liked the idea of negroes having the vote, but didn't want one moving into their neighborhood. Kansans did tolerate black men on their basketball team. Wilt Chamberlin was a legend in the city, having dominated college basketball in the late '50s. This year, the Jayhawks had growing excitement for their football squad, which was led by Gayle Sayers, the best running back in the country. Black athletes, said Patrick, were the anomaly which proved the rule. Kansans were agreeable to cheering for negro gladiators but weren't likely to invite them to dinner. Chris did not disagree because disagreeing with Patrick would require speaking. He mainly did not. Of course, during debates he did, but those speeches were rehearsed, like lines in a play.

Piper told Chris his association with Patrick Lakke made him a pariah with the cool kids at the school. Chris laughed at that comment. There was no way he was going to be accepted by the cool kids at Lawrence High, not ever. Chris was half a foot shorter and forty pounds lighter than most of the girls in his grade. His IQ was forty points higher than anyone, except Patrick. He was a freak to them. Patrick was an East Coast, long-haired beatnik; hippy was not a word that anyone used yet. But Patrick tolerated Chris as a colleague, if not a friend. Then later, a true give-and-take friendship formed.

As the school year progressed, Chris found it nice to have a friend, and that relationship helped his transition from the farm to the city. One friend was a win.

Piper, on the other hand, fit right in. She was selected as a junior varsity cheerleader that first fall and joined the backstage crew on the drama team. Piper also went to the fall homecoming dance with a junior football player. Her life seemed to take off just as her teenage awkwardness tilted from tripping down the stairs to a willowy grace. Her freckles faded and her figured rounded, though she remained trim. Boys called every night. Chris found it aggravating to his homework and often chose to do his studies, quickly and with ease, at Patrick's so they could spend the balance of the evening in chess games.

In short, both children found their place, and life became routine and good.

Their last week of school in Hardtner had been anything but. Henry's role in the Conway Twitty robbery caper was in the newspapers, on TV, and on the radio. Reporters from *The Kansas City Star, The Oklahoman, The Wichita Eagle and Beacon*, and *The Dallas Morning News* were all in Hardtner, and a reporter from an OKC radio station came to the house and knocked on the door.

Jeff sent him away. "Shoulda come to my door with my Peacemaker is what I shoulda done," he said to Grandma Gwen after he closed the door, lighting a Camel and blowing the smoke out the crack in the kitchen window.

Chris laughed.

With all the media attention, the most in Woods County since Pretty Boy Floyd's appearance in 1932, Lillian pulled the kids out of school after an OKC TV truck and reporter set up a camera outside the Kiowa High School, hoping to catch Piper walking out at 3:30. Other camera crews waited by the mailbox at the farm, hoping for Jeff to pick up the mail. For the second semester in a row, Piper and Chris did not finish the term.

On their last day before the move to Lawrence and after the scavenger news teams moved on to other calamities, Lil let each child have a friend come to dinner.

Piper chose to invite Shannon Gill, and Chris, with no other option, asked Barton, Shannon's step-brother. Shannon, now with her learner's permit, drove over with Barton in tow. Grandma Gwen served porkchops with gravy with all the fixin's. The food was ready as the guests arrived. Shannon and Piper dominated the conversation. The boys quietly ate.

Gwen looked on at Barton as he put away a second porkchop with no trouble. "Chris, you watch your friend eat," she said. "Follow his lead and we'll put some meat on your bones."

Afterwards, Bart and Chris shot Jeff's .22 down by the garage, punching holes in the green beans can Gwen had opened for dinner.

Jeff got them set up and then went to attend to the dogs.

"Sorry about your dad being on the run from the police, Chris," Barton said. "It is kind of exciting, though. Right?"

Chris shrugged as he reloaded a .22 shell into the single shot chamber.

"In some ways, you're better off than me," Bart ventured, nodding his approval as Chris hit the mark making the can dance a little on the fence post.

"How so?"

"Your daddy ain't around to beat you, you know, like mine."

Chris looked at his friend and nemesis. "That needs to stop. You're as big as your pa these days, Bart. He hits you, maybe you hit back."

Bart smiled, surveying such a moment in his mind. He took the rifle, loaded a shell, and plunked the can once again.

Chris smiled and paced off another ten feet back. He nodded for Barton Meeks to join him farther from the target.

"I oughta plug the bastard like one of these tin cans," the boy said. His eyes were glassy.

"Waste of copper and lead, you ask me," Chris replied, laughing.

Barton laughed. "I'll tell the cops you suggested it iffin' they catch up with me."

Chris curled his lip like the gangsters on TV. "I'll plead the Fifth if you rat me out. Us Fairchilds got a reputation, and no Sgt. Joe Friday is gonna crack me, buddy."

Bart laughed, fired, and hit the target again. "You're not so bad for a city kid, Chris. Tell you what. I'll write you up in Lawrence if I ever take a poke at my old man."

Chris took the rifle. "You can get the address from Shannon. I know Piper gave it to her."

The smaller boy took aim and fired. Nothing.

"Right over the top," Barton Meeks smirked. "A clean miss. You owe me a dime."

"Double or nothing?" Chris ventured.

Lillian's job at the Haskell Institute was all that she'd imagined and more. The school was just now coming into its own. Over 500 Native Americans from over thirty different tribes attended classes there. Some were completing GED programs and getting their high school degrees while others took college classes, finishing an associate's degree before moving two miles east to the University of Kansas.

Every day brought something new. Helping those hungry minds find their life's destiny was a joy to her. Lillian spent more than her eight hours a day on campus among the students. She became a fixture and friendly face. Evenings were spent with her children working on homework, that is, if either were home. Chris was often at Patrick's, and Piper had so many friends and activities. Given their absence, Lillian often made evening plans at the Institute. Lillian started having homework, too, as she began her Ph.D. in Native American Studies at KU. She would be the first woman at Kansas to ever complete such a program.

———

After the fall debate season ended, Patrick and Chris took on a paper route for the Lawrence *Journal-World* for its afternoon edition. Picking up their newspapers every day at 4:00 p.m. at 7th and New Hampshire, Patrick drove his father's paneled station wagon on their route. Back then, Kansan teens could drive at age fourteen with a learner's permit for work. Patrick was now fifteen and an experienced driver with a year on the road and only one fender bender. A cracked reflector on the driver's side of the old Dodge remained as a reminder of his family's dented mailbox each time he took the wheel.

Afterward delivering to the 115 clients on their route, Patrick would drop Chris by the Institute. Chris would try to get his mother to put aside her work to come home and fix some dinner. The truth was Piper had become the primary meal provider in the family. Piper had learned a thing or two from Gwen in the previous year. She was a better cook, in Chris's mind, than his mother. But it was a low bar. Chris knew his mother had found her calling, so he cut her some slack as a chef. He was happy to see her happy. Food was just a source of fuel for him, and he usually went back to Patrick's each evening for a game of chess after eating, anyway.

———

One afternoon, a young Indian man, thick through his upper body like a weightlifter, stood in the lobby of the institute's administrative building near Lillian's office.

Chris entered the building, carrying a lunch box and a book about Franklin D. Roosevelt. Chris was reading biographies about all the presidents in order. This book was the thirty-second he had read in his pilgrimage.

The college-aged Indian man had double pigtails, braided past his shoulders. His denim shirt was faded almost to white. His jeans were tight and flared at the bottom. His flat-toed boots made him seem taller than he truly was. He, too, held a book and showed it to the boy, *The Ballot or the Bullet* by Malcolm X. "Just finished it. Want to trade, little man?"

Chris did not like being called "little man," so he replied. "Can't trade. It's a library book." The pig-tailed man smiled at the comment, so Chris added, "Roosevelt was the best president since Lincoln."

"Kennedy would have got there. 'Ceptin' they killed him to stop progress."

"They being Lee Harvey Oswald?"

"Tip of the spear, little man, tip of the spear." The Indian set the book on the desk and stuck out his hand. "I'm Tate Laughlin. You must be Mrs. Hart's boy."

Chris, in turn, set his book down. "Yes, my name's Chris, but I still got my dad's last name. Christian Fairchild," he said, taking the Native American's grip. The man's hands were calloused and meaty. Chris thought Tate Laughlin must be very strong. Then, he asked, "What tribe?" His mom had taught him that.

"Cheyenne."

Chris nodded. "Do you speak Algonquian?"

Laughlin raised his eyebrows at the boy's question. He smiled. "No, my grandmother knows a little. Me, not so much. My folks moved to California during the Okie migration. Came back late. I'm the youngest in my family. I don't know the native tongue, but I learned to surf when we lived in Oxnard."

Chris smiled. "Definitely cooler."

"I used to think so, before the war. Now, I'm in college, half the day here, half over at the university. I spend my evenings learning the old ways at night with my brothers. In the day, I take classes to burrow under the white man's skin like a rabid tick. Maybe make some changes once I burrow good and deep. Insurrection from within."

"That's an unusual major," said the boy, smiling.

Tate laughed hard at that comment. "Right now, like most guys my age, my main goal is to keep the grades up above a 2.0 and keep my deferment. Don't plan to go to Indochina anytime soon, especially not to shoot fella's your size with yellow skin."

Chris didn't like the small comment once again. "I skipped two grades, so I'm not so small, just young."

Tate said, "Smart guy, huh?"

"Navajos served in World War II as radio operators. Wind Talkers, they were called," Chris offered as evidence.

"Navajo is a really hard language," Laughlin said. "I have some Navajo friends here and in California. Their language doesn't sound like anything else I ever heard, like Martian talk."

Chris nodded, intrigued. "I'd like to hear it sometime."

Tate pondered something in his mind. "I'll tell you what. I'll loan you this book. You read it and we'll get together and talk next week. I'll take you to hear two guys talk in Navajo. Deal?"

It was Chris's turn to grin. "Deal."

They shook again.

Tate Laughlin handed Malcolm X's book to the boy and stepped to the exit. "By the way, I'm your mom's new work-study student. I'm here in the afternoons on Monday, Wednesday, and Friday. She's gone to a meeting. Should be back anytime soon. I supposed to lock up when I leave at 4:30. I'll leave it open if you're going to be here, but don't go anywhere. It's my first day on the job." Laughlin started through the door.

Chris called after him. "Are you Suhtai or Tsitsistas?" referring to the two main branches of the Cheyenne.

Laughlin stopped and laughed. "Suhtai," he said. "You *are* a smart kid. See you next week. Read that book. Okay?"

"Deal," Chris said again.

With that and with a flip of his pigtails, the blocky Indian strode down the hall.

Oklahoma Territory
February 12, 1899

Tanner delivered Anthem down to the main house the next morning. Everett was surprised by the news of the nuptials, as Carson had not returned the previous night after talking with Tanner. Everett's relief at seeing the young stallion, healthy and strong, gave his brother-in-law a pass for any questionable behavior right then. Things at the Salt Fork were awry. Renfro was still laid up. Carson and Everett had spent the last two days doctoring cattle suffering from frostbite. Many from the herd had tipped ears and damaged eyes. The two men had to put two head down and spent a good bit of time using the team to drag dead cattle away to a pit created between two sand dunes. It had been a harrowing time.

Avery and the girls were still in town. Renfro, himself, was still confined to the house, his face, ears, and fingertips in various stages of scarring and healing. The mess was almost too much to talk about, so the two men did not talk of it. Tanner and Everett spent the day putting the barn back in order. They marveled at the amount of work Renfro had accomplished to save the ranch. It really had been heroic. Losing twenty-five percent of the herd in a day was devastating, but it was not a death blow. Everett could not stop singing Renfro's praises and saying how they would forever be indebted to the old Confederate. After that day of hard labor, Tanner rode home to his bride, who awaited with a hot meal. The newlyweds were blissfully happy.

The following day, Everett did ride up to the north house to pay his respects to Tanner's bride. The introductions were awkward, but

Everett was civil and polite, telling Marie that Avery would be ecstatic to have another woman on the ranch. The snow, he explained, was still too deep on the trail back for the buckboard to navigate safely and Everett was waiting on a big thaw to bring the family home.

Then, for the next two weeks, the newlyweds were left on their own. Tanner worked the cattle herd during the day. Many of the remaining cattle needed doctorin'; he spent a lot of time treating those with damaged ears with salve. Sometimes, he trimmed away dead flesh with shears. Carson was home and working, but he stayed with Everett. Tanner and his brother had not spoken again about his marriage to Marie. In fact, he, Carson, and Everett seemed to never find time for pleasantries, only stopping for a cigarette or to chew some hard tack or jerked beef. The herd had been hard hit; they lost forty-three of the 158 head to the blizzard. Yet most other ranchers in the territory lost the majority their herds in the deep freeze, so only losing a third of the livestock was in some way a cause of celebration for the Salt Fork Stations.

However, the mood around the ranch was not celebratory. Carson's temperament had soured, and his poisoned mood kept everyone quiet and edgy. Carson, a refugee from his own bedroom due to Marie's arrival, blamed Tanner that he was forced to sleep on the floor at Everett's house. Everett avoided the conflict by retiring early, choosing to read by lamplight in bed after dinner. Carson was surly and spent his evenings throwing his knife at a corner post of the living room. His relations with Everett had been strained by the confrontation in town on the night of the blizzard's arrival. Neither had forgotten, but they did not speak of it. Tanner left the two as soon as the day's work was done. It was only Renfro, in recovery, who was cheerful and spent his days teaching his dog, Stu, new tricks.

In the evenings, Everett cooked and brought the old cowpoke

his dinner. Renfro had never in his life been waited on hand-and-foot, and he clearly enjoyed Everett treating him like visiting royalty. Renfro spent the evenings by the fire playing his harmonica or playing solitaire while sipping Everett's best whiskey. Carson was not offered any of the Kentucky bourbon.

Each workday, Tanner felt more disconnected from the others, caring only about getting back each evening to Marie. Everett talked incessantly as they worked about getting the word out that Anthem was available for stud fees. Carson was sullen and without words. Renfro was eager to get back into his saddle as soon as his fingers worked well enough. For now, Renfro sat on the corral rail and gave advice that the other three did not need but tolerated. Four men, four different agendas, and no Avery to keep things in line.

One evening after a week of silent labors, Tanner and Marie sat together with coffee. It was the highlight of each's day, the quiet time after supper before they settled down for the night. The weather had changed, and these first warmer days began to melt the deep drifts. The cabin, for the first time since Marie arrived, was not so cold to see one's breath in the lamplight.

"Before I came along," asked Tanner, "did you have a fella you were sweet on?"

Marie was thoughtful for a moment. Her dark brown eyes were full upon him as she spoke. "There was a soldier there at Jet whom I thought might take me in, yes." She paused. "It was not love, but it would have been a safe place. He was kind to me. But all that changed when you showed up."

"Because of the violence?"

"No, because of who you are, Tanner. I knew even before we arrived to the switchbacks that first night that we were meant to be together. I just knew. I felt it."

Tanner nodded. "I did, too. On our ride, the moon cut through and lit your face, I knew."

Marie laughed.

Tanner lit a cigarette. "Who is this soldier fella?"

Marie shook her head. "It doesn't matter. I was grateful to him. He showed an interest, and after that happened, my father did not sell me anymore. The soldier's interest in me made my life better. Because…" her words trailed off. "Because there wasn't the other."

Tanner nodded, understanding.

"His name is Staff Sgt. Richard Spaulding. He was in the stable, playing cards that night."

"Along with Harris, Wells, and Crups."

"Yes, Sgt. Spaulding, too, was playing that evening."

Tanner pondered a minute. "He a big man, bit of a belly, yellow mustache, shaggy like?"

She nodded.

"I saw him once when he had a patrol coming back from the reservation. I know who he is. Just got a gander at him that once."

"Uh-huh," she said, "he is a big man. Strong, but kind. People say he is a good soldier."

Tanner nodded, quietly smoking. The lack of conversation in the room was not uncomfortable. He finished the cigarette. "Then, you were sweet on this Spaulding?"

Marie laughed. "You *are* jealous, aren't you, Tanner Station?"

He grinned. "Maybe just a smidgen."

Everett fetched his family home that next weekend. The entire family was reunited the next evening as Avery brought food stores from town. It was the best meal any of them had eaten in a coon's age. It was a feast! Avery knew of her brother's marriage, as the preacher who hitched them had been into town. That's how Avery got the news. She had been careful not to react with shock or dismay at her brother's choice in his betrothal.

Avery and Marie spent the afternoon putting together the meal. The three girls were more trouble than help, but Marie felt comfortable.

Autumn set the table and Viva and May stared at Marie and her braids. She, in turn, kept peeking over at the two little ones, making them laugh.

Avery did everything she could to make the Cherokee woman comfortable.

At dinner, they ate ham and canned yams, a special meal usually reserved for Easter. Fresh biscuits and gravy also filled out the meal. Avery had also purchased an apple pie from the baker in town. All agreed it was the best meal since they'd been at the ranch.

Afterwards, the men drank coffee and smoked cigarettes.

Avery looked joyous that she had another woman on the ranch.

Carson, obviously, did not feel the same as his sister, and it was difficult to read Everett, who, as usual, played his cards close to his vest.

Marie felt happy and reasonably accepted.

Tanner watched her with pride. It was enough. More than enough.

Avery and Marie cleared away the dishes. As they did, the older woman looked at her sister-in-law and spoke, "I heard there was trouble when you met."

"Tanner saved me from a bad situation," Marie said, soberly.

"He tends to find trouble."

"I hope you are not referring to me."

Avery laughed. "No, it is just that we are Quakers. My mother raised us to avoid violence. Tanner has always had difficulty avoiding it."

"No one was badly hurt. He removed me from men who would have..." she paused, her voice cracking as Avery touched her sleeve. "They would have hurt me badly. Tanner stopped that. I was grateful, and now I am more than that. I am in love with him."

Avery nodded. "That's good enough for me. I can see the light in his eyes. I can see my brother feels the same way about you. I wish you two much happiness and peace. We don't want any trouble here."

Marie nodded. "I wish for the same."

The next afternoon, shortly after Tanner returned from the pasture, six soldiers arrived at the north house. They dismounted as one, tying their mounts to the hitching post in front.

Tanner emerged from the stable door, curry brush in hand. "Afternoon. Don't usually see blue boys this far afield. I'm Tanner Station." He pointed at the trough. "Feel free to water your horses. Don't have a lot, but you're welcome to eat with us. My wife's inside putting on supper."

The leader of the tiny patrol looked a bit shocked at the cowboy's words. He stared for a moment at the house. "I'm Sgt. Richard Spaulding," he said, haltingly. "We thank you for your hospitality. Might I give my regards to your missus?"

Now, it was Tanner's turn to be shocked. He raised an eyebrow at the sergeant's name, trying to not reveal his sudden curiosity about the man in front of him. He had not recognized the man after all. The soldier seemed smaller than he remembered. Diminished in some way.

"Marie," yelled the lanky man to the house. "We got company. Come out and say hello."

Marie opened the door of the tiny cabin. A bit of corn flour was on her cheek. Her black hair was pulled back and tied behind her ears. It was now her turn to be surprised. She stood before them, brushed the flour away as best she could, and put her hands on her hips. She wore the same clothes as she had when she'd left Jet. In fact, she owned no others.

"Hello, Marie," said the sergeant.

"Hello, Richard," was her reply.

Spaulding was a not as tall as Tanner, but then again, few were. The sergeant was not short, though. He was perhaps six feet tall, above average for the time. His shoulders were broad. His nose and cheeks were ruddy from the brisk wind out on the prairie from where the patrol had come. Spaulding wore that straight-line mustache many soldiers adopted. It was blonde with no gray. He was thick through the middle and a bit bow-legged. After a long moment, he allowed his eyes to leave the Indian woman's.

He turned to his troops. "Water your horses. Then, with Mr. Station's permission, build a fire and fix some coffee and beans. We'll be heading for the fort in an hour."

Tanner waved them back. "No sense building a fire. We have one a-burnin' in the hearth. We got coffee on already. Can fix some more. And as far as y'all heading back to the fort tonight, that'll take you until dawn. Best wait until first light. It'd be a cold ride. We can shelter you in the stable. It's not much, but it would be out of the wind. Bed down in some straw. Expect you've had worse accommodations."

Spaulding shook his head. "Got my orders. Troops, carry on." His face turned solemn. "We need to speak inside."

Tanner nodded, nearly imperceptibly. "Come on in."

Marie's eyes were dark with thoughts. The two men entered, and she followed, closing the door behind them.

Inside, Marie poured the men coffee.

Tanner took a bottle of whiskey off the shelf and offered it to Spaulding.

The sergeant declined. His eyes examined the contents of the room as if taking inventory. After he scrutinized the room, his eyes seem to lag as they reached the bedroom door.

Marie motioned for Spaulding to sit on one of the two chairs at the dinner table.

Tanner sat on the stool beside the fire.

Marie sat across from the soldier.

"Saw your herd on the way in. Glad to see you made it through the cold spell. There were those who didn't," said the sergeant. He took a sip. "Always did like your coffee, Marie." He looked to Tanner. "I am friends with Joe, her father."

Tanner nodded. He didn't speak, giving the floor to Spaulding.

The sergeant paused. "Especially glad you're okay, given the events in Jet."

"We sheltered in the switchbacks," Tanner said. "Found a place kind of out of the wind, much as you could be. Got through okay."

"In the switchbacks," said Spaulding, introspectively. "That would be why they didn't..." His voice trailed off.

"That would be why Harris and Crups didn't find us?" Tanner said, finishing the thought.

Spaulding nodded. "And you two are married?"

Marie smiled. "Yes, we got married in Cherokee last week."

Tanner smiled, graciously. "We got hitched alright. Love at first sight it was."

Spaulding smiled, ruefully. "I guess congratulations are in order."

Tanner thanked him. "Sure you won't have a shot of that whiskey? A toast?"

"I'm on duty until I return the patrol to Jet. We're on an assignment, I'm afraid."

Tanner raised an eyebrow. "Some Indians use the snowstorm to cover their tracks?"

"No, nothing like that. I have bad news. I'm afraid Buck Wells died of his injuries."

Marie closed her eyes in sorrow and silent prayer.

"I see," Tanner said. "You need a statement or to hear what happened?"

"Captain Mulvaney will. I've got orders to bring you back, Mr. Station."

"What do you mean? Bring me back?"

"Mr. Station, I've got orders to arrest you and bring you back."

Marie said, "Richard, you've no call to do this. Tanner's done nothing...." Her words trailed away, pain in her voice.

The sergeant stood and shook his head, vehemently. "Please understand, my implementation of this order is nothing personal. Our history, as it were, is not a factor. The captain issued an order. I'm to carry it out. Nothing more than that. Nothing personal. None."

"If I'm being arrested, then what is the charge?" Tanner asked, rising above the sergeant. He noticed Spaulding loosened the button on his pistol cover. He turned sideways to do it, sheltering Marie from the action. She had not noticed, but Tanner did. He abruptly sat back down to settle things down a might.

"Murder in the commission of a felony," said Spaulding.

"Murder?" Marie said in a strangled tone.

"In the commission of what felony?" Tanner asked. "What crime was I up to when I am said to have killed Buck Wells?"

"The attempted rape of Marie Wolf Walker."

After the soldiers departed with Tanner, his hands bound to his saddle horn, Marie rode to the main house, finding Carson, Everett, and Renfro at the table. Coffee mugs set in front of each man, Renfro's dog at their feet. She burst into tears entering the cabin.

Avery came in from the bedroom, where she'd been putting the girls to bed. "What's wrong, Marie? What's happened? Is something wrong with Tanner?"

Marie told them breathlessly of the arrest and the soldier's return to the fort.

Everett, their leader, took charge.

"Carson, you get to Alva. I know you're spoiling for a fight with your brother, but this ain't no time for attitude. Tell Max to find a lawyer who'll go to Jet. I don't know how long before this Captain Mulvaney will hold his tribunal or whatever it is that the military does. It's a hard ride at night, and it'll be cold, but time is in short supply. I'll head to Jet, see what I can do. If the telegraph is up, I'll wire in the morning. We'll figure out how to handle this."

Carson smirked. "Looks like big brother might get his neck stretched."

Avery gave him a look that took the dirty grin off his face.

Renfro stood. "Let's have no talk like that. You fellas get. Me and the dog are up to watching the cattle long as we don't get another one of them Arctic blasts. Go on. I got this."

Everett arrived in Jet just after Tanner was placed in the stockade. Tired though he was, Everett gathered facts at the café in Jet. Evidently, Buck Wells had been taken to the fort infirmary by Joe Wolf Walker and another man. Wells was unconscious and bleeding from the ears, nose, and mouth. The bleeding from the mouth seemed to be only a cut in his tongue. For the rest, though, the camp doctor could do little except pack snow around the man's head.

Mel Harris and Charlie Crups got a lantern, found their guns in the deepening snow, then mounted up and attempted to find Tanner and Marie. However, the snow and wind filled any tracks quickly. The two cattleman, angry and ready for retribution, travelled to any ranch, farm, or shelter they could think of in the mile or two surrounding Jet. The weather was too bad for the two runaways to go far, they figured. The two had to be holed up somewhere close.

Harris and Crups checked barns at a few farms south of Jet. They also checked west. They did not bother looking north onto the salt flats, which was by then white with snow instead of sodium. The two men, growing frustrated, never considered the switchbacks, a place where nobody went in good weather, let alone bad.

According to talk at the café, Harris and Crups' story was that the two, along with Buck, came upon Tanner Station attempting to rape Marie Wolf Walker after they left the poker game. Buck attempted to intervene, but Tanner hit him with the butt of his Henry rifle. Then, he held the other two at bay while he forced Marie to leave with him in the storm. By the time, Harris and Crups got Buck medical assistance, they lost Tanner and the girl in the storm. Based upon their report to the fort's colonel, an order was issued for Tanner Station's arrest.

Buck Wells stabilized after a couple days and was moved from the infirmary to Jinny May Benchley's boarding house. Wells had regained consciousness, but he was very weak and could not stand without severe dizziness. With Jinny May watching over him, Wells repented all his bad deeds. He told her this close call had been his "come-to-Jesus" moment. The cowboy felt bad, he said, for what he had planned to do to poor Marie Wolf Walker. He asked often for his friends, Harris and Crups, but they were nowhere to be seen during the deep freeze.

The second morning after the cold spell broke, Buck Wells was found dead at the boarding house. Jinny May was gone when Buck passed. She had walked to the neighbors for some cream and butter, leaving the boarding house for the first time since the Artic blast hit. Upon her return after an hour of chatting with the only other woman within two miles journey, Jinny May found Wells dead, his eyes wide awake in a lifeless stare.

By all accounts, the case was weak against Tanner. Buck Wells himself said he intended bad things for Marie Wolf Walker, but the only person to hear those words was Jinny May. Now Buck was dead, and Tanner was charged with his murder. Yes, Jinny May Benchley's testimony contradicted that of Harris and Crups, and she'd told others of Buck's words, but those words were hearsay, and no one but her would be allowed to testify. Jinny herself was petrified with fear. Harris and Crups were well known for their vicious nature. The woman was afraid to cross them and wished to recant her story.

After Buck's death, people began to speak about how Tanner was known for his violent behavior. Perhaps striking Buck was just another incident. Everyone knew he killed those Indians up in Kansas. Plus, Tanner had history with Harris, Crups, and Wells. There was bad blood between them. Maybe Tanner Station *did* attempt to rape Marie Wolf Walker. Maybe he *had* struck Buck Wells down after getting caught.

The truth was most folks had no use for either Tanner Station or Buck Wells. Buck Wells was dead. Good riddance. As for Tanner Station, nobody much cared what happened to him either. Who'd miss him? Nobody knew him well, so he had no one to give testimony of his good character. Maybe the rope was a good option for a fella everyone knew to use his gun a little too quickly. Of course, he had married that Indian whore, too. There was that to consider.

Plus, there was some pressure to side with men employed by the biggest ranch in the territory. Colonel George Washington Miller carried weight, and his 101 Ranch shifted public sentiment to Harris and Crups' side of the ledger. Nobody wanted to draw Col. Miller's ire. Miller having even knowledge of the trial was unlikely, and no one knew how he even felt about Wells' death, but he carried a lot of weight in the territory. Harris and Crups were his employees. Jurors would feel heavy regret to side against the most powerful man in the territory. But there would be no jury. This was to be decided by military tribunal.

Of course, the family felt differently. Avery and Everett knew it was Marie who'd hit Buck to protect herself. She'd told them herself. Naturally, Tanner would not allow that fact to ever come to light. Harris and Crups were liars, but they declared Tanner responsible. Those statements would not be disputed. Tanner would never allow his freedom at the expense of his wife's. He knew the jury's decision would be open and shut against an Indian woman in the killing of a white man. Therefore, Tanner stayed behind bars, his word against Harris and Crups.

Over that first day in Jet, Everett spoke to Joe Wolf Walker and to Jinny May. He also spoke to the fort's doctor who had signed the death certificate on Wells. At this point, the situation was stymied. Jinny did not want to testify about what Buck told her. Joe Wolf Walker was also afraid of Harris and Crups, but his statement was inconsequential, as he had not seen or heard a thing from inside his little shack at the livery. Sgt. Spaulding was not approached. It was assumed his words would not help the man who took Marie away from him.

Everett filled Tanner in on the progress, or lack of it, that evening. Tanner was taciturn and surprised anyone would believe Harris and Crups. Everett reminded him that at least those two talked. And they spent money around town. People in Alva and the territory only knew what stories were told about Tanner Station, and they weren't good. Everett reminded his brother-in-law of his reputation. Tanner raised an eyebrow, but he didn't reply.

Avery took the carriage to Alva from the Salt Fork with the girls. Billy agreed to watch the wee ones, taking time off from dealing cards. Carson, who had accompanied the four females, promised his sister he'd go home the next day to assist Renfro, who was not as spry as he let on. With his word given, Carson headed for south of the tracks. Avery gave him a disapproving eye, figuring he was off to find Pokey Arthur. She was not happy, but she had bigger fish to fry. Caron's corrupted morals were less concerning than Tanner's indictment.

The next morning, Avery and Max made the day-long trip from Alva to Jet by buckboard. They arrived tired and cold.

Everett paid Joe Wolf Walker to care for the livestock at his livery and then took his wife's bag. He carried Avery's things from the buckboard to Jinny May's.

Max walked beside them, offering his arm to Avery as they

navigated the frozen mud rutted with horse tracks past the fort's front gates toward the only hostel in town.

"Who'd you get to represent Tanner? Trial starts day after tomorrow."

Max, tired but still standing straight and tall, looked like the disheveled southern gentleman he was. He shook his head. "Ain't nobody coming. Not a lot of affection for Tanner in the territory. People know about him and the stagecoach. Killing those Injuns. They know about his showdown with Harris during the land run. And with that story getting around, most of them think of him as a Sooner. A lot of folks resent him for it, too."

Avery took her husband's arm. "And you know Tanner. He probably hasn't said twenty-five words since we got here seven years ago. He doesn't have a friend in the whole territory."

"Carson's reputation is hurting Tanner, too," Max added. "People think he's an extension of Tanner. Folks think Tanner is running with Carson and that creature, Pokey Arthur."

Everett paused, acknowledging their words. "Guess I'll be representing Tanner myself."

Avery pulled her husband close and kissed his cheek. "Everett, you're sweet to try to save my brother, but folks think you're a little stiff. Max, though, knows everybody in the territory because they've all been in Cutler's Dry Goods sometime or another. Max and I talked on it during the ride here. Please, don't be upset, but I think Max should represent Tanner. He's had more schooling, he's better with words, and he's got a soothing way about him."

Everett started to object, but his wife put her finger to his mouth. "Shush. It's decided. Now, let me get freshened up. I'll see if the commanding office will let me see my brother. Then, we'll rustle up some supper."

Benevolence
Lawrence, Kansas
October, 1964

Chris Fairchild read the entire book by Malcolm X the first night. He couldn't wait to discuss it with Tate Laughlin. Laughlin was unlike anybody Chris ever met. The young Cheyenne was dark and mysterious with long hair in braids, and the ideas in Malcolm X's book were unlike anything Chris had ever heard anyone espouse. He was sure most people in Kansas and Oklahoma where'd he grown up would disagree with most of them.

When next he saw Laughlin at his mom's office, Tate seemed to enjoy their discussion and Chris's questions. He also brought another book for the boy. It was Dick Gregory's biography, *Nigger.* The title shocked Chris. This book's title was so taboo that Chris stuck the paperback deep inside the pocket of his jacket to make sure no one saw it. He took it out only after he saw his mother's light go out that evening, and with his door closed, he read Gregory's words. It was not what he thought it would be. The pages contained a thoughtful memoir of how difficult it was to grow up black in America. Chris decided the title was for shock value and the boy didn't approve, but he was glad he read it.

Other books followed those first two: Erich Remarque's *All Quiet on the Western Front*, then Steinbeck's *The Grapes of Wrath,* next up was *India of My Dreams* by Mahatma Gandhi. Chris was fascinated with his new friendship with Laughlin. He knew the Cheyenne student was directing his reading with an agenda, but the books were so interesting, and for Chris, who had few friends, the now standing once-a-week meetings on Thursday afternoons were a welcome respite for his too often solitude.

Patrick, his debate partner, one day commented about sleepy Kansas. "No one even realizes we're at war in Vietnam. There's a flippin' youth movement in the country," Patrick complained, "and it doesn't center around 'Up with People.' No one gets it."

Chris disagreed. "There's a counterculture here. But you wouldn't know it because they don't want you to. I know some people at the Indian school. You'd be surprised."

Patrick pressed him for more, but Chris felt his friendship with Tate Laughlin should be kept secret and their discussions, the stuff of conspiracies, mysterious. Chris would not reveal them to anyone, not even Patrick. He also felt that having more knowledge about the underground than Patrick somehow increased his value in their relationship.

———

One night at a rare family dinner, Piper brought up his reading. "Chris, not that you aren't always studying, anyway, or prepping for debates, or whatever you do, but you're even more reclusive than before we moved here," she said. "What gives? There are movie theaters in Lawrence. There are good TV shows. Have you watched *Bewitched, The Man from U.N.C.L.E*, or even *Flipper*?" She took a drink of milk. "I mean, you used to have Patrick over at least. Now, you just lie on your bed with your nose in a book. What gives?"

"Debate is over," Chris said, matter-of-factly. "We don't have anything to prepare. I'm just reading for fun."

Lillian, who was more like her son than she would care to mention, hadn't really noticed that Chris was reading more than usual. Truthfully, her head was always stuck in a book or a case file from work. She was as self-absorbed as her son. But when her daughter noted a change in behavior with Chris, she poked at it.

"Chris," she said, "what are you reading right now?"

"*Siddhartha* by Herman Hesse," he answered. "It's about India."

Lil cut him off. "Yes, I know it. Hesse is in vogue right now. Interesting choice. So you've been reading a lot?"

"Yessum."

"For school?"

"Not so much. School's easy. Just reading for fun."

"What did you read before Herman Hesse?"

"*Civil Disobedience*. *Walden*, too. They were short."

"Henry David Thoreau. I see," Lil said, smiling. "You're quite the little revolutionary. What's next on your list?"

"*Ten Days That Shook the World*, I think. I've already checked it out from the public library."

"John Reed's Russian revolution book?"

Chris shrugged. "Don't know. I haven't read it yet."

Lillian smiled back. "And where are you getting your reading list?"

Chris felt he needed to tread lightly here. There was the potential for trouble. He was in deep water. His mother did not know of his weekly meeting with Tate Laughlin at the public library. The boy would prefer to keep it that way.

He also knew his mother might question the subject matter of the books. He was in ninth grade, but he was only twelve. Chris worried his mother would halt his friendship with Tate Laughlin. He didn't want to jeopardize that. The two's discussions were now the highlights of Chris's week. They met at a far back table on the second floor of the library on Massachusetts. There were few people back in the stacks at that time of day. Retirees visited the library in the morning; students would come after supper. Late afternoon after the newspapers had been delivered, the place was deserted. It felt like the two conspirators had the run of the place. And after all, he and Tate were talking about books. How bad could it be?

Despite his reluctance, Chris did not lie to his mother. "Tate Laughlin gave me one book and I've been asking him what I should read."

Piper sucked in air to note her surprise, and Chris gave her a look.

"Tate Laughlin, my student? He's nineteen." Lillian pursed her lips, her brows furrowed.

"He likes to read, and so do I."

Lillian began gathering the dirty dishes. "I have to think about this situation, Chris."

"Tate hasn't done anything wrong. He just recommended a book he read, and I read it, too. He lets me ask him questions sometimes."

"And where does this questioning happen?"

"At the library. I had to get a card from the public library because the high school doesn't have most of the books Tate and I read."

"I'm not surprised, based upon your selections," Lillian said, walking into the kitchen. The conversation was at an end.

Piper gave him the one-eye "you're dead" look as she left the room.

No one spoke much. Piper washed, Chris rinsed, and Lillian dried and put things away. Tension was in the air.

Chris made a point of not reading that evening. He lay on the floor and watched *Bewitched*. His mother walked into the room and saw him there. She reversed her field, left the room, returning to drop a book on the floor in front of him.

"I've decided that censoring your reading list from Tate will only make those books more attractive to you. But I want you to expand your reading list. And I'm going to expect Tate Laughlin to read my suggestions, too. You can read your revolutionary counterculture stuff every other week. I get to pick the titles on the evens. Is that a deal?"

Chris nodded. "Yes, Mom."

"That's the first one. It's short. Tell Tate to read it, too. I'll ask him what he thinks of it, and I'll give you a little quizzing on it, as well. Is that a deal?"

Chris shrugged.

"What's the problem?"

"I'm not sure I can tell Tate what to read. He is seven years older than me."

"I understand that. Tate works tomorrow, and I'll put the deal on the table to him myself. I think he'll agree. That Cheyenne boy has about the sharpest mind I've seen in a student." She paused. "Maybe except for you. I think he'll take the deal. If not, I'll put a stop to it. You got that?" Lillian smiled that smile when there was no choice but to agree, so he did.

His mother left the room, and Chris examined the book in front of him. It was a slim volume. It was *Profiles in Courage* by John F. Kennedy. He finished it before he went to sleep. It was not a chore. It was one of the best books he had ever read.

Oklahoma Territory
February, 1899

Tanner awoke from his second night in the brig. It was his third night away from Marie. The first had been spent on horseback riding back to Jet in the custody of Sgt. Spaulding's patrol. Everett, who'd arrived on his first day of captivity, brought him his first meal that day. By the time sentries brought him his evening meal, Tanner knew Marie was now there in Jet, back at her father's. However, Tanner was not allowed to see her, for the commanding officer forbade the entry of any Indian inside the military installation. It was incredibly frustrating to know his wife was not maybe two hundred yards away, yet he could not see her.

When Avery brought him breakfast on day three, she was shocked at her brother's condition. He seemed to have not slept in days. He was dirty, unshaven, and distraught. Tanner seemed even taller than normal in the smallness of the cell. It held a bench too low to the floor for him to sit well and too short for him to sleep without his legs splayed over the end. Avery worried for his health and sanity.

The brother and sister ate from the meager supplies she was able to bring into the jail. Tanner was hungry for the first time since his arrival, and there was not near enough here to fill him, but he insisted on giving half to Avery.

She finally accepted when she realized her brother would not eat without sharing. She'd eat, she said, if Tanner said the grace. He did, and she squeezed his hands with the "Amen." She added a silent prayer for Tanner's deliverance.

After their meal, Avery put the plates and cups in her basket. "Marie sends her love," she said. "They don't let Indians in buildings into the fort, except for the PX, and they don't let them inside the walls at night. Jinny May, the boarding house owner, is a nice woman, but she said she couldn't let Marie stay at the boarding house, either, so we took her back at her father's. He seems a nice enough man."

"Maybe sober, he is."

"What do you mean?" Avery asked of her brother.

Tanner just shook his head, sparing her the details. "Marie going to be able to come to the trial today?"

"Yes, and her father, as well. The base commander will allow that. But only because they may be called as witnesses. The prosecution will be calling her father. Max will call Marie."

"The judge should just let her talk first and clear this whole thing up. She can tell Captain Mulvaney that it was Buck Wells who grabbed her, not me, and we'll be done with it."

"We all know you did not lift a hand in violence," Avery said.

"We'll not talk another word of that," Tanner said, cutting off any talk of telling the truth about who struck Buck Wells.

"God's will," Avery said, and with the words, she rubbed the gold cross on her necklace It reflected the morning light through the cell's only window.

Avery called the guard to bring Tanner the suit of clothes she had brought her brother. It was Max's best suit. It would be too short for him, but it was all they had. She had brushed and ironed it at the boarding house with Jinny May's assistance. She turned as he dressed. It was a black parson's suit with a white shirt and a string tie. Avery helped him with the collar stud and with tying a tie. She told her brother he would not be allowed to wear a hat.

Avery asked the jailer that Tanner be allowed to shave before his court appearance, but the man, kindly enough, refused to let Tanner have possession of a straight razor. Avery asked that she be allowed to shave her brother in the jailer's presence through the bars, and a compromise was reached. Tanner's hands were bound behind his back while his sister shaved him. His face stung with shame at the predicament.

"Remember, Tanner," Avery said, ever the big sis to this lanky man, "do not speak, no matter what the lieutenant prosecutor says in court today. Max is your voice."

"Captain Mulvaney is acting as judge?"

"Yes, he is. Do you know if he's a righteous man?"

"No, I've just heard his name, Avery. Don't know a thing about him."

Avery smiled at her brother. "I'll pray he is a just man. Remember now, all that happens if you speak out is that this Captain Mulvaney might get mad and then have it out for you."

"More than he already does?" Tanner asked, sarcastically.

"There," Avery said, "done." She wiped the lathered soap on the trim at the bottom of her petticoat. With a puff of air, she blew her black hair from her face. One strand fell loose onto her face as she leaned forward for one last scrap with the razor. She handed it to the jailer.

She smiled. "I've got a good feeling about this trial. It's scary, but you'll be okay. God is just testing your love to Marie. Marrying her was the right thing for you two, but it wasn't the easy thing. We'll just have to repair the bumps in the road as we navigate it, won't we? God will deliver us His blessings this day."

Tanner snorted. "Hey, bailiff, come take these bindings off my wrists. This barber lady is starting to preach."

The siblings' laugh was interrupted by the bars of his cage clanging loudly as she exited.

The military tribunal was a simple affair. Captain Thomas Marvin Mulvaney would preside as judge. Lt. Linus Moore would prosecute the case. Max Hart would represent the defendant. Tanner sat at the table with his father-in-law, Max. The older man wore a three-piece suit of deep blue and a bowtie the color of sky. His pocket watch chain looped from his pocket. He sat with his eyes on the pad in front of him. He scratched some words there.

Tanner turned in his seat to see his wife. Marie wore Avery's

Easter dress, and she was more beautiful in that moment than he could believe. The dress was brown and covered with print flowers of pink. Marie's hair was up and she had powdered her face. It only softened her brown skin and did not hide it. Her eyes warmed to his and she mouthed, "I love you."

He returned her sentiment.

Then, Captain Mulvaney called the court to order.

The lieutenant was a precise man with speech as clipped as his tight mustache and goatee. He looked every bit like a young Custer as he addressed the court. First, he called the Army doctor to explain Buck Wells' injuries and his cause of death.

"The victim's death resulted from complications of a severe head injury. Loss of motor control led to the man's inability to breath. Wells ultimately died of asphyxiation."

Max's redirect to the doctor took a different route. "Doctor, you say that Buck Wells died of asphyxiation, loss of muscle control. What happened? Did his lungs cease to function?"

"Yes, essentially, his lungs failed to bring him enough air to live. We all have to have oxygen."

"I see," Max followed. "And who was with him when he died?"

"No one. Jinny May Benchley, operator of the boarding house, found him upon her return. Wells was the only guest at the boarding house, and Jinny May had gone to the neighbors for some cream. She found him dead upon her return."

"And are there other ways to asphyxiate?"

"Certainly, a person could, say, choke on food."

"Could illness, like pneumonia, cause such a death?"

"Yes," the doctor replied, "but there were no signs of illness when I examined him after his injury that first evening, or when I saw him dead."

"I see," Max said. "Could another person cause asphyxiation?"

"Yes, but I saw no signs of strangulation. There were no signs of foul play whatsoever. There is no evidence anyone but Jinny May saw Buck Wells after my last visit before he died."

"But no one was there at his time of death to witness the cause?"

"No, but..."

"Sir, you testified there were no signs of foul play whatsoever, but did you not find something in Mr. Wells' throat while inspecting the body?"

"Yes," the doctor guffawed at the insignificance of the question. "A feather. Just a feather. Buck's head was reclining on a feather pillow. He was obviously in respiratory distress, sucking at air and inhaled a pillow feather. I assure you the feather was small and was not the cause of his passing. It was insignificant to cause of death."

Next, Jinny May was called to simply verify she'd found the body upon her return with the bucket of cream. "No," she said, "no one was in the boarding house during my absence. Yes, I feel terrible that man had to die alone, no matter what he done. Nobody should die alone."

Max asked Jinny May his first question not thirty seconds after Lt. Moore left her side. "Who'd you tell first about Buck's passing, Miss Benchley? Did you run back to the neighbors? That's a half mile. Did you hook up a team and ride to the fort? What is it, better part of two miles over there?"

"Oh, goodness," she said. "I don't have any horses, or a carriage. In truth, I didn't do anything for a little bit. I was a bit in shock. I admit I sat down and cried a bit. I was having some hot tea when Mel Harris and Charlie Crups rode in to see their friend. But they were too late. Buck died maybe a half hour before they arrived."

"Jinny May, did you see them arrive? Is it possible they showed up earlier?"

"No, I don't see how..." she didn't finish her sentence, thinking.

"Can you see your place from the next farm over?"

"No, there be a stand of cottonwoods, big ones, between us. Sometimes in the winter, you can see smoke from the chimney. But you..." she began, but Max cut her off.

"You've really no idea if Mel Harris and Charlie Crups were in the boarding house while you were gone?"

"All I can say is I didn't see any sign of them in the house."

"Except for that feather."

"Objection," shouted Lt. Moore. "The witness has never said she saw any feather."

Max turned to her. "Did you see a feather?"

"No," she said. "But Doc told me he saw one."

Max pivoted, feeling he had made his point and offered an alternative to the doctor's cause of death. He was gathering steam. "You have any conversations with Buck Wells before he died, or was he unconscious all the time?"

"No, Buck was awake some. He slept a good deal, of course," Jinny May said, "but we spoke. Buck was my only guest, and he was hurting, so I spent a lot of time with him. Nursed him as best I could. I feel awful that he died under my roof."

"He ever confess anything to you, Jinny May? He admit to rape, or even attempted rape?"

Lt. Moore objected.

Mulvaney asked Max to revise his question.

Max nodded. "What did you two talk about? About what happened? How he got hurt?"

"Yessum," the woman said. "We did talk of that. I took the Bible up and read to him. After I spoke of repenting his sins, he professed he wanted to."

Max followed up on that. "Just what did Buck Wells tell you he done, Miss Jinny?"

The woman hesitated, her gnarled hands and arthritic fingers interlocked like a secret, but then she moved her hands to grip the arms of the chair before she spoke. "Buck told me he regretted grabbing that girl. That poor man said he regretted what he had planned to do to her; have his way with her, he meant, though he never said those words to me, beings I'm a woman. I told him to pray to the Lord, and he told me he would."

The lieutenant objected. "This is hearsay, Captain Mulvaney. Such testimony is not allowed in military court."

"Your honor," argued Max, "death bed confessions have long been accepted by the courts as legitimate testimony and an exception to the hearsay rule, Your Honor," Max, used the honorific twice to appeal to the captain.

Lt. Moore turned to the doctor now sitting in the third row. "Doc, did you believe, and more importantly, did Buck Wells believe he was on the mend and going to live through this blow to the head?"

"Yes to both queries," the doctor answered. "Buck and I both believed he was going to be back to riding a horse in a month's time. His death was a sudden occurrence. Nothing about the death could have been foreseen. It happens that way sometimes. The good Lord just decides to call someone home."

Lt. Moore turned to the captain. "Sir, I ask you to not let Jinny May's hearsay testimony impact your judgement in this case. It is not a death bed confession, as Buck did not believe he was dying. In addition, we have no ability to judge its veracity. We also ask you instruct Mr. Hart here to discontinue this path."

The captain nodded. "I agree with the lieutenant," said Mulvaney. "Please refrain from asking Miss Jinny any more questions about the decedent's words. Have you any more questions of this witness?"

Max smiled, grimly. "Jinny May, have you lied up here on the stand today?"

The lieutenant stood again, "Sir, she is under oath—"

Max waved the question away. "No more questions."

Next, Joe Wolf Walker was called to testify. He confirmed that Wells, Crups, and Harris were playing poker in the stable when the snow started in earnest on the night of February fifth.

"Who else could verify their attendance?" asked the lieutenant.

"Two other fellas," said the weathered Indian, "and of course, Marie, my daughter."

"Who were these other men?"

"Sgt. Spaulding and Miller Smith, an old muleskinner who stops in his travels now and then. He moved on the first break in the weather. Think he was headed to Amarillo."

"Miller Smith would not be around for us to talk to?"

"No, I reckon not," said the Indian.

"Did you see anything about your daughter's attack?"

"No."

"So, you cannot tell us if Mr. Harris and Mr. Crups' account of the altercation is wrong?"

"What's altercation mean?"

"It means fight, Mr. Wolf Walker," said the lieutenant.

Joe Wolf Walker looked to his daughter and then to Mel Harris and Charlie Crups seated across the room from her. His head pivoted slowly before he answered. "I reckon not."

Lt. Moore turned and looked into the gallery at Sgt. Richard Spaulding. The two men's eyes met for a long moment before the lieutenant turned back to ask an additional question of the Indian. "Do you know if Sgt. Spaulding saw the fight? Did he say anything to you later?"

Joe Wolf Walker glanced at Spaulding. "Now, he did go out of the stable about then, but we haven't spoke none since Buck got hit. I don't know if he saw nothing."

The lieutenant nodded. "No more questions."

Max approached the chair next to the captain, where Marie's father sat.

"Good morning, Mr. Wolf Walker. Can you tell us about that evening before the attack? Are you sure you didn't see anything or hear anything from your daughter's attackers that evening?" Max added to the question, "How about before the attack? What occurred earlier?"

"No, I don't know nothing about the attack. As far as earlier, all I can tell you is that Harris, Wells, and Crups were drinking pretty heavy and losing pretty heavy because of it. Miller Smith was the big winner. Sgt. Spaulding was playing, but he probably broke even. The other three were drunk. They started making comments about Marie, things that should not be said in front of a father, things that should never be said to a woman, and things that would not be said by sober men, so I asked Marie to go to the General Store PX over to the fort."

"You feared for her safety at the hands of Buck Wells and his companions?"

"I object," the Lieutenant shouted. "The defense has no way of knowing the intent of Misters Wells, Crups and Harris at that moment."

Max shook his finger at Lt. Moore. "I was not asking about their intent. I asked Mr. Wolf Walker his intent in sending his daughter to the fort's PX just before the attack occurred."

Mulvaney nodded. "Continue."

"Why did you send Marie to the PX? I believe you sent her for coffee. Were you out of coffee?" Max rephrased.

"Nope, had plenty of coffee."

The courtroom laughed.

Everett watched Max with awe. Avery had been right to insist on the older man as his representative. The old man's insistence came across as earnestness. With Everett, it would have come across as belligerence.

Captain Mulvaney banged his gavel, the laughter subsided, and the gallery's attention returned its attention to Joe Wolf Walker.

"Joe, you didn't need coffee. Then, why'd you send Marie off in a blizzard? To get her away from Harris and his two sidekicks?"

"Objection, Mr. Hart is putting words into the witness's mouth."

"Ask it differently, Mr. Hart," the captain ruled.

Max nodded. "What about Harris, Wells, and Crups? Did you already know them?"

"Knew them and knew of them. Bad hombres, people said. Hard drinkers. Drink, screw, and fight is what they like, people say. They do bad things down in New Mexico, people say—"

"Objection!"

"Mr. Wolf Walker, did you send your daughter away because you feared Harris, Crups, and Wells might harm Marie?"

"Well, more because they were runnin' her down the road with their drunk talk, but yes, I was some worried."

"No more questions."

The next two witnesses were Mel Harris and Charlie Crups. Their two stories mirrored each other. The two, along with Wells, had lost their money at the card game in the stable. They didn't like losing to the muleskinner Miller Smith, but he was a tough old coot. They wanted no part of a fight with him. Plus, the weather was getting bad, so they went outside to decide whether to risk riding back to the 101 Ranch bunkhouse, but that was a long ride drunk. Outside, they came upon Tanner, up to no good, wrestling the girl to the ground. Both made a point of saying the tall cowboy seemed to be grabbing the woman between her legs. Their testimonies were nearly identical.

Buck, they said, attempted to pull Tanner Station off the girl. Tanner, in return, struck Buck in the head with the butt of his Henry repeating rifle. Wells dropped to the ground. Then, Tanner turned the gun on the other two. According to their testimony, Tanner threatened to kill them. Then, he disarmed them, threw their weapons out into the snow, and led the girl away. Harris and Crups said they attempted to follow, but they were without weapons. The blizzard made it impossible to see anything in the dark, and most importantly, Wells needed medical attention. The lieutenant seemed satisfied and turned over Harris as a witness over to Max.

Harris wore dirty jeans but seemed to have purchased a new white shirt for the occasion. He wore a black Sunday-go-to-meeting coat over it. Harris wore no tie but had a weatherworn blood-red handkerchief tied around his neck. His cheeks were covered with stubble, and his skin seemed as leathery as his boots. Max turned his keen eyes on his witness.

The contrast to Max could not have been starker as the older man stood facing the 101 Ranch's ramrod. The captain at his desk viewed the two men closely. Today, he served as judge and jury for a third man. His eyes watched intensely as Max approached Harris.

"Mr. Harris, you say the three of you were on your way out of the stable. Did you have your horses with you?" Max inquired.

"No, we was just sizing up the weather. After talkin', we figured it was snowing to beat the devil and we'd have to hole up in the stable. Couldn't get a room over to Jinny May's, as we'd lost all our funds at the game."

"And you saw the defendant attempting to subdue Miss Wolf Walker?" Max asked.

"No, sir," Harris replied. "He was trying to poke her."

The courtroom laughed again.

Harris frowned. He did not like folks making fun of him.

Captain Mulvaney banged his gavel. "Everyone, shush. I'm trying to hear."

The room settled down once again.

Mulvaney turned to the witness beside him. "Subdue means to control, maybe tie up."

Harris nodded, and Max continued. "Did Mr. Station have the girl on the ground?"

"Almost. Just about had her legs where he wanted them."

"And would you say you, Buck Wells, and Charlie Crups are experienced in fighting? Good in a scrap? Good gun hands?"

"Not gunfighters, no. Handy enough, I guess. Not like Tanner Station. He's known to be real fast. A killer-diller."

Max said, "Captain Mulvaney, I ask you not to consider that testimony. Mel Harris has no idea how fast or good with a gun Tanner Station is."

"But you asked the question," Lt. Moore piped in.

The captain asked Harris himself, "You ever see Tanner Station in action with a gun?"

Harris nodded. "Yessir. Twice. Once on the day of the land run, back in '93. He and his no-account brother pulled guns on us three when they soonered us out on the Salt Fork. Then again the other night. Tanner Station is the fastest I've ever seen with a gun. Plum scary, he is. Got them dead eyes of a killer."

The captain nodded. "Back to you, Mr. Hart."

Max gave up on that direction. He was losing ground. "So it is your testimony that Tanner Station was attempting to rape this girl. You three men saw him on the ground with Miss Wolf Walker, and you attempted to stop him? He knocked out Buck Wells by striking him in the head from his position on the ground and then got the drop on you and Crups while he was wrestling the Indian girl?"

"Yes."

"It seems the three of you are not near as tough as your reputations."

The crowd roared with laughter.

The lieutenant objected, as Max knew by now he would. Max waved it away, indicating he was taking back his observation.

Captain Mulvaney asked., "What do you think of Tanner Station's skill with a gun?"

Mel Harris ran his index finger down his scar line and then rested it on the black stubble on his chin. "Tanner Station is snake-fast, Judge. Like nothing you ever seen. Thought for sure he was going to kill us all, but instead he drug off that Injun girl, Marie. Guess he was more worried about a poke than killing us this one time."

Max wanted to object, but the captain had asked the question. He gave up. "No more questions," Max said, feeling he had lost the case in that moment.

Max's interrogation of Charlie Crups did not go any better, with one exception. "You told Lt. Moore that one reason that you didn't go to save the girl was that Buck Wells needed medical assistance. Is that right?"

"Yep," Crups said. His brown leather vest showed dust, and he was in need of a shave, and a bath. His hair was greased back, and the cowpoke held his tan felt Stetson in his hands. Max could smell stale whiskey on the man from six feet away. "Buck was in a bad way. Figured getting him help was bigger than finding Station and the Injun girl."

Max turned to the doctor. "Who brought Buck in for medical treatment?"

"It was Miller Smith, the mule skinner, who woke me up. Joe Wolf Walker was out in the buckboard with the injured man. Fort doesn't let Indians inside after dark, so he waited with the buckboard."

Max turned back to Crups. "Were you there bringing in your friend or not?"

Crups curled his lip. "Must of been hunting down Station by then. Didn't find him in the snow. Guess he got what he wanted. Married her, I hear."

"Your earlier testimony about getting your friend help was a bit off the mark?"

"We loaded up poor Buck in the buckboard, sent old Joe and the muleskinner to the fort. Couldn't a done no more."

Max excused the witness, and Lt. Moore concluded their case.

Mulvaney acknowledged it, approvingly. The defense would present after lunch. The case would be completed before taps. Good. February days were short, and the captain longed for this trouble to be behind him. He banged the gavel down twice. "Mr. Hart, the defense will present its case in one hour."

———

Back at the jail, Max was beating himself up something fierce. "I should have just passed on interrogating Harris and Crups. I knew they would lie. Why'd I give them a chance to lie to all of us and especially to Captain Mulvaney? Oh, my boy," he said, looking to Tanner in the cell, "I think I may have bought you a hanging."

Max held his eyes on Tanner's. The length of the man was Gulliver-like sitting on the tiny bench, and his face was even longer. Everyone was glum. It was crowded in the tiny jail room. Everett and Avery stood, hand-in-hand. There was only the one chair outside the cage. Max, who looked fatigued sat, even though as a southern gentleman it rankled him to have his daughter stand while he rested.

"What's the plan this afternoon?" Avery said, trying to rouse Max out of his depression.

"I'll ask for a continuance until we find Miller Smith, but Mulvaney will say that codger won't have anything to add. Joe Wolf Walker already said Smith never left the stable during the whole time. Not until after Buck was down and out."

"But Sgt. Spaulding did," said Avery. "He was outside."

"Probably won't do me no favors, Sis," Tanner said. "He's sweet on Marie. Looked kind of gut shot when he came to arrest me and found out we was married."

"I already spoke to Spaulding," said Everett. "He didn't see nothing. Said the wind was howling so that nobody could have heard nothing, either."

Tanner nodded. "That's true enough about the wind." He paused. "Then, why not just put Marie on the stand and have her tell it was all Buck doing the attempted raping, and it was me doing the stopping the rape?"

Everett said, "You know, Max brings her up, they's going to call her a whore."

"Everett!" Avery exclaimed.

Max nodded to Tanner. "They would do that. Call her morals into question. A whore is a liar. That will be the tact they take."

Tanner said, "Then, it will come to down to me. Put me up there."

Everett reached through the bars and put his hand on Tanner's shoulders. "Brother, you'll have to keep it together. Calling these two-bit sons-of-bitches what they are to their faces will be what will feel right, but you can't do it."

Avery looked at her husband. "And we don't even do it here," she said, matter-of-factly. "We will not stoop to lying or cursing, even in these trying times."

Max looked at Tanner. "Might have to finish up with you on the stand."

Tanner nodded. "You do what you need."

Max said, "Just tell the truth when I get you up there. I will do better this afternoon."

Back in session, the room was hot, despite the winter chill outside. The stove had been restoked, and with a room full of people, it was hot. Max wished that one of the windows could be opened. He feared the captain's impatience would become a factor in the heat. He asked a young soldier who was functioning as a bailiff if the rear door could be opened a crack.

The soldier asked Mulvaney, who nodded his approval, and they were underway.

Max began the afternoon with a request for a continuance.

With the request, Captain Mulvaney called to Joe Wolf Walker for information. "Joe, did Miller Smith ever go out of the stable before Buck got hurt?"

"No, sir," the aged Indian said.

"Think he knows anything about what happened more'n you?"

"I 'spect not. Inside counting his money. Must a won a hundred dollars off those drunks."

The gallery laughed, but the captain ignored them. Mulvaney turned back to Max. "Motion denied," he said. "Call your first witness."

Max called Richard Spaulding.

Spaulding rose from the gallery and approached the stand in his dress uniform. It was freshly pressed, and he looked as if he had shaved a second time over lunch. His boots were shiny but worn at the heels. However, Jet was a backwater fort next to the Cherokee reservation out in the territories. Spaulding's old boots were as nice as most men owned. It had been at least Christmas since most of the folks in this room had been this cleaned up. Nobody noticed the boots, except maybe Avery and Max, who always cared about his own attire.

"Sgt. Spaulding," began Max.

"It's corporal, now. I got busted down a rank being out of the fort gambling."

Max nodded. "That was on the night in question?"

"Yes."

"Corporal Spaulding, then you *were* at Joe Wolf Walker's poker game on the night of February fourth?"

The soldier turned his head ruefully to the captain and then answered, "Yes, sir, I was."

"Were you on duty?"

"No, sir. I worked the six-to-six days. I was off duty. We have two staff sergeants on base. Sgt. Trawley has been on nights this month."

"I see," said Max. "And is Indian Joe Wolf Walker's stable on base?"

Sgt. Spaulding faltered for a second. "No, sir, it is not. It is just outside the walls, but it is technically off base."

"You were off base without leave?"

"Well, maybe technically, yes. But only by a quarter mile at most. I just went over there for a bit before I went to bed. Nothing was going on with the blizzard coming in, and—"

Max cut him off. "So, we're clear. You were absent without leave?"

Spaulding looked at the captain again before answering. "Yes, sir," he said to Max.

"Lt. Moore," the captain interjected, "see me afterwards regarding off-base gambling."

Spaulding paled. His beefy frame seemed to wither a mite. He rolled his cap in his hands.

"Were you present when Harris, Crups, and Wells made derogatory remarks about Marie Wolf Walker that evening?"

"Yes, I was."

"What did they say? Was there any indication they intended to rape Marie?" Max asked.

"Objection," Lt. Moore shouted as he slapped his hands on the table. "Prejudicial!"

Max raised his hands in exasperation. "I just want to know what the three said about Marie that night."

Captain Mulvaney looked to Spaulding, sternly. "You may answer."

"Harris said he hoped he had enough cash left at the end of the night to buy Marie for the night. He said it was so cold out it would be nice to have an Injun gal in the sack. I believe those were his exact words."

Harris stood at the back of the room. "You're a damn liar," he shouted.

Mulvaney banged his gavel. "One more word out of you" he said, pointing his gavel at Harris, "and you'll do thirty days in the brig for contempt, no matter what the outcome is today." Mulvaney's eyes were aflame.

Harris sat muttering under his breath. His scar was a white line on his red cheek.

Crups stared at Spaulding with malice in his eyes.

"Did you follow the three outside after the game?"

"Yes."

"And what did you see?"

"Nothing, I went out south of the corral. I wanted nothing to do with those three, especially after they'd been drinking and then lost at poker. They were in a foul mood."

"Do you think they intended you harm?"

"Nah," said the sergeant. "I didn't take any of their money. If they were spoilin' for a fight, it was with the muleskinner, but he's a handful. I don't think they really wanted to tangle with him. Be like fighting a badger in a flour bin."

The crowd erupted in laughter.

The captain banged the gavel twice, and Max proceeded once

the volume decreased. "When the three left the stable, which way did they go?"

"North. Toward the entrance to the fort. Gate was open, but there were sentries there. They was hole up in the shed out front. Weather was as bad as it gets. It might have only been a couple hundred yards' walk, but far enough in that snow and darkness, them sentries wouldn't have seen nothing. When I came out, I saw them three and I went the other direction."

"Did you see who attacked Marie?"

"No, I did not. I was urinating off south."

"Hope your hand wasn't too cold," a husky voice yelled from the gallery.

There was tumult in the courtroom, and Mulvaney banged his gavel several times.

"I'll clear this room if we have one more outburst like that one," the captain threatened.

"What did you hear?" Max asked.

"Nothing. Just the wind. Roaring like a train."

Max nodded. He knew that answer was coming, but it didn't mean he wasn't disappointed. "Sgt. Spaulding, would you have any reason to wish Mr. Station convicted today? Any relationship with any of the parties involved that would make you less than impartial?"

Lt. Moore started to rise but then hesitated as Spaulding cleared his throat. The seeming import of his forthcoming words left everyone on the edge of the seats.

He hesitated for what seemed a minute before uttering a word. "No, sir, I know everybody involved alright. I was there, although maybe I shouldn't have been. But I don't have a dog in this fight, and I don't have any evidence to add to the proceedings."

Next, Marie was called. Max did not beat around the bush. "Marie, who attempted to rape you the night of February fourth outside your father's stable?"

"Objection," Lt Moore shouted. "Mrs. Station, as she can now be identified, cannot be called upon to testify against her husband."

Max threw up his hands. "She cannot be forced to, but she can testify of her own volition. And she is sworn to tell the truth."

Harris' guffaw could be heard throughout the room. Mulvaney did not speak but did point the gavel once again at the man with the scar.

The lieutenant disagreed with the possibility of Marie's veracity. "Who's to say her words would be of her own volition? Tanner Station took her away, had his way with her, and married her, perhaps without her approval. Or worse, who's to say she wasn't paid off with the marriage to protect him here today? Maybe he offered her marriage to a white man in exchange for her falsehoods on the stand today?"

It was Max's turn to be outraged, but he saw Tanner rise in anger. The old man stepped back to the red-faced Tanner and pressed his shoulder down, keeping the defendant in his seat.

Everett reached over the rail and grabbed his brother-in-law's arm, holding him. "We talked about this. Hold your temper," he whispered to Tanner.

Max waved his arm at the judge. "Lt. Moore's conduct and comments in the last minute have been at best speculative and certainly unbecoming an officer, sir. Lt. Moore has no basis to his charges which shame this woman. It is simply conjecture and shameful conjecture at that."

Lt. Moore said, "You want factual? I could call numerous witnesses to testify regarding Marie Station's known prostitution. Captain, this woman is an Indian, not an American. She is a known prostitute, and she is in league with the defendant. As his wife, she should not be allowed to testify. We have other means to ascertain the facts here today. I ask that she be removed from the stand, as her testimony is inherently tainted. In fact, I asked that she be removed from the courtroom. It is highly irregular to allow an Indian to these proceedings."

"That's ridiculous," Max bellowed. "Let's hear her words and then decide her veracity."

"You cannot un-ring the bell of falsehoods, Captain Mulvaney," Lt. Moore exclaimed.

The gallery squawked as one. The volume reached a fever pitch.

Mulvaney banged his gavel. "For now, Mr. Hart, I'm going to rule in Lt. Moore's favor. Before closing statements, I'll make a determination whether Marie Wolf, er, Station will be allowed to testify. For now, she is dismissed."

"But judge…" Max stammered.

Captain Mulvaney raised a hand for the defense to be silent.

"I've ruled. Now Miss, er, Mrs. Station, if you would step down." The captain turned to Max. "Call your next witness."

Max looked to Tanner next to him. "You are all I have left."

Tanner nodded and stood. "I reckon it's up to me."

Tanner took the stand, telling his side of the story. He arrived to the fort late, bringing the colt Anthem to Jet. It had been snowing hard for perhaps two hours when he arrived. He was danged near frozen stiff. He heard the altercation but couldn't see anything in the dark. Recognizing trouble if not the exact words said, he grabbed his Henry rifle and approached what appeared to be some kind of melee. He saw the attempted rape in progress and popped his rifle butt into the head of the man who was assaulting the girl. Tanner didn't know it was Buck Wells until the man was on the ground. Then, in the moment directly after, Mel Harris threatened his life. Charlie Crups attempted to draw his weapon too. Tanner held them off with his Henry until he and the girl vamoosed.

Max followed up his question. "And what did you do or say after Harris said he was going to kill you?"

Tanner looked abashed. "I told Harris he'd sober up in the morning and realize an Indian girl was not worth anybody dying over."

A murmur went through the courtroom.

Tanner held his head down in shame. Then, he lifted his eyes to

Marie's. She was crying. "I'm sorry," he said. "That was wrong for me to say. I didn't mean it even then. I just didn't want anyone to get hurt."

"Did you know Buck Wells was severely injured?"

"Had no idea," replied Tanner, his eyes still rimmed with tears. "I really had no time to reflect on it. Charlie there, with Harris, they're dangerous men. They were hell bent on tanning my hide. Have been for six years since '93. I knew out there in the blizzard where nobody could see they'd be set loose. They'd kill us if they found Marie and me, so we just lit out."

Lt. Moore objected once again. "The defendant does not know Mr. Harris and Mr. Crups' states of mind during the incident. I asked those words be stricken and not considered in deliberations by you, Captain Mulvancy."

Tanner laughed. "Y'all know what those buzzards are about, Lt. Moore. All the time, they're looking for trouble. They just happened to have found it that night. I was in the wrong place at the wrong time for trouble, but in the right place at the right time to help Marie. I thank the Lord, he put me there when he did."

Max nodded. "You never assaulted the girl?"

"No."

"Did you marry her to keep her silence?"

"No, I married her because I love her."

"No further questions."

Max sat down.

Lt. Moore stood and approached Tanner. "Would you say you're a dangerous man?"

"No, I would not," Tanner replied.

"But your reputation is that of a gunman. You've been out to New Mexico with your brother, Carson, and the outlaw called Pokey Arthur, isn't that right?"

"I've never even met Pokey Arthur, and I've never been to the New Mexico territory."

Lt. Moore raised an eyebrow to the gallery to signal that Tanner had just told a whopper. "I see. And I suppose you're not a killer.

How many men had you killed before you took Buck Wells' life? Is it two or three Indians, is that all? That's the story on you. You started in your teens, killing a couple Comanches. Or are there more? What about that fellow and his travelling wagon of pots and pans up toward Medicine Lodge? Garinger, I believe was his name. They found his body with a .44 hole in it. You have anything to do with that?"

"Objection!" Max shouted. "Talk about prejudicial. Those are warrantless accusations. In fact, I ask that the lieutenant be held in contempt. His last words are outrageous."

Mulvaney looked at Moore and then to Tanner.

Tanner stared back at the man who would decide his life or death.

Captain Mulvaney met his eyes.

Tanner never blinked, and neither did the judge.

Finally, the captain spoke.

"What say you, Mr. Station?" Mulvaney asked. "I think everyone in this community has wondered about you since first you showed up in the territory with the reputation of Billy the Kid or some such. What *is* the story with you? You killed those Indians who attacked the stagecoach. Blasted them after they killed the shotgunner. Everyone's heard Everett tell that story one time or another. We've all heard it. Most of us have read about your exploits in the newspaper. I think there was even a dime novel or some such about that stagecoach attack.

"I know you tend to be a lone wolf, Tanner Station. Word's you're an unfriendly sort, but since your family staked out that ranch out on the Salt Fork of the Arkansas, you've not been in trouble that no one can tell on you. Not that I know of. You ain't been arrested. What is the story on you? You a killer like they say? How many notches are there on that Army Colt .45 of yours?"

Tanner's eyes narrowed as the captain asked his questions in his role of judge and, as it now appeared, accuser. The lanky cowboy stood before he spoke. He took his sweet time, rising slowly, his head swiveling as he took in the gallery in the hot room. He gazed at Marie, then to his sister, Avery. Finally, he looked to Everett. His brother-in-law was tight-lipped, his shoulders squared, locked. Tanner looked to Max, and Max shrugged, encouraging him to speak.

"Y'all don't think much of me. That's okay, I don't like any of ya any better," Tanner finally said.

A series of grumbles and growls cascaded over the courtroom, but Mulvaney let it go. The floor belonged to the accused man.

"Y'all should listen to yourselves tell stories about folks. Gossip, gossip, gossip. Heck, I've heard people say I've killed a dozen men, that I'm a murderer and a back-shooter. Folks say I've robbed banks and trains. That I killed that Garinger fella up to Medicine Lodge. You think I can't hear you talk? You wonder why I stand away and don't join in the festivities when you bad talk me when my back is turned?"

Lt. Moore raised a hand, but Mulvaney waved him down before the subordinate officer spoke a word.

"And the things you've said about my wife today," uttered Tanner, his eyes boring holes into the gallery of Jet's citizens, ending with his stare on Lt. Moore. "Well, God offers forgiveness, but I'm not sure I got any grace left in me. Your actions are just self-righteousness. All high and mighty, you are, but then hateful to an Indian woman who never did nothing to you. So I ain't gonna give you what you want today. None of you deserve it. I stand by my woman. I did right by Marie, and she knows that. The rest of you can go straight to Hades. That's all I got to say on it." He sat, his face black with rage and despair.

Avery grimaced and turned her face down away from her brother.

Marie began to cry.

Tanner took his eyes from the dumbfounded audience in front of him. He looked to the captain who would decide his fate. "I said my piece. You do what you got to do."

Mulvaney said, "You made your bed, son. I won't be going easy on you." He turned to the crowd and banged his gavel. "Silence. It seems these proceedings are at an end. It's time for me to be deciding where the chips'll be falling."

The crowd quieted down, except for Marie's soft wail. Tanner closed himself off to it. There was nothing he could do to change those people's minds. They had decided long ago on him. There was no mercy in them.

The captain stood and cleared his throat. But before Mulvaney spoke, one voice intruded. "I need to say something." It wasn't spoken loudly, but everyone heard it.

There are times, it seems, for humans to sense a change. Like when a big thunderstorm is bringing hail and the sky has gone to green. Or when an elder is drawing his or her last breath. Or when the truth hits folks smack dab between the eyes. This was one of those moments. Every eye turned to the voice, and it belonged to Corporal Richard Spaulding.

Spaulding stood. His face was pale. He blinked quickly and a drop of sweat dangled from his nose. "I got something to say. I have to stop things before they go too far. Captain, I had hoped to get out of this situation from the outset with no one knowing I was even at the stable that night. I knew it would go hard on me if I was found to have been off base. I'd been warned by Lt. Moore once before about going gambling afterhours at Joe's. Plus, nobody much knows it, but I was going to the stable pretty much every day to see Marie. To see her and play some cards. But I really just played cards down there so's I could see her. That's why I was there the night of the blizzard. I'd been sweet on her for a while."

Captain Mulvaney sat down, disapproval in his eyes. He nodded to Spaulding to speak.

"Captain, I know I've been disciplined for being off base, and I know I'll bring more trouble on myself for admitting I committed perjury, but the bigger crime would be in not telling the truth on what I saw after the game broke up."

"And what is that, soldier?" Mulvaney asked.

"Captain, it happened just like Tanner Station said. He came on them three, Harris, Wells, and Crups, as they were fixing to rape Marie."

"And you saw this abuse taking place, but yet you stood by?" The captain's voice was fierce. The anger also began to show in his face.

"Yessir. That's why I said nothing. I was ashamed to have seen it all and then be too much of coward to help her. Them three are bad medicine. I'm scared of 'em. Harris is real bad."

"That is a shameful admission, Corporal Spaulding. One unbecoming a soldier who serves under me."

"Yes, sir."

"You were sweet on this woman, but you left her to these jackals?" Captain Mulvaney asked, his fervor causing a quake in his voice.

"Yes, sir, I feel shame, sir. I am ready for any punishment meted out by you, sir. I just do not wish to see these proceedings end in injustice."

Max rose from the table. "I ask that the bailiff take Mr. Harris and Mr. Crups into custody, and they be charged with attempted rape."

Tanner said, "And they smothered Buck Wells. The feather in his mouth tells us that."

Mulvaney stared over at the defendant, not six feet away, who returned his glare, defiantly. "This situation is not yet resolved, Mr. Station. I would recommend you keep quiet."

Tanner nodded. "Yessir." He looked to Marie, who was still crying. Avery had moved to her, and the two hugged like sisters.

Mulvaney turned his attention back to Corporal Spaulding. "You saw Buck Wells manhandling the Indian woman?"

"Yes, he grabbed Marie, had her on the ground. Yes, he did."

"Did Harris or Crups have their hands upon her or say anything to her? Was there any action on their part that would indicate without a doubt the other two also planned to rape Marie Wolf Walker?"

"Without a doubt? No, sir," replied the sergeant. "I expect

Crups and Harris were up to no good, but Tanner Station showed up just in the nick."

Mulvaney nodded and banged the gavel once more. "My decision is as follows: Buck Wells died of injuries he received in the commission of a crime. We are well rid of him. All charges against Mr. Tanner Station are hereby dropped. The court apologizes for the inconvenience to you for the last three days of confinement, Mr. Station."

The captain looked menacingly at Spaulding. "Corporal, we will deal with you privately after these proceedings. Lt. Moore, you'll see me in chambers afterwards."

Then, Captain Mulvaney turned to the defendant. "Go in peace, sir." He banged his gavel. "These proceeding are adjourned."

Tanner nodded his thanks.

The crowd began to talk as one. The crescendo made it impossible to hear anyone.

Tanner stood and stepped close the captain's table. He shook Mulvaney's hand.

Max threw an arm around the tall cowboy's waist.

Together, Max and Tanner waded through the gallery. Most folks who lived in Jet were there, and they liked a good spectacle. They had certainly received one today. They didn't like Tanner Station, but there was no love for Harris and Crups, either.

Those two nasty hombres slunk out the side door, avoiding the crowd.

The mass began to disperse, but Everett and Avery stood beaming, arm-in-arm.

Tanner found his woman and swung Marie around, hoisting her up. He kissed her.

After a bit, Everett walked to the buckboard and brought back both his and Tanner's pistols and holsters.

"Expect we both better wear these. Made some enemies in there today."

"Harris and Crups?" Tanner replied, putting on his weapon. "They were already enemies. We headed home tonight?"

"No, we'll stay 'til the morning. You going to stay with Marie or at Jinny May's with us?"

Tanner looked at him, quizzically. "With Marie, of course."

"She can't come in the boarding house. They got rules agin it. You okay with the stable?"

"Not to worry. Better men than me have slept in one."

Everett laughed. He looked over and saw Avery. She was walking across the pasture in front of the fort toward a solitary figure. It was Richard Spaulding. He held a cigarette and his hands were shaking.

"You did a good thing in there, Richard," Avery said. "A lot of men having lost her would have been bitter. They might have just kept their mouths shut in revenge. You spoke out. Spoke out for good. You told the truth when it counted most."

"It'll cost me my stripes permanent like. Might get drummed out of the cavalry. I'll do some weeks in the stockade for sure. I'll be takin' your brother's place by tonight, I figure."

Avery pursed her mouth. "For doing the right thing? I doubt that. I think Captain Mulvaney will offer some compassion for what you did in saving a man's life today."

Spaulding laughed. "Mrs. Hart, you don't know the Army. Somebody's got to pay for the time wasted today. Lt. Moore was embarrassed to have lost. I'm surprised the bailiff didn't take me into custody before folks left the mess hall with the verdict."

"I hope not," Avery said. "I came over to thank you, to thank you for telling the truth."

Spaulding laughed. He raised his eyebrows with mock surprise. "That's what you think I did, huh? 'Cause it wasn't any such. But if you believed me, well, then if I get drummed out of the calvary, maybe I'll go to Denver and become an actor, Mrs. Hart."

Avery looked at him, confused.

Spaulding tossed his cigarette and ground it out with his heel. "I didn't see anything, Mrs. Hart," Spaulding said. "I didn't see Tanner save Marie. But we all know what really happened that night. Buck Wells, Harris, and Crups were up to evil. They are downright bad to the bone. They'd of killed Marie once they'd had their way with her. I know in my heart that is what would've happened. But I never saw nothin'."

"You lied?"

"Yes, I lied. I could see there in the courtroom that she loves Tanner Station. I spent the whole trial watching her. I love her. Just wasn't bold enough to marry an Injun while I had Army stripes on my sleeve. And Marie knew that. Knew I was weak. She never really cared for me. She never looked at me as anything other than a way to escape her father; Marie needed a way out of a terrible life as a hanger-on outside a no-account fort that won't be here in five years. From a life where her father would sell her when he got tight on funds. I think if I'd of asked her she would have married me to get out. But I knew the ribbing I'd get at the fort. I was a coward." Spaulding shook his head, ruefully. "Look where it got me."

"You lied," Avery said softly, as if trying to take in the fact that the trial had ended well because of falsehoods. She lowered her eyes. "All the same, Richard Spaulding. I thank you. My family owes you a debt. Thank you." She walked back to her family. Her eyes welled tears.

Everett met her as she approached. "What's wrong? What'd he say to you?"

"Oh, he just wished Marie and Tanner well. He had feelings for her, you know."

Everett nodded. "But the look on your face as you walked back?"

"I'm just tired. The stress of this trial is finally getting to me. And I miss the girls."

Everett smiled and put his arm around his wife. He looked to Max shaking hands with well-wishers as folks mounted up and headed back to their farms. Max might become the most popular man in the territory after today, but soon the crowd got sparse. Everyone was still nervous about being out at night after the deep freeze.

They soon mounted up and left Jet behind, hoping to get home 'fore dark.

Everett watched Tanner with his long arm wrapped around Marie's waist. Everett said to his wife, "I'll have us to the girls before sundown tomorrow."

Avery smiled at him, but there was sadness in her heart. "Deal," she said. As she said it, Avery wondered about deals and truth and love. The world was a much more wicked place, she decided, than she'd ever have believed before today.

Darkness
Lawrence, Kansas
1965

Lillian Fairchild held a Christmas party on the Saturday after finals were over. The first semester had been a big success for her at Haskell. She'd worked an inordinate number of hours, so much so she worried about the children being left on their own. To their credit, they both thrived in the new environment. For the first times in their three lives, they all fit in at their current locale. Both children had friends and were thriving. Lil found herself sleeping well for the first time in years. Her face, having been stretched thin with stress in her marriage with Henry, seemed to relax in his absence. Her children were graced now with her smiles.

Career moves are often as not about being in the right place at the right time. America in general and Lawrence, Kansas, in particular, were in the beginnings of institutional change, societal change, and political change. With those changes came new voices. The term "Native American" just was beginning to be adopted, and those "Indians" were demanding a seat at the table.

Lillian, it just so happened, was standing at the vestibule when the door was unlocked for Native Americans. A white woman who represented those with brown skin, she made the most of the offers to sit on boards or committees with the city and with the college. And once in the door, Lil worked hard for the betterment of those she represented. People began to notice her within months of her arrival. She was effective, unassuming, and attractive. She soon had offers at the best academic soirees. Official functions were many, but she declined most dinner invitations. She was still a little shy and she was technically still a married woman, albeit one waiting her divorce decree on the ground of abandonment. For now, her life was full. It was enough. She was happy. Lillian had found a home.

Lillian's Christmas party, scheduled for December 12th, was her first at her family's new home. It also happened to be the day Lillian also got her last name back; she was once again a Hart, Lillian Hart. Her divorce was final. Lil wished she could also change the children's names. She no longer found any charm in Henry's last name or in anything about him. The children were both still Fairchilds, but she did not have the ability to change that.

Henry's whereabouts were still unknown. Even if found, Henry would have to agree to relinquish his rights to both Chris and Piper, and there was small chance of that occurring. Her husband would be charged, if apprehended for his part in the robbery; the sentence to be given was fifteen years to life, but the clock would not start running until his apprehension, conviction, and imprisonment.

For now, the children would continue with their father's name. It was something Lil worried about sometimes at night, but the law was clear. Unless Henry was captured, or Lillian attempted to have her ex-husband declared dead, she had no legal ability to change her children's names. With no other options, Lillian decided Chris and Piper could decide for themselves what name to take when they reached adulthood. She hoped some day they would abandon the Fairchild name.

All three were glad for a semester completed in entirety. That stability alone was cause for celebration. The semester was over, and the family was beginning a four-week holiday, half of which they would spend in Oklahoma. Chris was ecstatic to be returning to the farm. He loved it there, even in winter. He enjoyed riding to the pasture to throw hay off the back of the pickup in the morning while the hills were still purple and the steam from his breath joined the cloud of the herd's in the dawn chill. He liked his grandfather's easy silence. It matched his own. Chris was never one to make much conversation. Small talk was an art lost to him, so the farm was an ideal setting. Jeff Hart was not a talkative man, and certainly not one so early in the morning. Chris could not wait for a full two weeks at Jeff's side.

For Piper, the idea of two weeks on the farm did not give her joyous thoughts. She kept a busy social schedule as a high school junior. She also had a boyfriend who had taken her to the snowball. The glint of first love was in her eyes, and the thought of two weeks away at the farm was an eternity to her.

However, the trip to the farm was for next week. This night was one for celebration. All three had accomplishments. Piper had a boyfriend and was very popular at school. Chris had performed in the fall play, once again as a child, this time as Tiny Tim in *A Christmas Carol*. He also lettered in debate with Patrick as his partner. Lillian had completed her first term in her Ph.D. program.

Patrick and Chris were the most unlikely pair to ever letter at Lawrence High. Chris was only twelve and barely five foot tall. Patrick was an East Coast elitist with his nose out of joint toward all things Midwestern. They were certainly an odd couple.

Chris invited Patrick to the party, naturally, but he also invited Tate Laughlin. It made the boy nervous. It would be the first time his two friends ever met. For Chris, and even for Lil, those two guests were the biggest cause for celebration in the family. Chris's integration into Lawrence and to high school life had been the family's biggest worry, and he had two real friends.

Upon arrival and introductions, Patrick was amazed to learn that Chris and Tate Laughlin had been meeting for an hour or two every Thursday for two months to discuss revolutionary literature, now supplemented by Lillian's more balanced selections. Patrick thought his East Coast cred made him the radical par excellence at LHS, and it turned out his twelve-year-old debate partner was the true counterculture warrior. Patrick could not wait to pull Chris aside after the boy had introduced him to Tate.

"Chris, I can't believe you didn't tell me about this Laughlin guy. You know Tate Laughlin is like the next tier down from guys like Jerry Rubin and Tom Hayden? He's been mentioned in *The Village Voice*. He's like the Indian version of Bobby Seals."

"Native American."

"Yeah, yeah, you know what I mean."

Chris nodded but was only vaguely aware of Rubin and Hayden. He replied with his new cool, "Yeah, I knew all that. I was just keeping it low-key."

Later, Tate sat at the kitchen table with Patrick, Chris, and Lillian. They all drank cider and ate pumpkin cake. "You know, Chris," Tate said, "you have just about the hippest mom in the world. I mean, when I showed up for work that day and she asked to speak to me about giving you books to read, I thought I was going to get chewed out; maybe lose my work study! Something, anyway, but then she hands me the JFK book to read. Says she'll pick the book every other week. That was cool, man. Super cool."

Lillian raised a finger. She stood and moved to the Christmas tree in full view of the kitchen and the three's rapt attention. She brought three wrapped packages and handed them to Tate, Patrick, and Chris. "Go ahead," she said, "open them."

Each present was the same. A hardcover book. *Catch 22* by Joseph Heller.

Tate Laughlin smiled a crooked smile.

Lillian raised an eyebrow. "You've read it?"

"No, just heard about it."

"It's about the insanity of war. I'm afraid all of you will be facing war. Vietnam is coming at America like it's a train and we're in a tunnel."

And at that moment, Patrick joined the reading club.

On the morning of March 8, 1965, the weather was cold, and it was spitting snow as if winter bitterly disagreed with leaving. Patrick met Chris in the hallway between classes.

"Did you hear about the sit-in?" Patrick asked. His hair was now in full Beatles' phase. He looked a bit like a chubby Ringo.

"What's a sit-in?"

"It's where a bunch of students just sit down on the floor to protest something unjust. It's happening on campus today."

Chris wasn't following. "At Haskell?"

Patrick snorted. "No, on *campus*. Do you think Tate will be there?"

Chris nodded yes. If there was a counterculture event in this city, Tate would be there.

The two boys were among the first in the city to know much about the demonstration, as they took the time to read the article in the afternoon printing before they rolled the newspapers for their route. The newspaper's editorial board was scandalized by the sit-in. City leaders complained vigorously. An editorial denounced it. Chris thought the sit-in was cool. It didn't seem like that big of deal that the city fathers should be all up in arms about it.

The newspaper reported the following: At 10:30 that morning, 150 supporters of the Lawrence Civil Rights Council, including both black and white students, gathered outside the chancellor's office. The students were there to protest the university's role in racial discrimination in campus housing and approved organizations, like fraternities and sororities. The students did nothing too outrageous. Most simply sat on the floor completing homework.

Many came and went during the day as they left to go to class or lunch, but for everyone who left, another arrived. Several carried signs which they leaned against the wall during their sit-in protest. The students listed grievances for which they wanted university action. The worst behavior seemed to be the chanting of, "Hell, no! We won't go." Protestors refused to leave and planned on sleeping in the hall until a meeting with the administration was scheduled and the seven issues addressed. The article had gone to press before the event had been resolved.

When Chris arrived home at dusk from delivering newspapers,

he turned on the TV, hoping for an update on the sit-in. But there was nothing and the house was quiet. Not even Piper was home. Soon, however, he saw headlights pull into the driveway. It was his mom's car. She stopped before the garage, and both she and Tate Laughlin emerged from the vehicle.

As Tate entered, Chris stood before his hero. "Were you at the sit-in today, Tate?"

Lillian sighed. "Tell him. I'll get some dinner going." She left the two in the living room.

Tate looked more weary than usual. His lean face had a tiny bit of a stubble at his chin. His black flag of hair fell loosely behind a red kerchief. He wore a black leather jacket, jeans, and moccasins. The Cheyenne fell back to the couch.

Chris sat facing him. "What happened? Were you there?"

"Yeah, I was there. I was there pretty much the whole day. And for the most part, nothing happened. I read the Hurston book for this week from front to back. Then, a whole lot of nothing happened until 4:30, when the building closed."

This week's selection was Zora Neale Hurston's *Their Eyes Were Watching God*. Chris had finished it last weekend, but he didn't want to talk books right now.

"What happened when they went to close the building?"

Lillian entered. "By the time happy hour arrived, four hundred students were blocking the halls in the administration building. The police arrested them all and loaded them on buses. It filled up both the city and county jails. I went looking for Tate at the city jail and had to call the sheriff's department to find our intrepid hero. I posted his bond and brought him home. That's all the news that fit to print."

"Except a cop slapped me." Tate leaned his face toward Chris for inspection.

"Not in front of anyone," interjected Lillian. "He'll deny it."

"How much was Tate's bond, Mom?"

"Only $25.00. I should have left him in until Rev. Henning of St.

Luke's Episcopal arranged for bail for all the rest, but I took pity on the fool."

"Thanks for that," Tate said, "but this ain't over. There's a sing-in tonight in front of the chancellor's house. I need to get down there."

Lillian shook her head, vehemently. "No, you don't. I will have to defend your scholarship to the Board of Trustees at the institute's monthly meeting Friday. I want them to know you regret your actions and stayed home after the first incident."

Tate laughed. "I don't regret anything, except not getting a fist to that cop."

"Oh, Mom, can I go? I mean, just to watch? I'd stay across the street," Chris begged.

Lillian's eyes flashed anger at the young Native American man before her. Her eyes turned slowly from Tate Laughlin to Chris. "No, nobody is going anywhere this evening. It could be dangerous. Big crowds with everyone's stirred-up emotions. Emotional contagion, it's called in sociology. Look it up." She looked to Tate. "It's bad medicine. Going down there is not a good idea" she paused, "for anyone." Lil glared at Tate.

He met her gaze for a moment but could not meet her intensity. Tate looked to the floor and rubbed the red mark on his face. He was silent while he thought out his words.

Chris watched his friend's face. He knew Tate's deliberative pauses.

Then, Tate stood and spoke. "I'm going, Miss Hart. You don't have no say in stopping me. It's just something I got to do. I was in on the start of it. I got to be there for the duration."

Lillian drew her lips into a line. Finally, she spoke, "I can't take you down there. Haskell's board won't stand for that. Just stay. Stay for pancakes and bacon. Breakfast for supper."

"I *can* stay for that," Tate laughed. "Then, maybe you can drop me on Massachusetts. I need to get a couple things at the grocery store before I head back to Haskell."

"Short walk up the hill from the store to the sing-in."

"Far enough away for deniability. You'll have taken me to the grocery store."

Lillian nodded and then walked into the kitchen without speaking.

Chris watched his mother in the kitchen. He'd never seen her lose an argument before.

Oklahoma Territory
Spring, 1899

Captain Mulvaney's words, *"Go in peace, sir"* seemed to be a good omen for Tanner and Marie, who returned to their tiny home just north of the Salt Fork River.

Carson lit out after Tanner and Marie's return. The tension between the two brothers was palpable, but they did not argue. The relationship was past that now. They had no words for each other and nothing to give. Tanner was steadfast in his love and loyalty to Marie, and Carson could not accept his brother's marriage to a redskin. Their kinship was at an impasse, and with Marie installed with Tanner at the north house, Carson felt he had no home, not at the north homestead and not with Everett, Avery, and the three girls returning to the main house.

The family all agreed Carson and Renfro would stay at the main house until good weather when they would build a bunkhouse. The truth was, though, they didn't really fit in the main house, not with the family of five there. It was not a workable situation. Carson, who considered, rightly or not, that one third of the ranch belonged to him, resented he should live with the hired man, anyway, so thoughts of residing in the bunkhouse rankled. Plus, the dug-out and its stable were both uninhabitable after having cattle closed inside them for four days and nights. It had been deemed best to push the hillside walls down from which they'd been cut. Renfro volunteered for that duty.

By spring, little remained of the eastern structures. Soon, prairie grass sprouts appeared on the soil where the dugouts had once been, erasing their history. The men reclaimed the tin roofs and used them for the chicken coop and the main house's barn.

Renfro, now back to work, spent his time out of the way of

family squabbles. He cared for the herd, nourishing it back to health.

Finally, after stops and starts, spring arrived. After the deep snows, the prairie turned emerald green. The cattle were happy in the plentiful grass, but calving was light, as few pregnant cows made it through the blizzard. Everett and Tanner spent a good bit of their time building the bunkhouse for Renfro, who was receiving the best treatment of any hired hand in the territory. Carson worked his share but chose to camp near the herd in a pup tent, roaming to God knows where when he could be spared. He spent time indoors with the family only in the worst of spring rains. Life proceeded. The family felt as if God had granted them a reprieve as both the blizzard and the trial had left them mostly unscathed. Plans were for Autumn to attend the new school building at Rose Hill in the fall.

Life seemed good. In fact, things went easy like. Days became routine, but by summer, things were not the same between Avery and Everett. The husband did not know why his wife had cooled to him, but one night after dinner with the girls asleep, the couple, married now nearly ten years, walked out onto the grassland south of the house. An owl called in the distance, and the moon bathed the mesas across the river in a peach-colored glow.

"Avery," Everett said, taking his wife's hand, "what is wrong?" His voice was low, and his face showed concern. Lines furrowed his brow. "You've had a burr under your saddle for a month. Something is wrong. What is it?"

Avery took her hand from his. She turned her face to the evening wind but said nothing. Everett knew the look. Avery was not saying nothing was wrong. She was saying she didn't want to get into it. Her silence sent a strong message.

Avery was still a handsome woman, beautiful in fact. In truth, her husband still found her desirable. He took her hand, but she pulled away.

Avery hesitated, but then turned to him. Confrontation was at hand. Before she spoke, her hair caught the breeze and it swept from her neck. "I spent a goodly amount of time in Alva these last months after the blizzard. We've been in town nearly every Saturday night and Sunday for church. And I met most of the people in town. I mean, most of the people worth meeting. Not those who just move on."

"You've met someone? A man?"

"No. I mean, yes, but not in the way, you're thinking. You really believe I could be disloyal to you, Everett Hart? Unfaithful? I would never do that. But I did meet a man. Doyle Bremmer, the attorney. You know him?"

Everett flushed. Instantly, he knew where the conversation was going. He did not like it, either. The rancher merely nodded.

"Oh, yes, yes you do," Avery said, bitterness in her voice. "Well, I do, too. I met him one Sunday after church when you went to cut a deal on Anthem Song with some mare. Mr. Bremmer told me quite the story. It seems the morning after Tanner's arrest, with my brother in the stockade up in Jet, you sent a telegram to Mr. Bremmer from the fort. I didn't know you'd been trying to get Bremmer to utilize your new colt for stud."

"Avery," he interjected.

Everett's wife overrode his objection with a strident tone. Avery's fury steadied to a cold iron tenor. "Mr. Bremmer told me you asked him in your telegram to represent Tanner in his murder trial, that you needed him in Jet the very next day."

"Darling, you're only getting his side."

"Oh, I'll let you tell your side in a moment. You know what Mr. Bremmer told me? He said he would be glad to represent Tanner, but he wanted Anthem in payment. He said he wired you with the proposed payment of the colt, and you wired that you would defend him yourself. Said Tanner wasn't worth that horse. That's what he said you told him. Those exact words."

"Bremmer made an unreasonable request. He knew I was over a barrel. We didn't have any money. The ranch had just lost more than forty head of cattle a couple weeks before. Bremmer was taking advantage of the situation. It was just the first round of negotiations."

"Did you say Tanner's life was not worth that horse?"

Everett was not a good liar. He hem-hawed. "I said words to that effect, I guess..."

"You gambled my brother's life for a horse." Her voice was trembling with anger. Everett had never seen such rage in her. It was a quiet rage, but it had heft. Her face scared him. He felt a tremor in the earth. A new force. He did not know where it would take them.

"But it all worked out," Everett said, shrugging. He reached to take his wife's arm, but Avery stepped back. His arm was left there dangling, soliciting solace that would not come.

"You admit it?" Avery almost hissed her words. Her volume stayed low, so Renfro did not hear from where he sat on the front porch whittling at a willow stick. In her, she felt such emptiness. Avery knew her brother would have been found guilty if not for Richard Spaulding's lies. Her husband and his love for that precious horse would have allowed it to happen.

"You make it sound worse than it was," Everett argued. "Anthem is a way for us, you and me and the girls, to get ahead. That lawyer sharpie was trying to take our future away."

"My brother was falsely accused of murder, and you chose a horse over him."

"You shouldn't look at it that way. I put our family first. That's my job."

Avery smiled, grimly. "Oh, I know how I'll look at it; that's for sure. I asked Mr. Bremmer to keep those negotiations between the three of us. I expect he will remain silent, as I told him we would use him for our legal remedies, should we need them in the future. I would not want Tanner to hear you valued that horse more than him. Carson, either, although I don't think my little brother's opinion of you could be much lower, but it would break Max's heart. You know he feels he failed Tanner in representing him. Your father believes Tanner would have been hanged, if not for Richard Spaulding's…" she searched for the word, "er, confession."

Avery knew she would never tell anyone of Spaulding's revelation that he had lied to save Tanner. She didn't know what impact that knowledge would have on Tanner's freedom, but she was sure Captain Mulvaney's knowing would not be good for either Tanner or Spaulding. She was a woman with secrets, and no one could wrest them from her. Some secrets can never be shared, she decided. For a woman of faith, keeping secrets locked away soured within her.

"Avery," Everett begged, "let's not stay mad at one another. It won't be good for the girls."

Avery, a practical woman, nodded. "I won't be mad, Everett. I just won't forget."

She walked away with those words, and he let her go. Everett was correct that the horse, Anthem, would make the family financially secure. Indeed, the horse paid for himself within the first two years. For nearly a decade after that, the family made a decent income from the stallion.

To Avery, it was bittersweet. The stud fees were blood money to her. Thirty pieces of silver year after year. But she kept her tongue. If she was anything, Avery was true to her word. She never spoke of the matter again, even when, on occasion, Everett tried to bring their conflict to the fore. Avery now realized with a heartsick lurch how her husband measured the world, how low people ranked with him, and how everything came after the ranch. She didn't like it. The cut in his character was so deep that the chasm between them could not heal. Things would never be quite the same. Later, she would come to believe that conversation was the day she fell out of love with her husband.

For all the difficulties arising in Everett's and Avery's relationship, Marie and Tanner spent that winter and spring in an extended honeymoon of sorts. It was a life with ritualistic consistency. Tanner worked from dawn to dusk, returning to the house to wash up as the sun faded behind the cottonwoods to the west of the house. Marie would have spent the day cooking, cleaning, and bettering the homestead. She cleared out ground and turned the soil for a large garden. She fixed a fence where they could maybe get goats or maybe a piglet come summer. She mucked out the stable each morning. Each day the northern homestead looked better and better.

Life on the Salt Fork Station ranch went on. In the evenings, both tired from their labors, Tanner and Marie would lay in bed together and speak of their day, their plans, and their dreams. Tanner would always look at these days as the very best of his life. And they would last quite some time, nearly a decade in fact. That is, before change came. Blessings during that period were many and significant. For in the spring of 1900, the two welcomed their first child into the world, a boy whom they named Gabriel Joseph Station.

Everett and Avery also added a boy to the family, despite their differences. Robert Jefferson Hart, but called Jeff, was born only two weeks after Gabriel's arrival. The two infants were healthy. Farm life suited them, and the two were steadfast friends from the cradle.

Gabriel, as they grew, was a lean string bean of a boy. He was dark, but not as dark as his mother. His personality was reflective, like his father's. He was a thoughtful son. Spending much time alone at the northern homestead as an only child, Gabriel loved his time at the Hart home, surrounded by Jeff and his three sisters.

On the other side of the coin, Jeff, the baby of the family, longed each day for Gabe to come visit to give him relief from the three girls. As soon as either could ride, they spent their days together, learning the ranch's every mysterious nook and cranny. Soon, they were assigned chores, like the girls, who treated not just Jeff, but his cousin, Gabe, as their two little brothers.

One day, the two boys, Jeff and Gabe, were chasing chickens across the farmyard. Marie was peeling potatoes, and Tanner, back from the pasture at bit early, took a turn at hoeing weeds.

But then it happened; boys tend to push things too far. Some learn moderation, some never do. Gabe, racing on foot through the barnyard, tripped as he harassed a rooster, grabbing at his tail feathers. The boy tumbled, scraping a knee. The sight of blood mixed with red dirt startled the boys. Gabe began to cry. He ran to his mother.

Tanner turned at the ruckus and set down the hoe. He ambled across the sizable garden toward his son and nephew. He heard Marie talking to their child.

"Tut-tut," she said, "Gabriel, it's just a scrape. Nothing that every boy who ever ran hasn't had one time or another." She patted his head. "Now, stop your crying. It ain't nothing bad." Marie dipped her dress hem in the potato water of her pail. With a ginger touch, the bronze-skinned woman dabbed dirt off the wound until it was clean. With the blood and gravel wiped away, the boy no longer cried.

Tanner watched from a short distance.

"Gabriel, my son," she said, smiling, "I have found that scar tissue makes for personality. Life is hard. It is the healing from our wounds that makes the Cherokee strong. You will be stronger when your knee heals, and it will heal very fast. Now, go finish your chores before dinner. You've run wild long enough."

Tanner approached his wife as the boys headed to the barn to tend to the horses. He took her hands. "Scar tissue makes for personality?"

"I could not think of the English word. In Cherokee, it would be *nu-li-ni-gv-gv.* It means strength or good character."

Tanner smiled. "When you said scars cause personality, it took me back a step, Seems I might be better at conversation by now if that was the case. Character, now that makes more sense."

Yes," Marie replied, pertly. "Do you not agree?"

"Let's raise our boy to have some of that *nu-li-ni-gv-gv,*" Tanner said, stumbling over the word.

They both laughed. Then, Tanner went back to his garden, and Marie fixed supper.

Despite the tranquility of those years with the two couples and their children, things were not as happy for Carson. Even after the bunkhouse was completed and he had a small bedroom with a shared living room with Renfro, he felt slighted. He deserved more respect. He was entitled to a third of the ranch's assets. He let the family know. Everett chuckled, saying in response, "Thirty-three percent of our cash reserves wouldn't get you a dinner in Alva, boy."

Carson often disappeared during the spring and summer of that first year after the birth of the boys. After that, he would leave during the cold months. Upon his return, Carson would tell the family of his travels in New Mexican Territory and even into Old Mexico itself. His eyes would glow in happiness telling his tales. Remembering life down south, though, seemed to be the only time he was happy at the Salt Fork Stations.

Living with Renfro was an insult he could not bear. His unhappiness spilled over, and finally it was Avery who gave him an ultimatum. Carson needed to straighten up or leave for good. His continual grumblings were bad for the children, and the children were the priority. Carson sneered in response and said give him his share and he'd leave tomorrow. Tanner heard the conversation, left the family dinner, and rode home. He returned with ninety dollars, all that he had saved.

"Iffin' you take two horses, you can be back to warm weather a'-fore Christmas. I hope you find yourself a pretty senorita." Tanner handed Carson the wad of cash, most of it in singles.

Carson, though ashamed, took the money, nodded, and stuffed the cash in his pocket. He packed to leave before the dawn.

Renfro lay in his warm bed in the other room. His new dog slept at his feet. Renfro hushed it as he heard Carson leave the bunkhouse. The latch on the door clicked on his way out.

"Shush, Brew buddy," he said to the animal. "You settle down, dawg. That's just a goose headed south for the winter."

Unveiled
Lawrence, Kansas
April 20, 1970

More than five years had passed since that first Christmas party at their new house in Lawrence. Chris was now in his second year at the University of Kansas. Five years had passed since the sit-in. Things had changed. After the Civil Rights Act of 1964 passed, Democratic racists had left the party and become Nixon Republicans. Tricky Dicky changed his platform to adopt a "southern strategy" in Orwellian fashion. The music was rock-and-roll. The country's social scene was directed by America's youth. Movies were filled with ambivalent endings and anti-heroes. The news was filled with Vietnam. Hair was long. Time was short. The university campus classrooms often wafted ever so slightly of the scent of marijuana smoke lingering on student clothing. Republicans called for the end of college deferments for the draft. Take those hippies to war! The chasm between the establishment and America's youth had fissured. "Say hey, what's that sound? Everybody look what's going down!" sang Buffalo Springfield. Battlelines were indeed being drawn.

The city of Lawrence had changed a great deal, too, but Chris's world was much the same. He was still in school, albeit now the University of Kansas, not Lawrence High. He studied law but chose not to participate in college debate. He'd been offered a scholarship after winning the state championship as a senior. And that first-place finish was a story in itself.

In his junior year, Chris teamed with Patrick Lakke for the third year. Patrick and Chris were undefeated throughout the season, but throughout each week and each tournament, Patrick's demeanor, dress, and hair grew more and more defiant. He seemed to be daring someone to attack his politics or his dress. Finally, in the state finals against a terrific team from the Catholic boys' school in Hays, the two lost. Chris had since reexamined the loss in his mind.

He knew they had won on fact, evidence, and their ability to apply their arguments. It was on style the three judges awarded the win to the opposition. Short hair, conservative values, and bow ties still carried weight in Kansas.

Patrick graduated and chose Columbia University in faraway New York. Saying goodbye to his first real friend had been difficult for Chris. Patrick could not wait to leave. That left Chris, perhaps the best debater in the state, without a partner for his senior year. However, since he was only fifteen, Chris was still not a likely match for the other young men on the team. A week into school, he was approached by Katie Mills, likewise fifteen, but just a sophomore. She was a petite blonde with unfashionable bangs. Her smile made up for any detriments.

"Chris," she said, "let's be partners. You're the best and being your partner in my first year would be a challenge, I admit. It will take work on my part and coaching on yours, but it might work. I'm a quick study. I work hard. You can teach me the tricks. It would be fun, wouldn't it, to be two fifteen-year-olds whopping those senior boys with their prep school ties?"

Chris smiled at the mental picture she gave him. He agreed with a grin.

The two debaters worked very well as teammates, and while Chris had a bit of a crush on her, Katie kept space enough to make sure that no romance would ruin their partnership. Katie prepped more than Patrick ever did. That is not to say Chris was lazy. No, he was well-prepared and memorized his openings and lots of his evidence. Chris thought he was the master of evidence, but Katie bested him on some occasions. Soon, they became the favorites to win their region of the state. Chris was a solid presenter, earnest and true. Believable. Katie turned out to have a rapier tongue. She would cut opponents' mistakes into gaping holes. Her blonde hair was actually a lion's mane. Often after Katie's first interrogatory, the decision was *fait accompli*. Together, despite their skilled and precise presentations, people's first comment was how cute a couple they were. "Aren't they just darling? So smart? So young!"

Chris hated that part of it; in some ways, they were a carnival attraction. It was, however, hard to argue with their success. After the season, his senior year, ended in a championship, scholarship offers from college forensic teams started arriving.

Once he mentioned it to his mother. "Mother," he said, "do you know Patrick was a superior partner to me than Katie?"

Lillian raised an eyebrow and filled a coffee up. "Because she's a girl?"

Chris looked shocked. "No, not at all. Patrick was superior at debate, but he came across as rude. Like a know-it-all. People didn't like that. But the thing was, he was!"

Lil nodded. "It's all about how the message is delivered."

"Yeah," Chris said, "I get that. Katie isn't as good as Patrick, but people could accept her packaging more easily."

Lillian raised her eyebrow and creased a smile across her lip.

"I didn't mean her body."

Lillian smiled. "I think I get where you're going."

"I've been thinking about it." the boy continued. "Patrick was deeper than Katie. Katie has all the evidence. All the right lines, all the take-downs and she has them so she can access them in a second, but when I asked her feelings about our debate topics, she didn't have any."

"She is only fifteen."

"I'm only fifteen."

Lillian laughed. "Hardly. You might be the oldest soul I've ever met."

"What does that mean?"

She smiled. "Give Katie time. She doesn't have to have it all figured out as a sophomore. You didn't. Look who helped you along the way. Two amazing teachers, Patrick Lakke and Tate Laughlin. She certainly wouldn't have the guidance you had."

Chris considered that. "Do I tell her?"

"Tell her what?"

"That to take the next step, she needs to not only be able to debate about topics, but she needs to have a position on them herself. She has to feel. Even if she isn't arguing that side. For her, it is always just intellectual…" he paused, "maneuvering."

"You want to tell Katie Mills, who just won the state championship in debate, as a sophomore, that she's shallow," Lillian raised an eyebrow. "I think that might go badly."

It was Chris's turn to laugh. "You're right. I'll give her time."

"Big of you, senior man."

Tate Laughlin graduated from KU with a degree in political science in the spring of 1968. Chris saw him occasionally after that, but Tate moved in much different circles these days. He was rumored to be a member of the SDS, Students for a Democratic Society. But the SDS, more commonly called the Weathermen, based on the Bob Dylan lyric, "You don't need to be a weatherman to tell which way the wind blows," were considered provocateurs and rabble-rousers. There had been violence attributed to the Weathermen.

Tate, upon arrival to any city with a protest planned, was routinely stopped, frisked, and occasionally brought in for questioning before any crime even occurred. His face was routinely printed on police handbills. In turn, Tate routinely called police officers "Custer," and his reputation with the Lawrence PD was very bad. Very bad, indeed.

It went from bad to worse in the summer of 1968. It was August, and the eyes of the country, if not the world, were on Chicago and the Democratic Convention. It was there during the riots between police and the Yippies the world got a good look at Tate Laughlin. As the delegates voted inside the International Amphitheater adjacent to the Union Stock Yards, the national news organizations moved their cameras to the *battle royale* taking place at the Conrad Hilton. There the police rioted, although the fact was disputed by Chicago's city officials.

Hand-to-hand combat between the hippies and the police ensued. Tear gas cannisters flooded the streets with smoke, and in one particularly memorable scene, a young Native American rushed toward a fresh tear gas cannister roiling smoke. He grabbed it in full view of the CBS cameras, garnering comments on the nightly news from Walter Cronkite. Taking three running leaps, Tate, ponytails flying, hurled the gas cannister back at the police. His face is very visible, lit for the moment. Lips curled, eyes wild. Curated in a single iconic photo for all time.

Andy Warhol would have said in that moment Tate Laughlin had his fifteen minutes of fame, or infamy. Both the local newspapers and television stations mentioned him by name constantly. While Jerry Rubin, Abbie Hoffman, Tom Hayden, Bobby Seale, and the others stood trial as the Chicago Seven, Tate Laughlin, Lawrence's hometown boy, was declared a renegade on the run. Tate Laughlin was Lawrence's original angry young man.

During the fall of '68, Tate returned to Lawrence, and Chris noted a change in his friend. Tate was now a man. He was harder, his body leaner, his eyes darker and his mood less ambivalent. Less joyful. Tate was headed down a dark tunnel. It made the boy upset, but Chris could not see what he could do to help. Tate believed so deeply in the cause. Even if Chris disagreed with Tate's assessment of the Vietnam War, and he didn't, it was hard to dismiss the body counts on each night's evening news. America's young men had become cannon fodder.

And it's one, two, three,
What are we fighting for?
Don't ask me, I don't give a damn,
Next stop is Vietnam…

The two met at Lil's kitchen table and spoke of old books they had read, but things were not the same. Laughlin did not even stay at the house long enough for Lillian to get home from work. The war had come between them. Time was short and Tate Laughlin had to get back to the front.

A year later, Tate showed up again on April 20th. It was 1970 and the new decade started with the same war. Chris was studying at the table when a car horn bleated in the driveway. It was not yet noon that day, but Tate carried a six pack of Coors beer under his arm as he stepped out of a beat-to-hell paneled station wagon. The Cheyenne warrior, and that is the first description that came to Chris's mind, greeted him with a wide grin. Tate wore a blue U.S. cavalry shirt stuffed into bell bottoms. He wore lace-up boots. His hair was not braided and was the longest that Chris had seen on his friend.

"Happy belated. You're eighteen now. Old enough to drink beer."

"Just almost."

"Almost is close enough."

Chris laughed. Perhaps the old Tate was back. The pre-law student waved his friend inside, and they ate lunch while catching up. Chris made them baloney sandwiches with mayo. They ate Hydrox cookies, both claiming they were better than Oreos. It was like old times.

Tate looked at him across the table. "What's with the hair?"

Chris frowned. "My hair's the same."

"That's what I'm talking about. Time to let your freak flag fly! Girls dig it."

Chris smiled. "Law firms don't. I'm looking for an internship to help pay for the next couple of years. I can be a social warrior on the inside, Tate. But only after I get inside."

Tate nodded, smiling. After a time, the Cheyenne opened his second beer and shared the stories of his travels: San Francisco, New York, and of course, his infamous moment in Chicago. He also mentioned his notoriety. He'd been interviewed by *The Village Voice, The San Francisco Rag*, and *The Chicago Seed*.

"Oh," Tate said, "I almost forgot, I saw Patrick."

"You did?"

"Yeah."

"How is he?"

"Good, man, and his hair is really long. Maybe longer than

mine. He's got it stuck behind his ears in this Che Guevara hat. He's gone, man. Totally gone. In law school, too. But he's a total freak. Dresses like he's in a rock band, plans to ace the bar exam next year."

Chris laughed. "You know he'll do that."

Tate nodded. That was a no doubter. But soon, the conversation stalled like six months before. Tate seemed lost in his thoughts. Something seemed to be bothering him.

"What's wrong?" Chris asked.

"Nothing, man," answered Tate. "Things are just heavy. Real heavy."

Chris spoke to his friend. "Tate, why are you doing all this? You've graduated. You wanted to go to grad school. To become a professor. What's your plan? You can't just absorb all that knowledge and not use it. Demonstrating is not a full-time job. Or at least it shouldn't be."

"We shouldn't be in a full-time war. You know, man. Twelve thousand American kids died last year over there. For what?"

"For nothing," Chris answered.

"I'm in for the duration. We got to end it. And I am using all that knowledge I got in class, using it against the man. Mainly, I'm using the information I got from the books we read. Here's something I learned: Isaac Newton said, 'For every action, there is an equal and opposite reaction.' Right?"

"Yes,"

"Fascists acting out. Me and the Weathermen are reacting the hell back."

"You're a Weatherman?"

Tate smiled. "I didn't say that exactly."

"Didn't say you weren't. Why join the Weathermen?"

"Walter Cronkite already messed up my resume. Why not?" Tate raised an eyebrow.

"What does being in the SDS get you? Besides a rap sheet." Chris was livid.

Tate rubbed his neck, ignoring Chris's question. He formed his words slowly. "I'm an outside agitator these days, at least according to the Lawrence Police. I became a radical here in this city, but according to my arrest report, I'm from the Northern Cheyenne Reservation. Hometown, Lame Deer, Montana." He smiled, sadly. "I was born there, I guess. Not sure where I'd say my home was if someone asked me right now."

Chris, without hesitation, said, "Here."

Tate looked to Chris. "Mind if we go out on the back stoop? I want to smoke a cigarette."

Outside, the Cheyenne warrior offered a cigarette to the boy, but Chris refused. Patrick once got him to try one, but even menthol tasted bad to him. Chris just didn't like them.

After lighting up, Tate offered a question. "You ever been around tear gas?" A pause. "I guess not. Well, it burns your eyes, of course, but that's not the worst part. It gets in your skin, I mean, for days. You itch, like a chemical itch you can't wash away. And of course, in lock-up, the pigs are not big on letting you wash up."

"That must be horrible."

"My skin burned for all three days I was in stir in Chicago."

"I'm sorry. Those cops were out of control. Everybody says so."

"I'm not sure everybody."

"Was it bad?"

"I've seen worse." Tate rubbed out his cigarette. "I've seen cops act worse."

Chris went inside and poured them both glasses of iced tea. He ignored the beer on the table. He thought Tate's mood called for something non-alcoholic. Chris remembered Tate liked lots of sugar in his tea. He returned, and Tate had lit another cigarette.

Laughlin took the drink and smiled. "You're a good friend, Chris."

"You, too, Tate."

"I can't stay long. I have to go agitate on campus this afternoon."

Chris nodded. "I heard there was a demonstration. Can't go. I have calculus."

The Indian laughed. "Different strokes, eh?'

Then they sat in silence for a while dwelling on their different paths.

When Tate left a half hour later, Chris felt ancient, though he was just turning short of turning eighteen. He stood on the porch, feeling old as Father Time as the clock struck noon in his mother's house. He watched his friend walk toward that beater jalopy.

Tate waved in leaving, and later Chris wished he'd walked Tate to his car. The weight of the world was in the air. Things had been going badly for Tate Laughlin. Chris felt they were to become worse. Chris wished he could do something for Tate. He did not have to wait long.

That afternoon, Chris attended his calc class and then came back to his room to study. The house was empty. Piper was attending her end-of-year get-together with the KU cheerleading squad, so he knew she wouldn't be home. Lillian was always late. After Patrick left, Chris no longer delivered newspapers, and tonight he wished he had the busy work of rolling 150 newspapers to deliver. Tonight, he could only read the paper when it arrived, but there was no news about any demonstrations.

Evening had fallen with a blood-red sunset. The air was heavy. After attempting to read and comprehend his criminal law text, Chris lay on his bed and closed his eyes. He couldn't concentrate. He knew things across the whole city were a mess. He watched the local news. A TV station reporter stood on the lawn just north of hallowed basketball site, Phog Allen Fieldhouse. Chris knew the visual of the reporter with the best-known building on campus in the background would give the report gravitas on the planned evening demonstration.

The reporter seemed nervous telling the story. A crowd of approximately 200 African American students stormed out of a university board meeting. Those exiting said their demands for an expanded black studies curriculum and more representation in student activities had been rejected without consideration. The crowd was angry and impatient.

Chris put his textbook away and surfed through the four channels looking for more news. Lillian and Piper were still not home. He watched TV for hints of what might be happening. He learned police were on campus in heavy numbers. One report said that as of yet, the African American demonstrators were peaceful.

Later, another newsbreak interrupted the local NBC station. Now it was reported that at 9:13 p.m., the Lawrence Police and Fire Departments received reports of vandalism and even acts of arson at Lawrence High School. Some concerned citizen reported seeing people in the crowd with lighters, candles, and flammable materials. The crowd of college students was now interspersed with outside hippie agitators. There were unsubstantiated reports of gunshots and police were on alert. The city seemed in full lawlessness. Several store windows were broken, and some fire damage was discovered at a private home. Firemen arriving to the arson scene told local police they could hear gunshots in the distance. Chris wished his mother and sister were home and safe. He also feared for Tate Laughlin. In his gut, Chris knew Tate was in trouble.

It was full dark and there was no moon. Chris decided he had to act. He couldn't just sit there. He would save Tate Laughlin.

April nights in Kansas can be glorious or they can be filled with thunder, lightning, and hail. This evening hinted at the latter. Bolts flashed on the western horizon. Thunder, just barely audible, rumbled. The air felt kinetic. Chris was excited, despite his trepidation. The impending storm seemed to make his pulse race.

———

Chris left his street and headed to campus. Taking a deep breath, Chris pulled onto 15th Street but saw flashing lights ahead at the Iowa/54 intersection. Chris turned north and took Oxford, eventually parking on Hilltop behind fraternity and sorority row.

From there, he trod his way onto campus and began to climb to the Campanile and the university bell tower. He could see most of campus from his position. Below him, near the Memorial Union, a crowd gathered in the evening's shade. He could see the flicker of candlelight and the flashlights among the students. Chris descended the slope toward them and soon found himself intermingled with several hundred students.

He heard some male student call out, "Hey, check out the little dude." He knew that most would assume he was a high school student masquerading at the demonstration. Chris cringed inside. Didn't they know he was a radical? Didn't they know he was at least as much with the cause as any of them? He'd read every book about the counterculture movement. He knew more than any of them. Heck, he was friends with the infamous Tate Laughlin. Everyone there would know that name. But still his face flushed with embarrassment at the jibe.

Then, Chris realized with an epiphany he had been a fraud. In his mind, Chris was against the war, but he had never been to a demonstration. He had never carried a peace sign. He had never protested. He had never spoken his mind. He dressed like a square. He was a fake. Chris realized in that moment that protest is action. His involvement had been only a mind game, an intellectual exercise to impress Tate. Chris resolved to do better.

Soon, he was embroiled in the crowd. They milled in front of the union with Memorial Drive at their back. Most carried signs, candles, or in some cases, flowers. Nearly all the men and all of the women had long hair. Chants of "Hell, no, we won't go!" and "Stop the War!" echoed between the limestone lecture halls. Chris was jostled as he made his way to the front where he could understand the shouting. He figured his friend would be leading the protesters.

Chris searched the crowd for Tate. He thought it would be easy to see Tate's long black mane, but many people had long hair, and in the dark, he did not see his friend. Along the protracted battle line, students shouted at the riot-gear equipped police. Not three feet separated the two sides. Chris figured there to be perhaps fifty officers and four hundred students. The students shouted and pumped their fists. Chris did the same. At first, the young man felt self-conscious, but soon he lost himself in the moment.

Someone threw a pop bottle at the police line. The glass bottle bounced harmlessly off one the plastic shields, but it changed the event.

Now, the police surged forward. Chris was pressed into the maelstrom, trying to keep his feet and found his face pressed against a shield. He felt a baton's blow crease his back and Chris cringed more out of surprise than pain. Against the plastic shield, he peered through at his attacker, a young policeman, maybe only five years older than him. The young man's eyes were wide with fear. The two were just inches away from each other. They eyed each other through the plastic. So close but no communion of spirit occurred. Chris only felt their separation.

Then came the tear gas.

Chris spun backwards as the smoke burned his lungs and eyes. He began to run, battering his way through the crowd, seeking oxygen. The students, or at least most of them, were in full flight. Cops now waded into the crowd and took batons to those remaining, the most militant of the demonstrators. A few young men threw ineffective punches at the officers and their shields. A scant few of those throwing wild haymakers donned gas masks. They swung signs at the police. Those agitators were taken down and arrested.

Chris gagged as he quickly made his way south.

At the sidewalk before Memorial, a young woman tripped and fell to her knees.

He stopped and helped her to her feet.

Together choking, they retreated.

Without a word, Chris took her arm and led her toward fraternity row, veering away from the mob of retreating students.

The police followed the mob as it dispersed.

Chris and the girl slipped through enemy lines and found themselves walking alone.

Chris coughed.

The girl cried.

He pointed. "Here's my car. Get in. I'll take you home."

She got in, but then said, "I live in 'Schol' Hall on Tennessee." She pointed back past where they had run toward the far east side of campus.

"I don't think we can get back there right now." Chris stared back up the hill on campus. A red glow was emanating from beyond the Campanile. "What's that?"

The girl looked beyond and her mouth dropped open. "I think the union is on fire."

They sat in his front seat, mesmerized by the ever-increasing flames which overcame the structure. Chris turned on his radio, and they sat there until the station broke in with news report of a bomb going off in the union. No one was hurt, but hundreds of students and all the fire departments in the area were on scene fighting the blaze.

The girl eventually looked to him. "Thanks for helping. I'm Elizabeth."

"I'm Chris," he said, not taking his eyes from the flames up the hill. He was not thinking of the girl. He was thinking of Tate.

Soon, the young man did turn to inspect Elizabeth, and while she was pretty, a pert brunette, his mind was elsewhere. He tried with difficulty to put Tate from his mind. The girl needed help. Her face was streaked from tears. She was bleeding. Both knees were scraped. Blood trickled down her shins and the tops of her white socks were soaked red. The palm of one hand was angry and torn with gravel embedded in her wound.

"Hey, we need to get you some help."

Chris started the car. He didn't want to take her to his home. That seemed too creepy, even given the circumstances of the night. He decided on Haskell. Maybe given the bombing and riot, Lillian would still be there. He knew where the student infirmary was and he could certainly contact the school nurse who would be on duty to treat Elizabeth's knees and hand.

When Chris parked in the nearly abandoned administration lot, he saw his mother's car still in her spot. Her office light was still on. He helped Elizabeth out of the car and took her arm. He escorted the young woman up the sidewalk as he explained to her that his mother was dean of students, a recent promotion. He knew the nurse, too, and she could get her cleaned up. Maybe by then he could drive her back to her dorm. Chris decided he would ask the nurse to check Elizabeth's head. She seemed dazed.

Inside the lobby, Lillian stood with students around a TV. It looked all the world like an opening scene in *Billy Jack*. The news anchor spoke of the union ablaze and the riot on campus.

When Chris pulled the double doors open, the room's occupants' heads turned as if on a string. Lillian's eyes showed surprise.

"Chris! What are you doing here?"

Chris felt tears welling up in his eyes, but he steeled himself, not wanting Elizabeth or the other students see him cry. "Hi, Mom, this is Elizabeth. We were on campus and somehow got mixed up in the mess over there. The police chased us off the green. A bomb must have gone off at the union. I think it burned to the ground."

Lillian took her son's arm. "I know. We've been watching it on TV. What were you doing over there at this time of night?"

"I don't really know. I just got this really bad feeling that Tate was in trouble. Suddenly, I just found myself driving there. I didn't find him, though. I can't explain the feeling. It was like I knew what was happening before it did. Like the whole evening."

Lillian smiled. "Grandma Avery used to say she would get premonitions. Mom too.

Chris nodded. "Hey, Elizabeth is hurt."

Lillian looked down at the girl's scraped knees. "Oh, dear," she said, reaching out to Elizabeth. "Let's get you cleaned up." Lil turned to Chris. "How about you? Are your eyes okay?"

"What?" He turned and looked at his face in the reflection of the glass of the trophy case. His cheeks were streaked with the path of tears. His eyes were rimmed with pink swollen tissues, and the whites of his eyes could scarcely be called that. They were bloodshot and etched with fire. He was strangely proud. It had literally been a baptism of fire. Tear gas was no joke.

"Yeah, I'm okay. Just take care of her."

Lillian smiled at her son then pulled him away. "The police have already been here. They are looking for Tate. I need you to go home. He might be there. If he is, call me at my office. I'm not sure I'll get home tonight."

"Did he set the fire?"

"God, I hope not."

Chris didn't really want to leave Elizabeth, but he was concerned about Tate; plus, it would be weird to hover over the girl while the nurse treated her knees.

Halfway home, he resolved to seek her out again another day but then realized he didn't know her last name or in which of the scholarship halls she lived. The boy smiled ruefully to himself, knowing he was far from smooth with girls.

Chris put the Dodge where he always parked, along the side of the drive, leaving the garage for his mom's car. Piper was still not home. There was no sign of the beat-up car Tate had been driving. The house was dark.

Chris slipped in back, entering the kitchen. Flipping on the light, he opened the fridge.

A voice called from the darkness of the living room. "Looking at your face, I think both of us could sure use a beer."

"Tate!"

"Yeah, it's me."

"Where's your car?"

"Cops are looking for me. I had to ditch it by The Wheel. I'm sure it's impounded by now. I walked back here. Just now arrived." Tate opened a beer and handed one to Chris.

Chris took it and took a swig. It was impossibly good.

Tate also gulped down a cold swallow. "You mind turning the light back off? Some major shit went down, and I've seen the cops doin' drive-bys. I've been peeking out the drapes like a character in an Agatha Christie book." The young Cheyenne took a drink. His hair hung down his back in tangles. His shirt was grass-stained across one shoulder. One knee on his jeans was torn. "Maybe you could go move your car up the street?" Tate asked.

"Sure," said Chris. "Then, we gotta talk."

Tate shook his head. "No, no time for that. I have to get out of town." He thought for a moment. "Can I borrow your sleeping bag? Maybe your pack and pup tent? I need to get out of here. Get somewhere nobody is."

Chris nodded. "I'll be back in a second." But he didn't just move the car. He drove back down to 15th and filled the car with gas. His seventeen-gallon tank would get them where Tate needed to go, someplace nobody ever went.

He came back and told Tate his plan. It didn't take much convincing.

Tate was exhausted and surprisingly, out of ideas. For the first time, the Cheyenne radical let his younger friend take the lead.

Within the hour, the two left for Oklahoma. Until they cleared the city, Tate was in the trunk with the tent, the sleeping bag, and a bag of groceries from Lillian's pantry. It was a good thing. Chris was stopped by a cops on his way toward the highway entrance.

The highway patrolman motioned for Chris to roll down his window.

He did.

"Where you headed so late, son?"

Chris held his defunct *Lawrence Journal* newspaper ID up to the police officer. "I deliver papers. Got called in early. Guess there's a special edition after all the stuff over on campus."

The officer nodded, looking at the photo ID and then at Chris's face. "Not surprising." He looked twice at the photo. "You okay? Your eyes look bad."

"Spring allergies. Worst day I've had, and it would be today some fool does something crazy to make me miss a night's sleep." He smiled. "Oh, well, got to pay for school somehow."

"Y'all take care," said the flat-capped officer.

Chris took the laminated card back from him.

Soon, with city lights behind them, Chris pulled down a dirt road and let his friend exit the trunk. Tate was sweaty in the muggy April air.

"You're a pretty good liar."

Chris smiled. "Open us a couple of Cokes," he said. "It's a long drive to Oklahoma."

They took 59 south to Ottawa and picked up 35 at Emporia. Chris decided he would drive. If they got stopped, at least it would be his license they would give the police. He made sure to not exceed the speed limits.

Wichita was more than two hours from Emporia, but it was easy driving, and there was no traffic. It was now well after midnight.

After a time, they could get KEYN FM on the radio. The DJ was coasting, playing the entirety of side four of *Tommy* by The Who.

"They played Woodstock, you know," said Tate.

"Who?" asked Chris, and they both laughed. Chris paused a second. "Wait, are you saying you went to Woodstock?"

"Well, yes, I went to Woodstock. Never got there, but I tried. I was in New York, meeting with Jerry Rubin and Dave Dellinger, and we heard about the festival. I tried to get those two to go, but Rubin was too wrapped up in his own shit, and Dellinger had something going with his kid. Some of us young bucks headed off upstate. The traffic was just ridiculous. Impossible. After a day of that, we went to the Jersey Shore."

"I think you buried the lead there," remarked Chris.

"Huh?"

"It's a journalistic expression. It means you emphasized the wrong part of the story. You *know* Jerry Rubin and David Dellinger?"

"Abbie Hoffman, too, actually."

"I don't know whether to be shocked or proud."

"Me, either. Dellinger is interesting. I was there because he wanted me to speak at some Fifth Avenue Vietnam Peace Parade Committee events. Voice of a quote/unquote 'real American against the war' thing. I did a few. They were boring." He paused. "Unlike tonight."

Do you belong to S.D.S.?"

"Am I a Weatherman?"

"You're made reference but never said for sure."

"It's not like they have ID cards like *The Lawrence Journal*."

Chris snorted. "You know what I mean."

Tate nodded. "I've been to some bull sessions with guys who participated with S.D.S."

"But you're not in it, per se," said Chris, completing his friend's thought.

"Not until tonight," Tate said. "I mean, I didn't have anything to do with the bombing or whatever that was at the union, but they asked me to be on campus. Give a speech, rev people up."

"Create classic diversionary tactics."

Tate laughed. "Right, I forget you're a student of the underground."

Chris looked across the car at his friend. "They used you?"

Tate scratched his chin. "I don't know who set the bomb. I'm sure the cops in Lawrence think *I* did. They know I was on campus today. And that's all that will matter. I'm guilty. It won't matter if there's evidence or not. I'm an outside agitator. Essentially, a professional disruptor of society. I'll be lucky to get to trial. If they catch me, I'll get a bullet in the back trying to escape. Or maybe I'll commit suicide in my cell."

Chris grimaced sadly at his friend. Tate looked very tired and very old. "Let's not get you caught then, shall we?" Chris added, and it was the last they spoke for a long while.

It was past three when they cruised through Wichita. They took County Road 42 and passed through Anthony. "Good horse races here. I've been a few times," Chris noted.

Tate did not respond, and Chris noted the Cheyenne was asleep. The DJ was playing the entire *Chicago Transit Authority* album. Chris turned south, drove across the state line, realizing he had just broken federal law in transporting and harboring a fugitive across state lines. KEYN was playing the song "I'm a Man," as he did. Chris laughed to himself in the car.

An hour later, he passed Jet and arrived at the Great Salt Plain from the north. Seeing the salt flat in front of him, Chris shook Tate awake. As the Indian wiped sleep from his eyes, Chris crossed the bridge which opened onto the flat. There, he followed the same ruts his grandfather had driven the day his father Henry took flight.

Tate looked at the misty surroundings, the white ground covered with sodium. Chris's old Dodge creaked as he drove slowly across the flat, edging slightly west. It was 4:30 in the morning. Not a soul was out here. It was very dark. There was but a waxing crescent moon. Chris thought he might turn off his headlights, but there was no way. Trails of fog wound their way in front of the beam's path, twisting like ghosts in agony.

Finally, Chris stopped the car.

Tate leaned forward in his seat and rolled down the window. He stuck his head out, taking in the night chill. "What is this place?

"The switchbacks, a place nobody goes."

Chris turned off the vehicle. The cliffs of the switchbacks stood like castle walls before them. The height of the walls hid what little moonlight was left. It was so dark they could not see each other's faces.

Tate went to the driver's side and turned the headlights back on. When he came back around the vehicle to his friend, he held a Bowie knife in his hand.

Chris started.

Tate took the blade to his thumb. He cut a slit, and a line of black welled from the wound. He motioned to Chris.

"I thought that was just a *Daniel Boone* thing," Chris said. But he extended his hand, trusting Tate.

Tate grabbed him and pulled their hands together. "Take my wrist, too," he said.

He cut them both. Thumbs pressed together. Tate smiled. "We're brothers now. Forever brothers."

"I'll be back tomorrow with water. More supplies. Do you need anything else?"

Tate shrugged. "Smokes, a bottle of hooch maybe."

Chris nodded, wiped the blood on his jeans and trying not to show his pain, he got back in the car and left his friend in the darkness of a place nobody goes.

With the sun just rising, Chris pulled into the Salt Fork Station ranch. He saw the lights in the kitchen were on and the screen door opened before he was ever out of the car.

Jeff stood in his undershirt, his bony frame tucked into his dungarees and boots. "What the hell, boy? Your mom has the highway patrol out looking for your body, you know that?"

"Sorry, it was just a terrible day. I wanted to be here to start the next one. I didn't mean to worry nobody."

As Chris walked in, Jeff noticed the blood on the boy's pants. "You okay?"

"Cut my thumb," he said. "I'm fine."

The havoc in Lawrence made it impossible for Lillian to drop everything to retrieve her son, but he got a good reprimand from her over the phone.

He was lucky, she told him. Classes for the remainder of the week had been cancelled. His professors would post a reading schedule. Piper would get them for him. Did he have his books? No, he didn't? Well, it really doesn't matter then, did it? And how he left things? All the lights on and the front door open? The house was a wreck? The food all gone from the pantry? The garage torn apart? His camping backpack gone? Why did he need that for the farm?

"Oh, never mind," Lillian said. "I know you were upset. When we're upset, we do stupid things. But not leaving me a note and driving all night with no sleep? That was dangerous, and stupid, Chris." She gave a tired sigh. "I've never known you to do something stupid."

And it went on from there. It was a long call.

Afterwards, Grandma Gwen scuffed his head with a loving cuff. He ate ham and eggs with four slices of toast and then slept.

When Chris awoke, the day was sunny and nice. It was just past noon. Jeff was piddling down in the garage. Chris went down to join him.

"Thought you might sleep the day through."

"Sorry, it was a long drive after a long day," the boy said.

Jeff set down the screwdriver he was using to tighten a bolt on the lawnmower handle. "Anything you need to do?"

"Want to go fishing? Got some talking to do. Maybe we could do it fishin'."

"Always ready to fish, son, always."

On their way toward a pond about ten miles south, Chris asked Jeff to pull over.

Jeff raised an eyebrow. "You can't tell me while I drive?"

"I think this is a pullover one."

Jeff smiled. "Okay, let me find a place."

When they stopped, Jeff lit a cigarette and retrieved the bottle of 7 Up he kept in the back with a cork in it. It was filled with warmish soda pop and bourbon. He took a swig and for the first time, he handed the bottle to his grandson. "Looks like you could use a swaller yourself. Make the words flow."

"I don't want to go fishing. I need to get some groceries, maybe up to Kiowa and head over toward Jet. I need to deliver them to somebody."

"Who we be deliverin' this food to? That Indian your mother told me about?"

"Yessir. But he wasn't involved in the bombing. He was on the green with me. Not that it would matter. The law has it out for him. I took him to the switchbacks. He's hiding out there."

"The switchbacks?"

"Yessir."

"You took an Indian boy out to the switchbacks to get away from the law?"

"Yessir."

"You trust him?

"Yessir."

"You know for sure he wasn't involved in the bombing?"

"The people who asked him to be at the riot maybe were. They used him to misdirect the police. He doesn't know for sure."

"He's in a spot, then."

"Yessir, he's in big trouble. We talked last night. He's going to lay low for a while."

"Can't live in the switchbacks forever, son."

"No, we figure he stays out there until I get out of school in a couple of weeks. Then, I drive him to Mexico."

"Pretty stupid plan."

"It's all been pretty stupid so far."

Jeff laughed. "Okay, sounds stupid enough for me to get involved, too. Never did like Johnny Law much. I ran moonshine, you know. One time, after delivering a load up to Hays, Kansas, we got so drunk on the way back we ended up in Colorado." He laughed, thinking back. "Didn't get caught, though."

Jeff and Chris bought ten one-gallon jugs of water, a case of beef stew, several cans of Chef Boyardee, a combo Swiss knife with a can opener, a bottle of Old Forrester, and a carton of Camels. Chris wanted to buy Marlboros, but Jeff insisted that they buy his brand so no one would ever be the wiser.

It was late afternoon when they arrived back at the flats. A wind was blowing, and the sodium in the air burned their eyes. Chris's were still raw and bloodshot from the tear gas the night before. Had it really been less than twenty-four hours ago?

They parked and walked back into the switchbacks for a bit but did not call out. There was always an outside chance someone besides Tate might be up here. But there was no one.

Just before dusk, they heard somebody scrambling down the slope. Soon, Tate approached. He hugged Chris. His clothes were chalky white with salty dust. The Indian grinned. "You must be Chris's grandfather. He speaks very highly of you. I know your family history. Your family, especially your uncle, has served the red man well. Thank you."

Chris looked at his grandfather with curiosity.

Jeff seemed to take in the Indian with an appraising eye. He liked what he saw. "Expect any decent sort would have done as much or better."

"The history books say otherwise."

Jeff laughed. "Hell, son, let's not be so stupid to believe the history books."

Tate nodded. Chris knew he had done the right thing. Jeff liked Tate, and Tate liked Jeff.

Jeff lit a cigarette. "Not long to dark. Them's a lot of supplies. Need us to carry them up?"

"It's a ways back to my hideout," Tate paused to laugh at his own words. "Too far for you to help me carry in the dark and then come back down these cliffs. Let's just get them hid over there behind that scrub. It will give me something to do tomorrow."

Jeff nodded. "Chris needs to get back to school, but I can come back. Salt flat is less busy weekdays and even more so evenings. I can bring whatever you need, iffin' I can get it."

"I couldn't involve you. It might get you in trouble with the law."

Jeff laughed. He reached out and grabbed Tate's wrist. He pulled the man's hand to him in the dim light. He inspected the cut on Tate's thumb. "Expect I need to, seeing's as you're family." He laughed once again and looked at the other two. "I watch *Daniel Boone*, too."

Two weeks later, when the university let out, Jeff and Chris hatched a sudden trip to the San Juan River, just the two of them. Jeff and Gwen showed up to Lawrence the Saturday the college let out. Chris's grandfather dropped off Gwen at the house for a girl's week with Piper and Lillian. Chris loaded his things. The two men left, made it to the switchbacks before dark, picked up Tate, and drove all night to the Mexican border. Both young men cried at parting, and Jeff, who might not admit it, also wiped a tear or two from his eyes.

Chris lost all track of Tate that night. His heart ached, and every day he went to the mailbox, hoping for a letter from his friend, but one never arrived. Tate was gone like the words in a book burned in a fire. There was a national manhunt on to find him, too. Tate Laughlin was hot. Plus, the counterculture war was in tumult. The Kent State Massacre occurred two weeks after the burning of the union in Lawrence.

The Kent State president, fearing an uprising of violence like at Kansas two weeks before, called out the National Guard. Four college students were shot dead by their own government. The anti-war movement was now in full bloom, and for the first time, mothers and fathers began to side with their children. The Neil Young song "Ohio" was number one on the charts. "Tin soldiers and Nixon coming. Four dead in Ohio…."

Jeff and Chris listened to a lot of news on the ride back from Mexico. On the way home, Chris finally asked Jeff about Tate's earlier comments on the missing link in their family tree. "I'd like to hear about your uncle. Why has no one ever mentioned him? What happened to him?"

Jeff pursed his lips before he spoke. "Boy, it was a long time ago. My mom, your great grandmother, Avery, had a falling out with her brother. He done some bad things. Killed people is what I hear. Mom was a Quaker, and she didn't abide violence. Cut him out of her life. He's dead. Dead to all of us. She said to never speak of him. I do not."

Chris wanted to ask more, but the look on Jeff's face said there was no more to tell.

Woods County, Oklahoma
May, 1910

Theodore Roosevelt signed a proclamation making Oklahoma a state on November 16, 1907. In many ways, it helped things. There were better roads, better schools, and better times. The Harts and the Stations were still not rich, but they were getting by despite more than a decade of living on the land with almost no money. During the last seven years, Anthem Song had paid for himself many times over and carried the ranch financially, but the horse was nearly the ranch's only income. Cattle prices remained depressed after the Panic of 1893, the run on gold, and the closing of nearly three thousand banks across the United States. A nation without capital could not buy beef.

Since the Depression of 1893, a world event the family didn't even know by name, many of their neighbors had gone bust. Wheat prices dropped from fourteen cents a bushel to nine. Prices of getting grain to market on trains had become prohibitive. Farmers found they owed more after harvest than they had before sowing their crops. Thousands of destitute farmers in the Oklahoma Territory joined with wheat farmers in Kansas to support The People's Party.

Oklahoma seemed a strange place for a socialist uprising, but empty stomachs make folks seek new answers. Right then, it seemed the deck was stacked for the rich folks. Next to New York City, the subversive People's Party had more members in the Oklahoma Territory than anywhere else in these United States. There were lots of homes with the Bible, a Sir Walter Scott or two, and *Das Kapital* by Karl Marx as their only reading. However, most folks weren't so political. To be honest, they were just pissed off.

From 1892 to 1896, the Oklahoma Territory played a major role as a left-wing force in American politics. Years of back-breaking labor ending in bankruptcy and loss of land fostered a hotbed region of disgruntled Okies. They met in secret and plotted schemes that most did not have the guts to carry out. The covert meetings usually ended up in drinking, bitching, and little else. The enemies were the banks and the railroads who kept farm prices low and getting products to market expensive. Oklahoman Reds imagined everyone in New York City, except their communist friends, owned a bank. Oklahoma became radicalized.

The People's Party reached its peak in the 1892 presidential election, when its ticket, composed of James B. Weaver and James G. Field, won 8.5 percent of the popular vote and actually carried five states: Colorado, Idaho, Kansas, Nevada, and North Dakota. Oklahoma was not yet a state, but the People's Party would have won there had its citizens been given the right to be represented. The strength of The People's Party was finally noted in the 1894 House of Representatives elections when it won nine seats. Poor cotton and wheat farmers were the largest contingent of members in the movement. A few crimes were committed in the name of freeing farmers from the grip of the banks. The number of votes for the communist candidates doubled in every election until the U.S. entered the war in 1917.

Statehood did not end any of those subversions on the home front, but it did allow farmers the illusion that prosperity would find them. They would be sadly disappointed. Socialism was realistically discussed as a replacement for failed capitalism but not by the nation at large. Nonetheless, Oklahoma, at the time of its entrance into the union in 1910, had the largest number of Socialists in the United States.

In 1907, the Salt Fork Station Ranch was stable, and the herd now numbered over two hundred head. Tanner turned thirty on an April day in 1907. He would look back upon these times as the best in his life. He and Marie lived a quiet life at the north house on the ranch with their too quickly maturing son, Gabriel. Gabe had enriched Tanner's and Marie's lives to such a degree they wished to fill their lives with as many children as time and Marie's health would allow, but she had not become pregnant again. Marie feared she was now barren, but it was hard to be sad about the lack of more children. Gabe was a light that filled their world.

One evening, down by the river at the main house, after the families had all eaten together, the three girls, now old enough to be little mother hens, watched the boys skip stones along the flats of the Salt Fork. Avery, Everett, Renfro, Marie, and Tanner rested outside on cut logs used as stools. Max and Billy, fresh from town, were there, as well.

After dinner on that fine spring day, Max asked if he could have the family's attention.

Avery seemed prepared for the request. She yelled to the girls. "Autumn, take the children down to the river. See if you can catch us some breakfast."

The eldest girl, now fourteen, nodded and passed out cane rods to the other four. Viva May was thirteen and taller than her older sister. She had flaming red hair and a striking face that already had young men stopping by the ranch to "water their horses" and say hello. Madge was eleven and the two boys, Jeff and Gabe, both seven.

It took a minute or two for the children to wrangle worms from a can onto the hooks of the cane poles. Soon, they were settled along the river bend, hoping for a nibble upon their lines.

Everett stood, stretching as he investigated the long red smear of a sunset to the west. "What is this all about?" He looked suspiciously upon Max and Avery.

Max, too, stood. "As you are all aware, I will be turning seventy-three this fall. I hope to last a while longer, but I will admit standing at the general store all day is not as easy as it once was. Age, though reserved for the lucky, is not an easy task."

Billy laughed and took a nip off his flask. "Ain't that gospel."

Everett nodded and took the flask from Billy.

Avery frowned.

Max nodded at Billy with a brief smile. "As you know, the Cutlers, who own the store, are even older than me. I recently found out they wish to sell. I've discussed it with Avery. The two of us wish to purchase the property."

Everett dropped the flask on to the hard-baked clay beneath his feet. "With what?"

"That is what I wanted to discuss with you. Billy and I have saved some for a rainy day, and he's agreed to give Avery and me that which is his. Avery herself has tucked away nearly two hundred. I do not know what you, my son, have, nor do I know what you have, Tanner. But perhaps you would like to invest in the general store. I have the accounting for you in town. I can assure you it makes a good profit each year."

Everett looked to his wife. "You knew about this?"

Max interceded. "I came to her. I knew I would need her assistance at the store. If she was not willing, it would not be possible."

"Then, it's not possible," Everett said, flatly.

Avery slapped her hand flat on the table. It resonated, even in the out-of-doors. "I expect that is my decision to make, not yours."

"You want the family's money, then I get a say."

Tanner spoke. "Avery, I don't have a lot. Still trying to make up for giving Carson my nest egg a while back, but what I got is yours."

Everett looked scornfully upon his brother-in-law but didn't speak for a moment. "And how much do the Cutlers want? Doesn't seem like we'd have enough money. And without the Cutlers, you couldn't work it with just the two of you. I don't want my wife in Alva full-time."

Avery nodded, agreeing with her husband. "Yes, and you are right, we don't have enough money to buy the store. With all of our funds, even if you agree we can invest the money we have, Everett, altogether we could barely scrape up a thousand. They want twice that."

"Two thousand?" Everett exclaimed. "There's no way. And don't think I'm borrowing against the herd or the land."

"No, no," Max interrupted. "We will not jeopardize the ranch. That much is certain."

Avery nodded. "That's why we're proposing taking a partner. Max has been in correspondence with a man and his wife in Galveston, Texas. They have a thousand and are experienced merchants."

"Galveston?" Everett asked. "And how did you come in contact with this fella?"

"Well, I've known for a while that the Cutlers were fixin' to sell. I wanted it to be me who got first dibs," Max replied. "I just didn't have the capital. Then, one Sunday, Reverend Wellesley was talking about the Galveston Project. You remember that?"

Avery nodded, but Everett's face was blank.

"It's a project to get Jewish families out of Tsarist Russia. They've been targeted by horrible people. There are organized plans to harass and even kill Jews. Pogroms they call them."

"I don't follow," Everett said.

Tanner smirked, seeing what was coming and knowing Everett wouldn't like it. Marie took her husband's hand.

"I wrote to the fella in charge down to Galveston," Max said.

"In charge of what down in Galveston?"

Avery frowned at her husband. "The Galveston Project. They have brought three thousand Jews to Galveston to save them from persecution in Russia."

"I thought Jews went to New York."

"New York doesn't want them," Avery replied. "That city is run by the Irish now. Sending them there would just be more of the same violence and discrimination."

"And Galveston wants a bunch of Jews?"

"Everett!" Avery exclaimed. "They are God's chosen people. We will not be uncharitable."

"Agreed," he said, "but it doesn't mean we want to go into business with them. Never even met a Jew I know of."

"I've been in contact with the head of the project down in Galveston, a Rabbi Henry Cohen. I told him of my situation, that I was looking for an experienced merchant, that I was looking for someone with enough capital to invest," Max explained.

"And this Rabbi found someone willing to give you a thousand dollars?"

"Yes," Avery answered. "a Mr. and Mrs. Jonah Gideon. The wife is named Miriam. She goes by Mimi. They have two children. They ran a store, but then lost it in the riots of Odessa. They left out of Bremen, Germany six months ago. If we agree to take them as partners, The Jewish Immigrant Information Bureau will pay for their passage to Alva."

"You two got it all figured out."

Max nodded. "Yes, son. I have a good head for numbers, and this is a good deal. There will be passive income, plus equity. When I can no longer work, then perhaps the Gideons will buy us out for a profit, or perhaps one of the girls would like to take my place at the store."

"Where will these Jews, the Gideons, live?"

"Upstairs above the store," Avery said in a determined voice. "The Cutlers plan to go back to St. Louis. They have kin there." She paused. "The Gideons are homeless for all intents, Everett. Can't you see it's the Christian thing to do, plus it will bring us security long term. Anthem is getting on, and none of your sires are cutting the mustard like he done."

Everett sat down as a mark of surrender. "I am not seeing any security in this. You're taking all of our cash reserves. Cleaning us out. Anything happens, we're in trouble."

Billy picked the flask up from where it had laid during the interaction. "Sometimes can't win a big pot without going all in."

Everett realized he was alone. "Okay, Dad, just make sure this all works out."

The Gideons arrived within two weeks. Jonah surrendered his one thousand dollars at the sale with Max matching the pot. The deed was signed. They were officially partners.

Within another week, the Cutlers had vacated the upstairs apartments, and the Gideons moved into their new home. Their children, ages eight and seven, a boy and girl, were shy and reserved.

The boy, Levi, once asked Gabriel if he, too, were Jewish. "Your name is Jewish, and your skin is like mine, too."

"I'm Cherokee, but my Aunt Avery says Indians come from the lost tribes of Israel, so maybe we are related."

Levi agreed. "It's good to have even a distant relative here. Being new and all."

"Sure enough, Cousin Levi." And with that, they were fast friends.

Jeff agreed.

Soon, Levi, nearly living at the ranch, learned to ride and fish from his two friends.

The girl, Frieda, was seven, and younger than any of the Hart girls. However, they adopted her as a little sister. She became closest to Autumn, who quickly became a fixture in the general store with her mother. Soon she declared she would take Max's place when he retired.

"Don't run me off yet," he laughed to his granddaughter, pleased she should want to become a part of the store's future. "I'm enjoying being a big shot, owning my own place. I'm not ready to quit, not just yet."

The change to the family's life was minimal, almost to Everett's chagrin. The "I-told-you-so" on the tip of his tongue never got said. The only change was that, instead of Saturday, the family now went to town on Fridays so that Avery could work in the store beginning the next morning, which was their busiest time.

As for the Gideons, it was Mimi whom everyone took a shine to. She was a boisterous woman, full of life, and despite the religious hesitancy of most the Baptist folk in town, soon no one could say they didn't like her. Mimi's hair was dark and full of bounce. She was loud, demonstrative, and always had a good word for everyone.

Max noticed she always gave a peppermint candy to each child who came in, whether with parents or not. Max once thought to say something, but he did not. Soon, he saw sales tick up a bit, and he realized it was children driving the sales. Their parents could hardly begrudge their little one's wanting a free piece of candy. All things being equal, parents brought their business where their children were best behaved. It was a winning strategy. Mimi was a hit in Alva.

Jonah was a bit of a mystery, but people kind of shrugged. They didn't know him well. But he was Mimi's husband. He must be okay, they reasoned, liking her. Jonah was quiet, he said, because Mimi never let him get in a word edgewise. People laughed and let him be. He seldom waited on customers, preferring to place orders, stock shelves, balance the books, and make the deposits.

It was understandable if he kept an eye out, looking cautiously over his shoulder. The Gideons could have lost more than just their belonging and livelihoods in Odessa. Many friends and members of their synagogue did not survive.

But then a good portion of Galveston was blown off the map during the hurricane of 1900. It had been a devastating event, the worst in U.S. history. A fifteen-foot storm surge and 130 mile-an-hour winds hit the city on September 8, 1900, officially killing 8,000. Many others also died but were of a transient population. Sailors in port, Native Americans, blacks, and Hispanics were not counted among the city's population and so were not counted when their bodies were taken out to sea. Perhaps as many as 12,000 truly died. Galveston, in rebuilding, discovered people were a valuable commodity. Jews, a people with no home, came cheap.

By 1909, 773 Jews arrived in Galveston. The next year, 2,500. In

1911, 1,400. Jonah and Mimi Gideon and their children were among the second wave. They were glad to arrive in Galveston, but also were glad to leave the port, which was too humid and hot for Mimi's tastes. Most of the new arrivals eventually moved to Houston which already had 2,500 members of the faith and several active synagogues. Joshua and Mimi had many connections to Jewish families in Houston.

Upon arrival in Alva, the Gideons proved to be hard workers, but Max had not figured on the problem of his new partners not working on their sabbath, Saturday. Max, Avery, and Autumn worked very hard those days. And truth be told, Everett moved and loaded stock onto store shelves more than once. The store proved profitable, and the times were good. The ranch was hard work, but Renfro, Tanner, and Everett were up to its chores. They found Carson's absence giving Tanner no time to leave the ranch, but the truth was his home and life was with Marie and Gabe. He didn't care about leaving. As for Renfro, he was so happy to have his own home. Though it was a simple bunkhouse, he, too, could see no reason to visit town. He and Brew were happy as clams.

Tanner and Marie did not care for politics, but they followed the news of what was now called the Five Civilized Tribes: the Cherokee, Choctaw, Chickasaw, Creek, and Seminole Indians, and their attempt to form an Indian state. In 1905, the Sequoyah Constitutional Convention was held in Muskogee just outside Indian Territory. General Pleasant Porter, the chief of the Creek Nation, led four other chiefs representing each of the tribes. They drafted an Indian Constitution, planned a government, and even proposed county designations across Oklahoma. Marie was excited when Tanner read to her about it. She and Avery spoke about the possibility of an Indian state, but Everett said there was no way a white Washington would ever allow that to happen. Tanner, though not liking to hear it, agreed with his brother-in-law. Nothing he had ever seen allowed him to believe an Indian state would be allowed to stand.

Of course, President Theodore Roosevelt rejected the Sequoyah proposal, but the pressure was on to provide some alternative. A proposed "unified" state joining the Five Civilized Tribes and the white settlers seemed necessary. Republicans brokered the deal, but Washington worried about territory's growing number of socialists. This communist concern in Oklahoma slowed statehood by two years. Still, many Sooners stayed interested in all things red. By 1914, Oklahoma boasted 12,000 dues paying members of the American Socialist Party.

Maria told Avery she was saddened to know an Indian state would never be. Avery told her not to worry, that politics would not affect them way out on the ranch. Tanner heard his sister's comment, but, as usual, did not speak. If he would have, the lanky cowboy would have said politics was just rich folks deciding what crumbs to let the poor folk have. He paid no dues, but his beliefs were quite socialist by the time Roosevelt named Oklahoma the forty-sixth state.

If things in Oklahoma seemed good in 1910, income was still a problem for the Salt Fork Stations, but maybe less so. The ranch, along with the income from the store, was enough to keep everyone fed and warm. Once or twice, Avery suggested the menfolk take some of the land and dedicate it to wheat. Everett reminded her that farmers were paying their entire profit on wheat to the railroad to get the crop to market. The truth was Everett, Tanner, and Renfro weren't farmers. They were cattlemen. Standing behind a plow was not something any of them cottoned to.

In the fall of 1911, the family fortunes turned. Billy collapsed one night dealing faro at work. The doctor said he'd suffered a stroke. Gamblers returned the stricken man home where Max helped them get Billy to bed. Neighbors sent for Jonah and Mimi to join Max at the house.

There, Mimi assisted the doctor, but there was little they could do. Billy died before Jonah could reach the ranch to let Avery and Tanner know their father was ill.

Two days later, they buried him upon the big hill next to Tanner and Marie's homestead. A slight plateau off the hill's eastern side became the site of the family's cemetery. Avery, Marie, and the girls took to planting sunflowers around the hillside. Some took hold.

The boys, Jeff and Gabe, planted some scrub saplings they dug up in the woods near their treehouse. Autumn found a catalog that sold tiny trees shipped in damp cardboard envelopes. She and Avery ordered a Caddo Maple, which arrived like a withered bouquet. Marie and Tanner planted it where they thought it had a chance at getting some run-off. Marie made frequent trips up the hill throughout the following year, even in the hottest of months, carrying a pail of water to nourish the tiny trees. When the weather broke and the rains came, the tiny cemetery with only one cross became a garden.

Stigmata
Woods County, Oklahoma
April, 1974

"A fella can't make a dime growing wheat these days, Chris," Jeff said the words as he stubbed out a Camel cigarette in the creek bank on the Hackberry. A car body, looking like a Model T to Chris, rose rust-brown out of the water. Jeff squatted on his haunches as was his way. His gray dungarees were cuffed, and telltale signs of ash lightened the hem. A willow stick was stuck in the stink bait, and his pocketknife was embedded in a hunk of sponge.

Chris was down at the farm on a Thursday. Piper was getting married in OKC on Saturday afternoon. The rehearsal dinner was tomorrow. It was just now noon on a warm April day. The two men patiently watched their bobbers for bites.

"What you know about this Johnny Fleet, son?"

"I know he's famous, at least a bit. Played running back. Drafted third, played pro for a couple of years and made a pile of money. Then, got his hip busted up by Dick Butkus."

"That man has ended some careers, ain't he?"

"Sure has," Chris replied.

"Then, Johnny came back to Norman and made a name for himself. Brings in talented kids to play football. City finds a place for a fellow who can recruit first class talent. Johnny opened a car dealership and sells Lincolns. Makes a good living." Chris paused, trying to decide if his bobber was moving to wind or fish. "It bother you he's a black man, Grandpa?"

"'Spect not. I wonder iffin' folks in Oklahoma will buy cars from a negro, though. And they'll be those who look down their nose on Piper for marrying outside her race."

Chris nodded. "Not the kind of people we should concern ourselves with."

Jeff nodded to that. He paused to light another Camel. "Gonna be good to have all of you in Oklahoma again," Jeff said, unsnapping his western shirt a couple times to flick a fly off his chest. "Lil going to work for the Bureau of Indian Affairs, you taking the legal job for the five tribes, and Piper on TV as the weather girl in Oklahoma City. I truly wish we could get that station up to here's so me and Grandma could watch her nightly."

Chris nodded again then bobbed his head at Jeff's line.

The old man picked up the pole and reeled in a smidgen on his Zebco. Jeff pursed his lips. "Just bounced it, didn't he? Water's still pretty cold. They's not moving much yet."

It was Chris's turn to nod. "I think people will want to buy a car from a football star like Johnny Fleet. He was runner-up for the Heisman. Rookie of the year in the bigs a couple of years before he took that shot from Butkus. Johnny is good for the university football program. Working his California connections to get black players down here to play football. Regular pipeline, according to the papers."

Jeff set his pole back down. Smoke from the cigarette tilted toward his ancient, felt cowboy hat. "I ever tell you about the time I got a big ole catfish on the line down there by those car bodies? I was wrasslin' him. He kept a-tuggin', and when he stopped, the bobber was floatin' right inside the car window of that ole Model T."

Chris looked at him. "What happened? You reel him in?"

"Well, sir, the water line was lower, and I waded out there and I stepped up on the roof."

"And?"

"Once I had my footing, I leaned over, reached in, and grabbed that line right up above the bobber. Then, the damnedest thing happened."

"What was that?"

"Damn fish rolled the window up on me."

"Really?

"No, son, fish can't roll up windows on cars," Jeff said, laughing. With a wide grin, he reached down and took the cork out of his 7 Up bottle, taking a sip of Old Forester and pop. "I hope you aren't as gullible in the courtroom when you get down to Oklahoma City next month."

The next morning, Jeff's stomach was ailing him. He asked Chris if he could take Grandma Gwen to Hardtner for her beauty shop appointment. The young man was worried for his grandfather, but Gwen assured him that Jeff sometimes had bouts with stomach acid and pain. They left him in his chair with the TV on.

After Gwen got her hair done, she decided Chris needed to take her to the café for some lemonade. There they talked. Gwen found having her grandson as chauffeur a treat and was positively cheerful. Chris, however, was concerned about Jeff.

"You think Grandpa is okay?"

"Heavens, yes. He's had that stomach thing come on for nearly all fifty years we've been married. He'll have the radio on by now, listening to what prices came in at the livestock sale over to Vinita. You aren't around every day. Jeff rests in that chair more than you think."

"Fifty years is a long time, Grandma Gwen. He still surprise you?"

"Not so much these days. It's a wonder we ever got hitched. My father was dead set agin it. This ranch and the folks who lived on it were the talk of the territory. And none of it good."

Chris took a sip as his ears perked up. "How so?"

Gwen smiled, knowing the boy was interested in family scandal. "Oh, by the time Jeff and I were an item, the Heralds knew all about the Stations and the Harts. I mean. by then, Avery had moved into Alva to run the general store with her husband's father,

Max. Now, that woman was a handful. Avery was the first of what they now call a 'women's libber.' Always doing something to get people up in arms. Opened that store with a Jew. Then brought in a Mexican fellow to work the shelves, and a black man to work the ranch. Us Heralds didn't care, but they's folks who did.

"Then later, Avery was downstate several times just before we got married working on the Suffrage. Avery marched around Alva with some other women. My folks thought it was unseemly, but the vote passed in Oklahoma in 1918. Your great-grandma was in the middle of that. Her daughter, Autumn, Jeff's oldest sister, was right in the middle of that mess, too."

"How so?"

"It was politics, Chris," Gwen said, "and I was just a girl then. I didn't pay no attention, but I remember my father talking about it. Had him shaking his head." Gwen paused for a drink of lemonade. "That oldest girl, Autumn, was in town with Avery early on. Jeff parents, Everett, and Avery weren't together for a long time, but folks didn't get divorced like they do now. Avery was headstrong. She just up and moved to town. Had her fill of Everett, I always thought.

"Later, Everett took a woman on the side in Kiowa. He thought nobody knew, but of course, everybody did. I mean if my kin, the Heralds, knew the scoop clear out on their Salt Fork homestead, then it was something everybody knew about.

"Of course, there was the no-account boys. Tanner, who was a gunman and married an Indian woman. Carson was a complete no-account. Just a highwayman, he was. Wanted by the law most of his adult life. But to start, they were a prominent family. Everett was smart with money. He was good with cattle and he had some stallions he put out for stud that brought in good money, I heard. But he was not a likeable sort."

Chris raised an eyebrow and said, "Was Grandpa Jeff close to his father?"

"To Everett?" Gwen laughed. "I'm not sure anyone was ever very close to Everett."

"What'd you think of him?"

"Standoffish fella. Smart, but cold," Gwen said. "I never knew him very well. 'Course I knew him some, beings he was my father-in-law, but anytime I talked to him, he always seemed to be thinking about the next place he needed to be, seems like." Gwen paused for a moment, lost in time long past. Her eyes had a faraway look.

"Jeff was closest to Gabriel, his Uncle Tanner's son. They were like brothers. To hear Jeff tell it, those two boys was pretty much raised by the Injun woman, Marie. That'd be Tanner's wife. Jeff set store by her. But she died young, and Tanner drifted after that.

"Then, Jeff was looked after by the two younger sisters, Viva and Madge. But they both moved away long, long ago. Viva is in Dallas, Madge in a place called Yorba Linda, California of all places. They married well. Have been happy, I hear. Couldn't wait to get out of Oklahoma, not like their older sister, Autumn, who stayed longer. All three girls left Jeff to run the ranch."

"The older sister, Autumn. What's her story? She stayed around here?" Chris raised an eyebrow. "I haven't heard much about her. She still living? What happened to her?"

Gwen dabbed a napkin at her mouth. "Oh, honey, that's a story for another day. We better get back. Jeff will be a-wonderin' 'bout us."

The rehearsal dinner was held at the VIP Supper Club in Alva, despite the wedding and reception being planned for the next evening in Oklahoma City. Neither Piper, nor Johnny Fleet were from OKC, but both were considered local celebrities. The ceremony was going to be private with only family attending. However, the reception would be a wingding of an affair with everyone from the local news anchors, the governor, the university president, the head football coach, the athletic director, and the biggest star of them all, next year's starting quarterback, all in attendance.

The attendees on the reception list who had RSVP'd to attend were a who's who in Oklahoma dignitaries and celebrities: Jane Anne Jayro, a previous Miss America; basketball coaches Henry Iba, Abe Lemons, and Eddie Sutton; Steve Owens, the state's last Heisman winner; Coach Barry Switzer; Lee Roy Selmon, a current NFL star; and even Mickey Hatcher, a current Yankee, who flew in since he had a broken finger and was on the injured list. Even William Skelly, head of Skelly Oil, would be there.

But all of that was one night away. Tonight, it was just family, Piper's family, in Alva. In attendance were Lillian, Piper, Chris, Jeff, Gwen, Uncle Landon, Aunt Etta Jane and their daughter, Libby, now a senior in high school. Her boyfriend, and soon-to-be husband, Linstrom, was there, too. Of course, the final member of the party was Johnny Fleet. Chris had met him once before when Piper introduced Johnny to Lillian. He knew Johnny played in the NFL, but it still surprised him how big the man was. Johnny was just a running back, for gosh sake. Chris could not imagine what lineman must be like. He guessed he'd meet some at the reception the next night.

The VIP Supper Club in Alva was mismatched to the tiny Oklahoman city of Alva in many ways. The décor was sleek; leather, glass, and mirrors. The dining room had piled high shag carpet in electric blue. The VIP Club had great dinner, dancing, and drinks in the bar on weekends, and if you knew the right person, it had a hidden backroom with gambling, including poker, roulette, blackjack, and slots. Most women in Alva kept their change, nickels, dimes, and quarters, to play the slots on Saturday nights at the club.

All the gambling was illegal and getting into the casino room felt like stepping into a time machine, back to prohibition. It was great fun for visitors to see the mechanisms in action as the slots disappeared into revolving walls if rumors of a police raid occurred. The slot machines vanished from sight like something on a ride at Disneyland.

The biggest attraction at the VIP was its Jim Beam bottle collection, said to be worth a cool million. The porcelain decanters came in every possible shape: cars, planes, horses, and even historical figures. Every visitor to the club was required, it seemed, to admire the collection's display case, one that went from floor to ceiling across the entire backwall of the cavernous dining room. Everyone picked their favorite. The kids, while awaiting their food, would beg to leave the table to go look at the bottles. Husbands would beg to leave the table to go behind that wall to the hidden casino. Wives waited patiently for the food and for a chance to plunk their purse's side pocket of dimes into the slots in back.

Jeff was enjoying the notoriety of having an NFL star at the table. It didn't seem to daunt him in the slightest that Johnny Fleet was maybe the first black man to ever eat at the club. But if anyone had a problem with a black man in the dining room, and not being among the servers, no one said anything. In fact, it was much the opposite. Several boys came to the table with pens and napkins, asking for autographs. Johnny always made a point of asking if they wanted his or Piper's signature. Her being Oklahoma's newest weather girl and star-to-be, it got smiles every time, but the autographs requested always read, *Johnny Fleet.*

Soon, several of Jeff's neighbors were at the table, and the old man was holding court, laughing and drinking a bourbon and 7 Up. Chris smiled at his grandfather's happiness. He left the table as Jeff introduced all the men to his soon-to-be grandson-in-law, Johnny Fleet. Chris slipped away before he was roped into the conversation. He never knew what to say in those instances and hated the awkward feeling.

In a moment, he was at the huge display case, gazing at the bottles. It was something he remembered doing since he was a small child. It was always fun to try and see what decanters had been added to the collection since his last visit.

"What's your favorite?"

Chris looked at his reflection in the glass, and Johnny Fleet stood at his side. In the glass, the man looked huge. Chris turned to face him. Nope, it was not an exaggeration. Johnny was just as big in real life. Chris was a very small man in comparison.

Chris pointed in the case. "The Caddy."

Johnny laughed. "'Cause I'm a Lincoln dealer. Very funny."

Chris smiled, "How about yours?"

Johnny scratched his chin for a moment. "Maybe the Brahma bull."

Chris studied the porcelain figure. It had flared nostrils and exaggerated horns. Its face was reminiscent of the Tasmanian Devil from the cartoons. "Good choice," he said then added, "I know the one I don't like, the rodeo clown. Never cared much for clowns."

Johnny laughed. Then, he swiveled his frame, gazing back at the table. Jeff stood with Piper under one arm and Lillian under the other. He blabbed to neighbors. Everyone smiled.

"Gramps having a good time, I see."

"He's entitled," Chris said. "Worked hard his whole life. Been lucky as of late. The oil on his land has given Grandpa Jeff and Grandma Gwen the ability to retire and to travel a bit."

"Good for them. They've been very nice to me. I thought they might harbor some hard feeling about Piper marrying me."

Chris met Johnny's eyes. "You mean 'cause you're black? No, they aren't like that. He just wants the best for Piper. He'll back you 'less you wrong her. If you do, he'll come for you with buckshot. He ain't no bigger 'n me, but I wouldn't be in your shoes if you did Piper dirty."

Johnny laughed. "No chance of that happening. You know, it was pretty much love at first sight for me. Saw her cheering up in Lawrence when we played there my junior year. Asked her out a year later when Kansas played down in Norman. Piper said no then."

This was news to Chris. "I thought you just started dating once she got to OKC."

"True enough, that. But only because she refused to go out with me back when. Then, when she moved down here and was on TV as a weather girl. Well, I decided to advertise my new dealership on that channel so I could have a reason to be hanging about the news set."

Chris laughed. "Persistence counts for something with Piper."

"Determination, I think I'd call it." Johnny grinned and then his thoughts seemed to turn inward. But they must have been pleasant thoughts, as the smile stayed on his face. He touched Chris's arm in brotherhood.

Chris decided he liked Johnny very much, indeed.

After dinner, Jeff took Lillian and Gwen back to feed the one-armed bandits. Uncle Landon and Aunt Etta Jane joined them. Libby and Linstrom had seen friends from home at another table and were there talking. Chris remained at the table with Johnny and Piper. Johnny had been invited back to the gaming room by Jeff, but he had begged off. Having just opened his dealership left him open to public scrutiny. A black man owning a Lincoln dealership in Oklahoma was too much for some. He feared a black man who owned a car dealership arrested in a gambling sting might cross the line for most.

Piper held Johnny's hand. Chris sat facing the couple.

"How soon will you be down?" Piper asked her brother.

"Two weeks until the bar exam. Got to get the house on the market. So maybe a month."

Johnny nodded. "Real estate market good?"

Chris nodded. "Lawrence market is always pretty good. Should sell right away. Mom had me hire painters and I've spent my spare time sprucing up the lawn. It looks good."

"And you'll be in Tulsa, too?" Johnny asked, sipping on a rum and Coke.

"No, I don't think so. I'll be defending clients primarily in federal court, U.S. District Court for the Western District of Oklahoma is on Fourth Street downtown. At least historically that's been the case load, so I'll live in Oklahoma City. I will get state cases in Tulsa or OKC too. Mostly in Oklahoma City. Problem is most prisoners will be held out at Big Mac, the Oklahoma State Penitentiary in McAlister. I'm guessing I'll be out there about one day a week."

"How far away is that, Johnny?" Piper asked.

"More than two hours," Johnny said, "although I never plan to visit." He smiled. "You'll need a good car to go back and forth every week. Make you a hell of a deal on a Lincoln."

Chris laughed. "I do need a new car, but I think the five tribes might wonder about paying for my schooling and salary if I showed up on day one driving a new Lincoln."

"Let me know what you're looking for. We take in trades all the time."

Chris nodded. "I was thinking a pick-up. Just to give me the right image, young earnest attorney defending the downtrodden red man."

Piper swatted his hand. "Shame on you, already thinking how to manipulate folks."

Chris shrugged and said to Johnny. "Low mileage, maybe black or dark blue, serious."

Johnny and Piper laughed. "A serious pick-up truck, got it," Johnny said. "I'll tell my manager to be on the look-out."

Piper raised an eyebrow. "Gonna get a Stetson?"

It was Chris's turn to laugh. "Probably should consider it. I'll take Grandpa Jeff to help me pick out just the right one."

"He'll love doing that," Piper said with a smirk.

Then, some more kids from a table near where Libby and Linstrom were gabbing approached Johnny and Piper, asking for autographs. Piper shook each child's hand as her husband-to-be began signing napkins. Chris excused himself and left the table.

———

The wedding the next day was beautiful, but a small affair. It was held at the Old Trinity of Paseo Event Center, built in 1842, the oldest chapel in Oklahoma. With warm amber lighting, ornate stained-glass and forty-foot gothic ceilings, it was the perfect setting for the family-only event. Johnny had only his brother attending. His parents had both passed years ago.

The surrounding neighborhood left a lot to be desired, but the chapel was perfect, and once Piper saw it, nothing else would do. When Chris arrived for the wedding, driving Lillian over, he remarked that the denizens of the Paseo were likely the kind of folks Merle Haggard didn't care for in the song "Okie from Muskogee."

"Yes, I would imagine a walk around the Paseo here might get a gal a snootful of marijuana smoke."

"Then, watch yourself. I'm not licensed yet in Oklahoma. Got to pass the bar before I can apply. They offer reciprocity, but I'm thinking having my mother in jail for smoking grass would be problematic."

Lillian patted his arm as he turned off the engine. "I think you can trust me."

The wedding was beautiful. Gwen and Lillian cried. Libby carried tissues for the two women and supplied them as needed, which was often. Jeff gave away the bride, his face radiant with happiness. He winked at Piper, who was emotional. Chris knew his sister's face well. He knew the quiver of her lip meant tears were close, but she held it together. Chris stood at the front with Johnny's brother, Ed Bruce. EB, as he was called, was also a mountain of a man, even bigger than Johnny, but with a belly. Gwen called them Big and Bigger. Jeff objected, calling "Hey, I'm over here, Biggest!" Everyone laughed as he barely came up to either's chest.

The reception was to be a huge event and it lived up to its billing. Guests spilled out from the Paseo Chapel's doors into the night. All the celebrities were there. *The Oklahoman* covered the event. A photographer was on-hand to document the night. Chris had to admit Piper had outdone herself. Johnny knew everybody. The photo that eventually made the front page of the society section of the paper was of Piper, Oklahoma City's new weather girl with her husband, football star and new car dealership owner, Johnny Fleet, on one side. Barry Switzer was on the other. The governor had also taken a photo with the newlyweds, but football is bigger than politics in the Sooner State. The coach got play.

The following week, with Chris back in Lawrence studying for the bar exam, now just nine days off, the phone rang. It was Grandpa Jeff.

"Hey, boy, whatcha doing?"

"Studying, just finished mowing the lawn. House goes on the market on Saturday."

Jeff laughed. "You're gonna pass, right? You being a smart feller and all."

"Yeah, I'll pass. I have pretty much memorized everything on the practice tests. The prep guides aren't so hard if you work at it."

"I won't take too much of your time. Just thought you'd want to know that we had ourselves a heck of an earthquake this morning. Heard on the radio it's the biggest in the state since the El Reno earthquake in 1952. That one was a 5.5 on the Richter scale. It centered just out on the east of Oklahoma City, iffin' you don't know where El Reno is. You might not want to get your apartment out there, seein' that these things kind of come in clusters, they say."

"No worries there, Grandpa. I decided to live out by I-40, get me on the highway quick when I have to go to McAlister. Is everything okay at the ranch? Did you get any damage?"

"Oh, it shook Gwen's sugar bowl off the table, made a mess, but it didn't even break. Got that bowl out to Pocatello, Idaho a few years back."

"I'm glad nothing's broke. No problems to the house?"

"No, but the damnedest thing. I drove out with Landon and checked the cattle. Spooked 'em something fierce. They's bunched together like they're in a corral. Scared 'em with all that shaking. It was something."

"How big was it?"

"They say they'll have final numbers soon, but around a 5.2 and centered right at Jet. Good thing your pal, Tate, ain't up in the switchbacks now. As prone to slides as that place is, I bet it was a helluva ride in there today. You ever hear from him?"

"Not a peep since we let him out to cross the border more than five years ago."

"Hmmm, well, I wish him well. Maybe he's got a new life, a new wife, and a passel of kids by now. Ain't that a thought?"

Chris laughed. "Not likely."

Jeff hooted. "Oh, boy, life has a way of happenin' for everyone. For instance, we had this earthquake today, and next week, we're expecting frost in the second week of May. Can you imagine? That's why you don't plant your tomato plants until after Mother's Day, son. My mom, Avery Hart, taught me that. God rest her soul."

"I'll remember if I ever have leave to plant tomatoes."

Jeff laughed. "You will, Chris. Life has a way of happenin' for everyone. Planting tomatoes and having kids just kind of happens to most folk. And speaking of having kids, I thought you were seeing that Elizabeth girl up in Lawrence. How's come you didn't bring her to the wedding? Seems like a perfect time to get her to a hotel room."

"Grandpa!" Chris exclaimed. "She's a nice girl."

"Nice girls have needs, too."

"You're pretty randy today for an old goat," Chris replied, laughing. "Anyway, she couldn't come. She had graduation ceremonies on the same day as the wedding."

"You get her something?"

"I did," the younger man replied. "A leather second American edition of *Gray's Anatomy* from 1866. Cost me a hundred dollars. Elizabeth starts med school in Kansas City this fall."

Jeff snorted. "Sounds like a pretty romantic gift, seein's you're so close."

"Gotta go," Chris replied. "A fella can only take so much abuse. You let me know if you get any aftershocks."

"You let me know if you get *any*, boy," Jeff replied.

Shaking his head, Chris hung up the phone.

Woods County, Oklahoma
April, 1911

Billy Station did not have to rest alone for long in his grave on that big hill. One chilly April day the next spring, Viva was out gathering eggs when she heard the young dog, Brew, barking from the bunkhouse. It was unlike Renfro to allow the dog to just let fly like that, especially for an extended time. He was particular about how his dog behaved. She walked to the bunkhouse with its door shut tight. Viva May could hear the dog inside. As she neared, he stopped his racket and switched to pawing at the door.

"Mr. Renfro," she called in the door. "Mr. Renfro, I'm going to let Brewster out."

She opened the door, but the dog did not emerge, but instead went back to barking. Viva leaned in and saw what had the dog excited. Renfro lay dead in bed. He went in his sleep, peaceful like. The next day, they laid him to rest on the hill next to Billy.

Afterwards, Tanner went to the burial site of the Confederate cowboy's first dog, Stu. He gently dug up the dog's body, wrapped as it was in an Indian blanket. He carried it up the hill, and placed Renfro's companion at the cowboy's feet before they filled in the hole. The dog and cowboy would spend eternity together. Gabe and Jeff kept Brewster as their own. The dog moved to the north house and seemed to get on just fine.

Renfro's death left the farm a little short-handed. Everett spent a lot of time in Kiowa booking his stud service via telegraph. He now owned two stallions; however, the operation just earned enough for Everett's own keep at a rented house up to Kiowa. Most folks found it strange that Everett had changed so much. A man who found nothing as important as his land now seemed allergic to it. With Avery living in town, running the store with Max and Mimi, Everett showed no interest in being at the ranch house without her.

Autumn had also left the ranch, going to business school in town and working afternoons, evenings and from dawn to dark on Saturdays at the shop.

The ranch work now fell to Tanner. Everett could still be counted on to work the big jobs. But the day-to-day operations of the ranch, what with Carson still gone, were Tanner's to worry about. He did them, sometimes with Marie on horseback beside him. He much preferred a hard-working life ending with going home to Marie to anything else he had known. Jeff and Gabe were now ten. The boys were a bit too young to really be cowboys working the ranch, although they stepped up as best they could.

Viva May was now sixteen, and Madge was now thirteen. The girls were now women as far as cooking and cleaning went. They did go to school over to Rose Hill, as did the boys, but school was always abbreviated by harvest, by holidays, by snow and cold weather, and of course, it was out for the summer. In the spring when Rose Hill lost its teacher, the children rode horses to school in tiny Capron about three miles due northeast of the ranch. It was a one-room building with a single teacher, but the education was good. The four children could all read and write. Viva May could even recite "Paul Revere's Ride" by Longfellow.

"Listen, my children, and you shall hear of the midnight ride of Paul Revere," she would call from horseback to entertain the others as they rode to and from school on two horses, the boys on one and Viva and Madge on the other.

Life was generally good for all, but Tanner felt the strain. His days were long, and they took a toll, though he never complained. Marie thought it shameful that Everett would leave her husband alone to do all the work. However, they weren't short-staffed on the ranch for long. One day at the general store, Avery received a telegram. It was from a town out east of Tulsa, Wagoner, Oklahoma. The telegram was from a woman doctor named Belle Cobb.

It read:

Have your brother in infirmary. Injured and needs transit. Need 300 dollars for me to bring him to Alva. Please wire money soon as. Await response.

-Belle Cobb, MD

Max left the store to see if either of Alva's doctors had heard of Dr. Cobb.

"Yes, indeed, I've heard of Belle Cobb, Max," said Dr. Davis Montgomery. "She's Cherokee. First woman physician in Indian Territory."

Doctors tend to talk about other doctors. Belle Cobb was perhaps the most famous doctor in the new state, even though she lived in the tiny city of Wagoner in the pine forests of eastern Oklahoma. Dr. Montgomery knew of Dr. Cobb, and he spoke glowingly of her. Max learned Dr. Cobb worked on the Creek Reservation. Her credentials were real, and her reputation was that of an honest, ethical doctor. Max was impressed with what he heard.

By the morning the next day, Everett was in Alva after Max tracked him down with a telegram to Kiowa. He stomped around the general store.

"Damnations," he cursed. "Every time this family gets a step ahead, Carson comes and blows a hole in our budget."

Avery frowned at her husband's profanity, which had worsened now that he now longer kowtowed to his wife's demands. "We sent this Dr. Cobb a response, Everett," she replied.

"Carson was badly beaten in a barroom fight. He owes some debts, a fairly large hotel bill, and medical expenses. And we're paying for Dr. Cobb to accompany him on the train home."

"An Indian doctor woman," Everett said, "of all things."

"Doc Montgomery said she was well-trained. Maybe the best physician in the state."

"It will completely run us out of money again," Everett said, then regretting it as he saw the disgust on his wife's face. He switched the direction of his comment. "I mean, we got to do it. I just hate it for the family. We'll be completely out of working capital for the ranch."

"There's calves to sell," Avery said, a determined tone in her voice. Then, she paused. "Oh, my God, we haven't even told Tanner. What kind of people are we? How could I not even have thought to send someone to the ranch to tell him?"

Everett frowned. "I didn't take the time after I got your wire. I'll ride there tonight."

He attempted to put his arm around Avery, but she acted as if she didn't notice and moved to stack a dozen cans of peas onto a shelf.

"Max," Everett said to his father, "can you make the arrangements to get the money from the bank? I'll tell Tanner. Avery, you arrange for the wiring of the funds to that doctor. We'll just hope we don't get swindled. Just have Doyle Bremmer make the arrangements."

Avery nodded. "Yes, I've already contacted Mr. Bremmer. He is my attorney, too."

The truth is always both better and worse than gossip. Carson Station certainly looked worse than the description of his injuries, but Belle Cobb said the young man was already on the mend. Avery was shocked at Carson's feeble appearance. He was just a mass of bruises.

Dr. Belle Cobb, a prim woman with a tight-lipped mouth and severe eyes, apologized profusely for making Avery send the three hundred dollars. Dr. Cobb explained to Avery privately later that Carson had been accused of cheating at cards by men at a Creek tavern near Wagoner. The Indians he'd cheated beat him within an inch of his life.

A bartender sent for the Injun woman doctor, knowing no other physician in Wagoner would come out to care for a crook like Carson. As for him, Carson was in and out of consciousness with a bad concussion for the first week. In fact, no one at that time knew his name. During his convalescence, the hotel manager, none too happy to have a cheat and a thief in his hotel, kept a running tally of the unconscious man's expenses. And later, when Carson came to, the Wagoner sheriff refused to let him leave town without reimbursing the other players who'd been at the table. Repaying his gambling debt accounted for half of the money Avery sent. Fifty went to the hotel. Dr. Cobb said the rest of the money went to buy a one-way ticket for Carson back to Alva and a round tripper for the doctor.

"Will my brother be okay?"

"I think so," said Belle Cobb. "Carson had some internal bleeding, probably because those who beat him broke some of his ribs. Damaged his kidneys. I taped him as best I could for the trip. His concussion was quite bad. He may suffer from headaches for some time. It would not be uncommon." She smiled. "Without giving those gamblers their money back, I was afraid they would come back and hurt him even more. It appears Carson is quite a scoundrel."

Avery nodded, grimly. "I can't thank you enough."

The two women had dinner, and Avery gave the Indian woman the last forty dollars she had squirreled away. Dr. Cobb, at first, refused.

Avery insisted. "Please. I've heard about your good works. The Five Tribes have been treated so unfairly. To have their own statehood plan taken by white men and used against them." Avery paused. "I am aware of the Cherokee's plight. My brother Tanner…"

"Yes, I know of Tanner's trial," Dr. Cobb said. "I heard your family's story a long time ago when I first got back from Ohio. Carson told me about it again during one of his lucid moments. Tanner Station is a name known throughout the Five Tribes."

"Unfortunately, I'm sure that is true," Avery replied with a sigh. Her brothers pained her.

Dr. Belle Cobb left on the morning train, and Avery regretted seeing her go. She was the closest woman to Avery's way of seeing things she'd met in Oklahoma. Dr. Cobb was truly a calm and progressive spirit. Sometimes, kindred souls meet and recognize each other instantly, perhaps from the eternal. That's what Marie explained to Avery when they spoke later about the Cherokee physician.

"You two have known each other from the eternal, I would say," Marie said.

"What do you mean?"

Marie waved her hand around, indicating the sky, the world, all things. "This that we see is just the temporary. The eternal is not affected by the every day."

"And you think Dr. Cobb and I are friends in the eternal?"

Marie shrugged. "It happens. Souls from the eternal are sometimes reunited in the now. It happened to Tanner and me. We knew in the first minute. We both did." She paused and smiled. "I know I did. He said he did, too. I believe him."

Avery said, "You can believe him. Tanner doesn't lie." But there were more words in Avery's mind than those. She wondered about her husband, Everett, and the eternal. She was not sure about him, not anymore. It made her sad.

Carson recovered quickly. Soon, he was back at the ranch. Stating simply that his injuries required a good bed, he moved into Everett's bedroom at the main house. The two girls, Viva and Madge, slept in the other room, anyway. Jeff, by this time, had moved full-time to his cousin's house. Now, he was a permanent resident with Tanner, Marie, and Gabe. Everett, when he visited the ranch, bedded down in the bunkhouse, a visitor to the ranch he owned.

Carson, now in the main house in the master bedroom, was considerably happier than when he left. Nothing gave him more joy than seeing Everett headed into the bunkhouse away from his children after a day's work in the field.

———

A third soul was laid to rest on that big hill on the Fourth of July that year.

Having planned in advance, Avery managed to get her family together for the holiday; Carson and Tanner brought Marie, Viva, Madge, Jeff, and Gabriel from the farm. Everett came from Kiowa, and being the day was to celebrate the birth of the nation which took them in, Jonah and Mimi allowed themselves a day away from their Shabbat. Mimi said, "It's a day of rest. We'll rest at the river."

Levi spent the time swimming and fishing with Jeff and Gabe. The three looked to be brothers. They wrestled, fought, and laughed along the bank, getting covered at times in the red Oklahoma clay, only to climb back into the water to cleanse themselves.

As the heat of the afternoon peaked, Tanner did come to his brother seeking a cold beer.

Carson lifted his seine net out of the river's stream. "Still got nine left," he said. "Take four. Give one to Max, Everett, and the Jew boy."

Tanner raised his eyebrow at the comment but did not allow himself to be baited into a dispute with his brother on this day of peace. Tanner simply nodded, took the beers, and ambled down the bank, distributing them.

Jonah looked up the hill and murmured thanks to Carson, whom he had only met when the man had been unloaded from the train, barely conscious.

———

Avery, Marie, and Mimi spread fresh table linens upon the grass and then set a meal ready. The supper was one of fried chicken, boiled roasting ears smeared with butter, canned beans, and strawberries picked just the night before.

As evening approached, sprinkles began to fall. The droplets quickly changed to rain. The crew scampered around the picnic site, gathering plates, cups, and blankets. Tossing the day's gear into the back of both carriages, the entire party began to pile in as Carson and Everett readied the horses for the two-mile ride back to town.

Jonah, who'd overseen the fishing tackle, called out for Max to stop his carriage. "The fish," he called. "I left the stringer down at the water." He jumped from the carriage and hurried back to the riverbank.

It was now raining quite hard, slanting in from the west. The girls huddled together under Everett's carriage's canvas roof.

Jonah arrived at the river's edge. He stepped along the bank, seeking the stringer staked in the mud. There it was: six catfish and two bass on the line. He stepped into the water, pulled the stake from the ground, and lifted the iron rod and its bounty toward the heavens.

"We'll eat like kings tonight! A-hah," Jonah said, laughing.

The lightning bolt arrived before the sound, Jonah jerked as if he, too, had been caught on a line. The man seemed to arch high onto his tiptoes, one foot in the river, one already in the grave.

Then the sound, the light, and Jonah's life exited with the fading of the flash.

In Jewish tradition, they buried Jonah quickly.

Max read from the Gideon's Torah after the family trekked from Alva to the ranch and up the big hill where Carson and Tanner had gone the night before to dig the grave. Max recited the kaddish over the grave as the other men lowered the blanket-covered body down.

Mimi cried, holding Frieda tight.

Avery stood, her arms around her three girls as tears flowed down all their faces.

A week later, Carson rode next to his brother-in-law. With a cigarette stuck on his lip, he said, "Might take a second act of God to get you and Avery back together, huh?"

Everett looked across at the smiling visage of Carson. "We sent the wrong fella after the fish, seems to me."

Carson laughed. "That Jonah didn't survive no whale, now, did he?"

Everett did not answer. He simply wished he was back in Kiowa, away from his family and his ranch. The irony of that thought was not lost on him.

Jonah's death had a direct effect on the family in a variety of ways. One, Mimi, at least for a time, sank into a deep depression. Max filled in her hours at the store, but as he was now nigh on seventy-five, it was difficult for him. Autumn was to head back to school in the fall and would only be available in the hours after school from four to seven. Jonah's passing led to the store losing two full-time employees, both he and his wife, at least for a time.

Secondarily, Mimi began to hold Freida too close. The girl, who had turned ten that summer, was not allowed to go out of doors to play, except for when Mimi slept, which was admittedly, too much. Avery watched over the children, both Levi and Freida. Max began to take his lunch upstairs, spending time with Mimi and attempting to lift her spirits.

As school approached, Avery was no longer happy with Viva

and Madge living on the farm with Carson—mainly that he was gone too much. Mimi's apprehension toward her daughter had leached over to Avery. She decided she wanted all three girls with her. She would have preferred Jeff to come, too, but she knew he would hate town. She never attempted to woo him away from the land that so held his heart.

Everett had no fight in him these days and the move was made. Avery now had Viva and Madge with her, along with Autumn. With the girls gone, the main house was now Carson's. Tanner and Marie kept the two boys, Jeff and Gabriel, at their place. Carson finally had the main house to himself. It was a lonely victory.

By late fall, Mimi was back to putting in full days at the store. Business was good. The community had felt Mimi's pain as its own. A lightning strike being such a visceral way to lose a husband made for much public sentiment. Folks often stopped by to see how the Widow Gideon was doing. That concern did have a way of turning into business. The family recovered financially from Carson's beating by Christmas. The general store now was supporting the family and the ranch.

Before Christmas of that year, at the peak of a lovely Indian summer day, Tanner was one day out with the herd. Carson had been gone wherever it was he went for the last few days.

That evening, Tanner, still as thin as ever, headed home from the herd. He saw smoke coming from the main house chimney. *Good,* he thought. Carson was back home. Tanner was glad his brother could help in the morning. They had some yearlings Everett planned to market, and they needed to be culled from the herd and taken to Kiowa for sellin'. It would be a hard job for just one man, but an easy job for two. For once, he would be glad to see Carson.

As Tanner ambled toward the north place on his chestnut gelding, a big horse named Elderberry, he saw an eastbound rider approaching. It usually indicated somebody from the Strawn place just north and west. Once in a great while, it was someone coming from Hardtner on the Kansas side. Truth be known, visitors were rare.

The sun silhouetted the rider, and Tanner didn't recognize the way the man set his mount. As the stranger came out of the sun, Tanner got a good look at the man. He was Indian, maybe fifty, and the markings on his beaded saddle bag indicated he was Chickasaw. His face was weathered and no-nonsense. The badge on his chest said he was a deputy U.S. Marshal.

The man brought his sorrel to a halt, and it was then when Tanner noticed the man's rifle lay free and easy across his saddle horn. The man didn't hold it with either hand. He had no case of nerves, not this one. He had one knee just kind of elevated enough to keep the weapon level across the horse's back. A very cool customer.

"You happen to be Carson Station?" The deputy spoke with a distinct accent found more often in eastern Oklahoma.

Tanner frowned. "No, sir, I be his brother, Tanner. What can we do for ya?"

"I heared of you, too," said the lawman. "You got a reputation."

Tanner laughed. "Ain't one I'm proud of. Now, I just spend my days babysitting cows." He paused. "But you have me at a disadvantage. What's your name?"

"Grant Johnson. Deputy Marshal. I'm looking to talk with your brother."

"Well, I don't know what to tell you. I haven't seen him in three days. He told me he was off to Alva or parts on south." Tanner, saying the words, thought to himself that nothing he'd said up to now was lyin'. Tanner turned his horse back toward the north. "You might as well come up to the house. My wife is Cherokee. Makes a good dinner. You can sit a spell and tell us what Carson's done this time."

Grant Johnson clicked his tongue. His horse stepped forward like they were a team.

As the lawman pulled even with Tanner, he slid his rifle back into its scabbard. Tanner noted the thong was still off the man's holster and that the Smith and Wesson Model 3 rested easy in the smooth and blackened leather.

"Grant Johnson, eh?" Tanner said. "Well, you got a reputation, too, sir, that is iffin' you're the Grant Johnson who arrested Chitto Harjo and those Snake Boys over to Muskogee about a decade ago."

The lawman smiled but didn't speak.

"You used to partner with Bass Reeves, the negro lawman, right?"

"Yes, Bass and I rode together for a while. We served as deputy Marshals together."

Tanner smiled, broadly. "I got some boys up to the house who set store by Bass Reeves. Arrested 3,000 outlaws, they say. Shot fourteen of 'em to hear the boys tell it. They's all the time riding around, playin' they's Bass Reeves and Grant Johnson. I can't wait for them to meet you."

"Carson won't be there?"

"No, sir. Carson took off three days ago. The boys'll tell ya if they seen him. They'll have been ridin' some since they got home from school."

As they neared the barnyard, Tanner stopped his horse.

Johnson rested at his side.

"Thought you were done as a Marshal. Quit a couple a years ago."

"Did. I'm Sheriff in Eufaula these days. Had delivered up a wanted man to Kiowa for extradition. A no-good horse thief named Pokey Arthur. He claims all the evil deeds he ever done were your brother's fault." Grant Johnson curled the side of his mouth into a bit of a grin, indicating he'd heard it all before. "I wired back to the Marshal's office and they asked me to put back on my U.S tin and stop on by on the way home to see if I could corral that skunk of a brother of yours."

"I reckon my brother done his share of bad. Nonetheless, I heared Pokey Arthur never needed any prodding to do an evil deed, the whole Cherokee Strip could vouch for that."

Both men laughed, then they rode on in.

The boys were waiting to see who the stranger was. They literally leapt in excitement to meet Grant Johnson. He wasn't Bass Reeves, mind you, but he was a real-life hero. Meeting Grant Johnson was the highlight of their young lives. He shook their hands and asked if they'd seen Carson. They said they hadn't, and that seemed to satisfy the Deputy Marshal. He asked to use water from the well to wash up.

Tanner and Marie never spoke over that dinner, as the boys were enthralled with tales by the famous U.S. Marshall.

Finally, after dinner, with the sun hanging low, the animals needed tended to. Still, the boys kept peppering the lawman with questions. They begged for one more story.

He gave them one as he smoked a pipe on the porch. Then, Tanner sent the young'uns to tend the stock.

Grant Johnson stepped inside. He spoke words of thanks in Cherokee to Marie.

She smiled upon hearing her tongue spoken so purely. She responded and they stood as kin in a strange new world. It may have been only ten minutes they spoke, but Marie glowed as the Chickasaw lawman left the cabin.

Jeff and Gabriel brought his horse.

"He's been grained and curried, Marshal Johnson," Jeff said.

"And I gave him an apple, too," Gabe said.

Grant Johnson laughed. "I expect Galahad will be one lazy critter for the ride home."

"You sure you won't spend the night?" Tanner asked.

The lawman shook his head. "Can't do it. There's a danger in it. I got a warrant to take your brother in. Wouldn't want him to come back in the night."

Tanner nodded. Somehow, he'd avoided mentioning all night that there were two houses on this ranch. Johnson didn't know, and nobody had bothered to tell him.

"Can I ask you what's on that warrant? What's Carson wanted for?"

Johnson reached into his saddlebag and took a folded document. He handed it to Tanner. "Cattle theft. The two of them, Carson and Pokey Arthur, rustled two head and drove them over to Waynoka. Sold them to a fella over there."

Tanner excused himself for a moment and went into the house.

Coming back, he held three twenty-dollar bills in one hand. In his other, he carried a set of Mexican spurs. "This ain't a bribe, Marshal Johnson. I wouldn't insult a man with your integrity. I am just wonderin' if the man who lost the cattle might take sixty dollars and these spurs for payment for those two cattle. The spurs are expensive. I have seen some like it into Alva, and they sell for better than fifty dollars. You think that fella would drop the charges for a hundred-ten?" Tanner raised one shoulder. "You think? It's all I got in the world."

Johnson took his reins, not wanting to answer. Then, he took the money and the spurs with the warrant and put it all in his saddlebag. "Tell you what. I'll sell the spurs at the fort. Soldiers always are looking for fancy hardware like this. Then, I'll wire the fella from Jet before I head to the railhead in Ponca City. He takes the deal and drops the charges, I'll see he gets the money. He doesn't, I'll leave it with the fort commander over to Jet." The lawman paused and laughed a mite. "I heard you already know him."

Tanner laughed in return. "Yeah, we met."

Both men smiled, liking each other.

Then, Grant Johnson stepped into the saddle and rode into the night.

After a sleepless night, Tanner rode the two miles south to the main house. His anger with Carson had cost him a night's slumber. Arriving, Tanner burst in the door. Inside, he was surprised to see a woman in a slip, moving from the Franklin stove, carrying a coffee pot to the table. She shrieked, nearly dropping the kettle in setting it down and moving to cover herself.

Carson stuck his head out of the bedroom door. "Tanner, what the hell?"

I 'spect that might be my question, little brother." He turned to woman to apologize but realized she was naked under the slip, and it left little to the imagination. Tanner turned back away. "My apologies, ma'am." He took a step back out the door. "I'll be waiting outside. Carson, we need to have a word."

Carson emerged in less than three minutes carrying two cups of coffee.

Tanner thanked him, taking one.

Carson was silent. There was still sleep and maybe last night's whiskey in his eyes.

"Well?" Tanner finally said.

Carson grinned, impishly. "What? No welcome home?"

Tanner nodded. "Welcome home. Didn't know you'd have company. Not sure Everett would like you havin' a woman in Avery and his'n's bed."

Carson sneered. "Don't give one good goddamn what Everett thinks."

"How about your sister?"

Carson pursed his lips. "Not sure Avery could think worse of me, anyhows."

"Who is she?" Tanner asked, nodding toward the door.

"Rose Kassik, we've been seeing each other for a while."

"Her father Frank? The Czech fella?"

Carson nodded, drinking the rest of his coffee. The dregs he rinsed out by dunking his cup in the horse trough. "Yep, married her yesterday. Same preacher man you used. Needed to make an honest woman of her. She's with child."

Tanner smiled. He patted his brother on the shoulder. "I got news for you, Brother. She ain't Rose Kassik any longer. She's Rose Station."

Carson laughed. "True, true."

"Good for you," Tanner said. "Got to tell you something, though." Then, he related the tale of the last evening and meeting Marshal Grant Johnson.

Afterwards, Carson whistled. "Bet you never thought I'd make something of myself. But here's the great Marshal Grant Johnson come to arrest me."

The two both laughed.

Strangely, given that Carson's news trumped Tanner's, the older sibling felt pretty good about things. He hoped that feeling would rule the day. Marriage trumped arrest warrants in his book. Tanner lit a cigarette and then handed it to Carson. He lit a second for himself. " 'Spect I'll take Marie over to Jet to see her father today. Find out if you're still a wanted man. If there's sixty dollars and a set of spurs waiting for me at the fort, we got trouble. Guessin' the two of us better go and find out. We'll be gone overnight. Can I hold you to watching out for the boys tonight, you and the missus?"

Carson smiled. "Yeah, sure."

"Good. You tell her I'm ill-mannered, but I'll knock next time."

"I'll tell her."

Tanner walked to his horse. "See you over east in a bit? Need to cull them yearlings."

Carson nodded.

"I like this partner of yours a lot better than Pokey Arthur, Brother."

Carson nodded and then went back into the house.

After checking the herd and driving the two yearlings back to the corral at the main house, Tanner said goodbye to Carson and asked his brother to give his regards to his wife.

Tanner rode back home and met Marie. She readied her horse, a white dappled gray named Patience. With the boys at school, the two gave the once over to the livestock. Then, they headed east toward Jet. Neither had been back to the town since the trial. Marie's father had come to visit a couple of times to fish, but the village of Jet held a lot of bad memories for the both of them, and they had avoided a return. Foreboding was heavy on their minds as they rode, but the weather was nice. They enjoyed riding together. It was good to be away from the chores of the ranch.

Once, they stopped along a creek and saw a red fox creep up to the water for a drink. "It is days like these that make up for those which have shook us to the core," Marie said.

Tanner agreed. After a stretch, he asked, "What'd you and the Marshal talk about?"

Marie smiled at him, tipping one shoulder into the muted light through the trees. "The end of the old ways. Our ways. How the days of our people are numbered." Then, she gave the horse a click and the mare moved to a trot, taking the lead, and ending the conversation.

They arrived at the fort late in the day. Night was falling. They met Joe Wolf Walker, Marie's father, for dinner, and then bedded down on blankets spread on fresh hay in the stable.

The next morning, Tanner went to the fort and asked if there was news for him left by Marshal Grant Johnson. He was escorted immediately to Captain Mulvaney's office.

The captain was cordial and shook his hand. The officer

inquired about Marie and said he'd heard they'd had a son. However, Tanner could read the man's eyes. Bad news awaited him.

The captain raised a telegram in his hand. "I have word for you from Marshal Johnson, Tanner. It seems that the rancher who had the two head of cattle stolen by Pokey Arthur and your brother would have been willing to settle for a hundred dollars. You provided sixty and a pair of spurs. It seems, though, that the spurs are listed on a circular of stolen items from a tack store robbery down in Guthrie. Marshal wired a description of the spurs down to the initials burned on the leather strap. It is a positive identification." He paused to light his pipe.

"That being the case, I'm to ask you how you came to have those spurs and if need be, take you into custody. Secondarily, Marshal Johnson wired Sheriff Abner down in Alva. He will be at your ranch today to see if he can apprehend Carson Station."

Tanner felt a sinking in his stomach. He could not go back into that jail in Jet again. He knew the pain and worry it would cause Marie. He decided he must tell the truth. "The spurs I got from my brother. Carson told me he bought them down in Mexico."

"I thought as much. When I saw them, I couldn't imagine a man like yourself even wearing big, silver, jangly, Mexican spurs like those. You seem a simple man with simple tastes. I'd just as likely see you in a purple hat and orange pants," the colonel said, smiling. He reached into his desk drawer. "Here's your sixty dollars. It won't be needed for restitution, as your brother will be arrested today for cattle rustling."

"Bad news, sir, but I thank you for the manner in which you delivered it, Captain Mulvaney. You could have taken a hard line with me today. I appreciate your faith in me, sir. I've walked the straight and narrow, I hope you know."

"I know, son. Take care of your family."

"I will, and thank you again," Tanner said, shoving the three bills into his vest pocket. He was sad, thinking of a pregnant woman back at the ranch about to lose her husband to prison.

It was early evening. Carson had just fed the horses some grain and a few sliced apples. He watched Rose in the barnyard, scattering grain for the chickens, letting them peck and feed for a bit before shutting them up for the night. It had been a good day.

The boys, Jeff and Gabriel, had been down to the main house for dinner. They'd met Rose with natural curiosity, but with an honest affability. The world was too full of new things for them to consider this woman as anything different than the daily dose of new.

After dinner, the boys were only too ready to head back to the north place. A night on their own would be an adventure, despite the evening chores which awaited them.

Carson smiled, thinking they might get skittish when tree limbs scraped the rooftop tonight. He wondered if they'd be back.

Carson was disturbed from his musings by a rider coming from the south. It was too dark for him to tell who it was. He felt a moment of trepidation. Carson wore no firearm and was too far from the house to get one before the rider would arrive. He walked toward the intersection of where he and the mounted rider would cross. He had no choice but to do so.

"Evenin', Carson," said the sheriff.

Carson recognized the voice just as he saw the badge on the man's chest. Sheriff Abner was a big man, maybe as tall as Tanner, but much heavier. He was in his late forties, but there was no middle-aged fall-off in him. Carson could see that. And he could also see the man held his rifle in both hands. This was not a social call.

"I suppose you know why I'm here," Sheriff Abner said.

"I ensure you I do not," Carson said. "But you might as well take a load off and get your feet on terra firma. I am not armed and bode you no ill will." He nodded toward the house with an invitation. "I imagine the missus has some coffee brewing. I like a cup at the end of the day. 'Spect you might could use one. What brings ya out here, arriving at nightfall?"

The mention of "missus" did cause the sheriff to raise his eyebrows. Carson's reputation was that of a man who visited the flesh pots of whatever town he was drinking in. With one hand still on the lever of his 30/30 repeater, the sheriff took a slip of paper from his wallet. "This does. I have a warrant for your arrest. Theft of a set of spurs from down Guthrie way, plus two counts cattle rustling. Your running mate, Pokey Arthur, gave you up. Says you were involved in both crimes. He's willing to testify agin you to get himself a lighter sentence." With those words, the sheriff did, indeed, step out of the saddle. "You need to keep better company, Carson."

As if it was a stage cue in a play, at this time Rose exited the front door of the house. "Carson, I don't know who your visitor is, but tell him the coffee is on and that I've got an apple pie cooling on the back windowsill."

Inside under lamplight, it was easy enough to see that Rose was expecting, and the sheriff felt awkward in explaining that Carson would have to come with him for trial and disposition of sentencing if he was found guilty. The lawman felt bad saying the words, but he knew Carson had ridden the outlaw trail for his entire time in the territory and the now newly formed state. It was hard to feel any pity for the man, although he did for the woman.

Carson seemed embarrassed for the situation in which he found himself. To be under arrest in front of his new wife seemed to give him chagrin, but the sheriff kept his rifle at his side and Carson in his sight. Carson sat easy in his chair across from the lawman. The pie and the coffee were both good. Indeed, they were so good Sheriff Abner let Rose talk him into seconds.

After she served him, she excused herself, saying pregnant women had to make frequent trips to the outhouse. Rose laughed and stepped out the door.

As she left, Abner said, "Seems to be a good woman. How long you been hitched?"

Carson smiled. "Three days. 'Spect she might be reconsiderin' things about now."

"No, a good woman will stand by you. You wait and see. It's time to change your ways, son. Life is long. You can get past these difficulties. It's just time to face up to them."

Carson nodded, but he did not speak.

A moment later, Rose stepped into the house, a flustered look on her face. "Carson," she called, "that darn bucket on the well is stuck again. The rope is tangled as all get out. I'm in the family way and I ain't bustin' a gut pullin' that rope up. You go on and fetch me some water."

Carson and the sheriff both laughed. "Sheriff, may I?" he said.

The big man took a bite from his second slice of pie and nodded in the affirmative.

Carson patted his wife on the fanny, much to the sheriff's delight as she followed her husband out the door. Outside, Carson's horse was saddled, and a gunny sack of provisions hung on the saddle horn. He looked to her with surprise. Indeed, she was a woman to ride the river with. He could not have chosen a better partner.

Rose gave him a peck on the cheek. "Ride to the territories. Don't stop until you are in New Mexico. Wire me in Alva from Albuquerque. Send it to your sister's store. Let me know where to find you. I'll come where you tell me."

Carson looked at her with astonishment. "The sheriff will be right on my tail."

Rose shook her head. "Nope. I ran his horse off into the thicket. He won't find that critter till daylight. Now, *git*."

Carson smiled, and then he did git.

The Passion
Woods County, Oklahoma
1974

Chris had just shut off the mower as he heard the phone ringing. He bounded up the front steps and swung the screen door open so hard it banged like a hammer against the exterior wall. He grabbed the phone on the fourth ring.

"Hello!"

It was Piper. "Hey, I worked all weekend and didn't get a chance to call you. How'd the bar exam go?"

"Fine, I'll pass. I studied hard and I have almost a photographic memory if I really study."

"Not me," Piper said. "I can't remember how to use a lot of the technology on the set. I have to come in early and re-read the tutorials. It's different and better than what we had in my meteorology program, but it's a lot."

Chris snorted. "You're being coy. You always ace that stuff. How are weekend shifts?"

"Bad. I'm there from 11:00 a.m. until after the 10:00 nightly news is over. Three broadcasts. And then back by 11:00 on Sunday, too."

"Reviews?"

"From my bosses? They just say to keep working hard. But Johnny says the public is eating me up. Even the racists watch me so they can call the switchboard to say they don't want white women marrying black football stars."

Chris laughed. "But they watch?"

"Yeah, exactly," Piper said. "I get some pretty nasty mail. I take it home and Johnny uses it to start the fireplace. Good kindling."

"And Johnny?"

"He's great. Dealership is going bonkers. He's in the middle of helping recruit a bunch of players from California. That gives him a lot of sway with the university. It's why I'm calling."

"I don't follow."

"Somebody at the station thinks I'm a good fit, I mean, with my ties to Johnny Fleet, and they want me to give the weather on football Saturdays, sort of my own show."

"Piper, that's fantastic," Chris replied.

"It's who you know," she said, her voice a bit distant.

"They wouldn't want you no matter your connections if you weren't good, Sis."

"The university president and the A.D. pitched it to Johnny over lunch. They want his dealership to sponsor it. He countered. Said he wants them to hire me to teach some broadcast journalism classes, too, if he sponsors."

"Did they say yes?"

"They also countered and asked him to buy the steady cams and the lighting equipment for in-the-field work for the college, then I could teach 'on camera' technique'."

"And?"

"And that's why I'm calling. Johnny told them yes, but only if they also hired you to teach some law classes, if you want to."

Chris paused before saying anything. He was floored. "Really? Had you guys talked about doing this? I mean, for me."

"No, Chris. Johnny is just a deal maker. You're family now to him, and he wanted to max the deal for family." Now, it was Piper's turn to pause. "Will you do it?"

"Sure, I guess. It's surprising. I couldn't let it get in the way of my work for the Indian Bureau Legal Defense Fund, but I think they'd like my higher profile. I'll have to ask if it's okay."

Piper gave a little yip of excitement. "I'll tell Johnny you said yes. Is there anyone he can call at Indian Affairs to grease the skids, so to speak?"

"Listen to you, wheeler-dealer."

Piper laughed. "Johnny is going places in this town. It's the right time for a black entrepreneur in OKC. But seriously, is there anyone he can call?"

"Mom, I guess. She'll know who to ask."

"That I can do. No Johnny needed for that. Okay, see you later, alligator."

"Say no slander, salamander." He could hear his sister laugh as he hung up.

No sooner had he hung up, the phone rang again. Chris picked up. "What'd you forget?"

Grandpa Jeff laughed. "Who you been talkin' to, boy?"

"Sorry, thought you were Piper. Just finished talking with her. What's going on?"

"How'd the exam go?"

"I passed."

"You already got your scores?"

"Nah, but I know. I studied my butt off, and I know what I got right. Figured it all out in my head. I'll be good, but I won't hear for quite a while."

"When you movin' down?"

"Monday, I figure. Hope it's warmer. Gonna be May Day tomorrow and they're predicting snow flurries tonight."

Jeff laughed. "Damned weather girls."

"Yeah, right," Chris smiled. "Damned weather girls."

Jeff laughed. "The weather is freezing down here, too. Strange times. That big ole earthquake last week and now this late season cold snap. Gwen has me to relighting the propane stove after I get off the phone. Says it's too cold to sit in the front room without it."

"Well, if Momma ain't happy…" Chris said.

"Ain't nobody happy. Yep, that just about covers it," Jeff replied and then paused like there was something on his mind.

Chris decided he needed to prompt the old man. "What can I do ya for? I was just about to get in the shower. Realtor lady has got a showing scheduled for later today. I've got to clear out. Gonna take Elizabeth for dinner."

"How's that goin'?"

"Fine, but I don't think that's why you called."

Jeff laughed again. "No, but I'm curious enough. Why I called is I wanted you to come by the home place on your way down to OKC, if you could find the time. I know it's out of your way, starting a new job and moving into an apartment and all..." he trailed off.

"Of course," Chris replied. "What's up?"

"Well, boy, Gwen and I been talkin' about it, and we think we owe you a story or two. Think eventually you'll hear about it from the legal eagle types you'll be running with. It'd be better to hear bad stuff about your kin from family."

"You mean about Henry?" Chris asked, referring to his father. He no longer called him Dad. "Mom told Piper and me all the dirty details, I think."

"No, not about Henry. About your great-uncles. My uncles, Tanner and Carson Station."

"That was all a very long time ago, Grandpa Jeff. I don't figure anybody downstate much cares or has even heard about them rascals anymore. Not to say I'm not curious. Those two do seem to be the skeletons in the family closet. But hell, they's been dead for fifty years, right?"

There was a pause on the other end of the line for a second. "Well, Carson, yeah. He got kilt a long time ago. But Tanner, he's still alive."

"Your Uncle Tanner is still living?"

"Yes, he'd be ninety-six now, I think. Maybe just ninety-five and nearin' a birthday, but I think this is a story better told with some whiskey and Seven Up, sitting with fishing poles. When'd you say you were headed south?"

"Monday, but I'm thinkin' of headin' down there right now to get this story out of you."

Jeff laughed. "It'll hold until Monday. Leave early and we'll get a line wet."

"Yessir," Chris replied and hung up.

That evening Chris was just sitting down to watch an episode of *Petrocelli* when the phone rang. Thirty minutes before, he'd dropped Elizabeth off at her apartment after dinner.

Things seemed to be getting serious with her, like she was a little desperate about him now that he was leaving. She'd been cool enough about their relationship throughout the last four years. He was attracted enough, but she'd kept him at arm's length. Just friends, she'd said. And they were both so busy with school. Hands off had been her policy. Not now. Tonight, she was all over him in the car. He was not complaining, but Chris *did not* understand women. Not a bit.

The phone kept ringing, and he realized he was just standing there. Chris picked up.

"How's my boy, the attorney?" his mother asked.

"Don't jinx it," Chris laughed. "It ain't official yet."

"Dad told me you were having dinner with Liz. How is she?"

"Good. Grandpa Jeff tell you about the bombshell he dropped in conversation?"

"About Uncle Tanner? Yes," Lillian's voice was flat. "I'll let him tell it how he wants, so don't try to pry it out of me."

"Deal. House looked good for the showing today. It snowed enough to cover the ground. Looked real pretty. Crazy weather."

"Snow on the last day of April," she said. "Strange days, yes?"

"Agreed, but good ones," Chris said, "Realtor had good news. She thinks the couple who looked at the place this afternoon will make an offer. Expect a phone call tomorrow, she said."

"That's great. I have news, too. I spoke with Louis."

"Who?"

"My boss, Louis Bruce. He's Commissioner of Indian Affairs. He's Mohawk-Oglala Sioux. Good man. He said it would be great for the attorney representing the Five Tribes on criminal matters to teach a law class or two for the university."

"Great, I guess."

Lillian's tone changed. "Oh, honey, Piper told me this was something you wanted to do. You think it will be too much with a new job? I can tell Johnny it has to wait a bit. He was so pleased to be able to do something for the family. He's a really good guy."

"I just have to get used to the idea," Chris replied. "Piper sprung it on me pretty sudden. How about getting Piper her own show, and Johnny paying for the cameras and everything?"

"Johnny's a mover and a shaker. He was a playmaker on the field, and he is in life, too."

"Yep, and this deal proves the ole point, it's who you know," Chris said.

"Honey, all of Oklahoma gets by on the good ole boys' way of running things. This time it worked out for my children, and that's okay, but I spend my days doing battle against the old boys' network. Native Americans always get the short end of the stick because of the way business gets done. When the contracts are signed, they don't have anybody at the table."

"Well, if you feel that way, then Piper and I can turn it down, Mom."

Lillian replied with alacrity. "Oh, no, getting sensitive people into important positions will help. You and Piper will make a career out of doing good."

"Okay, if you think so."

"Yes, and speaking about it's all who you know, did you know that the warden at Big Mac, the state penitentiary, where you'll be spending your time, is the brother of the athletic director at the university?"

"Johnny's buddy?"

"Yes, Arden Kilmain, that's the AD. His twin brother at the prison is Zane."

"A to Z. Are there any more Kilmain's in Oklahoma government?"

"A younger sister," said Lillian already laughing. "Apostrophe."

Chris groaned. "That joke doesn't even make sense. Have Piper tell Johnny thanks and that I owe him a beer."

"You should call him."

"I will, but I'm going to watch *Petrocelli* and hit the hay. Going to pack up the garage tomorrow. All those tools of Henry's."

"Thank you, dear. *Petrocelli,* eh? Is he still building that house?"

"About one brick a show."

"Goodnight, Son," she said.

"Goodnight, Mom."

It was about 11:00 the next morning when Chris headed back into the house to make an early lunch. He'd boxed what tools he thought he might use, and the rest he put in a stack to take the Salvation Army. Maybe they'd know what to do with them. As he sat down to a lunch of fried hot dogs and coleslaw, the phone rang.

"Jeez, all I do is talk on the phone these days."

He picked up. It was Piper. "Chris," she said, flatly.

"Yes, hey, I talked to Mom last night. I told her that I'd teach the classes. She got it squared with Indian Affairs. I thought she'd call you."

It was quiet on her end of the line.

"Piper?" he said, sensing something wrong. "Are you there? Did you hear me?"

"Yes," she said. "Are you sitting down?"

Chris felt the world collapsing. What had happened? He pulled the phone line close and sat on the piano bench. "Yes, what's wrong?"

"Uncle Landon went to the farm today to check up on the cattle."

"Yes, did he get hurt?"

"No, he found them."

Chris paused, confused. "He found the cattle? They get out again?"

"No, Chris," Piper said, struggling with tears. "He found

Grandpa and Grandma. In their bed. They were both still there in bed. They were…" she began to cry, "they were dead."

"What?" Chris called. "I don't understand."

"Uncle Landon couldn't even stay in the house the air was so bad. He opened the windows and then went out. Propped the door open, then when his head cleared a little, he went in and turned off the stove. The propane stove in the living room. It was leaking carbon monoxide. The chimney pipe was uncoupled up at the ceiling. That's what the state troopers said. But the county coroner…" she stopped speaking and just began to cry.

Chris leaned back and felt tears on his cheeks, as well.

When Piper gathered herself again to speak, she said, "They say the earthquake last week must have vibrated the chimney vent loose so that the stove was just dumping the exhaust into the room. Overnight it was enough to be deadly."

Chris nodded with a deep numbness. "Grandpa Jeff told me he was going to light the stove when I talked to him yesterday. How's Mom? Does she know?"

"Yeah, Landon called her first. She's destroyed. We're all meeting at Uncle Landon's house. How soon can you get here?"

"Leaving now."

Piper began to cry again. "Chris," she said.

"Yes?"

"I love you."

"I love you, too, Piper. I'm on my way."

But the truth be known it was more than an hour before he left for the ranch. Chris spent most of that time in the shower crying.

The funeral was the saddest moment of Chris's life, without a doubt. He doubted anything would ever surpass the sorrow he felt then. He'd called Elizabeth, and she'd insisted on driving him down. She was worried in his emotional state he would have a wreck.

They'd driven straight to the farm, where he stood in the pasture south of the house and listened to a covey of quail call out, seeking family.

Later, Chris drove Elizabeth in to get a room at the motel in town. He went from there back to the farm. He sat in the living room a long time staring at the ceiling and the loose chimney pipe in the living room.

Later that evening at Uncle Landon's, Piper asked him where Elizabeth was.

Chris was startled. He'd forgotten she had come with him. Chris was, like the rest of the family, numb with shock and pain. Lillian sent Johnny into town to fetch her.

Chris felt a hollowness inside; he was not sure if it could ever be filled.

People from town stopped by Uncle Landon's and asked what they could do.

There was nothing anyone could do. Chris, like the rest, was inconsolable. Feeling beyond aid himself, he, along with Elizabeth, assisted his mother and sister in their grief. Chris felt in them the same void he knew in his heart.

He asked Johnny about it that night back in Alva.

"Your grandparents have passed, right, Johnny?"

The big black man rose from the bed in the motel room. He poured some Scotch into a paper cup. "A-huh, parents, too."

"How'd you get through it?"

"Didn't."

"I don't get you."

"I been watching you," Johnny said, "looking like you're the out in the middle of traffic, like you trying to dodge your pain. Figure out a way to navigate through it. You're a smart guy, maybe one of the smartest I ever met, but you can't think your way through this. And you can't avoid it." He turned to the young man who seemed all the smaller with the grief he carried. "Avoiding things. That never worked for me." Johnny took a swallow and let the liquid burn on the way down. "I always figured if there was no way to get away from the pain, I might as well aim right at it. Take it head-on. Run right into it, then start a new world that included that pain. I don't mean no disrespect. Everyone has a way of dealing with pain. But that's how I done it."

Chris closed the blinds to the world. He felt tears in his eyes, but he held them back.

Johnny acknowledged the moment with a nod. "For me, I was a black running back in a game with mainly white defenders. They were trying to inflict pain on me, as much as they could. I figured out soon enough that there wasn't no outrunning them. I headed right into them. Put a helmet in their gut."

Chris motioned for Johnny to pour two fingers of Scotch for him. "And then what?"

"Slam bang. Started a new world with the pain in it. It becomes part of you. I started a new world where that kind of pain was just part of it."

"And it worked for you?"

"I lasted three seasons." Johnny laughed. "It was painful, sure. But then I was out of the league, and I faced right into that new world. I decided if I wasn't a running back in the pros no more, then I would become the best damn recruiter the university ever saw. I brought them black athletes from back home in L.A. Brought the team the best talent in the country. Turned black men over to those cracker sons-a-bitches to be made into elite football players."

"For their own good or for yours?"

Johnny looked at him with a raised eyebrow. "I had access to get those young men into the pipeline of one of the top ten football programs in the country. It was a way out of the hood for me and it could be for them. It made me indispensable to the university. Hell, it made me indispensable to the state. Both ends of the rope needed me. Those young men needed my endorsement. I pledged to them that young black athletes can come from Los Angeles to here and that they'll be treated well and have a shot at the big time. The athletic department understood what I brought to the table and in turn, they promoted me to the business community. They repaid me. Now, I'm set up for life with this Lincoln dealership."

"And how is facing into the pain going?" Chris asked.

"Knowing the bastards hate me for the color of my skin but still shine me on because of the young men who'll come on my promise?"

Chris nodded. "You feel you are betraying them? Those young black men?"

"Balancing act. The pros are changing. They care about winning more than color. Colleges getting there, too."

"How about you? You feel like folks will ever fully accept you?"

"Some always have. Bass Reeves, the basis for the Lone Ranger, was a black man and way more famous than me. They accepted him. As least mostly so."

"I believe they put a mask on a white man for that role on TV," Chris noted.

Johnny drank the last of his Scotch. "Hollywood. At least they got Tonto for Grant Johnson's part."

"Still discrimination throughout the whole country? Painfully slow on change."

"That's what I'm saying. I just know it's there. Racism always around. Hurtful shit. They wouldn't want us living in their neighborhood, but they'll accept an Orange Bowl win."

Chris frowned. "I'm not sure how all of that helps me."

Johnny shrugged. "May not. All I'm saying is I find it more practical to decide that life is full of pain and just plan on it being that way. I cope better knowing I'm about to get hit."

The outpouring of sympathy from the community was wonderful, but it couldn't reach Chris, Piper, Lillian, or even Uncle Landon and his family in this hour of distress and heartbreak. At the graveside, one double-wide hole was dug in the ground for the two who'd been married for fifty-four years. It was smaller, Chris thought, than the hole in his heart.

After the graveside service, a young redhead approached him. In his funk, Chris barely recognized her. It was Shannon Gill, the girl who'd starred in the school play in Kiowa all those years ago. She offered condolences, reaching out and touching his arm. He nodded thanks.

"Where are you now?" Chris asked her.

"OKC. I heard about your grandparents' passing on the news down home. I watch Piper. Everybody I know does. It's big news because of Johnny and her."

Chris nodded. "How's Bart?"

Shannon looked startled. "He died three years ago in Vietnam, Chris. I'm sorry, I would have thought you knew."

Then, Lillian called him away. He remembered only bits from that day. The look on his mother's face was the single moment etched in his mind. The devastation and sadness mapped itself from her face to his heart. After that, he only remembered pain. He understood Johnny's philosophy, but it was beyond him.

The next day, Chris and Elizabeth went back to Lawrence and the house, which was now pending sale, to pack up the last of his possessions. It was a quiet journey back to Kansas. At the house, Chris did not speak to Elizabeth, and she began to cry. Things were at an end.

Most of the furniture had been moved when Lillian took the job in Tulsa. The empty rooms in his childhood home seemed a perfect metaphor for the hole in his heart. Time and space seemed to be rendered mute. Elizabeth tried to care for him, but the truth was

Jeff and Gwen Hart had been the centerpiece of his world and now they were gone. He did not know how he would replace them. Chris was not ready to let anyone else in. He knew he could not. He did not know how to start his life again.

Chris spent the night with Elizabeth before he left the next day.

She gave her body to him as a balm to sooth his sorrow.

Afterwards, Chris felt tears begin to well in his eyes.

"Dear, dear man," Elizabeth said, "I'm here, I'm here. It'll be okay."

But of course, it would not.

On his last day in Lawrence, Chris received notification he'd passed the bar and was now an attorney. He called his supervisor in OKC and let him know that he was now official.

Elizabeth insisted they have a breakfast of biscuits and gravy before he left town. Chris could have felt nothing further from celebration, but he went and tried to put on a brave face.

Afterwards, as he held her beside his old car, it was her turn to cry. She seemed to know in his eyes it was the end of a chapter.

They made plans for her to come down over Memorial Day to see his new apartment. Chris promised to call her after he arrived and had things unloaded. However, she seemed to know, as did he, that their relationship was ending. Chris had nothing in him to give anyone else right now. He had a job, two jobs, in fact, awaiting him.

Elizabeth had kept him at arm's length for four years, and now, despite their closeness in the last ten days, he did not love her. He did not know if he could feel love. He did not know if he could feel anything ever again.

Woods County
Fall, 1911

Both Jeff and Gabriel had calves to raise. This autumn, the two were to enter their calves at the local fair in Alva. This year, the Livestock Association was offering twenty dollars for the best calf. However, when it came time to castrate the calves, Everett thought Gabriel's to be the biggest, strongest bull calf he'd seen out of their herd in the time they'd been running cattle. He decided to keep the bull as a stud for the farm, and Gabe's animal was kept home fair week.

The night of the competition, the family arrived early enough to get Jeff's animal from the rig Everett had borrowed to the arena and its pen. The girls were excited to see the rabbits and chickens, especially the fancy roosters, brightly feathered like peacocks in their splendor.

Everett paraded Jeff around like the heir to a ranching empire, maybe the 101 Ranch down to Ponca City, not a bone-dry spread of five hundred acres on the Salt Fork of the Arkansas River. But Everett was well-known. Anthem Song and his sire had bred a lot of good horse flesh in the last decade. Jeff, for once, had fun with his father.

Tanner was with his brother-in-law, but he felt awkward in this circle of ranchers all wearing new boots. He excused himself and moseyed his way off to the bunnies and chickens to find the womenfolk. He found them, took Marie's hand, and the two walked along with the four girls, and of course, Gabriel, who looked crestfallen to have had his calf pulled from the competition. He walked along like a fifth wheel.

Tanner, Marie, and the five children headed from the barn down the midway, where a few barkers were shouting for people to slide up and try their luck at ring toss or at knocking down milk bottles with a ball. They had few takers.

Then, at the far end of the lane, they came upon a shooting contest. The barker had repeater BB guns lined up. The goal was to X out a star on paper before the timer ran out. You had a minute. It cost a nickel. Normally, the family would not have spent any money on such malarkey, but Tanner felt bad for his boy not getting to show his calf. He gave the boy two bits and told him he could win each of the four girls a teddy bear if he was good enough.

Tanner pulled the boy close. "This is twenty-five cents. It'll get you five plays. Don't worry about winning on the first time. Figure out how the gun fires. How it shoots. Does it veer left or right? Does it go high or end low? Don't worry about the clock. Then, on round two till you're out of money, you can go for blacking out that X, you hear?"

Gabe smiled. "Yeah, Pa. I got it."

When Gabe began gauging the gun's accuracy, the girls saw his shots far off the mark. They were embarrassed and moved away. Soon, they were maybe fifty feet away, looking at quilts. Tanner stayed with the boy at first, but realized his presence was making Gabe nervous.

Marie joined the girls, smiling after her son and husband.

"Gabe, you can do this. I'm headed back over to the barn," Tanner said, kicking up a big cloud of dust to mark his departure. He tipped his hat at the barker and turned his back.

Gabe won two teddy bears on second and third tries. He was struggling on the fourth attempt, but he wanted to win all four times to give each girl a bear.

As he plugged away, a large man behind him began to be impatient.

The man leaned into Gabe. The boy could smell stale whiskey on the man's clothes.

When Gabe started his last try, the man swore and threw down an empty pint bottle. It didn't break, but he kicked it into the post supporting the front table for the barker. It bounced under the counter to the barker's feet.

The barker could see trouble coming. He set Gabe's timer once again and ducked out the back of the draped bunting, leaving the boy alone.

Gabe paid no attention. He was shooting the BB gun well, close to winning a fourth time.

Then, the man pressed against him.

Gabe lost concentration and experienced fear. His shots veered away erratically.

Marie looked across the midway to see a man dressed all in black leaning into her boy. The man, whose head was turned, wore a gun, which was not unusual on the range, but was in town It was certainly not common on the fairgrounds. She hurried toward her son, calling, "Gabriel, come here."

The boy turned his head and wrinkled his nose with a shake of his head. He had more than fifteen seconds to win another bear. He turned back to the target.

Marie called again, this time stridently. "Gabe, come here, now."

The man turned to her, and she recognized him. It was Mel Harris. He grabbed the boy's shoulder, yanking him to the side. "I'll show you how to hit a target, you little half breed."

With that, he pulled his revolver and fired at the target pinned as it was to three thick bales of hay. The roar was incredible, stopping everything on the midway. The sound reverberated off the barn down the way, sounding almost as if there'd been two shots. It was nearly as loud in its echo as its initial cacophony.

Everything seemed to slow down for Marie. She ran, as if in slow motion, to her son.

He was turning to her, tears welling his eyes.

The meaty fingers of Harris' left hand dug into the boy's shoulder.

Gabe wrenched himself away, ducking under the man's clawing hand as he bent low.

Harris' face was flush with drink, his scar a livid white stripe of lightning on his cheek.

"Run, Gabe!" Marie yelled, as the boy twisted free, darting away.

Harris looked at her, stupidly. He hadn't noticed her before so much was his intoxication. But now, as he was spun slightly by the boy's escape, she came into his full view.

"Goddamn Indians," Harris spat with venom as he shot Marie in the chest.

Burial
Oklahoma City
1974

Chris Fairchild was effective at his new job; everyone would say that. Not many would say they took to him right away. All his life, he had been quiet. He never made friends quickly. Now, after the death of Jeff and Gwen, the young attorney was positively silent. He was on time, his briefs were well-written, and he knew the law. His clients, usually reprobates guilty of the crimes for which they were accused, got less time with him as their attorney than they would have with a public defender, so the Five Tribes were satisfied. But Chris did not develop relationships. It was as if he were an automaton. His worst attribute, the inability to interact with people, was suddenly exacerbated. He seemed unable to connect at all.

That was not true for his sister. Piper grieved, yes. But she was married, and Johnny Fleet was a man who lived in the moment. He was always on to the next deal and made sure their lives were full. Piper was raised by his ebullient manner. They were on every guest list. They attended every gala. She was asked to work in charity. She became the face and focal point for a number of non-profits. She met every mover and shaker in central Oklahoma. By midsummer, they were the "it" couple. Piper, with her sassy looks and thin beanpole figure, Johnny found, was the key that opened high society's gates to him. In OKC, high society meant oil money. Twenty families in the state held eighty percent of the wealth. They were titans, but these oil scions did not fit in with the country's move toward long hair, smoking grass, and going to demonstrations. Nonetheless, these upstanding citizens wanted something new, and they found it in Piper Fleet.

The oil barons, and more importantly, their wives, had taken note of the charming young woman who was on their TV every night. They found her smiling face a bit of sunshine, and she tried each night at 10:13 to forecast some of it for them. The gates to the kingdom had opened for Johnny Fleet and his wife, and by inviting them in, these richest of households in the state could pride themselves on their open-mindedness and their willingness to accept diversity. One black man and his charming wife checked off a box, and those rich women liked checking off that box. It was a golden time to be in Oklahoma, to be inside the circle of wealth, and to be invited to all the best parties.

The fall arrived. Piper's new Saturday football show debuted to much fanfare. She did the weather looking like a London fashion designer had dressed her. Short skirts, tall boots, and neon colors were new for Oklahoma, but Piper brought it to the nightly news. Johnny grew an afro, but he kept it modest. He wore flared pants, but with cowboy boots. His shirt was unbuttoned showing chest hair, but he only undid one more button than what the sons of the oil barons would have. It was noticed, and tolerated.

Johnny and Piper were OKC's fashion plates. Piper ensured both the men and women watching the weather had something to talk about, and it wasn't tornados. Each morning, the outfit she'd worn the evening before was fodder for water cooler gossip. Oil money approved. The couple was OKC's most fashionable newlyweds. They were on every invitation list.

Chris was invited to many of the gala functions, but he did not attend. He went to work, and then he went home. Some days, he was at the federal courts; some days at Big Mac prison. Few days was he actually in the federal building at his desk. Evenings he worked from his spartan apartment on OKC's eastern side near the I-40 corridor. On weekends, he helped Uncle Landon with the cattle on the Salt Fork. Chris became pretty good on a horse. Saturday evenings, he did minor repairs on his grandparents' home as a tribute to their memory.

On the farm, Chris's silence was not taken as an affront. Uncle Landon was himself a man of few words. They could work together for a day and not write a paragraph with what they said to each other. Both liked it that way.

By early October, Chris's students in law classes at the university discovered him to be an able professor, but not one with any personality. At first, these second-year students stayed around after class to engage him, maybe curry his favor, but a month and a half in, those attempts had lagged. There was nothing there to be gained by hanging around with Chris Fairchild. He was a stiff. An empty suit, some said.

It was a Tuesday in the second week of October, and atypically, Chris was at his desk. He seldom had days like these with no appearances in court, no client visitations, and no meetings in chambers with judges. Most of his paperwork was completed at home at night. His legal secretary, Hazel Kingfisher ('tsa tlo hi' in Cherokee), could, by this point, read his scribble. She adapted his notes into legal documents, which allowed him to front the law office in the field. He was handling the caseload of two attorneys, but without a personal life, it was fine.

The tribes were pleased with his performance but had noted his lack of social skills. They were disappointed. His mother, Lillian Hart, was so endearing. She cared deeply about Indian Affairs and put her heart and soul into assisting the tribes every day. Chris, they reasoned, had too much of the white man in him. His soul was on ice.

On this day, with his secretary filing briefs at the courthouse, he worked alone in silence at his desk. His mind was in tune with the task at hand, so it was some surprise to hear the antechamber door open and close. He had a visitor. No one visited without an appointment. He set down his Dictaphone and pen.

Chris, dressed in dark navy trousers, a red tie, and white shirt, stepped to his coat rack and slipped on his jacket. "Hello, who's there?"

He opened the door to see Shannon Gill. Chris was stoic these days, but the appearance of Shannon's lovely face and red hair in his office caused shock to register across his face.

"Hi, Chris." Shannon stood before him in a business suit with skirt just above the knee. She wore stockings and black heels. Her lipstick was tasteful, and her makeup made her face even more pale than he remembered.

"Hi, Shann-on," he stammered. "Wow, this is a surprise. He looked around to assess his own office. He saw it as she must—stark and dull. The only item on the four beige walls was a large brass plaque. It was stamped with, *"The Seals of the Five Civilized Tribes"*. Other than that, the room held but the secretary's desk and a credenza with a coffee pot in it.

Chris reached out to shake Shannon's hand as she moved to hug him. It was an awkward moment, and they both laughed. Chris pulled back his extended hand, and they hugged.

"Come on in," he said, "it's good to see you. Thanks for coming to the funeral. Okay if I make some coffee?" The last line was rehearsed and he said it to everyone who entered his office.

Shannon nodded. "It's good to see you, too. You've lost weight." She nodded toward the coffee pot. "Sure, coffee'd be nice."

Chris opened the Folgers can and placed a new scoop in the pot, then bid her to follow him. He got Shannon settled in one of the two red leather chairs facing his desk, then he went into the adjacent restroom and filled the coffee pot with water. Putting it on to percolate, Chris landed in the second red chair, a technique he used to put the clients more at ease.

"What brings you here, Shannon, not that you're not always welcome. I just don't get many visitors. Sixth floor of the federal building, end of the hall. IRS auditors in every other office on this floor. It's not a place people want to come to visit."

Shannon smiled. "I sure don't want to visit an auditor."

Their laughter was real and comfortable until its volume trailed off awkwardly.

Chris tried to think of something to say.

Finally, Shannon took the reins. "I'm here because I heard something you should know." She scratched her wrist, nervously, with manicured nails.

Chris frowned. "Something about family?"

"No, no," Shannon said, crossing her legs. Chris could hear the nylon ripple. She still affected him, just like she had that first day as he watched her from Jeff's pick-up truck. "It's work-related" she said, "It's about, well, it's about Indians."

Chris furrowed his brow. "Wait, a second." He got up and left the room and poured them a cup of coffee. "Sugar or creamer?" he called from the antechamber.

"One sugar, and just a drop or two of creamer. Barely change the color, okay?"

A moment later, he came in. "I hope the coffee is to your liking. I'm not much of a cook, but Hazel, my secretary, tells me my coffee isn't too bad." He carefully handed her the cup and saucer. Truth be known, the saucers had never been used before.

Chris sat down. "Tell me."

Shannon Gill blushed. "This is something I wasn't supposed to hear, and I'd lose my job if anyone knew I talked to you about it."

"I won't ever say your name to anyone. It's just between us."

Shannon nodded and took a sip of coffee, swallowing slowly to gather herself. "Okay, I heard something. It struck me as wrong. It bothered me and knowing you, I thought maybe it could be put right." She had a catch in her voice. "I-I thought maybe *you* could put it right."

Chris could tell Shannon was about to cry. He put his hand on hers, and she looked up at him, surprised.

"Let's start slow," he said. "Where do you work?"

"Oklahoma Children Protective Services, only two blocks from here. I could have walked over. But I got in my car, drove out of downtown, and then I came by the bypass and parked on the far side of your building. I felt like a secret agent."

Chris smiled. "I'm sure no one saw you. How's the coffee?"

"Okay. Next time, a little less cream."

Chris took note of the words "next time". He liked it.

"You heard something at CPS that impacts my job. Something affecting the Five Tribes?"

She nodded again. Her face flushed. "Oh, I shouldn't be doing this. It will just open a can of worms."

Chris, his hand still on hers, patted it softly. "Wrongs that can be righted should be. Who said the thing that bothered you?"

"John Taylor, he's my boss. Well, really he's my boss's boss."

"Who'd he say it to?"

"My boss, Sandy McBride. She's married to Marshal McBride."

Chris nodded. He knew of Marshal McBride. He was an attorney and had been City Attorney in the previous administration. There was talk he would be appointed to the Oklahoma Supreme Court. "What is Sandy's title?"

"Director of Oklahoma Children Protective Services."

"What's John Taylor's title?"

Shannon looked nervous again. "He's head of Oklahoma's Health and Human Services."

Chris shook his head. "Taylor's on the governor's cabinet."

Shannon nodded. She pulled her hand free of his and put her fingers to her collar, taking a deep breath. She leaned back and took a moment to look at the ceiling.

"Okay," Chris said, "we know the principal characters. What did this John Taylor say?"

Shannon stood and went to the window. She looked out onto the roof of the adjacent building where three pigeons pecked at gravel along the rain gutter. "You should know John Taylor and Zane Kilmain are best friends. The Taylors and the Kilmains are thick as thieves."

"Zane Kilmain, the warden at Big Mac?"

"Yes, Taylor is a big law-and-order Republican. Hardcore Nixon guy. Has a photo in his office of him shaking hands with Tricky Dick."

"I'm at the prison almost every week, so I've met Warden Kilmain, but not Taylor." Chris smiled. "Most people would take down those Nixon photos after he resigned in disgrace."

"Not him. Taylor is hardcore."

"What did he say?"

"He handed Sandy some documents. I was later charged with distributing them to law enforcement. They were subpoenas. Subpoenas for Indian men on the res. From Children Protective Services to appear in state court."

"Is that unusual?"

"Not particularly."

"So?" Chris said, leaning back to see her face better.

"These particular subpoenas were unusual. They were all essentially bogus: cases that have been settled, cases that have been arbitrated, or even cases so weak they won't get to trial. Late pays claims for support that have been already paid in arrears. Petty stuff."

"Why would he issue those? Issue bogus paper? Waste everyone's time."

Shannon came back and sat down. She looked Chris straight in the eye. "Did you know state warrants and subpoenas can't be served on the res? Not on tribal land. Indians on the res are essentially in another country. Oklahoma can't get to them. Not even the FBI in most cases."

Chris nodded. "Of course, Indian land is policed by BIA officers. I can quote you the wording; they are there, 'to uphold the constitutional sovereignty of the federally recognized Tribes and preserve peace within Indian country.' I deal with it every day."

"Did you know the Tribes offer an exemption on state cases involving the welfare of children? They do allow citizens of the res to be served by Children Protective Services."

Chris nodded. "Yes, now that you mention it, but it never really comes up in my cases. Why?"

"Because John Taylor's working with the state prosecutor. With the AG. If they have an outstanding state warrant for an Indian on the res and they can't get to him, they get John to issue to a subpoena for him to appear in children's court."

"And then what? The case just gets tossed."

"Then, state police are always on hand to take the respondent into custody for the outstanding warrant; that's the real reason to get the Indian off the res."

"What if the outstanding warrant is on some guy who doesn't have kids?"

"Bogus paternity suits."

Chris was startled. The scandal would be huge. "How long has this been going on?"

"John Taylor took the job when the new governor moved in. I don't know if his predecessor did the same thing."

"So less than a year. How many times have you been asked to issue these subpoenas?"

"Just three times, but I was only promoted to be Sandy's secretary just about four months ago. I didn't think anything about them at first, but this last month, John Taylor was in with Sandy joking about how Zane Kilmain would be making a big bonus with all the Injuns they were putting in lock-up. They laughed and said Zane would be buying."

Chris's mind was racing. "Can I get a list of all the subpoenas your department issued since Taylor assumed the office?"

Shannon reached for her handbag. "Here they are. I made you copies."

Piper didn't start work until ten in the morning most days, and some days not until two or three. Today, she dressed in a pink and flaming orange mini, orange nylons, and pink heels. Now, she was putting on pink lipstick to match her shoes.

Johnny walked into the bathroom and patted her on the rump. "Looking good, Twiggy."

"Careful," she said, "Don't jiggle me. I don't want to have big ole smeary lips on camera. I have both the evening and the late shows tonight. You'll have to get yourself dinner."

Johnny looked himself over in the mirror. He wore a short

sleeve turtleneck, black jeans and boots, and a pick comb in his hair. "I'll just buy pizza for the salesmen. Have a slice," he said.

"You're not eating very good, honey," Piper said. "Don't go getting flabby."

Johnny laughed and flexed an arm in the mirror. "Look like your man getting flabby?"

"Oh, no," Piper said, laughing. "Remember. I see you naked."

It was Johnny's turn to laugh. "Yes, you do."

"And so you know," Piper replied, "I have better tits than Twiggy."

"So do I," Johnny said back, and they both laughed.

They exited the master bath and moved into the kitchen.

Piper poured two coffees.

Johnny took a sip, nodded in appreciation, and kissed her on the cheek. "Trick to a good marriage starts with good coffee in the morning."

"It does, does it? I thought it had something to do with the night before, too," she replied.

"That too; that too," he said. "You're heading in pretty early. What's up?"

"Going over to school," she said. "I am so excited about those steady cams you bought for us. My students are ecstatic to get to play with them now that they've arrived. I'm assigning outside projects in class today. It will be interesting to see my second years go out in the field and put together some footage. I'll see the rough footage and then let them edit in their studio shots. See what skills they got."

"Yeah, that reminds me," Johnny said. "That one chick you mentioned. I got her the interview she wanted. With Monroe Evans."

Monroe Evans was the newest wide receiver with the football team. Word on the street was he was the fastest man in the state. Football fans wanted more info on this young stud.

"Thanks, babe," Piper said, already getting her purse and

rolling out the door. "I'll tell her. By the way, that chick is Tobi Thomas."

"Right," he said, "her name is Tobi, and her cameraman is named Renée. The world is a confusing place."

"For old fuddy-duddies it is, sure enough," Piper laughed as she blew him a kiss goodbye.

At 5:00, Chris decided to call his mother and let her know he had business in Tulsa and was on the way and would spend the night. He wanted to tell her his explosive news in person. He vowed to Shannon he would not reveal where he received his info or where he got the list.

After the call, he went home to his spartan apartment and packed a duffel. Lillian was expecting him at bedtime.

By the time he arrived, it was past ten. His mother greeted him at the door in her nightgown and robe. She held a glass of wine and offered him one.

"No," he said, "I need to talk to you."

"Unless you're getting engaged, it can wait until morning," Lil said with a yawn.

"No, it can't," Chris said.

Then, in the living room, Chris told her what he knew and showed her the list. Lillian Hart was greatly alarmed at her son's words. Although it was nearing 11:00, she called the Commissioner of Indian Affairs, Louis Bruce, at his home. Like her, Bruce sounded fatigued and possibly awakened by the phone. Lillian explained the circumstances. With gravity in his voice, Bruce suggested they meet at eight in the morning at his home away from prying eyes.

Communication media students Tobi Thomas and Renée Ripley were captivated with the new camera given them by their professor and personal hero, Piper Fleet. It was state-of-the art equipment, capable of capturing images in deep focus up to a hundred yards away or within a foot, it also had a directional microphone good for clarity nearly fifty yards away.

The two tested the mic and discovered that, with a good wind, and there was often that in Oklahoma, the mic would pick up conversations at up to one hundred yards away. The two photojournalism students played with their new toy all afternoon after their class let out.

It wasn't until evening Tobi knew she needed to get home and start working on the questions she would ask the budding football star, Monroe Evans. Although the interview was not until the next week, Tobi knew it was a chance to get into the limelight.

Tobi was pretty, she was smart, and she was ambitious; interviewing Monroe Evans would get her a job. She was sure of it. Nothing was going to stop her.

Louis Bruce lived in a brick, one-level ranch with a large concrete patio. His two white shepherds greeted Chris and Lillian as they arrived.

Louis's wife greeted them at the front door before they knocked. She ushered them through the house to the patio, where Louis sat at a large redwood table.

He stood to greet them.

Lil and Chris shook hands with the man and then were seated.

Mrs. Bruce served them coffee, reentering the house, closing the sliding glass door.

The dogs moved about their feet, sniffing them, and asking to be petted.

"Don't mind the beasts. They're harmless. Big babies, really. John Wayne, Hopalong, go away. Git, you hear."

The dogs' ears perked with their names being said, but they obeyed and trotted out into the spacious backyard to play.

Louis Bruce smiled grimly at them. He looked tired. He wore a suit, but his jacket must have been in the house. The power tie was loosened at the neck. "Thanks for coming over so early. If you were like me, it was a restless night. I made some calls after we spoke. I have more information. Illuminating information, actually."

Louis Bruce took a sip of coffee before continuing. "It appears that your John Taylor is working in coordination with the state police and FBI to flush out American Indian Movement members, specifically one member of the movement. They believe this subversive to be hiding on the Muskogee Creek Nation Reservation. These spurious Child Protective Services subpoenas are directed at men whom the FBI thinks can provide information on that individual. They are using the threat of state charges to force those Native Americans to talk or face jail time. Mostly, they aren't charged. Not if they provide intel."

Lillian shook her head. "To me, it seems that Taylor in issuing these writs is violating our constituencies' civil rights."

Chris nodded. He had carried his Constitution Law textbook to his mother's last night, reviewing it during the wee hours when he could not sleep. He said, "I think what Taylor is doing violates the guarantees of the Fourteenth Amendment." Then, he quoted, 'No State shall make or enforce any law which shall abridge the privileges or immunities of citizens of the United States'."

He looked to Louis Bruce to speak, but the man didn't, so Chris continued. "And the third clause of the Fourteenth expands that protection found in the Fifth Amendment to cover state laws, as well. It says, '...nor shall any State deprive any person of life, liberty or property, without due process of law.' I think their actions clearly infringe on those rights."

Louis Bruce smiled at Lillian. "The apple didn't fall far from the tree, I see."

"He's his mother's son," she said with a grin. "In our perspective, they're illegally using Children Protective Services to flush an AIM warrior off of the Creek Reservation? Do we know whom they are looking for?"

Louis Bruce nodded. "Yes, he is a known radical. He's been off the radar for some time but was associated with the Yippie Movement and those in the anti-war movement. His name is Tate Laughlin."

Silence.

Lillian spoke first because she saw her son was incapable of it. "We're familiar with Tate Laughlin. He was an advisee of mine when I was in Lawrence."

Louis Bruce furrowed his brow. "That's unfortunate. The Bureau of Indian Affairs is not aligned with the political ambitions of AIM. They want to assist their brothers and sisters of our tribes, but their ways are too violent and too radical. We cannot support them." He took a sip of coffee and frowned.

"AIM has been very active in the last three years," he said. "They formed in 1968 in Minneapolis and came to national prominence when 200 members stormed and took over Alcatraz in 1971. They held that facility for two years. Later, members of AIM walked from the West Coast to Washington in a Trail of Broken Treaties. There they delivered a twenty-point list of demands of the U.S. government. It was too radical to consider. Just impossible. Last year, AIM had 500 members storm the Bureau of Indian Affairs in Washington and ransack the offices. Thousands of documents, including water rights contracts and other treaties with the tribes, were taken. $700,000 in damages occurred. It did not endear the political movement with Congress or with any of us at the Bureau of Indian Affairs.

"As Lillian may have told you, Chris, we are the verge of getting major legislation through the House, one that will greatly assist the many tribes still living and trying to survive in the white man's world. The bill is called The Indian Self-Determination and Education Assistance Act. It will, among other things, give the federal government the ability to license native tribes to fulfill government contracts."

"It will allow them to operate their own schools," Lillian interjected. "We can't allow AIM to screw all of this up."

"AIM opposes this bill?" Chris asked.

"No, they just believe working within the system will only give us what the system wants us to have."

Chris raised an eyebrow. "It has worked out that way so far."

"Yes," Louis Bruce said, "but it does us very little good to just stick a thumb in the eye of government. Working to better the lives of Native Americans through improved governance is what your mother and I have spent our lives doing. We are on the precipice of something terrific. Seventy school districts will soon self-govern but be funded by federal dollars. Many Native American businesses will be allowed to provide contracted services to the reservations. This bill is a wealth engine if administered properly."

"What do I do when I get to court on Monday? The first of these CPS cases comes to Children's Court then."

"I have some ideas on that, but first I need more coffee. Anyone?"

Both Chris and Lillian nodded.

Louis Bruce went inside and returned with a pot off the stove. "Are you familiar with an Oklahoma judge new to the federal bench? Judge Hiram Spence?"

Chris smiled. "I hunted quail with him once when I was child."

"Then, you know him to be an honest and good man. I spoke to him not an hour ago. He suggested we adhere to the following plan. I'll outline it, and if you approve, we'll implement the needed steps today."

The State of Oklahoma Juvenile Justice Center housed Children's Court. It was but a block from Chris's office. He walked over before the hearing and saw Judge Hiram Spence sitting in the small courtroom, which was more informal than most criminal courtrooms. Chris moved to the front and shook hands with the defendant, a young man named Kern Kopaka. Chris had looked up the man's last name in the Osage directory his mother kept at home. The name meant "flashing eyes." Knowing that, Chris looked closely into the young man's face as they were introduced. Kopaka's eyes were indeed filled with lightning and nervous energy.

The judge, a ruddy woman by the name of Ruth Miller, brought the court into session. She made immediate note of the addition of Chris Fairchild to the bench and to the presence of a federal judge in the gallery. "I must say, it is not normal for me to have such esteemed colleagues gathered in my courtroom. The Five Tribes Legal Counsel Christian Fairchild and Federal Judge Hiram Spence, we are glad to have you here, but are more than a bit curious than why you would be in attendance for the first item on my Monday docket."

"Good morning, Judge Miller, I'm glad to be here, as well," Chris said.

Judge Spence merely smiled and nodded. He was not officially part of the proceeding, although his mere presence in the room carried great weight.

The state attorney, when prompted, read the charges. Kopaka was charged with delinquency of child support payments. He was six months in arrears. Suggested proscriptions of garnishment had been unsuccessful, as young Mr. Kopaka was unemployed. The state was suggesting ninety days in state jail as a new alternative to motivate payment. "It appears," said the state attorney, "the American Indian Movement, in which Mr. Kopaka is quite active, does not pay its members well."

Chris stood. "Our client's political leanings are not subject to today's inquiries, Judge Miller."

"I agree," said the judge. "Please refrain, Mr. Lindor, from editorializing on my clock." She turned to the defendant. "Mr. Kopaka, you stand accused of being six months behind in child support payments. According to state documents, you have not responded to correspondence and have missed previous summons. What say you?"

She rotated her head toward Chris's co-counsel at the desk, an attorney for the res named Ernest Bloom-in-Sun.

"Judge Miller," said Bloom-in-Sun. "I have a receipt from Children Protective Services, dated last Friday, October 10th, for the entire amount of our client's current and past due support payments." He held a piece of paper toward the judge.

Judge Miller frowned. "Please approach."

She examined the receipt and then turned to the state's attorney, Mr. Lindor. "Were you aware that Mr. Kopaka's support was paid in full before this hearing?"

Lindor looked surprised. In fact, he'd been surprised to see Chris Fairchild as part of the defendant's counsel. He'd been doubly surprised to see Judge Hiram Spence in the gallery. "No, Your Honor. May I see the receipt?"

She motioned him to approach.

Lindor examined the receipt and then shrugged. "I would say the state now has no issue with Mr. Kopaka at this time. We would hope things in the future would not have to go this far to get compliance to the state's decision of child support."

"I agree," said Judge Miller. "Mr. Kopaka, you need to mind your P's and Q's going forward. However, I cannot punish potential future behavior. This court is adjourned." She looked to the gallery, where Judge Spence stood and buttoned his suitcoat. "As our proceedings took so little time, I would invite you back for coffee. My curiosity is piqued. Do you have time?"

"No, I cannot. Other pressing matters," Judge Spence said, "I'll fill you in later."

Outside, after descending three floors in an elevator, Chris and Kern Kopaka walked side-by-side toward Chris's office. They were joined by two Osage Indians dressed in denim shirts, brown slacks, black work boots, and flat-brimmed Stetsons.

Judge Hiram Spence and Ernest Bloom-in-Sun walked behind the other four by perhaps a half a block by design. Just as Chris and Kopaka reached the crosswalk, two state police cars pulled up, one on each side of the pedestrians.

Four officers exited the police cars with guns drawn. "Kern Kopaka, you're under arrest. Raise your hands." The gun barrels swept across all four men. "Hands up, all four of you. Let's not get anybody hurt here."

Chris began to speak. "Officers, I am this man's attorney."

"Zip it. Attorneys get their turn, but it ain't right now. Now, get your hands up. Iffin' you don't, you be arrested for interfering with police business. Now, up with 'em." The speaker wore a blue uniform. His gun was burnished steel.

Chris raised his hands.

Judge Hiram Spence approached with Ernest Bloom-in-Sun.

"Stay back," the state police officer said, "this ain't none of your concern."

"Oh, it is my concern, sir. I'm Federal Judge Hiram Spence. I have been asked to be here to see this arrest take place. It is an illegal action. See, these two men in the denim shirts and brown trousers? They are tribal police. May I introduce Lt. James Orson and Officer Nestor Chitto. Mr. Kopaka is in their custody.

"They escorted him from tribal lands to the court this morning under my order. He has remained in their custody throughout the proceedings upstairs, and he will remain in their custody until he returns to tribal lands to face charges on Indian land. Tribal land, you may know, is treated as sovereign soil, just as a foreign government's embassy. It is sacrosanct. Likewise, the tribe's vehicles and their personnel outside their prescribed territory while on tribal business are also off-limits to state arrest or detainment. I will ask you to stop your current actions, as they are forbidden under federal law." The judge smiled, benevolently. "I see attorney Mr. Lindor is seated in your backseat. Could you ask him to step outside so that I might speak with him?"

Lindor heard the judge's request and opened the door. The attorney rose out of the car and stood at the curb. His face was flushed with embarrassment. This was a story that would get told at every country club in town forever, the day Ted Lindor got bested by a federal judge and an Indian. He'd never live it down.

"Mr. Lindor, your illegal actions of today are at an end. Call off your dogs. If you would be so kind as to tell John Taylor, Secretary of Oklahoma's Health and Human Services, to give me a call, that would be terrific. I'd like to speak with him about what you attempted here today. You see, I am referring his actions to the Oklahoma Bar Association. I'll also give information regarding his egregious behavior to the state's attorney general, although on that score I probably won't get much action beings as they are drinking buddies. However, I am a federal judge, and I intend to make some noise over this bullshit."

Lindor nodded.

The judge leaned forward. "I didn't hear you."

"Yes, Judge Spence, I will tell him."

"Good. Now, tell these officers whom you directed to violate Mr. Kopaka's rights that you wish them to cease and desist at this time."

The four policemen turned to Lindor for guidance, but they were already holstering their weapons. It was over, at least for now.

Inside Chris's office, there was much laughing and rehashing the scene. Chris kept a bottle of whiskey on hand, and everyone drank a toast. Kern Kopaka was not exactly sure why the Five Civilized Tribes had paid his delinquent child support payments, and he was unsure why a federal judge had just saved his bacon, but he was glad. He, too, had a shot of whiskey.

"What charges am I facing on the res?" he asked Lt. Orson of the tribal police.

"Hell, I don't know. What say you to delinquent parking violations? Like you didn't pay a meter. That okay?"

"Res don't have no meters," Kopaka replied.

"I can come up with something with a jail sentence attached," Orson said.

Kopaka looked startled but recovered with a smile. "I'll pay the fine, sir."

Orson smiled and refilled Kopaka's glass with another shot of whiskey.

Later, after the adrenaline and the whiskey were gone, Chris pulled Kern Kopaka aside. "You know Tate Laughlin?"

The Osage brave's face clouded. "Maybe. I ain't saying. Is this what today was about? 'Cause I'm not telling nobody nothing."

Chris smiled. "Tate and I are old friends. If you have a way of getting a message to him, tell him that Chris Fairchild wants to buy him a beer. Will you do that?"

Kopaka did not respond, but he did not say no.

Before leaving, Judge Hiram Spence called Chris out of the office.

They stood in the empty hall.

He shook the young man's hand. His face was lined with years of difficult decisions on the bench, but his eyes held pride for the young attorney in front of him.

"Chris, my boy, I've seen you become a man today."

"Thank you, sir. You were my earliest inspiration at my first quail hunt."

The older man nodded. "Then, you'll take some advice from this old bird?"

"Of course, what is it?"

"Plan on practicing federal law. You're done in state court in Oklahoma. You'll never get a fair decision again. Your Native American clients will get the short end of the straw with you as counsel. The good ole boys will have it out for you, son. They hang together, protect each other, and scratch each other's backs. Time to move on." And with those words, the judge opened the door to the stairwell and was gone.

It did not take John Taylor long to hear that Judge Hiram Spence and the Five Civilized Tribes counsel, Chris Fairchild, foiled his operation and, in doing so, had done serious damage to his reputation. Taylor's political aspirations had taken a serious hit in the last hour.

Taylor's contact at the FBI met him in a parking garage near the federal building that afternoon. The mission was aborted. All the subpoenas issued by children's services were to be quashed. They'd have to find Tate Laughlin another way. The damage in the press, given Judge Spence's declaration on the street, would be detrimental. The civil rights movement was already with AIM. Journalists would have more political ammo to take to Congress and to lobbyists. Everything was off for now. John Taylor was on his own.

Taylor was scared. He began to call his allies. First, he called the head of the local bar association. It was too late. Word had already reached the head of Oklahoma's association of attorneys. They did not take his calls.

He tried the superintendent of the state police, but it was way too late to receive aid there. The officers present at the failed arrest had already reported. The wagons had been circled. His last two calls were to his closest friends, his childhood buddies, Arden and Zane Kilmain. Taylor called the prison and asked for the warden.

Zane Kilmain spoke before Taylor could even say hello. "I already heard. Don't call me here again. You got that? Reach out to my brother. We'll take care of this, but nothing on the phone." Then, he hung up.

Next, John Taylor called Arden Kilmain, the athletic director at the university.

Arden Kilmain answered his phone. "You're that stupid? Didn't my brother just tell you not to call?"

"Yes, but…"

"I'll be out on the practice field later. We've got some team photos going on this afternoon. Trying to get some good press. Something you should aspire to, dumbass. See you in an hour." Arden hung up.

Forty minutes later, John Taylor stood on the football practice facility endzone. He stayed far away from the press which gathered in front of the grandstands amid cameras and lighting stanchions. Football players gathered around the center of the practice field. Flashes of cameras among those gathered half a field away made Taylor squeamish. He did not want to end up with his photo in tomorrow's newspapers.

In a few minutes, the lawyer saw Arden Kilmain stride across the field of green toward him. Taylor had known the two Kilmain boys his whole life. He knew they were hotheads, and he could tell when they were mad. Right now, Arden was pissed beyond belief. With that angry stride, it did not take long for the athletic director to reach him.

"Screwed the pooch, did you?" Arden said, his voice a harsh growl.

"It went badly," was Taylor's reply.

Kilmain laughed. "It went badly? You tried to take down some radical Indian doing his I.R.A. impression, and a federal judge is on-hand to reprimand you and refer you to the bar for sanction and to federal and state Attorneys General for possible prosecution?" Kilmain laughed. "Yeah, you could say it went badly, all right."

"What do we do?"

"What do *we* do? There's no we here."

"Well, maybe not you, but your brother is in it up to his neck. He was at the meeting with the FBI. He's got AIM members in the prison. He wanted this leader guy, Tate Laughlin, brought to justice, by whatever means necessary. He even agreed to the bogus paper being served. The FBI will say he suggested it."

"Who's telling people that?" Arden said, suddenly white-hot.

"Nobody, nobody," Taylor said, backing up a step. "I'll never give testimony. I'd take the Fifth. I swear. You two have nothing to worry about from me."

Arden stood down. "John, I hope I can believe you. Zane and I cannot be involved. It's your neck on the line here, yours only, you understand?"

"You can count on me. I would never spill the goods on Zane or you. He's like my brother, too. I guarantee you I'd never talk. Never."

Arden looked over at the PR event which was wrapping up. All the interviews had been completed a half hour ago. Now, it was just final photos and the saying of goodbyes. He needed to be over there, not here. Public relations were built on relationships. He needed to be doing his job, not covering up for this screw-up.

Taylor seemed to read his mind. "Before you go, I want to say this. You know who's fault this shitstorm is? That one fucking family. Lillian Hart over at the Bureau of Indian Affairs, she's got her fingerprints all over this thing. Her kid, Chris Fairchild didn't figure the Judge Hiram Spence thing out on his own. He's a punk kid.

"That family's been a bunch of Indian lovers for a hundred years, picking red skin over their own. I mean, there's Lillian. You know her. There was her grandmother, Avery Station, a suffragette who got women the vote. She fought for Indian rights, fought for Indian statehood, for God's sake. She kept trying to put the Tulsa Riot back into the history books. Lillian's aunt, Autumn Station, a goddamned lesbian, involved in seditious politics her whole life. Her two uncles, Carson, an outlaw from day one, and 'course, you know about Tanner Station from Zane. Tanner married an Injun prostitute. Jesus. The oldest inmate in Big Mac. What is he? A hundred years old? Sits on the Indian Council. Traitor to his own people. Been inside since what? 1925?"

"You're not telling me anything I don't already know," growled Arden.

"I'm just saying Oklahoma has had about all it can take from this family. I mean, now we're supposed to suffer that nigger lover on TV every night? And that redskin-lovin' bitch Lillian Hart's son, Chris Fairchild, gets all high and mighty with a federal judge. Something has to be done."

Arden stopped him. "What are you saying?"

"I'm saying maybe your brother can get the job done on the old man inside Big Mac. That shouldn't be so tough. If he can do that, I'll take care of things out here."

"*You* can take care of things out here? You can't wipe your own ass, JT!"

Taylor looked serious. "You do it then. Get rid of the Station family, or I will."

"If I decide it needs done, I'll do it." Arden looked at Taylor with disgust. "Don't you do anything until I talk to Zane. You've done enough for a day."

Taylor nodded. "Let's make sure we have an understanding. You'll talk to your brother about taking care of the old man? This AIM movement must be stopped. The tribes got to be put back in their place. You two agreed to help. We need to break AIM in Oklahoma. It looks like this one family is in the way. Can I count on you?"

Arden sneered. "Have I ever not made good on a promise? Has Zane?"

"Will Zane be able to if a federal judge is in the Stations' back pocket?"

"I'll talk to him. Now, I got to get back. You lay low." He turned his back on John Taylor and hurried back toward the reporters and athletes.

In the grandstand, communication media students Tobi Thomas and Renée Ripley had completed the interview with wide receiver Monroe Evans. They were feeling great.

Renée saw the Athletic Director walking toward the endzone to talk to a tall, dark-haired man in a business suit. Renée turned on the camera. He aimed the directional mic at the two men and slid the earphones over his head.

Tobi saw him and looked curiously at the two men fifty yards away in a heated discussion. She made Renée share one headphone, which she pressed against her ear. Essentially, both of their heads were inside one headphone set.

Afterwards, Tobi looked over at her partner, Renée. "Was that other man referring to Piper and Johnny when he used the N word?"

"I think so. Let me run it back." He checked. "I got it all. Even the conspiracy to murder somebody named Tanner Station, the oldest inmate at Big Mac Prison."

"Who is he?" Tobi asked. "Is he some relative of Piper's?"

"I don't know," Renée Ripley said, raising an eyebrow. "But I think the Monroe Evans interview might have to wait."

Woods County, Oklahoma
Winter, 1911

Tanner Station, some said, lost his mind that day. They said the loss of Marie made him insane. Others said rivers eventually run to their low points. Tanner Station was known to have been a violent man. He simply returned to violent ways. Either way, by December, he had left his son and the ranch to find and kill Mel Harris.

Before Tanner departed, Max tried to reason with him. "Tanner, you have a son who is counting on you. He is hurting. He saw his mother killed in front of his own eyes. Gabriel needs stability. He needs his father at home."

Tanner stared back at the old man who had himself aged a great deal since the killing. "Max, I've never admired a man more'n you. You're the gentleman I would aspire to be, sir. But when I look at that boy, it's Marie's eyes looking back. I see her looking back and I just cain't take it. I know that I have a job to do. Harris must pay. He's deviled this family all of Gabe's life. I owe it to the boy to clear his way."

Max shook his head. "Marie would not want you to dedicate yourself to revenge, nor to violence. She would tell you to raise your son. Take care of Gabriel, that's what she would say."

Tanner nodded. "And I will, once that son of a bitch is in the ground."

And then he was gone.

With Tanner's departure, the ranch was without riders. Avery insisted Everett move back and run things. She even said he could bring his woman to the ranch, as scandalous as that might be. Everett laughed in her face. "I support the girls' schooling. I support Autumn going to the Territorial Normal School. I pay the rent on the home she lives in with…her friend. My horses keep us afloat, Avery, just as much as the store does. If you think I'd ruin my reputation by…" he paused. "By not being alone out at the ranch, then you're delusional."

"I'm delusional?" Avery said, her voice rising. She looked back over her shoulder toward those inside the store. The couple stood on the front walk outside. No one was about. "How about you're delusional if you think your relationship with Doris Detwiler isn't the talk of the county."

"She's a widow woman. I'm a lonely man. What's to guess at?" he said.

Avery stared at him. "How dare you? You, who've never put our family above either red dirt or a horse, now tries to justify your infidelity by saying that you must keep up appearances by sneaking to her house after the sun sets? Please."

Everett flushed with anger. "All I'm saying is I'd never embarrass you by moving her to the ranch. She wouldn't agree, anyways."

"Who's going to run things? Who's to take care of the cattle? The boys are only eleven. Carson's gone. Tanner's gone. Max is too old. Billy's dead. If not you, who?"

"I guess I'll hire two or three fellas to get it done," Everett said.

Avery said, "I thought you said the ranch was barely making money. That there was no money in it, except for the value of the land. And that the land will increase in value with time. Isn't that right?"

"Yes, but…"

"Then I'll run it," Avery spat at him. "I'll move back. Autumn and her friend, Joan, can take over my duties at the store. Mimi and Max are thick as thieves these days. He has dinner with her every night anyhow. He's always upstairs. He'll just have to come downstairs and work behind the counter at age seventy-four." She said it with a sneer. "I'll go to the ranch then."

Everett objected. "How will that help things? A woman and two boys? You'll still have to have to hire a cowman to help out."

Avery nodded. "Yes, but just one. It'll be me. It's decided. I should be out to the farm within two weeks. Can you cover things until then?"

"Sure, Avery," Everett said, seeing he would get nowhere. "Until you're able."

Later that evening when Avery revealed her plans to move to the ranch and take over operations, Max pulled Everett aside. "Son," he said, "that's your job. Avery is just angry about you carrying on with another gal over to Kiowa. She's rubbing your nose in it by taking over what should be a man's job to do. You gotta speak up."

Everett walked out back from the store toward the shed. He turned to his father. "I know all that, and I tried to tell her. All we can hope is that Tanner comes back soon. This mess is really all his fault."

Max raised an eyebrow at that comment, but his son did not see. "His wife was murdered, boy. I would expect a bit more compassion out of you."

"I know, and I am sympathetic. But men have obligations."

Max turned on his heel back to Everett. "Yes, they do. Is that woman over to Kiowa so important to you to allow your wife to shame you out of your obligations? Can you not find your way to right this thing?"

Everett looked to his father. "No, Pa, she ain't that important to me. I just ain't got nobody else. Avery's turned the girls against me. I made the mistake of letting Tanner and Marie raise my son. Jeff cares more for Tanner than me. He is missing Marie as much as Gabriel is. Tanner, too, now that he's gone."

"This thing is wrong, Son," Max warned.

"I know it. I just cain't find a way home," Everett said, and then he walked away into the darkness and the cold night.

Sleep didn't come any easier in Mexico for Tanner Station than it did on the Salt Fork River. Try as he might, Tanner could not sleep without the events of the day, that day, his wife's last day, running through his mind.

She was lying on the midway dirt, her lifeblood leaking out of her. The bullet wound had torn into her left breast.

Gabriel knelt next to her in the sand. His face leaned forward into the pooling blood on her. A small group of people had gathered around.

Just as Tanner arrived, Mimi, too, reached the scene. She took her shawl and rolled it into a pillow and placed it under Marie's head. One look told the Jewish woman there was nothing that could be done.

As Tanner reached his wife, he could see she was speaking to her son.

Gabriel was weeping, inconsolably.

Tanner slipped in beside his son, wrapping his arms around the boy.

Gabe folded into his embrace.

Tanner lowered his face to Marie's.

She attempted a smile, but a pain braced her. The expression ended as more of a grimace. "There's my man," she said. "I do love your face."

Tanner tore off his bandana to stanch her bleeding.

She reached her right hand to the wound and pushed his away. "There's no use, honey," she said. "But do not worry. Remember this is only the now. It is not the eternal. We will spend the eternal together. It will be all right."

Tanner began to cry. He sprawled alongside Marie, his tears on her cheeks.

She took her hand and with a finger moved some of his tears into her mouth. "A bit of you goes with me," she said. And then she died.

Tanner felt her slip away. The tension left her hand. Her eyes lost their gleam and closed.

Gabriel became to wail with new urgency.

Mimi pulled the boy to her. She took him into her embrace. It ended with the four of them on the ground, sand mixing with blood.

Tanner kissed Marie's lips. He didn't remember the rest.

The funeral was unlike the others which had been held at the ranch. This funeral was attended by hundreds of people. Marie, a pariah of society most of her life, became beloved in her death. Hundreds attended from Alva. Nearly a hundred from Hardtner, which was nearly all the population of the tiny burg.

There were many families from Kiowa in attendance. Ranchers across the county and their families attended. The trail from the house to the summit of the hill was lined with folks with bowed heads. The team of white horses, both brought down to the ranch by Everett, whinnied as they pulled the wagon through the crowd of mourners, winding their way up the hill to Marie's resting place. Tanner and Gabriel walked behind the wagon. The rest of the family trailed behind them.

When the service was done, Tanner and Gabe each tossed one of Marie's scarves onto the casket. It was too cold for anyone to have flowers. It seemed all the heat of the fall had left when her heart stopped.

Afterwards, all the people of the territory surrounded Tanner to offer their condolences. All those people who had thought him guilty of murder when he was brought to trial. All those people who snubbed him at gatherings because he had married an Injun, who had snubbed him because he was a killer, because he was a loner, because of his brother's crimes. Tanner took their hands but could not look into their eyes, such was the depth of his loss.

Somehow, Tanner and Gabe made it through that day. Avery stayed at the north house with the two of them when everyone else had gone home. She tried to console them. She could not reach them. She stayed in the house for a week, then two, but Tanner hardly spoke. He just rose every morning and went out to the cattle. Soon, Jeff and Gabriel returned to school. Avery decided to move both boys to the main house. The tiny north house was too small for three people and Tanner's grief.

The day after Christmas, Tanner left. He told Avery and Max he was going. Both objected. They could not change his mind. Tanner told Gabriel, too. His son's response was to the point, "Kill him quick, Dad, and come home as soon as you do."

Tanner hugged the boy, told him he loved him, and that he would, indeed, kill Harris as soon as he found him. But he did not find him. Time went by, and Tanner, his mission incomplete, did not come home. Three years went by.

Mel Harris was now a pariah. Yes, the judge had ruled only Buck Wells had violated Marie Wolf Walker that day, but Harris and Crups were branded as attempted rapists by the community. Both were fired from the 101 Ranch after Tanner's trial. No respectable ranch owner who knew of the two would hire them on.

Eventually, it was said Harris and Crups split up and hit the outlaw trail, but that made Harris more difficult to find. The scar-faced man was seen on occasion. He was spotted in small towns in Texas, Oklahoma, and New Mexico. He was rumored to be in Old Mexico. He was everywhere and nowhere.

Everyone in Oklahoma was on the lookout for the murderer, and many people stopped by the general store with tips or rumors. However, no one seemed to know where Harris had gone. Grant Johnson corresponded with Avery over the next few years about progress in the case, but there was none. Mel Harris, murdering outlaw, had disappeared. And so had Tanner Station.

One day in early 1915, Max arrived at the ranch with a letter. It was addressed to Avery in care of the store, but the handwriting was crude and nearly illegible.

"I didn't open it," Max said. "But I thought it might be from Tanner."

Avery looked at the soiled parchment of the envelope and the scrawl scribbled across it. "No," she said. "I don't recognize the hand."

She opened the seal. It was from Rose, Carson's wife. Avery read it out loud.

Dear Mrs. Hart:

We never got to know each other, so in case you forgot, I am your younger brother, Carson's, wife. Well, now I am his widow. I regret to inform you he died after getting laid up this last winter with the lock jaw. Once he got sick, we got Carson to a doctor down to Ruidoso in what is being now called as the state of New Mexico. He told us that Carson had something called tetanus. We got there too late for the doc to do much for him. It turned plain awful later that day.

Carson's muscles all seized up on him, and before you knowed it, he was having trouble getting air. He died that first night in town. We had been living south of there, having a ranch of sorts in the territory. Not far from the Mexican border. Carson had been living the straight and narrow since Cyrus was born. Oh, yeah, I had a healthy boy afters I followed Carson down here. Anyways, Carson never got over his outlaw way of feeling about things. He wanted to be close to the border in case he had to skedaddle 'cross to safety, even if it meant our land wasn't worth squat.

Running to Mexico wouldn't have done him no good against the lock jaw.

This letter is to inform you of your brother's death. Also wanted to let you know that we had Tanner visit for a time during the hottest part of this past summer. He was headed south to find Mel Harris to kill him, but there was no going into the desert during that stretch of hot weather. Tanner left when we got the first rain last fall. Carson wanted to go with his brother, said it would be like old times, which Tanner didn't understand. He would have none of it. This was his job to get done, man to man, he said. I have to say he was, to me, a man possessed. I only saw him a few times, but he was thinner and meaner than I had remembered. Guess I would want my man to love me that way, kill any man who took my life. I am sure you feel the same.

Anyhows, after Tanner went south, Carson ran across Charlie Crups, Mel Harris' old running buddy from the back in the day. Carson told me that night he died that he had kilt Charlie coming out of a saloon over to the town of Angus after Charlie had won a little in a poker game there. Carson caught up with Crups outside in the dark. Carson wasn't doing that kind of thieving no more, but he figured Charlie Crups had it coming. He said he tried to get Charlie to tell where Harris was, but Crups didn't know, so Carson cut his throat. No worry about telling it now that Carson is gone, too.

The boy and me are fine. We don't got much, but we don't need much. I am writing to you on Christmas Day, 1914. Probably a good thing that Carson's gone. Now we're a state, the U.S. Marshal's been here a couple of times to check on Carson's whereabouts. They don't seem to believe he's dead and still are thinkin' he's running around committing crimes. Maybe somebody's a-usin' his name. I don't like the thought of that, but God grant me the power to worry about just my own problems.

Your kin, Rose.

Max said, "Tanner has gone down a wrong road. Lost Harris and himself."

Avery folded the letter. "Yes, both of my brothers ended on the Devil's path."

Then there was no more word of Tanner for four more years.

Then one day, a scarecrow of a man, bent at the waist, limped onto the boardwalk in front of the store. He leaned with difficulty against the building.

"If it isn't the prodigal son returned," Max said, though he scarcely recognized Tanner.

Tanner Station propped his boot against the railing. It appeared to be keeping him from falling. Always thin, he was now cadaver-like. His shirt and trousers fit him like sails. Eight years had passed. It was spring of 1919, not quite the end of March, but for now winter seemed to be on the run.

"Howdy, Max," Tanner said, his voice a little rough from years of cigarettes. "Didn't know if you was still kickin'. It's been a while. Glad to see you."

"And back at you," Max said, smiling. "Haven't heard hide nor hair out of you for a good bit. Lots changed. Did you find your man?"

Tanner shook his head. "Fool's errand, that. Me being the fool."

"Carson died a while back. We got word from his widow."

"I was there a month ago. Cecilia and Cyrus are doing well. That's Rose's middle name. She goes by Cecelia Rose now. Her boy is Cyrus Rose. They changed their last name to Rose when they got to New Mexico all them years ago because of Carson's reputation. She's got another man now. He ain't married her but seems to treat her and the boy right. They're okay."

Tanner still leaned on the door frame.

Max motioned for him to come into the shop. A young lady was working behind the counter. She was wide-eyed at seeing the apparition of Tanner in the doorway.

"And who is this youngster?"

Max looked to the girl. "This is Freida, Mimi's daughter. Mimi and I married over four years ago. I live upstairs with Frieda and her mother."

"Where's Levi?"

"Back down to Galveston. Jewish family down to Houston reached out. Friends from their past in Odessa wrote to Mimi. Had a job for the boy. Training him in medicine. He works in a hospital. There's been a lot of sickness."

Tanner nodded. "Yeah, I was down with it for a month or two in Arkansas. Didn't think I'd shake it. A lot of folks died of the grip down there."

Max nodded. "Here, too. They're calling it the Spanish flu." He evaluated Tanner's condition and then brought a chair out to the porch. The old man set it before the rangy cowboy. Tanner gratefully sat down. "Thank you, Max. I been having back trouble. All my riding over the years. Doc down to Dallas said I got the bulging discs. Can't get comfortable standing never." He sat. "How's my son? How's Gabriel? 'Spect he don't remember me, or don't want to. I done him wrong. Spent his youth chasing a man who wasn't worth a single breath of my life."

Max asked Freida to bring the stool behind the counter to him. The old man, nearing his 82nd birthday, sat next to Tanner, who in some ways now seemed older than Max. "Gabriel has gone to war," Max said. "Avery was his legal guardian up till a year ago, but then he came of age and wanted to sign up for the infantry. Avery was dead set against it. She got him to enlist as a Quaker. He's a medic. He joined the service about a year and a half ago. Took the train up to Topeka, Kansas. Enlisted at Camp Funston. They shipped out in March of last year, I'm thinking. We used to get letters from him when Gabe was in basic training in Kansas, but we haven't heard from him since they reached Europe."

Tanner closed his eyes and took Max's hand. He spoke a prayer. Max was surprised. "I let the boy down. God, please look over my son who is at war. Bring him home safe."

Max reached over and patted the taller man on the shoulder. It felt all of sinew and bone. "Gabe'll get home, Tanner." He waited a bit, but the other man did not lift his head or open his eyes. Max spoke again. "Everett and Avery aren't one bit better, either. Don't remember the last time they were in the same room."

Tanner lit a cigarette and offered Max one. He declined. He said, "I expect Avery never goes to the farm, so they don't butt heads."

Max laughed. "Avery has lived on the farm since you left. She and Jeff run it. Jeff's married now. Married a Herald. You remember the family lived over east a'ways?"

Tanner nodded.

"Her name is Gwen. Good woman. They live in the north house. Avery is in the main house. Got a hired hand living in the bunkhouse. Black man recommended by Marshal Grant Johnson. Caused some talk back when Avery hired him. Young buck living on the spread with Avery all by herself."

Tanner smiled. "That's my sister."

Max nodded. "Young man is named John Joseph. Folks generally have calmed down, especially after meeting him. Quality fella. Then, there's those who never will."

At that stage, Mimi came down the stairs from the apartment above the store. "Good gracious, Max. What are you doing keeping this poor creature down here outside in the sun? Let's get him upstairs. I've got dinner going, and it looks like our long-lost boy needs some nourishment. Help me now."

She looked to her husband and Max stood. They each took an arm and helped the emaciated Tanner Station up the stairs.

Avery rode into town on horseback to see her brother two days later. He was laid up, not so much with an illness as a general malaise. Tanner was worn down to brass tacks. He was only forty-two, but he looked sixty. Mimi had thrown away his ratty, loose-fitting clothes, and Max had given Tanner a haircut and a shave, but the man could not be more gaunt and gangly. He was positively deathly looking. Avery was shocked at his appearance.

Tanner, on his part, was shocked at Avery's looks, as well. She looked like him now. Living on the ranch, riding a horse, and working the cattle had taken her soft, womanly looks and made her look wild. Her face had thinned, and her nose was now more prominent. Her freckles were now pronounced, and she was deeply tanned. Lines had formed around the corners of her eyes. There was also a discernable sadness that never left her gaze. Before, when things had been good, men folk would stop by just to get a look at her. Tanner thought those days were at an end.

"I tried to keep Gabriel here," she said to Tanner.

"Gabe's a grown man, Avery. You did what you could. I appreciate you keeping him out of battle at least. Gives him a better chance at coming home. Being a medic is better than being a cannon fodder in the Great War."

He paused to set the tea on the side table. "When's the last time you heard from Gabe?"

Avery handed him the letters.

He read them slowly while she watched. He noted the dates. They stopped after Gabe had written about the unit's deployment overseas. That had been over a year ago. There was no news and there was little they could do to get more. Tanner tried to put it in the back of his mind. Seeing his consternation, Avery told him of her life in his absence.

"Autumn and I have been busy while you were gone. We both worked to get women in Oklahoma the vote. I chaired the Cherokee Strip's Suffragettes. Once Woodrow Wilson got elected, the Democrats figured out the women's vote in the Northeast got him into the White House. Oklahoma Democratic Party leaders decided to push support our way. I made some enemies in Alva, but Autumn and me, we stuck to our guns, and eventually, the measure passed." She smiled, proud.

Tanner smiled, "Avery, that's something. That's something special. Women can vote. Next thing you know, they'll be running cattle ranches."

Tanner told them little of his eight missing years. Only that he had not found Mel Harris It had been wasted time and a mistake. He told them he and Carson made their peace during their last meeting, that Carson was happy his last years, that Cyrus was the spitting image of his daddy, and that Carson married well. Cecelia Rose was a strong woman who made something of her farm, even after her husband died when her son was too young to help. Now, she was with a new man named Bellflower. He was ex-Army, and was, in Tanner's words, Tex-Mex, meaning of mixed bloodlines. Good feller, he added.

Tanner did not travel north to see Everett until a month later. He was still rail-thin, but Mimi fattened him up considerably during the intervening weeks, at least in her mind. He felt good, although riding still gave his back fits. Tanner was used to pain a-sittin' astride a horse, though, and he enjoyed the ride, first to the farm where he met the hired man, John Joseph, a second-cousin of the famed Marshal Bass Reeves and friend of Grant Johnson. Tanner sized him up as a man to ride the river with. That was as high of compliment as Tanner could give a feller.

He also rode from the main house up to the north place, his old home, to see Jeff and Gwen Hart. The place looked better than he had ever seen it. The trees around the house had matured and gave shade. The shade gave way to grass. The house had paneled siding and a fresh coat of white paint. It looked fine. Prosperous, even. Gwen was a good woman, he could tell, and he had dinner with the newlyweds living in his old house.

They would not hear of him sleeping in the barn, so Tanner spent the night on a stack of blankets in the main room. Jeff and Gwen offered him his old room, but it was not a room or a bed he wanted to revisit. Marie was gone, and those wounds, nigh on a decade old, were still too fresh. It was a sleepless night in that house that had been his family's home. Ghosts would not let him be. He left in the morning in a hurry to leave those memories behind, but not before making a trip up the big hill to visit his wife's grave and that of his father, as well. He knelt and prayed in the shade of the maple which had grown and flourished in his absence.

"Until eternity, Marie, my wife," he said. Tanner stood and descended the hill.

He lit out after that and made Kiowa by lunchtime.

Everett was glad to see him.

"Look what the cat drug in," he said, smiling as the lanky cowboy stepped off his mount.

Both men were greatly changed. Everett had gone gray. His hair was not salt and pepper. It was full gray. He was thicker across the middle, and his clothes were finer. He was a man who now lived the city life, as much as one could in Kiowa in 1919. Tanner's face was lined. He was thin, and there was a fatalism in his eyes. He was thinner than when he had left. His clothes, though new, seemed outdated and shoddy against those of his brother-in-law's.

They walked down to the livery and saw the stables where Everett kept his breeding stock. The corral was big enough to be called a small pasture; seven fine stallions tugged at grass.

The wind ruffled their manes, and the horses whinnied as they saw Everett arrive.

He approached them with Tanner, offering them sugar cubes from his vest pocket. Life was, evidently, good these days for Everett.

"Let's go back to my place. We can unload you and then head over to the café for some late lunch. What do you say?" Everett said, pleasantly.

"Unload me?" Tanner said, quizzically.

Everett nodded down to the six-shooter on Tanner's hip. "Get rid of your hog leg. Nobody but the law wears a holster these days, except maybe out on the range. You look like somebody out of Bill Hickok's Wild West Show or something. Let's drop the gun off at my place, then we'll go. I'm hungry."

Tanner shook his head. "I never take it off," he said. "Never know when I'll come across that varmint, Mel Harris. I made a vow, and I plan to keep it."

Everett looked at him, not believing his brother-in-law was serious. "I expect the late lunch crowd at Thelma Darlene's to be safe enough. Leave it at home. Okay, Tanner?"

"No, sir," he said and wore the gun on his hip at lunch.

At lunch, Everett watched for reactions, but except for Thelma Darlene, nobody much was still there, and she was too good of a proprietor to let customers know what she was thinking. Tanner liked his lunch just fine with a gun at the table.

It was decided to let John Joseph go to save money after Tanner got up to snuff. The young black man went back to his people in Tulsa. There were no hard feelings, and his family was doing well in the Greenwood District of that city. Native Americans and people of color had flocked to Tulsa when it was thought to have been the possible capital city for an Indian Nation. That had not happened, but the community was flourishing. John Joseph left after the Harts, and the Stations threw him a going away party. They were proud to call him a friend and promised they'd soon see each other again.

Tanner spent the summer on the ranch, assisting his sister and Jeff in getting steers ready for market. They branded the spring calves, and come hot weather, they moved the herd down to the bend in the Salt Fork. Tanner remembered their first day there.

Avery read his thoughts and she put her hand on his arm as their horses drank from the river. "A lot has changed, but a lot has stayed the same, hasn't it, Tanner?"

He nodded but didn't respond for a moment. Then, he looked her in the eyes. "I need you to help find where my son is. I need Gabriel to come home."

It was not to be. The letter from the government came to Avery's attention at the ranch. Tanner was at this stage living there with her. He saw the rider coming from the north, probably having been to the north place first. He saw the rider was in military uniform, no longer Cavalry blue, but now U.S. Army drab green. The man, a sergeant by his stripes, dismounted. He looked somberly at Tanner. "I'm looking for Mrs. Avery Hart, aunt of Gabriel Station."

Tanner said, "I'm his father." He reached for the letter, but the soldier did not give it.

"I'm sorry, sir. I have to deliver it to Mrs. Hart."

Avery exited the house, and Tanner could see she was already crying. She opened the letter but gave it to Tanner to read. Her sorrow was too much, her eyes were filled with tears.

The letter told them what they already had surmised; Gabriel was dead. But the circumstance of his death was confounding. Gabriel had died at Camp Funston. He never went to war. He had died eighteen months ago.

It wasn't until Tanner went to the base not far from Manhattan, Kansas that he found out more. The base was much smaller now that the war was winding down. He enquired at the front gate if there was anyone on the medical staff at the base hospital who had been there during the flu epidemic. He was informed that a doctor would see him.

Tanner waited, expecting a wizened old physician, but what came through the doors to the wardroom was a young man, seemingly a very young man. He smiled but did not take Tanner's offer at a handshake.

"Sorry, handshakes stopped around here during the flu epidemic. I'm Dr. Dominic Dinsmore. You're Gabriel Station's father?"

Tanner nodded.

The doctor sat down. "I knew your son. In fact, he's why I'm becoming a doctor. I'm in my first year of residency. The V.A. paid for my medical training. I'm serving my residency here."

"You served as a medic here with Gabe?"

"No, sir. Not exactly. We were friends, I guess. He was a medic, and I was assigned to the hospital in janitorial duties. But when everyone got sick, staffing got juggled. One hundred the first day, March 4th, it was. A thousand before the end of the first week. Half a dozen dying each day. There weren't enough trained medics, doctors, or nurses to help sick soldiers. I got moved from cleaning up to become an orderly. I worked alongside your son. Assigned to be at his side. That last month before he died, Gabriel was one of the last medical staff who wasn't sick. He saved a lot of fellas. I don't know how many. Hundreds, I'd say."

"Then, Gabe got the flu?"

"Yes, sir, Mr. Station. Gabe got sick just about the time the battalion was scheduled to ship out by train. The field commanders should have changed the departure date, but nobody wanted to look weak, I guess. Plans for ships heading out of New York were already made. So they loaded up the better part of ten thousand men, including those who were too sick to be moved and shipped them to the front lines. Most of the sickest died on the way. Six hundred, I heard. Those others either got the flu on the train or on the transport ships over. Major General Leonard Wood made the decision. They won't tell you, but I've seen documents estimating that over 40,000 men died of the flu in the last two years over in France."

Tanner looked up, not believing the number. "And it started here? I thought it was the Spanish Flu."

"Looks like some Kansans from over to Haskell County brought it in when they delivered some beef to the base. We' heard from the doctor there, a guy named Loring Miner, who sent word that some of the hands who drove the herd our way died of a highly contagious respiratory illness. 'Course by the time we got his letter, we had a thousand sick. Thirty-eight died that first month. If it is any solace, Gabriel died quickly. Pneumonia set in.

He lost lung capacity and died in about two days after onset of illness."

"You're saying he didn't suffer?"

"I'm sayin' he didn't suffer *long,*" the young man said with a grimace. "You know, the estimates are that a half million Americans died of the flu, maybe more. Maybe fifteen million worldwide. Sending all those soldiers home from the war just sent this disease back to their families. Generals don't understand pandemics."

Tanner nodded, standing. His ability to take in the young man's words was at an end. He stood, stuck out his hand in thanks, and then pulled it back. Tanner, his back bowed, staggered on his way to the door.

The doctor stopped him. "Mr. Station, are you okay?"

"Son, I'm far from okay, but I'll be on my way. Thank you, doctor. I appreciate knowing what happened to my son more than you'll ever know."

Dinsmore stood. "Before you go, can I show you something? Two things, actually."

Tanner nodded and let the younger man pass him.

They exited the hospital.

Dinsmore pointed to some buildings in the distance. "You know what those barracks are? Why they have fencing around them?"

"Barracks are where men sleep. But the wire? I wasn't aware we kept prisoners of war here. Were they brought here, all the way from France?"

Dinsmore shook his head. "No, those were barracks where the Army kept the Mennonites and the Quakers. Conscientious objectors were imprisoned over there, those who wouldn't fight. Your son had that option. He chose to serve in the medic corps. He saved so many men. A true hero. Gabriel Station was certainly that. He's why I'm becoming a doctor. That's his legacy, sir."

Tanner looked at the young doctor. "Can't say as I ain't selfish enough to say I wish he had chosen a different path. But Gabriel was a better man than me."

Then the good doctor led him through a path of unmarked

tombstones, just white bricks each with a black number painted on it. Finally, Dinsmore stopped at the stone marked 28 20 285082 126.

Tanner looked down at the stone, noticing it was cleaner than the rest and decorated with a silver star. He looked to Dinsmore.

"The numbers?"

"His dog tag numbers. The silver star was awarded posthumously. I put it there. You're free to take it as a keepsake."

Tanner shook his head. "Reckon I'd rather Gabriel kept it."

Then, Tanner limped back to the main gate and got into his buggy. The men on duty had kindly watered and fed his team. He thanked them and left Camp Funston, what would later become Fort Riley.

Later at home, Avery asked her brother about it.

He told her, and they cried, knowing.

Afterwards, she said, "You've had sorrow enough for two lives, Tanner. Surely, the Lord will not give you more sorrow to carry."

Tanner looked back at his sister. He lay with his neck propped against the headboard of his bed. "I heard tell God doesn't give you any more trouble than you can handle. But those sayin' it are New Testament Christians. I believe in the Old Testament. Our God is a vengeful God. I got to say he's meted it out my way."

"What have you done to have deserved bad tidings?" Avery asked, disturbed.

"Oh, Avery, I ain't confessed so far, and I ain't gonna start now. But it would be a sin for me to tell you that Marie and Gabriel's death were punishments to me. Why would the Lord allow evil to come to them, good people who never hurt no one? I just figure there's a misery loosed upon the world and each of us is just waiting in line to get ours."

Avery shook her head. "Those are sinful thoughts."

"I'm a sinner. I admit it, and I am justly taking my place in line. I just wish that executioner man would hurry."

A month later, on June 2, 1921, Avery came back to her brother again at the end of a day. He was laid up, reading *Le Morte d'Arthur* by Thomas Mallory.

Tanner smiled at her. "Never been much of a reader, but when I was down sick in Arkansas, a nurse read this to me. I recognized myself in Gawain. Vowed vengeance. Paid back in spades."

Avery began to cry.

Tanner put his feet to the floor and awkwardly stood.

Avery leaned into him.

"What's wrong, Sister?"

"The Strawn boy just rode by. They heard bad news. Wanted me to know."

Tanner was alarmed. "Who's dead?"

"There's been a massacre down to Tulsa. White rioters went into the Greenwood District. They killed over three hundred people. They burned them out from the sky. Threw bottles of gasoline onto their homes from airplanes and then shot folk when they came out."

"John Joseph and his family?"

"Tanner, they're all dead."

Then, all she could do was cry, and Tanner could do nothing at all

---

Strangely, all this misery seemed to free Tanner for a time. He stayed at the main house with Avery, letting Jeff assume leadership of the ranch. Tanner became just a hand. Some days, Avery rode, but often she would drift away on horseback, riding to the river or somewheres that Tanner didn't know. It reminded him of Carson's disappearing in the old days. Except Tanner didn't figure Avery was sticking up people for their pocket watches.

Tanner, during these days, seemed bereft of thought. If anyone asked him, and sometimes it was Max who did, Tanner would say he was fine. Just waiting in line. No one but Avery knew exactly what he meant, but they could guess close enough. He seldom talked to anyone, except family. That was not unusual. Folks across Woods Country had been avoiding him for three decades. Tanner returned the favor, and that was just all right with them. If anything, he seemed content to work cattle during the day and to read at night. Avery allowed Jeff and Tanner to take the load, and she spent more time in town once again, but this time, she did not spend her days at the shop, allowing Mimi and Frieda to run things. Now, Avery was an activist.

She petitioned the state to find the murderers in Tulsa, but little was done. Neither her congressman, nor her senators, had interest. Avery was tireless, but ultimately, she and all who called out failed to bring justice to those lost.

In the end, no one was prosecuted for the three hundred deaths. Nor were the homes destroyed by fire-bombing covered by insurance. The policies had exemptions for "riot damage." Avery wrote a letter to *The Tulsa World* calling for those responsible to be charged. The newspaper editors agreed that because of police involvement in the violence and destruction the city, "must take on itself the responsibility of deciding to make full reparation for the losses sustained by the property owners." All lawsuits were, nonetheless, dismissed.

Avery fell into a deep depression after John Joseph's and his family's deaths and the lack of any semblance of comeuppance for those responsible. After a year of fighting the good fight, she returned to the farm and began her lonely rides into the tall bluestem and sage once again. She was a person alone, much like her brother. However, it seemed a ranch that size could only handle one iconoclast at a time.

There came a day soon after her return when Tanner found himself unable to mount his horse. His back, now bowed so he seemed almost to be a hunchback, caused him to be bedridden. Tanner could barely stand. He could not even comfortably sit.

After a week, Jeff cleared a flatbed rack onto a team of horses. Gwen and he moved a mattress aboard and loaded Tanner up. Then, with no help from Avery, whom they could not find, the two drove the team to Alva. It was a painful journey for all involved.

The doctor gave the hurt cowboy morphine and within the hour, he was asleep.

After two days of bedrest in the hospital, the doctor saw no immediate cure and suggested "gold salts," a radical treatment used for anti-inflammatory effect in cases of tuberculosis. Tanner, who could neither stand, nor sit, was willing to try pretty much anything. The shot was administered that night directly into his spine. It took two men to hold him down until Tanner fainted from the pain. While its effectiveness is still not understood, the "gold salts" treatment did alleviate Tanner's worst pain, but he could not stand but for mere moments after the needle had entered his spinal column. He became wheelchair bound.

Tanner became a fixture in the general store and developed a friendship with Frieda, who, like him, was a shy and reticent person. He was forty-four. She was a spinster already at twenty-four. There were whispers that a flame had caught hold, and that Tanner, who'd had such a hard life, losing his wife and son, would find happiness with the Jewish girl, but it was not to be. Neither felt passion for the other. They were just what they appeared to be. Friends.

Tanner talked Max into taking a small section of the store's backroom and converting it to a bedroom for him. He became a clerk. Tanner even ordered himself a child's red wagon which he tied to the back of his wheelchair, allowing him to load a case of peaches or a bolt of fabric on it. Then, he would wheel his way up and down the aisles stocking shelves. There were times he would even entertain questions from folks on where to find a product. He might have even smiled once or twice, but those were just rumors, though, people said with wry grins.

Time passed. Two years after his back gave out, Tanner was ensconced in his cocoon in the back of the store. Some nights, he played chess with Max. Some nights, he would read. He was a good reader these days. He made friends with the librarian lady who would deliver books to the store when she stopped in for eggs. She learned his likes and dislikes. He was not a fast reader, but he was a deep thinker. The librarian spoke well of him and of the books he chose.

Folks noted that Tanner Station's name, for the first time in more than twenty years, was not mentioned either in scorn or fear. There was talk by the church ladies about trying to save his soul and get him to come to church. The librarian lady suggested that she broached the idea and that he seemed amenable. People began to believe that a leopard could change his spots. Tanner Station, a man whose life was so blotched by violence, might see the error of his ways and come into the light. That was the general drift. So it saddened many when the day of reckoning did come. Surely, the events at the Alva Rodeo in fall of 1925 stunned the community. It was the final undoing of Tanner Station.

It was the day of the Alva Rodeo and Carnival. Carnivals were not events Tanner was likely to attend, but Everett had used Tanner's affliction to get front row seats to the rodeo.

"You have to go, Tanner," Everett said. "I told 'em you wanted to go but can't get into a regular seat, beings as you're in a wheelchair. They put the whole family up front. You gotta go."

Tanner relented, and truth be known, once there, he had enjoyed seeing cowboys riding and roping. He liked seeing 'em thrown even more. Everett, who always managed an iron in the fire if there was a buck to be made, had a couple of young colts involved in the proceedings. He might have owned them. He might have been thinking of buying them; Avery was not quite sure. It didn't matter. Days were few that the family all got together, and Avery was happy. She was with her three girls. Jeff and Gwen were in from the farm. Max and Mimi were there. Things were so good Avery even sat next to her husband with a smile.

Afterwards, Max herded the womenfolk back toward his home for ice cream and cake.

Jeff, now a rancher and a grown man, stayed with Everett as the animals were loaded into trailers for transport home.

Tanner stayed, as well. He sat in his wheelchair, the only person still in the stands, watching the proceedings. He smoked and enjoyed watching. He missed livestock and interacting with them.

As things wound down, nearly all the participants and those with livestock in the rodeo moved out. It was full dark, and the lights of the rodeo arena were off. Everett and Jeff went to the buckboard. They hitched the team and stepped to the carriage.

In the distance, back toward the arena, the two heard bottles breaking. A rough voice growled in the gloom.

Everett reached into the toolbox and brought out his .44.

Jeff gave him a look, and Everett shrugged.

"Probably nothing, but I'll stick some insurance into my belt just in case," he said.

The two men strolled back toward the grounds from the side lot of the livery. It was not two hundred yards, and they heard no more calls or any other sound to alarm them.

"Probably some young bucks raisin' hell," Jeff suggested.

"Always happens after a rodeo. Get laid, get in a fight. That's the goal. Not necessarily in that order," Everett remarked with bravado.

Inside the arena, the two could not see Tanner, except for the glow of his cigarette. It was very dark. They walked toward him.

As they reached the grandstand, what they saw alarmed them.

Tanner sat in his chair. A large man stood facing him. Both held weapons at their side, though neither had yet raised them.

Everett yelled, "Tanner, we're coming!"

Tanner called from his wheelchair in the dark, "It's him, Ev. The man who kilt Marie. It's him. It's Harris."

Everett turned and told Jeff, "Run to the midway. Find the sheriff." Then, he drew the gun from his waistband. Everett strode toward the trouble.

Jeff looked back once and saw his father converge on the other two men.

Jeff lit out as fast as he could, but before he reached the gate, he heard the shot.

The trial took no time at all. Tanner admitted guilt. Mel Harris kilt his wife. He kilt Mel Harris. Close the book on it. Tanner showed no remorse for Harris's death. Not one bit.

The jury was given instructions that could have resulted in first degree murder charges, beings as Tanner carried that hog leg hanging from the handle of his wheelchair from his holster with the express wish of encountering Mel Harris and killing him with it. One shot through the heart was the plan and the result. If ever there was a case of premeditation, this was it.

However, folks wished they could have a different outcome. Mel Harris, after all, had killed the man's wife. Harris, all knew, was the worst kind of misery a man could be. However, there were those who thought the Cherokee Strip got lucky in one bad seed getting rid of another. It would rid the community of two bad men.

The final stake through any chance Tanner might have for leniency was hammered home by Avery Hart, the defendant's sister. Known as a devout Quaker opposed to violence, she was called to the stand for the prosecution. Avery testified that her brother had actually killed Buck Wells all those years ago. Sgt. Richard Spaulding, she told the judge and jury, told her he lied on the stand for Marie's benefit. Spaulding, now dead, told Avery he had not seen Buck involved in any wrongdoing. She said it could have just as easily been Tanner after Marie in the first place, that maybe Mel Harris had lost his job as ramrod for the colonel's 101 Ranch based on a lie, and that Harris had been driven mad by the falsehoods against him. Avery said of her brothers that the both of them went down Satan's Road. They were killers and she'd written them off.

The judge and jury showed no remorse at sentencing, and the prosecutor regretted not asking for a first-degree murder charge. Tanner was found guilty of second-degree murder. He received the judge's words with the emotion of a dead man, "Life in prison without parole."

Time stopped. Nearly fifty years passed. Tanner Station waited to die, but he did not. He remained entombed. Entombed in concrete. His punishment was to seek the eternal and be denied it. He remained in a cell, separated from Marie and Gabriel and the Council Fire of his people. Hell had, indeed, a place on earth. It was Cell Block C at Big Mac; Tanner knew it well.

Resurrection

Tanner Station sat in his wheelchair as the prison physician examined his chart. The angular cowboy had now not been astride a horse for fifty years; he had ridden in a wheelchair now longer than he had ridden a horse. The year was 1974, but not so he would know it. The world had moved on without him. Concrete walls changed little with time.

Tanner was a very old man; ninety-six was ancient for an inmate, an age beyond most convicts' understanding. He had been born in 1877, son of an Irishman, a refugee from Civil War Reconstruction. He had seen the settlement of the American West and the decimation of the buffalo herds. He was there for the Oklahoma land run and the Depression of 1893. He was there for Oklahoma's statehood, the Great War, and the Tulsa Massacre. He lost his son to the first great pandemic. His wife died as part of the extermination of the Native Americans.

But Tanner had missed much.

Inside his prison, he had missed the Dust Bowl years and how Jeff and Gwen and their two children, Lillian and Landon, survived while others moved as Okie refugees to California. He missed the development of radio and television. Until prison, he'd never been in a place with electric lights and indoor plumbing. He did not see America in World War II, the Korean War, and he knew only vaguely of Vietnam. He had never heard of rock 'n' roll. He had never ridden in a car. He had never seen a movie. His solitary nature had not changed. To say he was a man living in a time which had forgotten him was an understatement. Most of his Indian inmate companions, if he was said to have any, were in their twenties. He had done twenty-five years of incarceration before they had been born.

His brother-in-law Everett and sister Avery both committed suicide ten years after his incarceration. Their home, the main house of the Salt Fork Stations, burned a year after Avery's death and was never rebuilt. Tanner did not know the house was gone. All that happened nearly forty years ago. The world he knew was long gone, and yet he remained.

His hair, now stark white, not gray, was long and braided in two ponytails. His face was lean; his cheekbones rose upon his face like ancient mountains. His nose, always long, was now more bent as a mountain leveled with age. His skin, even with half a century stuck inside a prison, was still leathery and dark. Lines etched alongside his eyes gave him a permanent squint. His mouth and thin lips were a dry stream bed. He looked all the world like an ancient Indian chief or shaman, except for the white t-shirt and jeans required of all prisoners at Big Mac State Penitentiary. Prison had not changed him, it seemed; it had only distilled his essence. He looked like an Indian. He looked like fifty years of wanting to be one had created him as such.

Tanner sat, waiting. He was not impatient. Impatient men suffer much in prison. Tanner no longer suffered. When asked by younger inmates how he did half a century behind bars, Tanner responded the same way each time. "I died before I arrived. Still waiting on paperwork."

The doctor, at the facility for just over three months, a newbie, spoke. "Mr. Station, the records and the recent tests show you have an erratic heartbeat."

"Sometimes, my heart skips like a flat rock on a river."

The physician smiled. "That is poetic, but not great for a heart. You know, with your heart condition, I can recommend compassionate early release. Why don't we do that for you?"

Tanner smirked with one side of his mouth. "It requires contrition. And you said 'early' without the proper ironic tone in your voice."

The doctor laughed. "Still have your wits about you at your age, I'll say that. Still not contrite at ninety-six?"

"Contrition requires feelings of remorse or penitence. Someone with contrition should be affected by their guilt. I am none of those things. I wished a man dead. He died. I don't regret my wishing him dead, and I am not contrite, nor am I a liar. At least I no longer am."

"You did more than wish him dead. You were convicted of murder. Shot a man in the chest with a .44 Navy Colt. Big gun, that. You entered a plea of guilty. I read your file."

Tanner's eyes glittered with words he did not say, but the doctor forced his hand. "Well?" the doctor asked.

"Sometimes, a fella gets just so far down a road it's hard to turn around and head back."

The young physician had other patients in the waiting room. He was no psychiatrist, nor did he want to spar with an old man who spoke in cryptic riddles. "Okay, I prescribed nitroglycerin tablets for you. Are you taking the tab each day and putting it under your tongue?"

"I feel better after the orderly brings it to me each day," Tanner answered.

"Good. Stay well, Mr. Station, and if you decide you want to go home, you let me know and I'll fill out the paperwork for a compassionate early release."

"Home?" Tanner said. "My home is in the sky."

Anger was Piper's first reaction after seeing the raw tape that Tobi Thomas and Renée Ripley showed her. Then, professionalism took over. She spoke with the two students about what they had and its significance. It would be a huge news story, given the prominence of football in this state and that one of the men caught speaking was the athletic director for the university and at the time of the recording was on the field at a press day for the team. Secondarily, there was not an alumnus with a higher profile than Johnny Fleet.

Thirdly, he was married to an on-air personality, namely Piper. It would be explosive.

Her second move was to take the students to the TV station. She showed the raw tape to the News Director, Evan Diggs. He agreed to the importance of the tape and the chances for real blowback. They first made several quality copies of the tape, sending one to the station's legal firm in a sealed cannister. No one was to see it, not even the station's attorneys. Anyone who saw it was in potential danger, they believed. Watching it was like handling kryptonite.

Next, Piper and Diggs helped the students, who retained rights to the tape, write copy for a news story. They previewed segments on the tape, interspersing cuts with Tobi's explanatory comments on who the two men were discussing.

After the edits were spliced in, the four previewed the finished segment. It was inflammatory. It was dynamite. It was great. It would ruin the men on the tape.

Diggs decided to hold the tape until the evening news on Tuesday. It was then the news director pulled Piper aside and suggested she take a tape home and show Johnny. She looked at the clock and realized with a start that it was 11:00. They had spent five hours in the studio.

When she arrived home, Johnny was at his desk. His face was full of questions. "How come you weren't on the air tonight? They had Janice in for the weather."

"I was working on something big. Evan Diggs, the new news director, and I were working on a story."

"A weather story?" Johnny raised an eyebrow, only halfway paying attention. "Have you eaten? I cooked burgers earlier. I have one I can heat up."

"No," Piper said, "a news story. And yes, I'm famished. Heat up that burger, please. I'm going to change clothes and then I'll tell you all about it. In fact, it's finished. I'll show you."

That moment was the first time Piper felt real fear. She worried about Johnny's reaction. She went into the bedroom and took Johnny's gun from the nightstand. She removed all the bullets from the revolver and hid them in her jewelry box. Piper didn't want Johnny to storm out and go out hunting John Taylor and the Kilmains.

Then, she went into the living room, slipped the tape into the player, and showed her husband the tape. She never got to eat that burger.

After Johnny Fleet's predictable reaction to his wife being called a "nigger lover," Piper spent the better part of an hour cooling him down.

Her husband did retrieve the gun but noted the absence of rounds.

"You hid the bullets?"

"Yes, I don't want you to go to jail for killing racists." Piper stood at his side. She stroked his cheek. It did not distract him.

"You do realize those bullets came from a box in my desk? I can reload."

"I know they also sell them at Kmart. I thought the process of deciding to reload would give me time to convince you of another course of action. Reloading would also be a sign of premeditation, greatly increasing the number of years until we could have sex again."

Johnny couldn't help but smile. "You have convincing arguments. Do you have a better idea than me shooting those assholes?"

"Yes, definitely."

"That being?"

"Getting them all fired? Ruining their reputations?"

"Would it? Or would their cracker-ass friends like them better?"

Piper said, "Some might. The ones who matter would not."

Johnny turned to her, realization on his face. "Do you think your life is in danger? Lillian's? Your brother's? What about the old convict? Tanner Station? Who's that?"

Piper was suddenly petrified. "We need to call Mom and Chris. They need to be here. We can keep them safe at our house. The story runs tomorrow at 5:00. We need to hunker down until then, and definitely after."

Johnny was a decisive man. Now calm, he poured himself a Scotch. "You sure we shouldn't kill them?"

Piper smiled. "Yes, let's prove to my students the camera is mightier than the sword."

"Call your mom first. She should drive over tonight if she's awake enough."

Piper laughed. "Oh, after I tell her about all of this, she'll be awake. Then, I'll call Chris. Hey, I'm not hungry anymore, but I would take a shot of that Scotch."

Chris didn't arrive home from the courthouse until after dark. His apartment was clean, if stark. He had loosened his tie and hung up his suitcoat when he heard a knock on the door. It might have been the first time he'd had a visitor. He opened the door and was somewhat surprised to see a young man, Hispanic or Native American, holding a pizza. It was a welcome sight. Chris was hungry, but he had not ordered a pizza.

"You Chris Fairchild?" the young man asked.

"Yes, but…"

"Just listen. There are instructions in the box from Tate Laughlin. Pay me for the pizza. Then, follow the instructions. Your apartment is being watched."

Chris retrieved his wallet. He returned to the door. "All I got is a twenty."

The kid took it from his hand. "The FBI will think you're a good tipper." He laughed and handed the box over. He turned his back and was gone into the gloom of the evening.

Inside, Chris pulled free a slice as he read the note:

At 11:00, turn out your lights. Wait thirty minutes. Go out your sliding glass door to the rear of the complex. Stay to the tree line in the shadows. Go north down Empress Blvd. At the first intersection, you'll see a pick-up parked in the barbershop parking lot. Ask the guy what the first book you and I discussed. If he answers correctly, get in and he'll bring you to me. We need to talk. -T

Chris changed into jeans and a turtleneck, thinking the whole thing was very cloak-and-dagger. He snuck a look out his living room windows, peering between the curtains, but he could not see any wayward FBI agents keeping tabs on him.

At 11:00, he turned off the TV and all the lights, thinking on a regular night, he would have done so earlier. Chris slipped out the back door and hurried next to the evergreen hedge at the rear of the property. He saw no one and took care to remain silent.

At the intersection at Empress, he saw the truck and approached. The same Indian teen was behind the wheel as had delivered the pizza.

"What was the first book Tate and I discussed?" Chris asked him.

"Treasure Island?"

Chris recoiled. "No," he said, shocked.

The kid laughed. "Tate told me you'd freak. *The Ballot or the Bullet* by Malcolm X, right?"

Chris smiled, knowing that, indeed, the prank was exactly Tate's idea of a joke.

Inside, Chris stuck out his hand. "Chris Fairchild."

"Terrance Embry. Laughing Dog."

"What tribe?"

"Caddo," the young man replied, pulling away as he turned on his headlights.

"Where we going?"

"Lake Thunderbird, south and east of the city."

"I've heard of it. Never been."

Embry curled his lip. "Nice lake, but they bulldozed roads and camping sites all through the park. Might as well have painted it white." Then, he was silent for a long time.

Chris Fairchild and Terrance Embry entered the park gates, now unattended by rangers, just before one in the morning. They pulled past Calypso Cove Marina, taking a rough road into the woods on the west side of the lake. It was very dark.

Soon, as they neared a fork veering right, Embry stopped and turned off his headlights.

They sat in the dark for a minute before Chris spoke.

"Are we waiting for Tate?

Embry smiled. "No, we're waiting for me to get my night vision. After my eyes adapt, we'll continue. Don't want anyone to see a vehicle's lights go up into these hills. We'll be on private land, but the access is best from the park."

Then, they proceeded, nearly scraping mirrors on pines close to the trail.

Eventually, Embry stopped the pick-up in a clearing. He turned off the engine.

As the two men exited the vehicle, four Native Americans appeared from the shadows.

Tate Laughlin, looking little changed in weight or stature, but having the face of a prize fighter, stepped forward and hugged his friend.

"Chris, it has been too long," he said. Then, Tate turned and told his comrades how Chris and his grandfather had taken him first to the switchbacks and later to the Mexican border. "They are truly our friends and allies," he said as he finished his story. Tate added,

"I was sorry to learn of your grandfather and grandmother's passing."

Chris nodded. It was his turn to talk. "This is very *Spy-vs-Spy*. You really think the FBI is watching my apartment? Watching me would have been pretty boring."

Laughlin smiled. "After this week, you have powerful enemies. You realize the Kilmains, and this John Taylor are powerful men. They have powerful allies."

Chris raised an eyebrow. "How so?"

"John Birch. The Klan. Other organizations having to do with white supremacy."

"For real?"

Tate nodded. "For real."

"And they're after you? Helping the FBI get you? Why?"

"I am in AIM, the American Indian Movement. I was at the occupation of Alcatraz, I was at the takeover at Wounded Knee, and I was at the storming and vandalism of the Bureau of Indian Affairs. They know I am trouble, and they know I will not stop." Tate waved his arm at the other three men beside Embry. "These men, my brothers, believe as I do. We must continue to push the white man to return our lands, to return our water rights, to return our homes."

"But surely you know about the legislation that is about to pass, allowing reservations to open their own schools," Chris said.

"We should not need permission to educate our own children how we see fit."

"Your actions, particularly if violent, might jeopardize that bill. You don't want that."

"Any demonstration against the status quo which is acceptable to it will be ineffective. Our actions must interfere with monetary flow. Otherwise, the white men don't care."

Chris stomped his foot. "No middle ground, then?"

"Our violence is having an effect. They would not have thought to appease us if they weren't afraid of our next act."

"Which is?"

Tate shook his head.

Chris put his hands on his hips. "I don't agree that violence is the way to better the lives of the Indian Nation."

Tate nodded again. "I know you believe as you do. We will just have to disagree. That is okay because we are on the same side and because we are blood brothers."

"There has to be another way. Things are better, don't you think?"

"Do I think the soldiers who committed the atrocities in the Mỹ Lai massacre were notably better than those who committed the same atrocities against my people at Wounded Knee?"

Chris frowned. "There are good people in law enforcement. I work with them daily."

"Ask the descendants of the people slain at the Greenwood District of Tulsa if they agree," Tate Laughlin spat. "I've heard from ex-DEA that they are importing cocaine from South America to our ghettos. Cultivating a criminal class."

Chris shook his head. "Why would they do that?"

"Our government can't fight drugs, but it can fight drug lords. There must be an enemy in order to increase appropriations."

"Then, you just do their bidding by playing the villain."

Tate Laughlin pondered that for a second.

There was a noise in the trees, and each of the Indian men pulled a firearm free.

Chris looked at them, shaking his head. "Not a great way to live, in my opinion."

There was no more commotion, and eventually the guns were put away.

"It is not ideal," Tate agreed, "but the red man has always had enemies. Now, Chris, you have taken a side. We both have the same problem, I reached out to you because I do not believe you realize the hate in the heart of your foes. We both have men wishing us dead. You need to be prepared. You need to go someplace safe. Have you such a place?"

"I guess I could pack up and go to my sister's. She's married to Johnny Fleet."

Tate laughed. "Yes, your sister married into trouble herself. It is in your blood. Your mother raised you two well. Did you ever hear from your father?"

Chris did not answer. He shook his head.

Tate too was quiet for a moment. "Yes, go there. Johnny Fleet is well-known. Piper, as well. It will be more difficult for those who wish you harm to act out there. But you cannot go back to your apartment and pack. We'll return you to your sister's. Go during daylight with others to get your things. Take this threat seriously. Your enemies are real. The evil is tangible."

"Okay, I'll go to Piper's. But I can't stay there forever. How do we fix this mess?"

"We kill the bad guys?" Tate said, partly kidding.

Chris frowned. "No, unacceptable. Come up with something different."

"Okay, oh, Great Attorney of the Five Civilized Tribes, we'll try. Remember, the Cheyenne are not considered civilized."

"Duly noted. Didn't y'all get forced into Wyoming or something?"

"Ask Custer."

Chris laughed. "Us blondes could resent that comment."

Now both laughed.

"Hey, Chris?" said Tate, as he turned to walk back into the trees.

"Yeah?"

"It's your mom's turn to pick a book. Ask her. We'll discuss it next time we're together."

"When will that be, Tate?"

"Soon, very soon. The fates have decided our arms are locked in brotherhood. Our friendship is eternal."

"Deal, brother."

And then Tate Laughlin disappeared into darkness. He was good at that.

Laughing Dog Embry took Chris to his sister's home. When they arrived, it was nearly 4:00 a.m. A dark sedan was parked at the curb a block down from their home.

"Feds," Embry noted, nodding his chin at the car.

Chris wasn't sure whether to believe him or not. He just knew he was very tired. The young attorney stepped out at the curb, letting Embry pull away sharply. He accelerated at the corner and then sped through the next intersection. The young Native American did not want to give the sedan time to think about following him.

Chris went to the front door and rang the bell.

To his surprise, Johnny answered the door on the first ring. He was not in pajamas. He wore yesterday's clothes, crumpled from twenty-four hours of wear. "Where the hell have you been?" the bigger man complained. "Your sister has been calling you all night. Your mother was in a car accident. She was run off the road on Route 66 on the way here from Tulsa. She's in the hospital in Edmond. Piper is with her."

"Mom was in an accident? How bad is she?"

"Lillian will be all right. She was forced off the road by another car. She hit an embankment, hard. Broke her nose. But lucky, given everything."

Chris was dubious. "Are you sure?"

"Yeah, we're sure. Piper talked to the doctors. Lil will be fine, especially because I hired bodyguards to stay outside her room."

"Bodyguards? I don't understand." Chris was confused. "When did this happen?"

"About three hours ago. Piper called Lillian around midnight. Told her to get up and drive here. We thought it was an emergency. We tried to get hold of you, too. We think your lives are in danger. Decided we needed to circle the wagons."

"Because of Tate Laughlin?"

It was Johnny's turn to be confused. "Who's Tate Laughlin? No, it's about the tape. I have something you need to watch. Then, I'll take you to see your mother."

Lillian was in a private room with two big black linemen at the door. Nobody was getting past, except doctors, nurses, and Johnny Fleet.

Once Johnny and Chris entered, they saw Piper, looking exhausted, and Lillian, who looked the same, except with a bandage on her nose. Both of her eyes were black.

Lillian looked past the white gauze to her son, "And where were you catting around all night? New girlfriend or did the forces of evil come after you, as well?"

"I went to see Tate Laughlin."

Lillian leaned forward and groaned.

Piper sat up. "Really? Do tell. What did our counter revolutionary have to say after his long absence?"

Chris smiled, grimly. "He said our lives might be in danger."

Lillian laughed, and then she groaned again, holding her ribs. "Tell him his timing is bad."

"I thought about that after seeing the tape," Chris replied. "He also said it was your turn to pick the book."

Lillian smiled again. "Tell him I suggested the U.S. Penal Code."

Chris shrugged, too tired to laugh. "At least I've already read that one."

Lillian cackled but then frowned. "Don't make me laugh. I have cracked ribs."

Piper looked at her brother. "You've seen the tape?"

"Yes, and I need to go see Tanner Station. He deserves to know his life is in danger."

Johnny nodded. "I agree. Chris should go home and pack up some things. After that, he can clean up and go to McAlister to the prison. This Tanner Station relative of yours, no matter what he's done, deserves to know someone wants him dead. I will send one of the bodyguards with Chris. Once we get Lillian to our home and settled, then I'll take the tape and go see the university president before the story runs this afternoon. Maybe they'll want to at least fire Athletic Director Zane Kilmain before then. It would keep me in good graces if I gave them a head's up, even if only by an hour or two."

Tanner sat in his wheelchair at lunch in a large canteen. While it was a room that seated perhaps five hundred men, one hundred seats remained empty. Those tables in the middle were no-man's land. Three factions ran the prison; whites, blacks, and Latinos. Whites counted for just over forty-five percent of the prison population. The black inmates would fill in another third. The remaining twenty-five percent would be Latino, although forty percent of those were Native American. Altogether, Native American inmates, at the current time, numbered at right around forty. Most all of them were in maximum security.

Big Mac, during the 1970s, was not a good prison to be in, not that there is actually a good one. From 1970 until July 27, 1973, the year prior to now, the prison had nineteen murders; forty inmates were shanked, and another forty-four took serious beatings requiring hospitalization. The big house was a rough joint. A man inside needed assistance to make it through. Not belonging to one of the three prison gangs meant an inmate was on his own and in jeopardy, but even belonging to a gang did not ensure safety.

Lunch for Tanner was two pieces of bread and a slice of baloney. A scrawny apple and two slices of cheese were also on his paper plate. There were no utensils. There were never any utensils. Tanner sat in the Latino section, the only white man who had ever done so. He had been convicted of killing a white man for killing his Cherokee wife. That was enough to earn him a spot with the Latins and Native Americans. He was sheltered from his own people, many wanting him dead for betraying his white skin.

Today, Tanner sat with his bodyguard, his constant companion. As a member of the Latino's leadership council, he had a guard with him night and day. Killing the old man would make some young white punk's bones. The Latino gang, the Nuestra Familia, held him in high regard. No one could approach Tanner without a fight. Today, the man with Tanner was a Navaho convicted of killing two men in a bar fight. He was not a good conversationalist. Tanner did not mind. His thoughts were elsewhere.

But then things changed. It was rare day unlike all the others. Today, a white man crossed no-man's land, walking across the open space and the empty tables to face Tanner. He stopped ten feet from the ancient man.

The Navaho bodyguard started to circle the table, preparing for violence.

Tanner waved Navaho Joe to a stop.

"You wish to speak with me?" Tanner asked the white man.

The white man's arms were covered with jailhouse tattoos. Scar tissue surrounded his eyes. He was perhaps fifty years old, but he was not in good physical condition. His muscles had withered, leaving his arms thin and sinewy. He stood silent for a moment, choosing his words.

The large room went silent as hundreds of men watched the proceedings, but none were close enough to hear them speak.

"You are Tanner Station?"

"Yes, you have endangered your life by speaking to me. Merely crossing into our territory puts you in danger, but I fear you may have more to fear from your own people after speaking to me, at least in speaking to me civilly." Tanner said, keeping the Navajo in check.

"Do you know me?"

Tanner raised an eyebrow. "I have been here since the dawn of man. I know everybody. You are called The Fixer, but I do not know your Christian name, if you are indeed a Christian."

"Perhaps a failed one."

Tanner smiled. "Yes, that is the most common kind in this facility."

"Yes, I am called The Fixer. I fix cars. I go by Walter Donohue now."

"But you have not always."

"No," the white man smiled. "Not always."

Tanner nodded. "Why do you risk your life to speak to me, Mr. Donohue?"

"There's a contract out on you, Tanner Station. You are not safe in the library where you spend your day, nor in the trustee cell where you spend your night. Someone wants you dead."

"Do we know who this person is?"

"It doesn't matter who ordered it. I am supposed to do the killing. Word came down I'm supposed to steal a screwdriver from the auto repair shop tomorrow and kill you."

Tanner pondered that for a second. He turned, looking at the white side of the room. The motion moved his ponytails to one side. "And yet you tell me this information, essentially guaranteeing your death when you walk back across the room? Why?"

Walter Donohue laughed. "Oh, I'm not going back across that room." He nodded with his head at the guard nearest the door. "You see that poor schmuck? When I leave you, I'm going to go and punch him in the face."

Tanner and the Navaho laughed. "Thirty days in the hole for that, all right!"

"Maybe then I live that long."

"And why would you risk your life for mine, Mr. Donohue?"

"Why would I take your real last name is the question you should be asking, Tanner Station. Truth is I was on the run and needing a new identity. I remembered hearing a story from Lillian about how your father took a new name to get away from the Irish gangs in New York. I thought it would be fitting to take the original family name, for my son's sake."

"Ah," Tanner said, "You are the father of Christian Fairchild, the Five Tribes attorney?"

The Fixer nodded. "Henry Fairchild, at your service."

"It is always a pleasure to meet family. You are the first I have seen since Everett died in 1935. Thirty-nine years ago. No, that is incorrect. His daughter, Autumn, visited me to tell me of Everett's death." Tanner was silent, then spoke slowly, "Your son is coming to see me."

"He is? Why?"

"I do not know. I dreamed it several times. And I was told Avery's offspring would visit me by a medicine man when they allowed such men here. Long ago, before World War II."

Walter Donohue smiled a bit. "You really believe in the whole Indian thing, don't you?"

Tanner smiled, sadly. "The white man's way was my undoing. I sought refuge with my wife's people. It was a decision I do not regret. Shall I tell your son about your circumstances?"

Walter Donohue frowned. "No, I died a long time ago. Just waiting on the paperwork."

Johnny Fleet held sway on campus. When he arrived unannounced at the president's office, he was not shooed away. No, Johnny brought first-rate talent to the football team and that was not to be taken lightly. Johnny Fleet had a voice that even the president of the institution recognized as powerful. It was not five minutes, and Johnny was escorted into the office, an ivory tower and edifice of institution.

The university president sat behind an impossibly glossy mahogany desk. The desk was big. Johnny was well over six-feet tall, yet the athlete could have lain across the desktop with room to spare. It was a desk and a room designed to intimidate. It was not having that effect. The president, white-haired with a youthful face, wore suits more customary in New York than Norman. He saw the look on Johnny's face and knew today was the beginning of big trouble.

"What can I do for you, Big John?" the president said.

Johnny reached into his coat. "I have a tape you need to see."

Five minutes and twenty-three seconds later, after the tape had run, things started to happen very quickly.

The first call the president made was to the governor. That conversation, including the president reading sections of the transcript as provided by Johnny, resulted in the governor deciding to ask for John Taylor's resignation as Secretary of Health and Human Services. The lieutenant governor was tasked with delivering the bad news.

The university president then called his Athletic Director, Arden Kilmain, to ask him if indeed he was party to a conspiracy to commit four counts of murder, and if the first attempt had been made last night on Lillian Hart.

Arden Kilmain took the call but replied only with stony silence. After the president's words of inquiry, words not quite rising to the level of accusation, he was after all an attorney, Kilmain replied only to say he needed to consult his lawyer.

The president, in turn, told the AD he was suspended with pay and banned from campus, pending an investigation into the recorded conversation and its allegations. The assistant AD would take over all functions of his office.

"None of it's true, and an investigation will show that," Arden said.

"John Taylor said to you, 'Take that Station family off the board, or I will'." said the president. "And you replied, 'If I decide it needs done, I'll do it.' That response will be hard to explain away to the alumni, Arden. I think your days are numbered."

Arden Kilmain hung up the phone.

The president then turned to Johnny with a smile. "Any chance we can get the TV station to spike the story?" He knew the answer but had to ask.

"Not a chance in hell."

"Then, please inform the station we'll have a statement to

accompany the story. I imagine the governor will likewise have something to add.

The governor, after some reflective, was less motivated to make a move than the university president. He spoke with Zane Kilmain, warden of the Oklahoma State Penitentiary, and afterwards, he did not suspend his state penitentiary warden.

Zane Kilmain was a huge figure in Oklahoma politics. A king-maker, he was. He would not go down without a fight. He swore he had no knowledge of the so-called conspiracy. Zane stated he was innocent and completely unaware of any conversations between his brother and John Taylor.

"John Taylor asked your brother to participate in four murders, and he didn't let you know?" the governor asked.

"Aw, hell, JT talks so much shit. Arden and me have known him all our lives. Someone listenin' in might take something for real when we know it's just John blowing off steam."

"You have an inmate, a Tanner Station, in maximum security. Make sure nothing happens to him."

"No worries."

"Okay, keep your head down. Arden has been sidelined. John will have to resign. If everyone does his job, we can weather this."

"You got it. Thanks for the head's up."

Then, the call ended.

Lillian was released from the hospital. By mid-morning, she and her daughter were installed at home with two security guards. Lillian was resting, if not comfortably, at least well enough to sleep. Piper did not like being at home with this big of news story going down, but she knew her presence at the TV station would be a distraction and might put others' lives at jeopardy. She tried to read a book but was interrupted by the doorbell.

One of Johnny's football recruits, now a bodyguard, answered the door. He stuck his head into the kitchen where Piper drank coffee. "Mailman says you have to sign for a letter."

She signed and opened the slim parcel. It held but a single page.

Piper read the words and then went and woke up Lillian. "I've been fired from my teaching job at the university. They say my high-profile is a distraction and Johnny's steady-cams will be returned."

Lillian looked at her, fatigue showing in her eyes. "Playing hardball, aren't they?"

Chris arrived not fifteen minutes later. "Guess what?" he said, setting down a suitcase.

"You got fired from your adjunct job at the university?"

Piper's little brother registered surprise and then understanding. "Oh, you too?"

Lillian called from her bedroom.

Chris stepped in and showed his mother the letter. Afterwards, he went to shower.

Piper poured her brother coffee. Chris did not want coffee. He wanted sleep. He was exhausted. But he needed to see Tanner Station. His bodyguard would drive him to Big Mac prison, and he could sleep in the car on the journey. Perhaps three hours would be enough.

The phone rang once again. Piper answered.

Chris entered the room, buttoning up his shirt.

"It's for you."

He nodded. "I left a message at my office that I'd be here."

It was Shannon Gill. She was crying. She'd just been fired, too. Chris tried to console her, but eventually Piper took the phone and soothed her. Piper asked where Shannon's home was. She got directions and sent one of the two bodyguards to pick up the redhead. The more, the merrier, eh? Who knew if Shannon was safe? No one knew how they knew she'd been the leak. It was better to be safe than sorry.

The story ran on the 5:00 p.m. news. The station had also offered the tape to the national nightly news, so it ran in a shortened form across America that evening. The additional news that there had been an attempt on Lillian Hart's life, that Arden Kilmain had been suspended pending a university investigation, that the Governor had asked John Taylor to resign, that Zane Kilmain remained on as warden of the state's largest penitentiary, denying all knowledge of the situation, and now that both Chris Hart and Piper Fleet were both fired from the university filled the news cycle. The story sucked all the oxygen from everything else. Only the weather remained with regular programming.

By evening, before Chris even met with Tanner Station, Johnny Fleet's attorneys were filing a wrongful termination suit against the university on behalf of both siblings. The university president called Johnny to say the decision to fire Piper and Chris had not been his, but instead their departments' respective deans. AD Arden Kilmain had directed the dismissals, saying a scandal involving Johnny and Piper would soon be revealed. Johnny replied he would no longer be able to speak to the president except through counsel. Everybody was playing hardball now.

When Chris arrived at Big Mac prison, he was awakened by his bodyguard and now driver, a middle linebacker named Elvis Fontaine. Chris was greeted in the parking lot by a bright blue pick-up truck. A Volkswagen bug was parked beside it. A rangy Native American man stepped from the truck. He was dressed in a western shirt, boots, and jeans. From the VW, a black man emerged in a severe black suit, white shirt, and black tie.

"You Chris Fairchild?" the Native American asked.

"Yep."

"I'm Douglas Talako. Work with Bureau of Indian Affairs. Excuse my attire. I was off today, headed fishing. Louis Bruce called me and asked me to run out here with this gentleman. This here is King Newberry."

They shook hands.

"How's your mother?"

"Banged up with some cracked ribs, but she'll be okay. Tough lady," Chris said.

"Somebody tried to kill her?" Talako asked.

"Ran her off the road, anyway. What can I do for you? I'm late," Chris said, impatiently.

"Yeah, given the possibility of your life being in danger, and with the court decision putting you in the crosshairs, Mr. Newberry will be taking your case load starting today."

"All of them?"

"Excepting your current meeting with Tanner Station, yes. Just for now. Louis thinks your clients, our constituents, might suffer retaliations through their association with you. Just for now, we want Mr. Newberry to represent members of the Five Tribes in court."

Chris nodded unhappily to Newberry. "Gotcha. I will call later and give you the lowdown on my caseload."

Newberry gave him his card. "I live here in McAlister. I appreciate your help."

Chris nodded, feeling very depressed, and then went inside.

Inside the visitor's entrance, a second man waited to see Chris Fairchild. This man wore a tailored brown suit with highly polished Tony Lama boots. He wore an old-fashioned string tie and a pencil-thin mustache.

"Mr. Fairchild?" he said, stepping forward.

"Yes?"

"I'm Paul Mabry, Prison Superintendent. I'm second in charge here. The warden asked me to bring you to him. He wants to talk prior to your meeting with Inmate Station."

"In his office?"

"No," said Mabry, "offsite at his residence. We have transports, essentially golf carts, to go back and forth. Shall we make our way?"

Chris followed Mabry out the door. He saw Talako and Newberry still talking beside their two vehicles. "Just a second," he said to Mabry.

"Talako?" Chris called as he got close enough.

The rangy Native American turned to him.

"Warden Kilmain wants me to go to his house off grounds. I'm going with this man Mabry. I wanted someone to know. You know, in case."

Talako nodded, the line of his lip tight.

Newberry said, "You must be onto something. Your enemies are forming ranks."

Chris nodded. "I'll call you, Newberry, when I get back to my hotel room." Then, he got into a golf cart with Superintendent Mabry, and they headed down a dirt path toward a large stand of cottonwoods in the distance.

Warden Zane Kilmain's residence was a very good replica of a Southern antebellum home. It had four columns supporting a large, covered porch. Rocking chairs tilted back and forth in the breeze as they approached. Today was windy. Cottonwood fluffs drifted by on the wind, leaving clumps in corners on the porch as Chris ascended the stairs. Two armed men, dressed in prison guard attire, nodded as he moved past them. Mabry, who had not left the cart, lit a cigarette and called after him, "He's expecting you, Mr. Fairchild. Go right in."

Warden Zane Kilmain was visible in an office at the far end of the long entryway hall. He sat at a large desk, his feet up on it. He wore red satin slippers. He did not immediately look up, and Chris could see he was trimming a cigar. He wore a white shirt, a bolo tie with a very large turquoise stone at his neck. Black jeans and a large rodeo belt completed the outfit.

"Excuse my slippers, Mr. Fairchild," Kilmain said, "but the lacquer on this desk has just been repoured. I ruined the first coat with my boots. My wife got me these slippers and told me no feet on the desk unless I'm wearing 'em." He laughed, then set the cigar down as if he decided he did not need the extra level of intimidation.

Kilmain stood and rounded the desk. He shook Fairchild's hand. His hand was much bigger than Chris's, but the older man didn't attempt to break the bones in Chris's hand. That would have been forthright. This man had levels. Chris was able to intuit his nuanced approach immediately.

"I've been wanting to talk with you for a while, Chris. Oh, may I call you Chris? We're not big on formalities here. Call me Zane. Or Warden Zane. Whatever floats your boat. We both come from prominent Oklahoma families. Both clans around for a century. My family involved in law enforcement; yours, in…" he paused, "I guess I'll call it civil unrest."

Chris tilted his head, but still had not spoken.

Kilmain motioned for Chris to sit in the leather chair in front of him. "You're seeing Tanner Station today?"

"Yes."

"I've arranged for you to see him in his cell in the Nuestra Familia gang wing. Tanner was moved from his private cell yesterday."

Chris looked concerned.

Kilmain shook his head. "Not my doing. He requested it. He asked to be moved in with a trustee medic. Caregiver, if you will. Said he might need some assistance." Kilmain tapped his chest. "Tanner has a bad ticker. Prison doc approved the move. I don't interfere in inmate's health decisions. Easy to move him out of a trustee single cell, anyway. We always have space problems. Can use the cell for two more inmates."

Chris considered Kilmain's words and decided to take them at face value. "Mr. Station should be given a compassionate release. His doctor says his health is poor. He is very frail."

"Dangerous man, Tanner Station. Killed four men. At the very least. Two Comanche back in the stagecoach days. I got no problem with that, but it does tell you some about him. Then, he gets off for crackin' the skull of that feller who messed with his Indian girlfriend. Plus, he most likely killed a skunk named Charlie Crups, who had his throat slit in New Mexico. Later, Station shot the man who killed his wife. Kind of long track record of remorseless killing. Killed at least four men. His sister Avery thought so too. Testified against him. And he probably killed more. He was off radar for eight years. A man like him can wreak a lot of havoc in eight years."

"All of that was half a century ago," Chris replied. "It's all been adjudicated. He's ninety-six with a failing heart. Tanner was convicted of second-degree murder and has spent forty-nine years in prison. The average sentence for second degree murder in Oklahoma is nineteen years. He's thirty years past the appropriate sentence. And he's dying. He should be freed."

Kilmain ignored Chris's words, picked up the cigar, and examined it. "I've been thinking about our families, yours and mine. My grandfather started as a constable over in Tulsa. He was born the year after the land run, back in 1894. Worked hard. Being a cop didn't pay well. Being second generation Irish didn't help his case in getting promoted. But he worked hard. Came into some land and money in 1921. Eventually, moved to the sheriff's office and was elected sheriff in 1930. Worked as sheriff for a decade and then ended up as warden of the Nazi prison camp over to Alva. Did you know they kept Nazis there during World War II?

"My father followed in his father's footsteps. He was elected sheriff back in Tulsa a few years after he got back from the Pacific Theater. Served honorably in the Navy. Saw some horrific things. Wouldn't talk about them. Never would. Damaged him some in the head, I think. He was tough on us two, Arden and me. Especially on Arden, who wanted to become a baseball player. Played for

Wichita State. Good program, that. Me, I went straight into law enforcement. Traffic officer straight out of high school. Now, I'm warden of the state's biggest prison and Arden is athletic director of the state's largest university. Success stories."

Kilmain lit the cigar. "And your family? It seems to me your family has spent the last seventy years trying to screw things up."

Chris shook his head, letting Kilmain know he was unrepentant.

"Your mother fights to turn valuable assets of the state over to Indians. Now, that's your fight, as well. Your sister is with Johnny Fleet, who caused Arden a lot of trouble this week. Your great-uncle Tanner is a murderer. His sister, Avery, fought to give women the right to vote and kept bringing up Tulsa every chance she got. Hell, she was with Carrie Nation, trying to get rid of booze. Now's that's some bullshit. She was a rabble-rouser, and her daughter, Autumn, got run out of the state as a lesbian. Her dad, Avery's husband, Everett? A skunk who kept a woman on the sly outside his marriage for half of his life. And the worst one of all was Carson, Tanner's brother. He was a murderin' outlaw by all accounts. I'd say you got bad blood in you, son."

Chris decided he'd had enough. "Look, I get it. Your grandfather used his badge to get rich in a community that ripped the wealth from black folk. Irish immigrant made good. Your father was a war hero. He came back with a violent streak and took over for your grandfather. Beat on you some and now it's your turn to beat back. Your family niche is in keeping minorities down. Racist has been your family's creed and job title. I don't like it, but I understand it. I'll deal with it. And I am going to get Tanner Station out of jail. You can count on it."

Kilmain just smiled. "Not if you need my signature, you won't." The warden was not angry. He scratched his chin. "I just don't get you. I'd say you must like that brown sugar those hippies sing about on the radio, but my contacts up in Kansas say you were seeing a nice white girl up there. No darkie nooky that we can tell. Can't see as you're tapping nobody much since you moved to OKC, and we keep tabs. Got eyes on you, boy, and we don't see no women. Although you somehow convinced that Shannon Gill girl to rat out Johnny Taylor. You got your sights set on her? She's out of your league, little man."

Chris stood. Kilmain raised his hand, like he had gone too far. He motioned for Chris to sit once again. Not sure why, Chris obliged him.

"My apologies," Kilmain said. "Gentlemen do not discuss such things. I was just saying I don't get you. What good is it for whites to help black folk and Indians get more? You and your mom use all your energies in a counterproductive way. It makes no sense to me and mine. Give them more and they'll just piss it away. Injuns always piss it away. Drugs and booze. Sex and violence. Them and the jigs are lower forms of humans. You're wasting valuable energies.

"Look, my grandfather had to turn back the tide in his day. Blacks in Greenwood getting uppity. Black fuckin' Wall Street. Laughable. That was then, this is now. Now, it is the red man making trouble. An uprising on the res ain't good for society. Ain't good for decent folk. AIM is just a terrorist organization. Tate Laughlin, their leader, needs to get the air let out of his tires. Let it go. You're a smart fella. Use your intellect in a positive way. Time to switch teams, Chris Fairchild. We got a place for you. Think about it." Kilmain was loving this moment. He rolled the cigar in his fingers like a teenaged boy hiding in a closet looking at a *Playboy Magazine*.

"You know even if people knew about the Red Summer of 1919, and most don't, do you know why they called Tulsa a race riot? Because we wanted it called that. Only failed insurrections are called insurrections. If you win, you don't have to bother putting flowers on your enemies' graves. You know what the headline said the day after Tulsa? ***TWO WHITES KILLED IN RACE RIOT***. We wrote that, and we told the story we wanted told. No one will be talking about how we took down AIM, either. The FBI will do our bidding. It'll be us writing the headline the day after Tate Laughlin is dead. Don't be on the wrong side of history, son."

Kilmain stood, indicating that the meeting was concluding, the message sent. "Look, John Taylor is a dumbass. We both know it. Let him lose his job, take the fall. Arden and me, we don't care one lick about him. John's just a kid we grew up with who became a fancy-pants attorney. We could manipulate him, so we kept him around. A lawyer on a leash was helpful, but he now screwed the pooch. You can have him. Win the round. Then shut it down."

Chris was now standing. "Did you try to kill my mother?"

Kilmain laughed. "Hell, no. Must have been a drunk Indian. Two o'clock in the morning on that highway? Sixty percent of the drivers between OKC and the res at two in the morning are piss-ass drunks. Ten percent of them going down the highway on the wrong side. Bad thing to be on the wrong side of things." Kilmain shrugged. "Nah, we didn't want your mom dead. Wasn't us. If it 'twas us, we'd have got it done right."

Chris felt bile in his throat. "If I take John Taylor down and back off, will you give me Tanner Station?" Chris was raising the ante.

Kilmain considered it. "I'll check with the others, but I'm thinkin' that's a bridge too far."

"Then, I'll do my damnedest to pull you all the way there. Tell the others I'm coming."

"You're spunky. I like that," Kilmain said and laughed. He reached out his hand.

Chris did not take it.

"Reckon the ground rules got decided today," Kilmain said.

"Those being?"

"Ain't gonna be no ground rules."

"Duly noted," said Chris as he exited the warden's office.

"One concession," Kilmain said to his back.

Chris turned. "Yes?"

"News reportage has all of this horseshit in high visibility. I will make sure you and Tanner are safe on prison grounds. Not because I feel any sense of responsibility to your homicidal great uncle, but because your deaths might hurt my reputation at the country club."

"If you're worried about your reputation, then you should let a frail old man out of prison," countered Chris.

"No," said Kilmain, blowing out smoke, the cigar lit like a fuse. "Tanner Station turned his back on his people Chose red skin over white. He doesn't get to come back into the fold when the going gets tough. I'll keep him in his tepee on the reservation, Cell block C, #338."

"That's white of ya," Chris said and stepped outside to far more breathable air.

"Hello, young fella. I've been waiting for you," the old man said. Tanner Station sat slumped, his back as curved as his long braids were straight. The cell was decorated with Indian blankets, and cedar incense burned in an ashtray sitting on the sink. A Navajo rested on the bunk. He looked at Chris with curiosity. He was a massive man, and his t-shirt was ripped at the sleeves. He wore his jet-black hair back, flipped up and clipped with barrettes. Chris wondered how the big Navaho got them. He wondered how they got incense inside the cell block.

Chris stepped forward and took the old man's hand. "You've been waiting on me? Someone told you I was coming to visit?"

"A medicine man told me way before the second Great War. Maybe 1940," he said, smiling.

Chris grinned. "Sorry I'm late."

Tanner Station shook his head. "No, no, your timing is exquisite."

"Exquisite is a fancy word. You're not what I was expecting," Chris said, noting that the old man's hand was delicate, like a bird's wing in his hand. He could feel the tiny bones.

"I read about three books a week. Three books a week for fifty years has increased my vocabulary."

Both men laughed. Their laughs sounded the same and it made them laugh again.

Chris did the math in his head. "So you've read eight thousand books?"

"You are quick at math. Only seven thousand. Many I read twice or three times."

Chris smiled. "I want the list of repeat reads."

Tanner nodded at the big man on the bunk. "This is my caretaker and my bodyguard. We call him Navaho Joe."

"Nice to meet you, Joe," Chris said, also shaking his hand. He turned to Tanner. "You need a bodyguard?"

Tanner shrugged. "Prison is inherently violent. One must accept that. However, I was told there was to be an attempt on my life. I moved from my trustee cell to here. I am safe inside the Cell Block C. It is exclusively Latino and Indian." He paused. "Except for me. They allow me to live among my wife's people."

Chris nodded.

Tanner motioned Navaho Joe to leave them.

Chris took his place upon the bunk across from the wheelchair.

Once settled, the young attorney spoke. "I am here because our family has learned there is a conspiracy to take all our lives, yours included. I will file a motion to have you released on compassionate grounds. If the warden does not approve, I will approach the governor."

Tanner waved the comment away. "I will not apologize to anyone for my actions."

Chris nodded. "I don't think given the amount of time you've served, that will be required. I will request compassionate release. The warden will refuse. I will appeal to the governor for commutation. There is now intense media pressure. Your name is on TV all the time. I think the governor will sign your release to kill the story. Are you okay with that?"

Tanner shrugged. "I have not seen TV. We have other things to discuss. Of them all, my release is perhaps the one I'm least concerned about. Let me start by telling you the overall lesson I've learned in fifty years. My time could end soon, so I'll tell you the last thing first.

"You must involve yourself in making others' lives better. I tried to stand outside. My mantra was simply to live and let live. To not bother others. I thought if I stayed away from everyone, no one would bother me. The world does not work that way. You cannot stand outside the fire. Learn that lesson, Moon-eyed Man. You know, that is what they call you in Cell block C."

"Why that?"

"The Cherokee tell of an ancient white race who lived in the Appalachian Mountains before the tribe moved to the highlands. The Moon People were friends. The tribe calls you that as a sign of respect; you remind them of an old friend."

"What do they call you?"

Tanner smiled. "The red gringo. Did you understand the import of my words? You must spend your life helping others. That is why we were put on Earth."

Chris nodded.

"I was slow to learn that lesson," Tanner said. "Marie, my wife, had to teach me. But even then, I could not bring myself to become a friend to others. I was a man unto myself. I have been punished for my reticence."

"I think I do spend my days helping people," Chris replied. "I am, or at least was, until this mess, legal counsel to the Five Civilized Tribes. I assisted Native Americans in their legal issues each day. I helped others. I learned from my mother, Lillian."

"Lillian, the daughter of Jeff and Gwen."

"Yes, you knew Jeff."

"Marie and I raised him until her death. Then, I rode a dark path. I lost Jeff during my lost years, and I lost my own son, Gabriel, too. Those are times I try not to think about."

"I'm sorry to bring up painful memories. I just wanted you to know I learned to help the red man from my mother."

"I know of your mother, though we have never met. She reminds me of my sister, Avery."

"Other people have said that about her."

"I spend my days much as you do, providing legal counsel to

Native Americans. I also help our Latino brothers navigate the white man's court system."

Chris nodded. "You have some expertise in the law?"

Tanner nodded, his white braids moving with his head. "Yes, what did you score on the LSAT?"

"738."

"That is a high score. I scored but a 652."

"Mr. Station, that is quite a respectable score," Chris nodded in appreciation. "You could get scholarships to a lot of fine law schools with that score."

"The murder conviction might be an impediment."

The comment stopped Chris in his tracks.

Then, Tanner laughed. "Do not worry of offending me. I have no ego. Just my soul remains. I am here to serve my brothers until my time comes. The end has been slow in coming."

"Yes, that was the other thing I wanted to ask about. I saw your medical records. You have a heart condition? You take nitroglycerin to steady your heart?"

"They provide a pill each day."

"Okay, I'll try to line up a comprehensive physical work-up as soon as we get you out of here. Are you okay if I proceed?"

"The medicine man foretold it. I will play my part. There is one thing you must do for me. And one thing I must tell you."

"Certainly," Chris said. "Tell me."

"First, there is a red-haired woman in your life. Do not worry about her. I have seen the two of you in my dreams. You are together in the eternal. She will stay by your side. Do you know of whom I speak?"

Chris thought of Shannon. "Yes, I know her."

Tanner smiled. "Stay by her side."

It was the young man's turn to nod and not speak.

Tanner spoke once more. "You must also allow me to provide you a bodyguard. My man is waiting for you to exit the prison. Let him be beside you. There are powerful demons who circle you like vultures. He will keep them at bay."

Chris nodded. "Sure, I'll find him outside. How will I know him?"

"You will know." Then, the old man looked impossibly old. He was fatigued from their talk. Chris and Navaho Joe helped him into the bunk. Tanner leaned back on a stack of pillows, the scent of cedar surrounding him like a campfire.

Chris touched his arm. "I will come back tomorrow with more news."

Outside the gates, a Ford Ranchero with a camper topper was parked by Chris's car.

As he approached, a huge man got out. It was Navaho Joe.

Chris stared at him. "That's a neat trick," he said. "How'd you get out like that?"

Navaho Joe shook his head. "Inside is Ira. I am Ezra. We are twins."

"Identical, I see," Chris said, shaking the man's huge mitt of a hand.

"No, he has killed two men with his bare hands. We are not identical."

"Okay, Ezra. Can you follow me in town to my hotel? I have some calls to make."

"Call me Navaho Joe. Everyone does."

"Sure thing." Chris opened his car door, leaning in. "Hey, Elvis," he said to the bodyguard football player Johnny sent to accompany him, "meet Navaho Joe. He's also on guard detail."

The lineman nodded. "Where we headed?"

"Back to the hotel. Need to call Johnny."

Johnny Fleet had news. "The university's law firm called. Said the two deans, law school and journalism school, fired you and Piper in error. They were instructed to do so by Arden Kilmain. He had no authorization to order your dismissal. You will be reinstated by today."

"What did you say?"

"I told them the wrongful dismissal reported in the press hurt both my wife's and your reputations. I told the reinstatement would have to come with a settlement for damages."

Chris laughed. "What'd they say?"

"Taking it under advisement. I told them no further calls to me. All correspondence must come through the university to my attorney."

"Anything else?"

"All the incoming freshmen I recruited are asking out of their scholarships. Going to investigate Nebraska. That kills these guys."

"How did the coach react?"

"Hope he was wearing brown pants," Johnny laughed. "Hey, Lillian wants a word."

Lillian got on the line. "Did you meet Tanner?"

"Yes, he's fascinating. Like meeting an old yogi in a cave or on a mountaintop."

"What's he like? What did he say?"

"He's very frail. Said he knew I was coming. Was told in 1940. Said there was to be an attempt on his life. He was told before we knew ourselves. He's smart. Introverted as hell."

Lillian said, "There's the pot calling the kettle black." She looked over to Johnny. "Present company excluded...."

Johnny laughed. "That will cost you some Scotch."

"What else did he say?" she asked Chris.

"Sent a bodyguard back to the hotel with me. Scary guy, much bigger than Johnny's guy Elvis. Also said our enemies circled us like vultures."

"True enough. Hey, I found the phone number you asked me about," Lillian said. Her voice was already stronger than this morning. "Autumn Hart, as far as I know, is still alive. She would be eighty now, or nearly so." Lil gave Chris the number. "What's next for you?"

"I'm going back tomorrow to visit Tanner. Tonight, I'll get the paperwork ready to file for his compassionate release. I will deliver it to the warden's office. He won't sign it, or so he said, so then we move to the governor to intervene."

"Wait a second," Lillian said, "you met Zane Kilmain?"

"Yeah, scary as they come. Outright racist. Said you and me were on the wrong side of history. That blacks and Native Americans are inferior. Same shit, different Klansman."

"Be careful."

"He did say he didn't want the publicity of me or Tanner getting hurt inside the prison."

"You're not inside the walls now, son."

"Yeah, but I got Elvis and Navaho Joe. I'm feeling pretty good."

But Chris didn't get to visit Tanner the next day, or even within the next week. A white inmate in solitary confinement was found murdered by blunt force trauma, beaten to death with nightsticks. The death seemed to tip the prisoners toward violence. Like a pot nearly at temp, adding additional fuel brought things to a boil.

After several scrimmages between guards and inmates, no one felt safe. A large fight occurred at breakfast in what was normally no-man's land. Warden Kilmain closed all visitation, even to attorneys for the present. Big Mac was on lockdown. Walter Donohue's violent and unexplained death considerably slowed down the process of getting Tanner Station released.

It was a week later when Chris Fairchild was allowed back in the prison to see Tanner Station. By that time, the university had attempted to settle with Chris and Piper but had offered little more than double the thousand dollars each was receiving for teaching their respective classes. Johnny, to whom they had given power to negotiate, explained Chris had lost both his adjunct position at the law school, but also lost his entire caseload with the Five Tribes.

Next Johnny submitted a friend of the court statement from Federal Judge Hiram Spence. The judge said he had advised Chris Fairchild to leave Oklahoma state practice as he would no longer be able to ensure his clients received fair treatment under the law. Such a statement caused the university to, in turn, argue Chris's dismissal was not the primary cause of his loss of reputation or income. Johnny explained to the university's attorney that Chris's representation would be glad to argue before a judge whether it was the dismissal from the university or the participation of its athletic director in a conspiracy to commit four counts of murder that was primarily at fault.

Johnny suggested they review their position once again. The attorney, sounding weary, asked Johnny to provide terms. The black entrepreneur gave them a big number and they ended the call sounding defeated. There was no way in hell either the university president or the governor was going to court to argue such a case. They would settle.

Chris entered Cell block C with his prison guard escort as before. This time, he received a hearty greeting from Navaho Joe. "How's my brother?"

"Looks about the same," Chris said, laughing.

Tanner greeted Chris with much joy. "I am sorry our second meeting took longer to occur. I have thought of many things I wished I had said to you."

"So start," Chris said.

And the old man talked. And talked. He had amassed a wealth of knowledge in fifty years and had none to tell. Thus, words flowed from him. It was an hour before Chris raised a hand.

"I have something to tell you, too," he said.

"Of course, I have been like a stream in spring flood. What have you to say?"

"I spoke to an eighty-year-old woman in Yorba Linda, California. Her name is Autumn."

Tanner's eyes warmed and then they teared a bit. He rubbed his ancient knuckles to them. "Then, you know."

"Yes, I know. She read me the letter."

"Everett's suicide note."

Chris merely nodded.

"Then, you know I never hurt anyone."

"Yes, Everett admitted as much in the note to Avery. That he had you lie about the two Comanche. He had you say that you had killed them."

Tanner Station nodded. "Yes, Everett was afraid that Avery, being such a devout Quaker, could never marry a man who had committed the sin of killing others."

"You let him tell everyone you did it."

"It was a terrible mistake. I hated being thought of that way. It corrupted Everett, too. The lie ate him alive. Everett felt his whole life with Avery to be dishonest. It poisoned their marriage. It also made the people around the Cherokee Strip afraid of me. I was already too quiet, too standoffish. They assumed I had a black heart. They scorned me. Eventually, after Marie's death, I gave them what they wanted. I wanted to become that bad man, that well-known gun they all thought I was. But hate was not in me. Not even against Mel Harris."

"And it was Everett who shot Mel Harris, too?"

"Yes, to save my life. I had my .45 in my hand. Jeff had gone for help. Everett saw in my eyes that I was not going to shoot. Harris was going to kill me."

"Everett called out Harris, who turned, and Everett shot him?"

"Yes, and then before Jeff arrived with the Sheriff, we exchanged guns."

"But Everett could have just claimed self-defense. It makes no sense," Chris said, arguing for logic in an emotional matter.

"If you knew how much he loved Avery, it would make sense," Tanner said, "and besides, my life was over. Marie and Gabriel were dead. I wanted to be dead. Still do. My life has been over since Harris shot Marie. I had carried Everett's sin, his lie to his wife, all my adult life. I carried it still. This time it led to prison."

"Then, Everett wrote a letter to Avery revealing all those things before he took his own life," Chris said. "Autumn read it to me over the phone."

"Yes, his suicide note. Everett shot himself with my gun a decade later. Autumn found him. Found the letter. But she hid it from the sheriff and the coroner. She showed Avery."

"And after reading it, Avery herself took her own life shortly after."

Tanner began to cry. "Yes, Avery blamed herself for me being in prison. Her statement at my trial for killing Harris trial saying Richard Spaulding lied on the stand about seeing Buck Wells attempting to rape Marie gave the judge all he needed to throw the book at me. Of course, Avery thought I was guilty by then. She said I was dead to her.

"When Autumn read her the letter, Avery knew Everett's words were true, I expect, because Everett used my gun. He carried a short barrel .44. I carried a Colt .45. His was shiny, mine burnished steel." Tanner again wiped away tears with a red bandana. "Everett lied when Avery asked why he had my sidearm. He told her the police gave back my .45 after the trial. But Avery looked for his and never could find it. Of course, she couldn't because it was the murder weapon."

"And after Avery committed suicide, Autumn left Oklahoma for good."

"Wouldn't you?" Tanner laughed. "By then, the whole generation was dead. Max and Mimi gone to old age. Billy with a stroke. Mimi's husband, Jonah, gone by lightning. Carson gone to lock jaw. Autumn's sisters had moved on, now they're dead, too. Mimi's kids long gone from Alva. Gabriel and Marie gone. Then, both Everett and Avery committing suicide? Who'd stay after that?"

"Jeff and Gwen were still out on the farm."

"Tanner nodded. "On the farm. Not in town. Autumn was a lesbian on her own in a redneck town. I'm glad she left."

"How did you know all this?"

"Autumn and I correspond."

Chris nodded. "That's a lot of secrets to unravel."

"There is one more I must tell. I have decided it is my final task on this Earth to clear the path for you. That means taking down your enemies. I have means of doing so."

"Tanner," Chris said. "We have all the ammo we need to win. Warden Zane Kilmain is a reprobate, but his kind will go the way of the slave master. We'll win in the long run."

Tanner raised an eyebrow. "Do I look as if I'm ready for the long run?" The old man laughed. "Zane Kilmain won the first round this week. The law was on his side."

The ruling had been in the warden's favor on refusing compassionate release. The prison board read the regs literally and ruled for Kilmain. It said a compassionate release must be to a "direct and close relative." Direct and close was defined as one of the following: father, mother, brother, sister, grandfather, grandmother, daughter, or son. If the inmate is requesting compassionate leave because of pressing health issues, he must meet the requirements of being in immediate extremis nearing death or express remorse and contrition for past deeds and have circumstances requiring release.

Kilmain simply stated in a news conference that Tanner Station met none of the qualifications required for release. He had no direct relative still living for such a release, he was not in extremis, and he had expressed no remorse. Kilmain ended by saying, "My hands are tied by our laws. I wish there were more I could do, but I follow the regulations of the state without the slightest deviation. I am a lawman, through and through."

It made Chris nauseous to compare those words to the racist ideas Zane Kilmain had spoken in private.

"We expected to lose that round. In fact, we needed to lose to force the governor's hand. This week, I'll formally file paperwork for a commutation of your sentence. Be patient."

Tanner laughed. "Be patient? That is quite funny, don't you think, to say to me?" Then, he rolled his wheelchair forward until he was at Chris's knees. The old man gripped the handles of his chair. "Hold the chair still, Chris."

Chris did, and then something happened.

Tanner Station stood. It shocked Chris. The old man was hunched when he came to an erect position. In fact, it could be hardly called an erect position. His back was bent like a bow before an arrow flies from it. Tanner, even skinnier than Chris had thought, held the rack of the top bunk for support. He grimaced with the pain and then reached under the pillow of the top bunk. Tanner pulled a document free of the thin blanket.

"Here, I wrote out all you need, I think. Zane Kilmain will release me after this reaches the newspapers and TV tomorrow. He will want to be shut of me for good."

Chris looked down on the document. "What am I looking at?"

"It is a record of the graft and corruption within the prison. The guards run it. It is overseen by Superintendent Mabry. You know him?"

"Thin mustache, fat mouth?"

Tanner smiled and nodded yes.

"How did you get all this information?"

"In fifty years, you hear a lot. People will tell things, brag to a cripple, things they wouldn't say to other folk. At least, I have found that to be true."

"Most of these accusations cannot be proven."

"There are enough names, enough vendors who pay the warden kickbacks for contracts, to get started. They hate him, and one of them will surely rat him out. And there is a kicker on the last page. That one last secret."

"And that is?"

"The man killed in solitary? Whose death closed the prison last week?"

"Yes?"

"He went by the name Walter Donohue. But he was your father,

Henry Fairchild. He asked me not to tell you, but I am done with secrets. They have betrayed me my whole life."

There are straws and there are concrete blocks. Both can break the camel's back. It was the latter in play after the revelation of Henry Fairchild's death became public. Chris used his connections with Judge Hiram Spence to get records pulled on the dead man, whose body was still held in the morgue at the prison. Those records, which included fingerprints, proved that the deceased man was, indeed, Henry Fairchild, Piper's and Chris's father.

During the 1970s, there was no organized national fingerprint record system. It took someone knowing there was a connection between two cases or from a crime to a specific perp to connect fingerprints. It was a difficult process even from city to city within a state. It was very rare for fingerprints to be used from one state to catch a criminal in another. Here, it took knowing the man's identity to connect him to his records.

Chris had no time to mourn his father's loss. Neither did Piper. There was too much going on for the two to examine their feelings. The news coverage after Chris's press conference, with Judge Hiram Spence and Johnny Fleet on the dais with him, was incredible. The young attorney simply announced the fingerprint analysis proved it had been his father who'd been murdered while in solitary confinement in the prison presided over by Warden Zane Kilmain. Chris then stated it was Warden Zane Kilmain's brother, Arden, who had been implicated in a murder conspiracy against the Station and Hart families not a week prior. Chris also read an accompanying affidavit from Tanner Station that Henry Fairchild had refused to commit murder for the Dixie Mafia who controlled the white gang operations in the prison. Refusal to kill Tanner Station led to Henry Fairchild's murder said Oklahoma's longest serving inmate.

Zane Kilmain was done at the prison before the day was

complete. He claimed no one knew Walter Donohue was really Chris's father, so his death was irrelevant. However, that excuse sounded a lot like "I would have never ordered his death had I known he was part of the family my brother and childhood friend John Taylor had previously threatened." Editorials in all the state's newspapers called for his head on a pike. The governor obliged.

After the press conference, the state offered both Piper and Chris $300,000 each to drop their lawsuits. Arden Kilmain resigned in disgrace from the university prior to the investigation into the tape and his involvement in the conspiracy. John Taylor was forced out from his position as Oklahoma's Secretary of Health and Human Services.

Chris and Piper decided to accept the state's offer, but Chris tied it to the release of Tanner Station and the reinstatement of Shannon Gill's position, plus, for her, a year's salary for her brave action as a whistleblower. Attorneys for both sides were billing hours, examining the offer as it went back to the governor's office for final consideration. Chris did not see Tanner Station on the day Henry's story ran. Chris went to bed early that night, exhausted from the proceedings but smiling because his name too had been mentioned by Walter Cronkite on the evening news. It was something to tease Tate Laughlin about.

At 6:00 am, Piper shook him awake. "Wake up, booger face. Navajo Joe is at the door."

"It's still dark outside."

Piper nodded. Chris, wearing only pajama bottoms, padded through the living room to the front door. "What's going on, Ezra? We're not leaving for Big Mac until about ten."

"The red gringo had a heart attack. They say for you to come now. There may not be much time. Tanner Station may die." Ezra was visibly upset.

Chris rushed into his bedroom, dressed quickly, and emerged to the hall. Shannon Gill was standing there in a robe, a shocked look on her face. "What is it?"

Chris pulled her tight in a hug. "It's Tanner. He's had a heart attack. I've got to go. I'll call you. Let Mom sleep. Tell her when she wakes up."

Then, he was out the door.

At the prison infirmary, the other Navajo Joe stood watch on the old man's door. A monitor inside beeped with each shallow heartbeat.

Chris left his prison guard escort and Superintendent Mabry behind as he approached the hospital's doors. "Ira, what happened? How's Tanner?"

"He's not good, man. He tried to kill himself. Took a handful of his nitroglycerin pills. I had no idea he wasn't taking them every day. He was stashing them. Took them all at once. The doctor said his heart just kind of popped."

"But he's still alive…"

"For now, but it's not good."

Chris went in and saw the old man. His face, now yellowish with illness, was impossibly thin. Chris wept. After a time, his tears slowed. He met with the doctor, who solemnly told the young attorney that his client would not likely ever regain consciousness.

Chris, reeling, went into the waiting room. He spoke to Ira once again. "Ira, are we sure he wasn't poisoned? That Kilmain or a Dixie Mafia gang member didn't get to him?"

"Nobody was in the cell all night, except me and him. He took 'em. He gave me a note."

Chris took it and read its words:

Christian,

I was so glad I waited for you. You were certainly worth the wait. I saw and felt the blood of my sister, which lives on in you. You shall make our family proud. I hope my words will guide you in some way as you move forward. I shall watch and assist as spirits are able. I do not understand those things and long to.

Now it is time for me to go to the eternal. My wife and boy call to me. I shall soon be by the council fire with my kind. Do not be sad. It is my time. Tell Warden Kilmain I now meet the requirement of "extremis." Ask him to expedite my release if he would. As I write this, Navaho Joe tells me Kilmain has been fired. Superintendent Mabry is not much better, but he will go along for now. Tell the press I want to go home to the Salt Fork. I want to be buried by my loved ones. Ask the people of Oklahoma to do me right this one time. Let me go home.

– Tanner Station

Tanner Station was released from prison that afternoon. An ambulance transported the old man home to the Salt Fork Ranch along the shallow branch of the Arkansas River, just south of the Kansas state line, a small parcel of land wrapped around a bow in the river there.

As the vehicle followed the highway north, other cars and pickups began to pull into line, much like a funeral procession, except the man in the ambulance was still alive. Chris and Ezra sat with Tanner, holding the old man's willow branch hands during transport.

It was sunset when the ambulance passed Jeff and Gwen's home, south into the pasture. It rattled across the cattleguard onto the ranch's dry ground. Chris guided them toward the ruins of the old main house.

There they stopped. There was no more road, and the ambulance was ill-equipped to go farther in the sand. Chris and Ezra stepped from the ambulance into the spreading night. Lightning bugs lit the prairie, still wet from an earlier rain. The heat of the day was gone, and quail called out for each other across the sage. "Bob white, bob white," the quail called mournfully for their mates.

Chris turned to watch the procession. Hundreds of vehicles

were stopping along the deeply furrowed, two-wheeled track leading to the main house's ruins. The walls of the old house had fallen, but the roof remained, rusted brown. The outbuildings were nearly invisible, lost in the sand and growing vegetation. The bunkhouse and the chicken coop were not discernable to anyone who did not know they had once been there. The barn walls leaned in the sand, desolate in their destruction. Time the conqueror.

Chris organized some Native American men in the faltering light. They found the thickest Indian blanket any had with them. They doubled it, and four of the men each held a corner as Ezra and Chris, with the ambulance attendant's assistance, placed the old man onto the blanket. Tanner Station was light as a feather. The men lifted him with little exertion.

Chris led them to the river.

Ezra walked behind like a massive grizzly following in their stead.

At the bank, Chris did not hesitate. He walked into the water of the Salt Fork. It had been nearly eighty years since first a member of the Stations clan stepped into that life-giving stream. Chris walked on until the water was past his knees. Then, he stopped and turned. He realized the four men, each wearing traditional tribal attire, represented the Choctaw, Chickasaw, Creek, and Seminole tribes. He wished there were a Cherokee among them to recognize all five tribes and then realized both he and Tanner would forever be tied to the Cherokee.

He did not tell the men to lower Tanner into the water, but they did. The water was cool, but not cold. It flowed over the old one like peace. Chris knew he was crying, but he also felt great joy. He would later be unable to express himself fully about that moment, not ever, but he would remember the feeling. It was of tranquility and of natural order.

He examined each man's face as they held Tanner. He knew

none of them. He had never seen any of them before, but they were his brothers.

Erza knelt before his friend and began to recite a death chant, a prayer for safe passage.

Chris heard the chorus picked up on the wind. He turned and the riverbank flowed with members of the tribes, Tanner's true lineage.

They sang the words as Ezra led them. Nearly everyone was crying, a cathartic release unknown in a modern world that hides death and stifles the real and the eternal.

Chris wept.

And then a miracle happened. Tanner awoke. He looked around him, at the fireflies hovering above him, at the stars beyond, at his people. He heard the words they sang to honor him. He understood the moment. His head began to turn about. Chris realized Tanner was trying to find him in the faltering light. Chris knelt by the old man and took his hand.

Tanner Station smiled joyfully, shedding fifty years of imprisonment and decay. He gazed upon the young man, kneeling in the Salt Fork beside him, up to his chest in the water which had been there forever, before the white men, before the Salt Fork Stations had homesteaded here. When only the buffalo came here. And the quail. And later the red man.

Tanner raised his eyes to the night sky, seeking the eternal beyond it. He called out, although it came as just a whisper. Yet all there, the hundreds, heard it. His final word was carried on the wind from the river to the heavens, to the big hill in the distance and to the mesas beyond. The old man said one word in his last breath. He said it with a relief of one coming home.

"Marie."

Gratitude

This book is not a memoir. It is fiction. I am not Chris. If he is anyone, he is an amalgam of cousins Rusty, Jerod, Zack, James, my brother Lance, and just a smidgen of me. Tanner is also a mixture of my uncles.

This book is not religious allegory, but hopefully it does have something to say that will stir your spirit. The organizational structure of the fourteen stations of the cross, plus Resurrection, was done with all reverence. The final section, "Resurrection" was engineered to provide an uplifting conclusion.

Mainly, this tale is a just a story for your entertainment, but one based on a place I once knew well and on people I know and love. I do not pretend to be a world class researcher, but I did attempt to portray historical events accurately. Oklahoma and Kansas during the period of this book (1893 to 1974) were fascinating places, and to think the book does not discuss the Okie migration, the Dust Bowl years, or the Nazi prison in Alva. Sequel, anyone? I apologize if any facts or depictions are wrong. The errors are mine alone. By the way, much from the original outline five years in the making did not make the final draft. Writing about memory and then enhancing it for a novel was fun.

As regards to the characters, Jeff and Gwen will be easily recognizable as my grandparents, Jack and Jessie Bond. Lillian and Avery have a lot in common with my aunt, Lela Madge and my mother, Peggy. Uncle Landon is based upon my Uncle Lowell. Etta May is his wife, Etta Marie. Lynette and her husband, Les, are represented as Libby and Linstrom.

The rest of the characters in the book are essentially compressions of various cousins, uncles, and aunts, plus my brother and sister. The house Lillian, Piper, and Chris leave in the opening scene is the Berry home in Wichita. The car ride, singing songs on a cold drive south, was a memory I have of being in a big sedan with cousins, Sandy, Patty, Verna, and Jenny, singing Beatles songs because that seemed to be all AM radio played. It was a joyous ride for a six-year-old boy.

Other events and tales in the book are sometimes true, sometimes partly true, but mostly fictitious for the sake of the tale. I hope no one takes offense at my liberties with the truth.

A book is far from a solo project. People imagine a writer sitting alone, staring at a keyboard with a cigarette and a bottle of bourbon. Yeah, it ain't like that. You get a little help from your friends. For this, my fifth book, many people tipped me about Native American music. Thanks to you all: Greg Peters, Ray Bachman, Justin Ervin, David Deming, Geoffrey Woolf, Aaron Kerley, Steve Garinger, Josef Matulich, Sheila Ediger-Phillips, Bill Rauckman, Ric Hickey, Jennifer Boblitt-Johnson, Bruce Bergsten, Peg Haas-Russell, Summer Caldwell Fletcher, Joe Shearer, Taylor Tyler, Rick Robinson, Brad Carter, Scott Galliardt, and last but certainly not, least, Kevin Faulkner.

Kevin gave this book the once (or twice) over, and it is much better for his careful eye. He is a voice in the wilderness that keeps me sane. Thanks.

Thanks also to Tony Acree for his confidence in publishing this novel. It is my best work. I appreciate all that you do.

Thanks to Jen Selinsky for the terrific final edit.

Thanks also to Brady Lantz and Mitch Keenan. You two will always be my co-conspirators.

I also thank my family. I am sure Lucy will review my words about horses. Finally, I thank my wife, Vicki, and all she does. This book is dedicated lovingly to her. I thank you for your love and patience with my strange ways.

Godspeed to you all.

Salt Fork Stations Playlist

"Rumble"Link Wray
"Come and Get Your Love"Redbone
"Heartbeat Drum Song"Robbie Robertson
"Stolen Land"Bruce Cockburn
"Indian Sunset"Elton John
"Ballad of Ira Hayes"Bob Dylan
"Big Alligator"Jim Billie
"Broken Arrow"Buffalo Springfield
"Running Bear"Johnny Horton
"Kalijah"Hank Williams
"The Spirit Trail"Don Fogelberg
"Cherokee Woman"Cher
"Pocahontas"Neil Young
"I Pity the Country"Willie Dunn
"Song of the Sun"Klee Benally
"Choctow Bingo"James McMurtry
"Bury My Heart at Wounded Knee"Indigo Girls
"Unbound" Robbie Robertson
"Cortez the Killer"Neil Young
"Snotty Nose Rez Kids"Boujee Natives

"One Tin Soldier"The Original Caste
"Warrior People"Nahko and Medicine for the People
"Cherokee People"Paul Revere and the Raiders
"Silence Is a Weapon"Blackfire
"Native Blood"Testament

Made in the USA
Monee, IL
05 March 2022

a2a84a65-1115-42b1-b5d3-6389a2d47b1cR02